This book is a work of fiction. The characters, incidents, and dialogue are drawn from the author's imagination and are not to be construed as real. Any resemblance to actual events or persons, living or dead, is entirely coincidental.



HarperCollins books may be purchased for educational, business, or sales promotional use. For information please write: Special Markets Department, HarperCollins Publishers Inc., 10 East 53rd Street, New York, NY 10022.

FIRST EDITION

Eos is a federally copyrighted trademark of HarperCollins Publishers.

Printed on acid-free paper.

---

Library of Congress Cataloging-in-Publication Data

Wilson, Robert Charles, 1953–
Magic time : ghostlands / Robert Charles Wilson ; created by Marc Scott Zicree.—1st ed.
p. cm.
ISBN 0-06-105070-9
I. Zicree, Marc Scott. II. Title

PR9199.3.W4987M34 2004
823'.914—dc22 2004050630

---

04 05 06 07 08 ❖/RRD 10 9 8 7 6 5 4 3 2 1

# Magic Time
## Ghostlands

Marc Scott Zicree
&
Robert Charles Wilson

*An Imprint of* HarperCollins*Publishers*

*Available from Eos in paperback*

MAGIC TIME
by Marc Scott Zicree and Barbara Hambly

MAGIC TIME: ANGELFIRE
by Marc Scott Zicree and Maya Kaathryn Bohnhoff

# Magic Time
# Ghostlands

*To Stuart Gordon Zicree and Christina Anne Zicree,*
*beloved father and sister, for all the inspiration.*
*And to the memory of SuAnne Big Crow,*
*who made magic in the real world.*

# Acknowledgments

Books are big, ungainly beasts, and it's a miracle they ever get written—and certainly they never do without the help of many.

First of all, as always, to my wife, Elaine, without whom none of this would have been possible. Then to Maya Kaathryn Bohnhoff, invaluable partner in crime.

Steven-Elliot Altman kept me writing when the darkness closed in, day by day, week by week. He *made* this book happen.

Harper Lee, Harlan Ellison, Ray Bradbury, George Clayton Johnson, Norman Corwin, Theodore Sturgeon, Richard Matheson, Barbara Kingsolver, Rod Serling and Ray Harryhausen all provided inspiration and guidance in a multitude of ways.

Thanks to Armin Shimerman, Mau Barklay and Richard Tanner for lending their prodigious talents and giving voice to the rogue's gallery of *Magic Time* and *Magic Time: Angelfire*. Diane Baker, Ken Mader, Jonathan Kaplan, David Simkins, Jim Cunningham, Dan Comins, Reece Michaelson, Merlin Stone, Allison Bingeman, Michael Reaves, Neal Romanek, Tony Tsou, Kelly Sumner, Angelina Swords, John Douglas, Jeff Larsen, Robert Cantrell, Dax Bauser, Robert Vaughan, Lamont Dixon, David Jansen, Henry Nagel, John Prendergast, the staff at Wolfgang Puck's on Sunset and Insomnia Café all lent help and support that were invaluable. Special thanks also to Mr. Kuriyama, my junior high school history teacher, who brought alive the travesty of the internment camps through his own first-person accounts.

A belated thanks to Marcy Ross, Ellie Hannibal and Sarah Timberman, who had enthusiasm for this project in the early days, and to

Iain McCaig, as always, for lending his genius (and to his son Inigo, for lending his name).

Diana Gill has been my terrific editor throughout all three books, and Lisa Gallagher and Jack Womack have supplied wonderful assistance and encouragement along the way. Deb Dwyer did a splendid job of copyediting, and her kind words were much appreciated. I also wanted to personally thank Michael Morrison, publisher of HarperCollins, and also the many others in editing, publicity and sales at HarperCollins who have done so much to help this book, among them George D. Bick, Jennifer Brehl, Brian Grogan, Olga Nolan, Kerry Morris, May Chen, Will Hinton, Jerry Marasak, Jeanette Zwart, Ian Doherty, Kate McCune, Michael Morris, Karen Gudmundson, Eric Svenson, Elizabeth Kaplan, Kristin Bowers, Cathy Schornstein, Robin Smith, Gabriel R. Barillas, Jim Hankey, Seira Wilson, Cheri Hickman, John Zeck, Diane Jackson, Becky Keiper, Denise DePalma, Kerri Sikorski, Debra Evans, Pat Stanley, Eleanore Gaffney, Brian McSharry, Mike Spradlin, Seth Fleischman, David Youngstrom, Judy Madonia, Kristine Macrides, Rhonda Rose, Pete Soper, Dale Schmidt, Chadd Reese, Stefanie Friedman, Bruce Unck, Donna Waitkus, Nanci Andersen, Ralph D'Arienzo and Angela Leigh. Without these remarkable, hardworking souls, not to mention all the bookstore managers and employees across the country, this book would not be in your hands now.

My ever-valiant agent, Chris Lotts, provided heroic efforts often on my behalf. Dana Wellborn, my trusty Indian guide, provided invaluable assistance to me during my researches in South Dakota. My heartfelt gratitude as well to my other Badland "angels"—Patti Etem, Milt and Jamie Lee, Leatrice "Chick" Big Crow, Ann Cedarface, Ida-Rae Estes, Cameron Ducheneaux, Patricia Catches and Nellie Cuny.

Michael Tennesen and Timothy Gogan kept my head on straight and my feet on the ground, while Mel Raab and the rest of the staff at Automagic kept my Toshiba 4090 processing words in reasonably coherent fashion. Also providing vital information and encouragement were Jeff and Karin West, Lita Weissman, Deb Yearout, Alison Kempf, Craig Black, Paul Coughlin, Josh Stanton, Haila Williams, Chris Wyatt, Alene Dawson, Krystee Cott, Raf Dahlquist, Todd Koerner, Frank Staniszewski, the ever-erstwhile Theo Siegel, Rob

Weaver, Lynne Weaver, Dennis Weaver, Floyd Red Crow Westerman, and Professor Walter Gekelman of the UCLA Department of Physics and Astronomy.

Thanks also to Jesse Larner, whose fine book *Mount Rushmore—An Icon Reconsidered* provided marvelous historical and cultural perspective.

If I've left anyone out, e-mail me at *marc@zicree.com* and we'll rectify the situation.

Sincere gratitude to all for their patience, their example, their courage and their wisdom. I once said that I thought our purpose in this life was to be happy, to be kind and to be brave. I'm lucky to be surrounded by a bouquet of people who do just that.

—Marc Scott Zicree

*If anything is taught here, it is simply the charting of the life of someone who started out to somewhere—and went.*

—Ray Bradbury

*We make our own ghosts, and then give them permission to haunt us.*

—*Magic Time: Angelfire*

# Prologue

## Grant Park, Chicago

*Life is loss,* Cal Griffin thought, standing in the chill wind off Lake Michigan, the dawn light like a held breath. Magic hour.

Magritte's flames were dying to embers now, the ashes whipping in the breeze to dust their hair and shoulders and eyelashes. Another friend gone: Magritte, the flare, who had found sanctuary of a sort with Enid Blindman, then a true home in Goldie. Magritte had known much of the streets and of loneliness, and little of trust.

She had trusted Cal.

Cal and Doc and Colleen had set the wood and primed it, and Goldie himself had laid the empty husk of the girl-sprite—still nearly weightless—onto the pyre. A new use for Grant Park, Cal reflected, as so many places and things had found new use. No more antiseptic Forest Lawn, where they carted the bodies off and sanitized them and put them on pristine display. *No, death is its true self here, and no one keeps clean hands.*

The somber-sweet a cappella of Enid's funeral song trailed away, his face turned to heaven, shining like cherrywood in the rose light. He moved off with Venus, who gulped back her tears, and Howard Russo, who bunched his shoulders and squinted his big grunter eyes against the pallid glare, despite his sunglasses.

A last stop for them as autumn waned, before they returned to the Preserve, to Mary McCrae and Kevin Elk Sings and the other strays and changelings. All the new combinations, the surrogate families, the desperate, brave attempts to find security and belonging in a world that had shattered to fragments.

Cal glanced at Doc and Colleen, grouped together in the unspoken way that declared a country with borders all its own. Cal felt a pang of loss, and yet was not surprised. They were right together, she so hard on the outside and sensitive within, he with his air of gentility and subtle inner strength.

They would need that in the days ahead. They would need each other.

As for Cal, whatever longings he felt or imagined futures he might once have entertained, he knew he needed to relinquish. He could little afford encumbrances now, attachments to slow him or bring hesitation or doubt.

He had an appointment in the West.

In the early days of last summer, a world away and a lifetime ago, a shock wave had spread out of the unknown heart of the country, a tremor that had stilled all machines permanently, had leeched away their energies to power other dread forces, and left its mark on every man, woman and child.

Most had stayed human—pitifully, inadequately human. A few discovered they had strange new powers to move objects at a distance, or cast fear, or otherwise alarm the populace.

And a minority—the outcasts, Cal recognized, the most fragile or emotionally distanced—found themselves changed physically in ways that reflected their inner natures. Some—like his own lost sister, Tina—metamorphosed into ethereal, radiant creatures that came to be known in some parts as flares or angelfire. Still others were compacted into grunters; loathsome, powerful homunculi that ran in packs and kept to the dark places of the earth. But even here there were eccentric loners, like Howard Russo, who eschewed the more repugnant pursuits of their fellows and who could be trusted—who could be *friends.*

Then there were dragons.

Ely Stern, lawyer supreme and Cal's former boss, had transformed into one of those appalling rarities, back in Manhattan, where Cal's long pilgrimage had begun. A brilliant man, Stern, and a monster, really, even before the Change laid its weighty hand on him.

Stern's extreme makeover had unshackled him, freed him at last to do things he had previously only dreamt of. So he had tried to kill Cal on several occasions, perhaps out of some sick need for payback, some attempt to quash traits he sensed in Cal that he himself could never have.

Or it might not have been that at all. Cal realized he had never truly understood Stern, that the man—the dragon—had in the end been a total enigma to him.

At any rate, Stern had been the first to abduct Tina, when she was wracked by fever in the midst of her transformation, mistakenly believing that only the two of them were changing, that somehow she was fated to share his road. Stern had spirited her away to an aerie atop the dead office building where he and Cal once worked, had oddly been something of a midwife to Tina during the final stage of her rebirth. Incredibly, in his twisted, halting way, Stern had been *gentle* with her, even solicitous.

Stern, who, to Cal's knowledge, had never spoken kindly of any woman—or man, for that matter. Who, as far as Cal had observed, had no kindness within him.

In the end, to get his sister back, Cal had been forced to put a sword through him, and Stern had fallen eighty stories and more onto a Manhattan sidewalk.

Cal stared up into the swirl of smoke from Magritte's funeral pyre, imagined it had taken on a dragon shape. Dead now? You would think so after a fall like that. But it was a world of cruel miracles and surprises.

Cal had been able to keep Tina with him for a time, as they had cobbled together their own makeshift clan out of friends and strangers: Colleen Brooks, who had been a mechanic in Cal's office building and a neighbor down the block (though Cal hadn't known it); Doc Lysenko, sidewalk hot-dog vendor, former physician, and veteran of Chernobyl; and finally Herman Goldman, Goldie of the subway tunnels, odd foragings and unreliable wonders.

They had set off in search of the source of the Change, to see if they could somehow staunch it, unmake what it had made. In the woods of Albermarle County, they'd come upon Secret Service agent Larry Shango, on his own urgent mission, and he had gifted them with the forbidden knowledge he carried—that the disaster that had upended the world had possibly stemmed from a classified program known, ironically enough, as the Source Project, its precise composition and location unknown. After his many tribulations, Shango had emerged with nothing more than a partial list of names of the scientists manning the project, and the towns and cities they had made their homes before relocating to the Source.

In Boone's Gap, West Virginia, Cal had ultimately met up with one of them, Dr. Fred Wishart, who was no longer human but something immeasurably more pitiless and powerful, single-mindedly bent on maintaining the life of his comatose twin brother, Bob, even if it meant draining the life force from all who lived within the town.

Cal and his friends had succeeded in saving Boone's Gap, but at a terrible cost—both Wishart and Tina had been yanked back to whatever dwelled at the Source, the malignant Awareness that seized not only the two of them but seemingly all flares anywhere not protected by some countering force.

As for the other scientists at the Source Project—Dr. Marcus Sanrio, who spearheaded the effort, his immediate subordinate Agnes Wu, all the other diverse talents who had likely unleashed this maelstrom on the world—Cal didn't know the least thing about them; whom they loved, who grieved for them, what had made them, in the end, living human beings.

Whoever or whatever they might be now.

After Tina had been seized from him, Cal had known only one goal, one drive—to find her, to safeguard her. Colleen and Doc and Goldie, bless them, had thrown in their lot with him, set off in search of Tina and the Source, carried where it beckoned, rootless as dandelions in the wind.

It had led them to the remarkable blues guitarist Enid Blindman and his companion Magritte, by whose symbiotic relationship each kept the other safe. They protected numerous other flares, as well, shielding them with a bizarre mélange of music and magic while they led them to a place known only as the Preserve—a place that had its own arcane defenses against the Source.

But Enid's gift brought with it a curse, and in trying to dislodge it, Cal and his friends, along with Enid and Magritte, and Enid's former manager, Howard Russo, had journeyed to Chicago. And in that journey, Magritte and Goldie had forged a bond as strong as it was unlikely. Neither had dreamed it possible—the manic-depressive transient and the hooker turned angel.

Cal thought for a time that own his answer might lie here, that he would find his sister and the end of the road, whatever that end might be. But he had found only a bizarre and terrible puppet called Primal—a puppet whose strings were pulled by Clayton Devine, former Maintenance Crew Chief of the Source Project. Maintenance and security had been his specialties, and he had maintained and secured Chicago, held sway over it for himself and his followers for a time, until Cal and his friends brought it all tumbling down . . . and Magritte sacrificed her life to save Goldie—to save them all.

Another soul distorted by the dark energy of the Source, Devine had disguised himself in stolen power—insulation from the scrutiny and reach of the more powerful Entity at its heart. A futile attempt in the end, as futile as Fred Wishart's last stand in Boone's Gap, West Virginia.

And who knew how many other last stands across the country, around the world, how many lives stolen or smashed or snuffed out?

*There's a power in the West, calling to us,* Ely Stern had told Tina on the roof of the world, the skyscraper summit to which he had flown her on that lost summer night.

And Stern had said too, *Soon it's gonna own the world.*

So there was a clock ticking inside all of them. Tick. Tock. Find it. Stop it.

If they could.

The fire was all but dead now, and Cal shivered against the chill that had seeped into his bones, despite the Gore-Tex and layering.

Goldie stood nearest the pyre, seemingly untouched by the cold. Cal and the others had let him keep his distance, and his silence. His eyes met Cal's, but what was behind them kept its own counsel. His jaw muscles were taut, his head cocked at an angle as if listening to a distant conversation. To the West.

Of all of them, Goldie was the least changed without, still had the hectic, beautiful black curls, the straw cowboy hat with the five aces in the brim—very much the worse for wear for having been lost, trampled and rained upon—the cacophonous ensemble of Hawaiian, plaid and paisley shirts. But he was the most changed within. The playfulness, the antic spirit that had greeted Cal at their first and subsequent meetings, was quelled now, seemingly extinguished, to be replaced by . . . what?

Grimness, and darkness, and a growing power.

How much Magritte—and her loss—had been a catalyst for this, Cal didn't know. But he suspected it played a great part.

Love was both a shield and a sword; it could protect and it could wound. The same emotion that bled Goldie drove Cal to find Tina. And it would determine the choices Colleen and Doc made, or failed to make, when the fire rained down on them all.

The sun was higher now, cresting on the stark branches as the city shifted and stirred and discovered itself. The last remnants of blackened logs fell in on themselves, threw up a firefly swarm of sparks and became still.

"We need to get the horses saddled and packed," Cal said.

They nodded, and turned from the lake to the road again.

# I

# Medicine and Storm

*Tomorrow never happens. It's all the same fucking day.*

—Janis Joplin

# ONE

## East of Storm Lake, Iowa

"All right, I admit it. Radio Goldman is stone-cold dead."

Herman Goldman stood like an iron spike driven into the rutted blacktop that had once been Route 169 heading north to Blue Earth—technically still was, Cal Griffin reflected, although no car had driven it in the nearly half year since the Change. No car could have, since cars ran nowhere on the face of the earth as far as anyone knew, as any of them had heard.

Horses, though, were a hot commodity again; and Cal and his friends had been hard-pressed to retain Sooner, Koshka and their other steeds from the depredations of roving smash-and-grab gangs that had lain in wait at numerous rest stops and Kodak moments along the way. "Horse thief" was no longer a quaint term out of a Western—it was a job description.

*And we've got the scars to prove it.*

You can't go through life without making enemies, his father had told him when Cal was barely four. That was just before Dad's first abandonment of the family, cutting out for the territories, the apogees and perigees of a roving life that had made enemies of his own family.

*Now I'm the rootless one,* Cal thought, and his collection of scars, both physical and emotional, formed the road map of his travels.

"Maybe you need new batteries," Colleen said, jolting Cal from his reverie.

Goldie glowered at her, stuck out his tongue. There were no radios, of course, and batteries didn't do shit. They were both speaking metaphorically, baiting each other as they tended to do when most frustrated. When it grew too barbed, veering into real venom, Cal would step in as he always did, smoothing their rough edges, reminding them of what held them together, of what bound them on this road. He was their moderator, their governing influence, and he knew well why they thought of him as their leader, despite how reluctant he had once been to accept that role.

Goldie tilted his head quizzically, as if listening for a distant, staticky station, and Cal realized that "radio" wasn't just a metaphorical term, after all. Goldie had been their crystal set even before the Change, catching the twisted music and voices on the winds of the Source, coaxing and wheedling and beguiling them on the daunting path that had begun that sweltering day in Manhattan when Cal had saved Goldie from being pulverized by a truck on Fifth Avenue—and Goldie had tried (unsuccessfully, of course) to warn him of the coming Storm.

Since Chicago, Goldie had led them by fits and starts through the blasted terrain of western Illinois and Wisconsin, past Rockford and Beloit, skirting the horror of Madison, where cholera and a newborn smallpox raged. In general, the most populous areas were hardest hit, and best avoided.

On the outskirts of Sauk City, by the banks of the Wisconsin, Goldie had found a cliff face with a faded petroglyph that he'd been able to coax into opening a portal that emptied onto the Effigy Mounds in Iowa. It had been murder getting the horses through—they grew frenzied at the prickling feeling of being transported—but it had saved several hundred miles of rough traveling.

They had continued west, drawn by the elusive call of the Source. Until now.

Goldie shook his head. "Nada. K-Source is not on the air . . . which certainly does *not* mean it's not still out there, doing it's nasty best."

"Great," Colleen enthused. "So we're stuck in *this* beauty spot." The afternoon light had turned long, the shadow of a bleached FOOD

GAS LODGING sign stretching out toward the horizon, browned prairie grasses tossing in the frigid wind. Route 169 opened ahead like a mottled black ribbon, and despite the signage, there was no food, no gas, no lodging anywhere in sight.

"Patience, Colleen," Doc advised from atop Koshka, looking every bit the brooding Russian horseman in his fleece-lined greatcoat. "I won't try to tell you it's a virtue, but it will save wear and tear on the stomach lining."

Goldie remounted his steed, took the reins from Cal, who was straddling Sooner. Goldie's horse had originally been called Jayhawk, but he'd taken to calling it Later. He'd wanted Colleen to rechristen her horse Further, but she had so far resisted the idea, merely commenting on an increase in Goldie's annoyance factor.

Not that it was inappropriate, actually. According to Goldie, this was the name Ken Kesey had painted on the psychedelic bus the Merry Pranksters had driven across America back in 1965. Cal dimly recalled reading the Tom Wolfe book on the subject, years ago. The irony was explicit. Kesey and friends had seen themselves as divine madmen embedded in a staid, magicless reality. *And we're the opposite,* Cal thought. *Reality has gone mad; we cling to sanity. Such sanity as we make for ourselves.*

Colleen pressed her heels to her gelding's flanks and the four of them moved ahead at a brisk trot. She turned to Cal. "How 'bout you, Cal? Anything off your map trick?"

Cal reached back and pulled a Triple-A map booklet from his saddlebag to open it across the pommel of his saddle. He had unearthed it in the looted ruins of a convenience store outside Osage. On their passage from Boone's Gap to Enid's Preserve and beyond, he had gained a fitful ability to read a map in a new and frequently useful way, to sense the changed terrain ahead, discern some of its tweaked geography.

But that skill had utterly deserted him since their showdown with Primal. And now, looking at the creased paper with its tangle of red and blue lines like arteries and veins of a body, he knew he had no special clue as to what lay before them. Only that Tina, if miraculously still alive, was somewhere due west of them, and that they had to keep moving.

Perhaps as they drew nearer the Source, it was leeching away such powers, drawing to itself the life forces of this new world, as it had seized Tina and the others like her. Or maybe Cal was generally tone deaf to such abilities, and his tin ear had simply returned.

Cal closed the map book, returned it to his saddlebag. "All I can say is Sioux Falls is about a hundred and fifty miles down the highway. If it's still there."

"And not somewhere in Luxembourg," Goldie added.

No telling.

They paused to let the horses drink from a roadside pond, dismounting to give them respite. It had rained yesterday and they'd collected the water in buckets, pans, whatever containers came to hand, transferring it later to bottles and canteens. The water was fresh—with any luck, not too contaminated with stale automotive oils or last year's pesticides. Had this land once been cultivated? Hard to tell. The prairie grasses had come back this summer, conjured out of the ground like ghost buffalo.

Colleen grimaced, angling her neck left then right to get the kinks out.

"Here, let me," Doc said, and moved to massage her neck with long, skillful fingers. There was a clatter from within her shirt, and Doc withdrew a long chain around her neck. It jangled with the dog tags Cal knew came from her late father, the Russian Orthodox cross Doc had given her in Chicago—and a triangular piece that resembled black leather, but which gleamed, even in the pale light of winter coming, with iridescent fire.

"Get your hands off my trinkets." Colleen playfully swatted Doc's hand away.

"Yes, but one of them is such an *interesting* trinket. . . ."

It was the amulet the old black blind man in Chicago had given her, the ancient sax player the refugee musicians in Buddy Guy's club had called Papa Sky. The talisman had burned the flesh of the demented half-flare Clayton Devine when he'd seized Colleen, had driven him back in the desperate, charged moment when they'd learned the servant was actually the master, that Devine was secretly Primal.

The powerful, vital charm had been given them from parts unknown, for reasons unknown.

*You have friends in high places*, Papa Sky had told Cal, and the memory brought no comfort, only the disquieting sense that such a friend might well see them as pawns in his grand design, not players in their own.

Doc was studying the leather triangle closely now. "Organic, almost certainly—"

"Speak English," Colleen said. "Or Russian, and then translate."

"I would say it came off an animal . . . but as to which in this brave new world, I would need another specimen for comparison."

*Another mystery*, Cal thought, *and one I'd bet hard currency we won't solve today.*

Colleen placed the chain carefully back inside her shirt. They remounted and moved on.

The wind kicked up out of the west, ran its cold hand across Cal's cheek. "This wind picks up, we may have to hunker down out here. Better keep an eye out for places to go to ground." But not for long, never for long, no matter what the flatlands threw at them.

He remembered the hard Minnesota winters of his childhood, where the snow flew parallel to the ground—a spray of fluffy white shrapnel you'd swear could peel off layers of skin. That's when you knew God was no Caribbean tour director but a stern taskmaster, and not one particularly inclined to like you. You found out who you really were in those endless gray months, not in the sunshine days. Good practice for what ultimately came down, Cal thought, and for what might lie ahead.

Doc clucked in mock disapproval. "America is for sissies. You haven't tried a Moscow winter."

"No," Colleen said as the horses continued on, "and I haven't driven a tank in Afghanistan, either. But I wouldn't lay bets on beating me at arm wrestling, if I were you."

"Which is why I take pains not to cross you, *Boi Baba*," Doc said.

Cal caught the slight smile Colleen shot him, the affection beneath. He would have to remember to ask Doc what that phrase meant when they were alone. Probably "pain in the ass" or "woman of sarcasm."

A distant cry sounded in the air, and he saw Colleen glance up sharply. He followed her gaze—nothing but a lone red-tailed hawk, its brown and white wings spread wide to catch the currents and float circling, scanning the ground for a lunch that thankfully was not them.

On several nights spaced over the last two weeks, Colleen had mentioned to Cal she thought she had heard a muffled beating like vast wings through the thick, obscuring cloud layer above them as they'd made camp. But it had been fleeting, and neither Cal nor Doc nor Goldie could corroborate the sound over the hammering prairie night wind that snatched away their body heat and drove them huddling into their tents till morning.

But whatever unseen god of hawks and demons shadowed them—if it was indeed more than imagination pricked by the brooding suggestiveness of this wide ocean grassland—it did not deign to make its appearance known.

"So what now?" Colleen asked Cal. "Homestead and wait for the crops to come up?"

"We continue west, see if we can find some people." Nowadays, short of tuning into K-Source, that was the only way to get current information. And also rumor, distortions and outright lies.

"Um, I don't think that's gonna be a problem. . . ." Goldie had pulled up, was scanning the fading light to the east.

Cal followed his gaze and spied the ragtag group of men and women emerging from the tall grass, about thirty in all, a hundred yards off, striding quickly toward them. Even at this distance and in this light, he could see they all held broken branches, stones, twisted lengths of pipe. A beefy man in front—a huge guy, like a refrigerator with a head—raised a pair of field glasses and scrutinized Cal and his companions.

He lowered them excitedly, shouted, "One in the middle, that's him!"

With a cry, the group broke into a run, came rushing toward them, waving their weapons.

"Your call," Colleen said evenly to Cal. "Hell-bent for leather, or . . . ?"

"Goldie?"

Colleen snorted. "Right, trust the one with the personality dis—"

*"Colleen."*

Goldie considered the mob, lapsing into a strange calm, as if there weren't a herd of buffalo stampeding toward him. After a long moment, he muttered, "Look like a nice group of folks."

A fortune cookie with a sting in its tail, like so much of what Goldie said. Was he being ironic, or . . . ?

Cal brought his horse around to face the attackers, unsheathed his sword. Colleen took the hint and unslung her crossbow; Doc freed his machete.

Goldie sat on Later and watched them come, began to hum under his breath. Cal caught a snatch of tune, realized it was "It's a Wonderful Day in the Neighborhood."

Refrigerator slowed as he drew near, raised his hands. "Easy, easy there, boss. We got no harm." He turned back to his followers. "Lay 'em down, folks." They set their weapons on the ground. Cal lowered his sword, nodded at Colleen and Doc to stand down.

Refrigerator strode up close to Cal, nearly his height standing on the ground. "You're Griffin, ain't you? Cal Griffin."

Cal hesitated a moment, then nodded.

Refrigerator squinted one big blue aggie eye, wrinkles fanning out. "You don't look like such a long drink of water." Then he bellowed a laugh like a volcanic eruption and seized Cal in a bear hug, nearly yanking him off his mount.

Colleen whipped up the crossbow reflexively, but Doc put a steadying hand on her wrist.

The big man let go and stepped back, still laughing, wiping tears from his eyes. His companions were all staring ardently at Cal, smiling shyly.

Up close, Cal could see now they were a weary and malnourished bunch, though leanly muscled as if used to hard labor. Their jackets and overcoats were buttoned against the chill, a sad attempt given the rips and tears that gaped like toothless mouths; their tattered clothes hung off them as if they were scarecrows outfitted by an indifferent assembler. Most were in their twenties and thirties, with a scattering of teens.

"I'm Mike Olifiers," Refrigerator said. "These others, hell, they can all introduce themselves. We been long traveling, out of Unionville, hugging the Missouri River mostly, but it's been worth it, yes *sir.*" He pulled a big kerchief from his pocket, blew his nose explosively, then fixed Cal again with an admiring gaze.

"We heard about you. You beat the Storm back in West Virginia, blew it clean outta Chicago."

"Well, sort of, not really . . ."

"You're famous in these parts, boy, don't you know that?"

"Hard to believe word's gotten around so fast," Colleen cut in. "I mean, it's not like we've got CNN or even *E! True Hollywood Story,* God help us."

"Word travels fast, even so," Olifiers replied. "*Good* word, 'cause there's so damn little of it."

Cal felt chilled rather than warmed. Oddly, he had a memory of when he was eighteen, when his mother died, and he had decided in that garish police waiting room to raise Tina on his own. He thought, then as now, *I'm not big enough.*

"I'm sure whatever you heard is mostly exaggeration," Cal said. "And besides, I didn't do it alone." *Or succeed,* Cal thought bitterly, remembering the slashing nightmare of the Source blasting into existence in the devastated Wishart house in Boone's Gap, spiriting Fred Wishart and Tina away.

"You're modest; I heard that, too," said Olifiers. He reached out to put a meaty hand on Cal's shoulder. His wrist came clear of his sleeve and Cal caught sight of a livid mark along the skin. Seeing this, Olifiers pulled his hand back as if burned, shame blossoming in his eyes. He pulled his sleeve down to cover it, looked at the others.

They shifted where they stood, tried to make subtle adjustments to their clothes at the neck and wrist.

Colleen picked up the vibe, looked in confusion from the group to Cal. But Doc had seen the mark, too. Cal nodded to him.

Doc dismounted, approached Olifiers and his band. "You will excuse me. . . ." With the expert hands of a physician, he examined Olifiers's wrist, turning it this way and that in the muted twilight. Then he drew near the others. Olifiers signaled compliance. No longer effusive, they stood as Doc lifted collars, pulled up pant legs to reveal thin ankles, inspected necks and shoulders.

He turned back to Cal, the expression on his angular face all the affirmation Cal needed. "Rope burns, lesions from manacles and shackles, welts—possibly from lashing . . ."

It was as Cal suspected. At the Preserve, Mary McCrae had told him of such things, but he had never seen it firsthand. Another wonder of this new world.

Cal's lips felt numb, reticent to pronounce the words. He forced them out. "You're escaped slaves, aren't you?"

The sun dipping low and every sign of a hard snow on the way, Cal elected not to question their new companions until he found them safe harbor for the night. As he, Colleen and Doc rode point through the grasslands, Goldie drew up alongside on Later, speaking low so the fugitives straggling behind couldn't hear.

"I hate to be the bearer of bad tidings—"

"Since when?" Colleen interjected.

Cal cut her off with a wave, but Goldie was unperturbed. "As long as we have Winnie the Pooh and the other residents of the Hundred-Acre Wood accompanying us on our jaunty way, it's virtually a sure thing we're gonna get a visit from the paddyrollers. Maybe not today, maybe not tomorrow, but soon and for the rest of our lives."

"The paddy—what?" Colleen asked. "They anything like the Tommyknockers?"

"No, Colleen, those are creatures from folklore and a Stephen King novel," Goldie said, with a patronizing air she would've liked to chop into little pieces and stuff down his throat. "I'm talking reality, or at least history here."

Cal nodded, remembering the lessons his mother had given him to augment the inadequate—and inaccurate—courses he had endured back at Hurley High. "The paddyrollers were men who made a living pursuing escaped slaves and returning them to their masters."

Doc added, "During and in the period immediately prior to your American Civil War."

Colleen groaned, reining Big-T back as the big gelding tried to surge forward. "Am I the only one here without the least excuse for an education?"

Doc smiled gently. "No, Colleen, you are educated in the skills that are most useful of all. The rest of us have simply accumulated a magpie collection of mostly useless facts."

Colleen grimaced. "God, Viktor, I hate it when you're charming." But her eyes were smiling. "Paddyrollers, huh?" She contemplated Olifiers and the group of footsore men and women gamely bringing up the rear.

"Or something with an alternate name but the same enchanting job description," Goldie noted.

"It may be a new world," Cal said, sorrow welling in his voice, "but it's a whole lot like the one that came before it."

Colleen let out a slow breath, considering. "If they've got a good tracker, or anyone with a map ability like yours—" She nodded toward Cal.

"Like I used to have, you mean."

"Whatever. We're in for a hell of a ride."

"An E-ticket ride, if I might elaborate," muttered Goldie.

"Yeah," Colleen said. "And no one would know what the hell you're elaborating about, as usual."

"Oops, sorry, I always forget you're of a generation without cultural grounding." Goldie plucked one of the five aces from his hat, toyed with it between his fingers. "Second vocabulary term of the day. It's an old thing from Disneyland—back when there *was* a Disneyland, I suppose. My esteemed mother and father took me there, a little side trip from a couple of symposia they were attending." A flick of his fingers and the ace was gone . . . appearing back in the brim with the other cards. "They didn't just use to have one pass where you'd enter and ride all the attractions. There were tickets with letter grades—A, B, C, D and E. The A tickets were really lame—trolley rides on Main Street, that sort of thing. But the E-ticket rides, now that was *real* magic, the monorail, jungle cruise, haunted mansion. . . . It was the highest you could go, the best."

"Thanks as usual for telling me more than I'd ever need to know," Colleen huffed. "Anyhow, if you're right about that paddyroller stuff, what's coming down the pike won't be the best of anything. It'll be a royal ass-kicking, and I'd just as soon it not be us on the receiving end."

"Ducking out on a fight?" Cal grinned devilishly. "That doesn't sound like the Colleen Brooks I know."

"In case you haven't noticed, I'm not Russell Crowe in *Gladiator.*" Answering their looks, she added. "Okay, okay, maybe I *am* Russell Crowe in *Gladiator,* but that doesn't mean I have to like it . . . at least, not all the time." Another glance back at Olifiers and his group. "All I'm saying is, just because these folks are charter members of the Cal Griffin fan club doesn't mean we should run interference for them till spring thaw."

"So what would you have them do, Colleen?" Doc asked. "Return to the life they so recently fled?"

"They *claim* they fled. Honestly, Viktor, we don't have to believe everything Joe Apocalypse and his brother tells us. I mean, look at the mess it got us into back in Chicago."

Anguish blossomed in Goldie's eyes, was quickly suppressed.

Colleen was instantly repentant. "Oh God, Goldman, I'm sorry. . . . I use my mouth like most people use a sledgehammer."

For the briefest moment, Cal flashed again on Agent Larry Shango, whom he'd seen use a hammer like that most effectively, and fortuitously, when Shango had entered the fray at a deserted creekbed in Albermarle County and saved Herman Goldman from paramilitary raiders; before Shango had shared the secret list naming the scientists of the Source Project with them. He wondered on what path that fierce, self-contained traveler might now be embarked.

Cal forced his mind back to the here and now, to doing what he did best . . . smoothing the rough edges, binding the four of them back together, keeping them on track.

"We're all worn to the nub," Cal said. "Let's get these folks bedded down for the night. Then we can recharge, get some perspective."

Goldie nodded, urged his horse forward. But for the rest of their ride, he was silent.

# TWO

## Outside Medicine Bow, Wyoming

Mama Diamond was alone in her house of rock and bone when she heard the whistle far down the tracks and over the horizon, and mistook it for a memory.

Mama Diamond was old. She was thin as chicken bones, and a cataract had clouded much of the vision in her left eye. She wore rings on her fingers, the rings fixed in place by swollen knuckles, a part of her now. The rings were cheap silver melted down from old forks and spoons, set with garnet and turquoise. She had made them herself, back when her lapidary and fossil business just off the juncture of highways 30 and 487 was a going concern, here at the foot of Como Bluff. One of the richest fossil beds in the world, it was a perfect spot for tourists to wile away an hour or two on the drive from Laramie to Casper, just a long shout out of Medicine Bow in the flyspeck little town of Burnt Stick. She was Japanese-American, but the tourists took her for Blackfoot. She made no effort to disabuse them of the notion; it was good for business.

But now there were no more tourists, only wanderers and marauders and crazy, lost pilgrims on the way from somewhere to nowhere or back again.

Mama herself was a long way from the place she'd once called home in the San Bernardino Mountains of California. There she'd had a different name, been called Nisei among other things, and had parents who told her bedtime stories of their growing times in Osaka and San Francisco, at least in the days before she and her family had been gathered up like raw cotton in a sack and carted off to the internment camps at Manzanar and Heart Mountain.

So she had set off on her own journey long years ago, been a wanderer and a pilgrim herself, traversing the Utah, Colorado and Montana ranges and even the far-flung Gobi, until she had come at last to Wyoming, to this place of long skies and fierce winters. She liked living in a place with hard weather and harder people, in the shadow of the mountains that told the truth of the land. Folks said America was a young country, but those granite spires put the lie to that. It was a realm like everywhere else in this old world, with layer upon ancient layer, and the history there in the rock if you just took the time to listen for it. The stones and bones of the buried past beckoning to be discovered, prized out, dusted and shined and revealed in their true glory.

She sat now on the porch of her old house in the bent-birch rocker, bundled against the gray noon wind in her weathered leather overcoat with the elk buttons and rabbit lining. Winter was coming on, she could feel it in the late November bite of the air, and she wondered if it would be harsh—where one ran a rope from building to building so as not to get lost in the demon-breath of blizzard—or the milder variety of the past few years. Since the Change, there was no telling what the future might bring.

Only the likelihood that today would be like yesterday and the day before. Forecast: solitude, with more of the same.

She liked to sit on her porch and read in the afternoon, now that Burnt Stick was a ghost town.

Or at least "depopulated." All the people had gone away, or died, after the Change. Without pumped water, Burnt Stick was simply too dry in the hotter months to keep a population. These days, you had to know how to find water, how to carry it, how to store the rainfall—skills only a scavenger rat like Mama Diamond readily possessed. She was not exactly the only living thing in Burnt Stick—she had seen coyotes in packs, pronghorn, mule deer, and those things, not quite human, that shambled through the streets now and again after dark.

The only living ordinary human person, that she was. Well, maybe not "ordinary" in the old sense. But un-Changed. Human flesh. All too.

She lifted her canteen, sipped tepid water, squinted her good eye at the book she'd carried out. It was a Tom Clancy novel from the Benteen Avenue lending library, more pages than pebbles in a quarry. It would last her a good long time. There were no new books anymore. But Mama Diamond didn't figure she would run out of books, not before her eyesight failed altogether.

The pace of the novel was slacking now. Everybody was lecturing the President about some crisis. *Boys,* Mama Diamond thought, *you didn't know a crisis from a wood louse.*

In these silly, diverting books that wiled away the time, virile men were always saving the world. But her dusty long experience had taught her that no one ever saved the whole world, not really, only their own little part of it. And truth to tell, it was more often the women doing the saving than the men, whatever the history books said.

All those submarines and aircraft carriers must have shut down at the Change, just like the TV stations and the automobiles. Maybe there were aircraft carriers still floating at sea, all the sailors long since starved to death. Had they taken to cannibalism as a last resort? Or would they have scattered to open boats and made for land, trusting themselves to the whims of wind and fate? As everyone now had, really. Amy Hutchins, who used to run the grocery store across the street, had had a boy in the navy. Amy was long gone now, of course. Everybody was gone.

The train whistle sounded again.

It *was* a train whistle, unmistakably so. The old-fashioned kind, not that bleating honk the freighters made; a whistle that called over the chill range land like a lost love, that brought strange, dark carnivals in its wake and disarranged time.

Mama Diamond stirred uneasily. She dropped the paperback and stood, bones creaking almost as loudly as the old pine planks. She shuffled down Parkhill Street to the old Burnt Stick railroad station, to where she could get a good long look at the tracks.

The depot had not been active for twenty-five years. Freight used to come through every couple of days, low-sulfur coal hauled from the Hanna mines in Carbon County. But the freights never even slowed at Burnt Stick. The depot was a relic, all flaking paint, planks and beams bleached by sun and cracked by cold. She guessed it was the smell she liked best. Old wood, wind-whipped, giving up ghosts of pine and creosote.

The old Union Pacific tracks cut due south into the Medicine Bow Range, north into the gray sage foothills of the Shirley Mountains, then east across the Laramie Range, where ages ago sharks the size of sperm whales had settled down to die, later joined by maiasaurs and T. rex. The call had come echoing off the hills, and Mama Diamond turned, facing their heights, squinting up her good eye against the ruthless slate light. But if there was a train, she couldn't see it.

She watched for a time, patient but vaguely alarmed.

Now came the whistle again, closer, almost taunting (no need, surely, to blow a whistle in all this emptiness). Mama Diamond had the unsettling thought that she should climb down off the platform and paste her ear to the steel track like the Indians in the old matinees. She'd probably pull a muscle if she tried it—get stuck there, and the train (if there *was* a train) would split her head open like a cleaver splitting a vine-ripened tomato.

But there was no need to listen to the tracks, because here was the train itself, suddenly visible winding out of the foothills like a black millipede scuttling from a crevice in a basement wall. It was blurred in the distance, so she couldn't be certain if it had topped the ridge or actually *burst* out of the earth itself. She tried to resolve the shape of the thing, peering into an ice-breath of wind that made her eyes sting and water, but all she could at first make out was a featureless assemblage of rectangular boxes, like a subway train.

As it approached, however, it seemed to take on complexity and ornamentation, and she wasn't sure if her eyes were playing tricks or—crazy thought—the train was actually *changing* as it drew near, deciding how best to present itself.

It came chuffing down toward Burnt Stick, and Mama Diamond stepped cautiously back into the shadow of the depot. Her mouth was dry again, but she had left her canteen on the porch, the chill air turning its surface cold as a tombstone as it lay atop the Clancy paperback.

The train began to slow.

*Sweet Jesus*, Mama Diamond thought, *what dark miracle is this?*

It was no ordinary train—as if she needed convincing of that, in a world without machines. It now clearly revealed itself as a single engine with a long string of passenger cars. The engine was antique-looking but shiny clean, like a coal-burner dragged out of a museum. The passenger cars were rounded and streamlined like the old transcontinental sleepers. Both the engine and cars were a carapace black, and the passenger windows, too, held the same darkness, no light piercing through. The insides, Mama thought, must be cold as a freezer. And who in their right mind would paint a passenger car that kind of black? If it *was* paint; the whole thing looked cast in onyx.

The train slowed, came huffing to a stop like something out of a dream, and Mama Diamond began to wish she had taken the trouble to hide herself, began to wish she had not even come here, that she had stayed inside like a sensible person. Though she suspected there was no hiding from whatever the train carried.

She thought about how peaceful it had been just a few minutes ago, when she was alone with her book and the sleepy hum of the town.

The train halted, hissing hot breaths of steam. Mama Diamond tried to get a look at the driver. But the cab windows were blacked as well.

From within the cars, Mama Diamond discerned a new sound, of movement and bodies, and a burbling of voices that might have been men or beasts or something in between. Her stomach tightened, she felt the bristly, gray-steel hairs on her neck rise.

A passenger door slid open on the first coach and Mama Diamond jerked her head in that direction.

A man climbed out. A man with long black hair pulled hard back and held by a white-gold clasp, wearing black fathomless shades, black shirt and slacks and belt with a white-gold buckle, his long black coat fanning out behind him. He held a dark cigarette with burning red tip, and smoke curled from his cold thin lips.

As he walked toward her, Mama Diamond knew this contained, silent man had not been one of the brute voices within. His voice would be as clear and sharp as a stiletto.

She stood watching as he came near, and in the merciless gray light it seemed as if he suddenly *shimmered* like ripples on a storm-wracked lake and changed, growing bigger and bonier, like strata shooting up out of a rock face. His black leather cloak altered, too, stretching out long fingers, gaining its own powerful architecture, becoming . . .

*Wings*, leathery wings big as box kites, supported by vast pebbled shoulders, which in turn supported a scaly head, ridge-boned and hard-angled, with eyes set deep in burnished sockets, eyes golden as Kazakhstan amber wrapped around a Jurassic spider. The cigarette was gone from his taloned hand, but a memory of smoke still curled from between his dagger teeth.

*I'm too old to run away*, Mama Diamond thought. Probably crack a hip if she tried, and then what? No 911, no ambulance out of the county clinic.

Anyway, she thought, when Death comes for you with bat wings and golden eyes in a black impossible train, running probably isn't much of a strategy.

Her knees trembled. She hoped they wouldn't buckle on her. The dragon drew up close to her now—slowly, smoothly, with the invisible majesty of great power—and fear bubbled through Mama Diamond like a dizzy drug.

The dragon-thing, this grotesque that had been a man—no, merely *seemed* a man—moments ago, stood glaring down at her.

"I couldn't decide what to wear . . . so I thought I'd give you a choice." His voice, clearly New York/East Coast, held the precision of a keen blade, plus a resonance potent as a boulder rolling down a rocky slope.

A *choice*, Mama Diamond thought. Like the train itself, changing as it drew near, somehow taunting, threatening.

"Which is the truth?" Mama Diamond asked, and was surprised at how level her voice sounded.

"Both . . . but this is the latest model."

Mama Diamond studied the razor claws, the teeth like a tyrannosaur. "If this is what I have to deal with, I'd just as soon see it."

"You've got sand," the dragon said. "Or I could say grit . . . or stones." Mama Diamond knew he was toying with her, playing his cruel games as he had no doubt often done even before the world had turned over, before he had become what he'd always been within.

Mama Diamond said nothing. Silence, she knew, could be a blade, too. Or at least a tool to make folks get to the point.

"Good of you to meet me," he said, and even in the gray light of winter coming, his black scales held an iridescence like the peacock pyrites she'd once hawked to city dwellers who'd only seen those colors in grease streaks on tarmac.

"I have to confess I didn't know you were coming."

"But you did. On some level. We know a lot of things we don't think we know. You are Judith Kuriyama?"

Not for a long time, not really. "People call me—"

"Mama Diamond."

"Uh-huh."

"Proprietor, Rock and Bone?"

"Yes. And you are—?"

"Ely Stern. Attorney-at-law. Once upon a time."

"What do you want, Ely Stern?"

"We'll start," the dragon said, "with a look at your shop."

Arnie Sproule, an old friend of Mama Diamond's, dead since '92, used to tell this joke:

*What's the difference between a dead lawyer in the middle of the road and a dead snake in the middle of the road?*

And before you could answer, Arnie would grin and say: *There are skid marks in front of the snake.*

An old groaner, and not a particularly funny one. But now here was Ely Stern, combining perhaps the worst aspects of the two, lawyer and serpent. Any skid marks in front of Ely Stern would surely have represented a fevered attempt to brake and flee.

The worst part, Mama Diamond thought as she slow-walked with the dragon down the main street of Burnt Stick, was how *calming* his presence was. Not *reassuring*—oh no, definitely not—but calming the way an oil slick calms a wind-whipped sea; calming the way a dose of Thorazine calms a lunatic. The energy, the madness, is intact, but it can't be expressed. Something about Ely Stern slowed the heartbeat and thickened the tongue. One was not *permitted* to panic in his grand and overweening presence.

Mama Diamond walked in the dragon's shadow.

"How 'bout you tell me," Stern asked in a conversational tone, "just why you're called Mama Diamond?"

"The native kids call me that." She was startled by the sound of her own voice, insanely chatty. "Called me that. They'd bring in dusty old quartzite now and again. I'd clean and tumble it for 'em. Making diamonds, they called it."

"But that wasn't your stock-in-trade—quartz."

"Surely not. No, I'm a rock hound and a purveyor of semiprecious stones." Her good eye glanced sidelong at his pebbled hide and vast muscles, the rough protrusions along his frame proclaiming the brute skeleton beneath. "And also bones . . ."

They turned off Parkhill onto Vaughan, and Stern halted abruptly. They had reached her shop now, and he peered at it, surprised—yes, he could actually be surprised—and impressed.

"The thing I so love about travel," Stern said, "is there's a wonderment around every corner. . . ."

No zoning commissioner in his right mind would ever have allowed Mama Diamond to build it, of course. Nor would the Geographic Society nor the Paleontological Research Institute nor Friends of the Earth nor the Sierra Club. Everyone from Robert Bakker to Jack Horner would have pitched a fit. And the press—at least, in the old, pre-Change days—would have had a field day.

But then, she hadn't built it. Old Esperanza Piller, grandmother of Mildred Cummings Fielding, from whom Mama Diamond herself had bought the place in '81, had hired the working men and former slaves who had quarried and assembled this structure ninety years back and more, before anyone had the least notion to raise an objection.

Back when farmers round here were still turning up triceratops skulls in their potato beds.

The Rock and Bone, Mama Diamond's fossil and lapidary shop, was a house built of dinosaur bones.

It had weathered the Storm—also called the Change, the Upheaval and the Big Friggin' Mess—without so much as a quiver.

In truth, the house wasn't wholly made of dinosaur bones; no, they were still held in their rock matrixes, the big blocks mortared into place. But it didn't take one whit off their grandeur, and Mama Diamond loved the place as much now as when she had first glimpsed it tooling down the blue highway of U.S. 30 in the dwindling light of that long-ago spring day.

Her Fortress, her Sanctuary, her Palace of Delights. Or, as the native kids only half-jokingly called it way back when, her Treasure Chest.

The chill sun glinted on Stern's gold-coin eyes as he canted his head and appraised the diplodocus bones flanking the doorway, the ribs of the house actual iguanodon and allosaur ribs. Bones not too different from the dragon's own, Mama Diamond reflected—at least, the therapods. And she realized, looking at Stern in his terrible saurian beauty, that he was as close as she would ever come to seeing an actual dinosaur walking. But then, *they* hadn't flown or talked or breathed smoke.

Not that anyone could really say.

As if the dragon had somehow caught the sound of her thought and completed it, Stern said, "I wonder what energies ruled their world . . . the old or the new?"

Mama Diamond said nothing—there was no answer—but she pondered, in the distant part of her mind held separate from the fear, if the Change might indeed be cyclical, like the great ice sheets that had once covered this land.

Another gust of wind flared up, stiffening the seams of her face. The handmade wooden sign with the words STONE AND BONE suspended off the overhang of roof creaked on its chains.

Mama Diamond opened her door and stepped inside.

"Come in," she said against her own better judgment, judgment reduced to a wheedling screech at the back of her skull, and she thought of Dracula inviting Renfield to step over the threshold of his castle. Only, the tables were turned in this case, she was inviting the monster into her lair, and she wondered how many before her had done this, and to what terrible consequence. She looked up at the molten-eyed, big-shouldered dragon. "If you can."

"I still know how to negotiate doorways," Stern said in his dry furnace voice.

The store was dim, but Stern blocked her when she reached for an oil lamp. Maybe dragons could see a little better in the dark than in the light, Mama Diamond considered. Or maybe they were just wary of fire.

He put out a razored hand to stay her motion, casually; it barely brushed her shoulder. But a sudden snap of blue lightning spit from his fingertip, passing into Mama Diamond's skin and bones, diffusing through her like smoke. There was a brief instant of her feeling like her insides were lit up, spectacularly energized and alive, then it was gone.

She and Stern looked at each other with an identical expression, and Mama Diamond realized that he was as surprised as she. For the first time since he had arrived, something had happened that he had not intended.

Stern blinked, dismissing it, then cast his gaze over the shop, taking it all in, not pausing at the oreodont skulls, the smilodons with their saber fangs, the hadrosaur eggs spirited out of China.

His gaze came to the faded photograph taped to the register, the snapshot of the blond child smiling by a riverside, her college chum Katy's daughter back when Carter was President. Stern studied the girl closely, his eyes lingering.

"She remind you of someone?" Mama Diamond asked.

"Yes." The dragon's voice was oddly softened, as close to human as it might ever sound.

"She safe?" Mama Diamond was surprised at her question; she hadn't thought to ask it. But it had been sparked by the sudden awareness there might be something, *someone*, this thunder lizard actually cared about.

The image came to her of the rough-hewn illustration from *The Hobbit* in her ratty thrift-store copy, the drawing old Tolkien himself had done, of the dragon Smaug wrapped around his treasure trove of gold.

*What might Stern hold as his treasure?*

For a long time, he said nothing, and Mama Diamond thought he wasn't going to speak. But then the words came, as muted as the wind held outside the bone-thick walls.

"In safekeeping . . ." the dragon murmured.

Stern said it as in a dream, and he said it to himself, Mama Diamond felt sure. But still it had been an answer, if one she herself didn't have the key to decipher.

Then, as if a switch had been thrown, Stern was again scanning the cases and shelves with that nuclear-reactor gaze of his. Mama Diamond knew somehow that on his walk from the station, and his ruminations on her house and the weathered photograph, Stern had been on his own time, taking a break for reflection and diversion. But now he was back on the clock.

"Well, well," Stern said, his wings folded and his head bent over one of the glass cases.

"They're not truly precious gems," Mama Diamond said. "No *real* diamonds here. Just desert rocks, minerals, oxides, carbonates, silicates from all over the world."

"I know what I'm looking for."

"Red beryls and morganite; almandine, pyrope, and other garnets . . ." Mama Diamond rattled it off, on automatic; she knew her spiel from years of practice and ease. But peering up at the dragon, she contemplated a new mystery. For while it was clear even in this dimness that these radiant stones *were* what Stern had been looking for, they were clearly not what he valued nor cared about. She had seen that covetous look in enough customers' eyes, the craving, the can't-live-without-it-whatever-the-price, to know it when she saw it. And when she didn't.

*This is merely a means to an end for him. A currency.*

But to buy what?

"Chrysoberyl in three varieties," Mama was continuing. "That's a cat's-eye you're looking at. . . ."

"Yes. Now bring me some bags."

"Bags?"

"Sacks, suitcases—whatever you have."

Mama Diamond felt heartsick. She had spent years accumulating this inventory. Trading it, selling it judiciously, increasing its net worth. She had always depended on the slow equilibrium of acquisition and exchange, never drawing down the true deep inventory faster than it could be replaced and upgraded.

And since the Change the shop had been a great comfort to her, though of course there was no money it in anymore—and what was money worth these days, anyhow? She cherished these stones. And they protected her, or so Mama Diamond had come to believe. Since the Change there had been strange characters on the street at night now and again, many clearly intent on doing harm. They never stopped, of course; there was no reason for anyone, any*thing*, to linger in Burnt Stick. But down the long hot summer and cooling autumn they looted, sometimes they vandalized. They had broken windows and emptied shelves at the 7-Eleven, the grocery, various houses. Mama Diamond had more food stockpiled in her basement than any of those places. But the half-human vandals had never broken in. Mama Diamond thought somehow the stones might be responsible. Bright, shiny, repellent to darker creatures. Except, apparently, this dragon.

"You taking my stock?" she asked Ely Stern.

"You're really very quick for a woman of your years."

"Maybe it's not for sale." She didn't mean the words to tremble so. She couldn't help it.

"Maybe I'm not buying. Maybe I'm bartering"

"What have you got to trade?"

"Your life. If I'm feeling kind."

This cool and absolutely convincing threat was too much for Mama Diamond. Her courage evaporated. Her knees buckled and she sat down right there on the floor of the Stone and Bone.

"Take what you have to," she wheezed. "You can get your own damn bags."

Then she passed out, or so it seemed. A few memories of that fading day (and evening, as it lingered on) remained. She remembered, or had dreamed, that the dragon looked on, huge and imperious, as huddled bunches of small gray men—or rather, hideous parodies of men, with stooped shoulders, pinpoint teeth and milky white eyes—carried out the gleaming stones of her inventory (the days of her life measured in peridot and tourmaline) in plastic grocery store sacks, in old luggage, in yellowed pillowcases, to the creaking Burnt Stick train depot and the impossible black train.

An impossible train in more than one fashion. It had arrived from the north, facing south, toward the Hanna mines. But now it was turned the other direction, though there were no sidings here, no rail turntable closer than a hundred miles away. It was as if the train had simply inverted itself, switched back for front.

Or maybe that was just part of the dream.

When she came fully awake, the moon was out, a thin sliver hanging over the Medicine Bow Range, and she was lying on her back on the platform, and the train was gone. That was good, the absence of the train, as if an abscessed tooth had been pulled.

The bad news—well, one small part of it—was that she ached in every bone and muscle. The night had turned bitterly cold. She should have been in bed with a fire crackling in the woodstove. Here she was instead, stretched out on these old unyielding boards, the night wind riding up her coattail.

She moved against the pain as if against an invisible weight, a whole ocean of pain bearing down on her in one inexorable wave. She flexed finger joints, elbows, then bent at the waist and sat up, an act that made the town spin on the pivot of her head.

She gained her feet at last.

The walk home was excruciating—worse, because she knew what she would find at the end of it. Her shop, stripped; her inventory, stolen; all that glittering magic lost and departed.

The bones—literally—would still be there. But so much gone, ripped away, amputated.

Her bed would be waiting, at least. Her bed, and the woodstove.

What she did not expect was the large man in a ragged trench coat squatting on her steps, an oil lamp lit beside him.

Mama Diamond thought: *What fresh hell—?*

But there was not much menace in this stranger, not as Mama Diamond sensed it. Power, yes. Great strength, yes, and great restraint.

The man stood up. He was a black man, and he spoke with the faintest trace of a soft accent. He had probably tried in his growing years to lose it, to cloak himself in the anonymity of Anyplace, America. But Mama's ears were sharp, and she caught the lilt she had heard in voices long ago, in her travels South, in the sultry, primordial places of the Louisiana bayou.

"I'm a federal agent," he said. "My name is Larry Shango, and I believe you've been robbed."

# THREE

## The Girl in Her Apartment

That night, she had the dream again. The one with the third blind man, the one who could see. It perplexed her, she didn't know how that could be so, but he told her not to worry, she'd know when they met. And in that telling, at least, she came to a partial knowing, that somehow his name was Blindman, and that it was not his eyes that were blind.

In the dream, they sat in a park, the two of them, the wind scattering the dry leaves like frightened children, and she could look across the street to the strange house, the one that was shrouded in night, lights shining within, yet a bright daylit sky above.

With that odd split consciousness of dreamer and dream, she realized she had seen this image before somewhere—in a book?—that it was a painting, and there was a name associated with it that at first she could not summon to mind. Yet she also knew that name had once been the Blindman's heart.

*Magritte . . .*

As if sensing her thought, the third blind man smiled, large even teeth dazzling against his young dark face, the old dark eyes. "The heart broken was Goldman's," he said.

She knew she should remember who the gold man was, too, but

her mind felt muted as it so often did nowadays, as if pale fingers had brushed against her lips and stifled the answer.

A rumble sounded in the azure sky, rolling in from the west, and she smelled a sharp tang in the air, like fresh sheets off a clothesline, and she knew a storm was coming.

"Time to get you home," the third blind man said.

There was a crackling and snapping in the sky like insane angry blue lightning. It swirled down at her faster than thought, seized her like the jaws of a big dog that was all the world. It tore at her and shook her and worried her as if she were a small dead thing, and it screamed and she screamed, too.

The Girl woke up in bed. The bed that looked just like her bed, under the blue and pink blankets that looked just like her blankets.

It was the same, and that was the really terrible part.

She threw back the covers and sat up and stretched, feeling the coil and ache of young muscles.

It was cold in the apartment, and she drew on the familiar terry-cloth robe that lay at the foot of the bed.

She rose and padded across her room in the darkness, lithe as flowing water—navigating with easy familiarity the clutter of dance magazines, souvenir programs, textbooks and, of course, the Nijinsky diary—and emerged out into the hall.

The door to the other bedroom lay half open. She commanded herself not to look again, not to give in to the tiny hope that was so akin to hopelessness. But as ever she lacked the will.

In the predawn gloom, the hissing lights from Patel's Grocery and the Amoco billboard shed just enough illumination to cast the room in noir starkness. The Marvin the Martian clock stood sentinel by the bedside, the covers tossed aside as if another had just awoken from unquiet dreams, too, and momentarily stepped away.

But it wasn't so, the Girl knew. There was no one else here. But there *should* be, a part of her memory insisted. She should not be alone. He had promised her she wouldn't be alone.

She continued on to the bathroom, where she showered and dried and did her morning things.

She looked at herself in the mirror, just like her mirror, the silvering coming away in the upper left and lower right corners. Her hair was dark and her eyes were dark—not blue at all, though strangely somehow she felt they *should* be blue—and her skin was smooth and pink, and her bare feet were planted solidly on the cracked blue tile.

What could possibly be wrong about that?

Her Danskin leotard and tights hung from the hook on the back of the door and she drew them on, feeling their snug familiarity with the subtle curve and flare of her body. She picked up the Grishko slippers from where they lay curled beside the cabinet and slid them onto artfully callused feet.

She glided out into the still, silent living room and switched on the television, turned the volume low. *It shouldn't be working,* she told herself in some dim back part of her mind—as she told herself every time she turned it on—but it glowed to life as always. Sometimes it showed TV series or movies she knew well, remembered from when she was little, or from more recent times. On other occasions, it displayed a puzzling multicolored snow or revealed disturbing abstract patterns.

But mostly it broadcast snatches of scenes the Girl couldn't place—disjointed moments in vibrant color or scratchy black-and-white, some in English but many in languages that sounded like they might be Japanese, Spanish, Portuguese, French. These she classified as being derived from Sakamoto or Sanrio, Monteiro or St. Ives, without clearly understanding what those names meant, or from where she summoned them.

The early daylight sun shone through the slats of the window blinds, painting the walls and the Girl with shadows like prison bars. She folded back the faded area rug, ran through her regimen of stretches. Then she assumed first position before the large practice mirror, went through her variations and barre work, felt the call and response of finely tuned muscle and sinew.

Once these motions had been primal to her, almost the totality of her past, present and future.

But now they were just something to do to fill the time, on the track of remembered action, like a train that returned you to where you started.

And beneath everything, like a low vibration just below the threshold of sound, the sense of *wrongness,* humming in the marrow of her bones, in the helixes within her cells.

Completing her routine in due course, the Girl ventured into the kitchen, nuked the coffee in its WNET pledge mug in the microwave. The level of instant coffee in the Sanka jar was always the same as she spooned it out, and the strawberry Pop-Tart always the last as she withdrew it from the box in the freezer and popped it in the toaster.

*Is it live or is it Memorex?* The Girl couldn't quite place who had told her of the commercial with the old lady jazz singer breaking a glass with her voice—only that it had been someone with a twin, someone who had had something horribly wrong with him. But the Girl herself had never seen the commercial, and—despite the melancholy variety of programming on the set now—it never appeared.

She remembered, too, the story someone—she had trouble remembering who—had read her when she was little (but not too little to comprehend it) by that bearded guy who had written for *Star Trek*, in which strange creatures appeared at night and rebuilt an exact duplicate of the entire world for the next day, so you would think it was all the same.

But invariably, of course, they screwed it all up.

The Girl walked back out to the living room. She set the Pop-Tart and coffee on a side table and plopped cross-legged onto the burgundy recliner with the tear hidden in back. She reached behind her and selected a volume from the big maple bookcase that displayed the round jelly-glass stain, exactly like the one that had journeyed with them when she and the companion now walled off from her recollection had come from Hurley, Minnesota, when she was small.

The book was a tattered leather copy of *Little Women*. The Girl knew it well; her mother had read this book to her, and that unremembered *other* had, too, and she'd read it many times herself. She flipped through it. All the pages were there, and all the words.

Not so with many of the other works on the shelf, she knew. They might hold only half the words, or a third of the pages might be blank, or the cover a blur.

She drew out another book, a dark blue one with a gold dragon on the spine, and the title *A Strange Manuscript Found in a Copper Cylinder*. She had not inspected this one before. With mild curiosity, she blew the dust off and opened it, saw scrawled in a childish hand on the inside front cover, "This Book Belongs to Agnes Hilliard Wu."

The frontispiece showed a group of mustached and bearded men in animated conversation around a table, with the caption "The Doctor was evidently discoursing upon a favorite topic." She fanned the pages. The words seemed intact, set whole. Agnes Wu must have cherished this book; must still, wherever she might be. There were other books on the shelves inscribed to Agnes, books in a lilting text that the Girl recognized (although she could not have said precisely how) as Thai; she wondered if Agnes Wu, whoever she was, might once have lived in that fantasy place.

The Regulator clock on the wall chimed the half hour—seven-thirty. The Girl returned the book to its place on the shelf, uncurled and stood.

Beyond her apartment, the city waited, and her regular classes, and the School of American Ballet.

The train on its track, circling.

The Girl emerged from her fourth-floor walk-up out onto the street, dressed in her school grays, the book bag with its toe-shoe insignia slung over her shoulder. The morning was bright and mild, with none of the weight of humidity nor razor chill she associated with so many of her days in Manhattan. Unseen, the robins and skylarks trilled their songs, and strangers bustled about on the brownstone street as if they were actually going somewhere.

Eighty-first looked exactly right; the streets she most often walked on were always as she remembered them. Some of the other streets were complete, too—maybe St. Ives or Monteiro or the others knew them. But sometimes she'd turn a corner and be back on the street she was on before, or it would just be fog.

Outside her place, the Girl passed the cherry tree within its circle of vertical iron bars, a prisoner of Eighty-first Street. It blossomed even in captivity.

As she strode toward Columbus and St. Augustine Middle School, a gentle wind detached some of the blossoms from the tree and they pursued her, floated about her like a scene from *Madame Butterfly*. She caught one in her hand and ran it along her lips, her cheek; it felt like her own soft skin.

Joggers loped past her and kids strolled bantering in easy, laughing conversation. The Girl knew by now not to try to speak to them. People looked real, too, but they wouldn't engage her in conversation; they were like extras in a movie.

Every now and then, though, someone would talk to her, and then she knew they were really real, or at least connected to someone who was.

The Girl slowed as she came to Mr. Lungo's home. It was the familiar curlicued Victorian wedding cake of a house she remembered. But really, with its warped and weathered shingles, its peeling paint, listing fenceposts and wild devil grass, it was more like Miss Havisham's ruin of a cake in *Great Expectations*, the symbol of abandonment, and broken promises, and time stood still. Even when she was little it had disquieted her, seemed an anomaly brutishly inserted onto this ordered street of brownstones with their weathered stoops and muted foliage.

It wasn't like this every day. Sometimes the lot showed nothing more than blackened timbers and twisted wreckage, smoke curling up and choking the air, the way the house had been after disaster had befallen it on that riotous, murdering night.

Other times it wasn't there at all—just the houses adjoining on either side, butted up against one another.

Lungo himself never made an appearance. But occasionally, his front-porch glider would rock with the slightest motion from the wind, in the shade of his scraggly jacaranda, and his twisted walking stick, like an arthritic, broken finger, would be resting against the rail.

*The realest people here are the ghosts*, the Girl thought, and turned onto Columbus.

She caught the sweet liquid sound from far off, way around the corner, like the smell of menthol, and honey on your tongue, and the azure sky at sunset when the stars were just peering through.

Then the husky, lulling murmur of the saxophone paused in midphrase.

"Well, if it ain't Anna Pavlova. . . ."

The blind black man turned his milk-sheened, useless eyes toward her and smiled with that smile that was like sinking into a warm bath. How he could know she was there before she spoke was always a mystery to her, and it felt right.

He was not young like the third blind man in her dream, nor pale like the other, malign one. His skin was a deep burnished brown, like old, oiled furniture, and when the light hit it just so, it showed a subtlety of gray, like a fine coating of ash.

"How they treatin' you today, sweet girl?" Papa Sky asked.

"Okay," she replied, and both the question and the answer soothed her, although she couldn't have said who she thought "they" were.

"Well, you just hang in there. You got friends in high places. What you wanna hear today?"

She shrugged, which was a request in itself. Dealer's choice . . . and when the dealer was this good, it was all flow.

Papa Sky put the shaved Leblanc reed of the 1922 Selmer alto sax (this instrument that was almost, but not quite, as old as he was) to his wetted lips, and it was an incantation and supplication in one.

The glorious sounds poured out, smooth perfection, throaty and soaring and exultant.

The Girl recognized the tune. The last time he'd played it, the old blind black man (the half *cubano* as he called himself) had told her it was called "Night and Day."

She closed her eyes and let the melody fill her, began to move to it. And this was no longer just going through the motions, nor feigning interest in the arabesque and pas de deux that had once been her universe.

*Night and day, you are the one. . . .*

She gave herself over to the river of harmony, let its cool voice fill every pore, engulf eye socket and fingertip, ankle and neck, liberated into expression and movement.

The way it had been before, when Luz Herrera had taken the photo (so exactly like the one atop her night table now) of her as Giselle at the March recital in mid-jété, enraptured, effortless.

Freed from the pull of earth, and its cares.

Weightless.

Before weightlessness had become a curse and a shaming, and a constant source of danger . . .

But that pang of memory was not for now; if that waking-dream existence lingered in her it was pushed far down and away, like a sliver imbedded and grown over with flesh, like venom lurking in a vein.

*Let it go. . . .*

There was only this moment, this gift, here and real and fine if she just held on to it. . . .

As she twirled and swayed, inseparable from the tumble of exquisite notes one on another, the image came to her of Nijinsky as the Faun and the Rose, posed with that excruciating, incredible mix of delicacy and power that only he could attain, so expressive and perfect that these weren't still images to her—she saw him in the glory and magnificence of motion.

The clear, undeniable message, the siren song that had drawn her so long and with such constancy . . . You are your real self when you are removed from self, when you give yourself over to what the cosmos calls you to be, and that thing might be called Destiny. Or simply Truth.

To *see* that truth, to not be blind to it . . .

And yet Nijinsky thought he saw it, heard what he took to be its call. He followed it, and that false god led him to his destruction.

She knew that god, too, now, had been snared by it.

But not in this moment, this sanctuary, blessed and released . . .

The song ended, the notes held, then drifting away, to unknown, unreachable places.

The Girl settled to stillness, exhaled a slow breath. She opened her eyes.

Inigo was there, watching her. As she knew he'd be.

Hanging back in the shadows against the cold stone wall of an office building, gazing at her through Gargoyle sunglasses. Though she could not see his eyes behind them, she knew from past encounters that they were white as pearl, with only the faintest vertical slash of gray for the pupil.

White like the old jazzman's eyes, like Papa Sky's. But not blind; Inigo could see as well as she could; better, particularly at night.

He was her age, but shorter—smart like her, though—bundled up not against the cold, because there was no cold, but against the light. The dark navy hood was pulled low over his broad forehead, the sides of it drawn tight against his bony face, that pale skin that was blue-gray and spoke of sickness but also, paradoxically, of strength.

The Girl couldn't say why he looked this way. But then, she couldn't say why she looked the way she did, wasn't sure she wanted to know, to hear the insistent thrumming deep in her bones. It was quiet now. Sometimes it seemed aching to scream.

*Is it real or Memorex?*

*Let it go. . . .*

"Hey," Inigo said to her.

"Hey yourself."

Papa Sky smiled his smoky smile. "Now we got enough to really make an audience."

"Nearly didn't get through," Inigo said. "The Bridge—"

He stopped himself, shot a worried glance at Papa Sky, whose face had darkened, a silent caution.

The Girl knew he hadn't meant the Brooklyn or Verrazano Narrows or any of the others familiar to her and to Manhattan. There were things that could be said here and things that couldn't, and the rules were always unspoken.

She remembered her friend Margie Daws once confiding about her own family, as the two of them had loitered after phys ed beside the volleyball net at St. Augustine's, "The best stories are the ones we never talk about." (And she wondered just now how she could so clearly recall Margie Daws, but not the owner of that other room in her apartment—the one who slept in that perpetually rumpled bed.)

The Girl was full of questions for her street-corner companions, but she invariably found herself faced with a silence that proclaimed, *You can't get there from here.*

Still, she was grateful to be here in this brief respite with two who were undeniably not mirages or puppets of the mist but actual people, regardless of what prohibitions they might have forced upon them.

There were other acquaintances she recalled, less as if she had met them on the way to her own daytime obligations and more as if they were characters in a story she had been told. Still, she could visualize them . . . almost: a Russian hot-dog vendor, she recalled dimly, and an impetuous, powerful young woman, and a wild-eyed homeless man. There was a veil there. *Was it real or was it . . . ?*

In some way she could not quite summon, she knew they were real; had become a good deal more than that in later times.

But none of them were here now, that was for sure.

Papa Sky had come first, appearing on this street corner or one much like it days and days before (hard to tell how long precisely, with each day so similar). Inigo had arrived some time later, suddenly standing there as he stood now, seemingly drawn by the music, transfixed by it.

There was a familiar quality to him, although the Girl knew she hadn't met him before, not this specific individual. But in the murkiness of memory she knew that she had encountered ones very like him, vague names in the cloudy waters coalescing into . . . Freddy? and . . . Hank?

The Girl had lingered on that day when Inigo made his debut, had drawn him aside into a shrouded alley curtained from prying eyes.

"Where are you from?" she demanded of him.

"Here," he said simply, and she knew from how he said it that he didn't mean these streets like her street, but *really* here, where this truly was, or at least what lay beyond her island home, the outside that was excluded from her.

Since then, she and Inigo had stolen moments away when there was a lull in her imposed schedule, blank spots to fill in. They went to the Guggenheim sometimes (the art was *always* different) or to Sbarro's at Times Square (where she always had *just* enough money).

They had both been shy of each other at first, and wary, too. But longing for company, in time they had opened themselves in a slow dance of growing companionability.

She assembled his past from the tiny fragmented pieces he revealed to her, like a jigsaw with more missing than revealed.

He was alone, his mother and father gone.

(As was she . . .)

The father had disappeared first, under mysterious circumstances. There was a curious irony to that, because Inigo had been named by his mother after a character in *The Princess Bride*, one whose raison d'être was to avenge the death of his father.

Then his mother had exited, too. Not departed into death like Tina's own mother, but on a voyage of some sort, a searching. Inigo had been left in the care of some woman . . . a friend of his mother's? At a place his father had worked?

The details were musty, uncertain. The Girl couldn't be sure of any it. . . .

Or that on a day back in summer, this friend of Inigo's mother had vanished, too, removed in some appalling, *different* way, had left Inigo derelict and stranded here, abandoned yet somehow shielded. . . .

Had that friend's name been Agnes Wu, or was the Girl merely confused again, mixing up what she saw and felt and remembered? It was all jumbled and scrambled together, smudged and blurring in her mind as she tried to hold on to it, elusive as steam hissing off a subway grate.

She knew this, though: On that specific summer day, at a certain very precise time in the morning, Inigo had begun to change.

The same day and time as when the Girl herself—

As if her thoughts had somehow prompted it, a dark rumbling swept through the sky like a giant clearing his throat, the ground trembling in sympathetic vibration.

The Girl and Inigo both shrunk away from it, and there was even a ripple of concern across the old jazzman's face.

But then Papa Sky began to play, and all grew calm.

The Girl knew this one, too, from her mother's record collection, the collection the dimly, almost-recalled *other* had brought along with the books and bookcase so long ago.

"Stormy Weather."

The Girl closed her eyes and danced and was free again.

But had she looked to see, she would have spied Inigo watching her from his place in the shadows, and would have known he needed nothing more to worship.

The music faded again and the Girl returned.

"Time you best be movin' on," Papa Sky advised. "Wouldn't want you late for lessons." She knew somehow that he wasn't referring to the mockery of the classes that were the same, but instead cautioning her not to light here too long, to draw a scrutiny she would not want to incur.

"Later," she said, already starting away.

"Bye, Tina," Inigo said.

The Girl paused and turned back. "Call me Christina," she said. A more formal name, but it suited this different time, this different place.

She headed off down the street to walk among the mists and shadows and echoes that were the same every day. . . .

Every Möbius-strip day.

"This part always creeps me out," Inigo said to Papa Sky.

New York was shutting down. Or at least this section of it, now that Christina was gone.

Growing dim, the people and buildings subsiding around them, losing detail, like clay sculptures submerged in water and drawn out again. Or Adam and Eve in reverse motion, God in an act of unCreation, returning them to the mud again.

The darkness encroached, not at all like a sunset with night coming on, but instead like the cessation of consciousness as death drew near.

The Place to Be turning into the Non-Place.

Inigo stowed the Gargoyle shades in his jacket pocket and threw back the hood, letting his blanched skin feel the caress of the thinning air.

"Quittin' time . . ." Papa Sky crooned. To one who knew the blind man less well than the boy did, there might be the assumption that he was unruffled by the darkness because darkness was his constant state.

But Inigo knew this was not the case—Papa Sky was just *cool,* in the way that eight decades of hard road and iron discipline had lent him a calm and strength that were rarely shaken by anything.

The old man bent his long, lean frame to the open case that rested on the pavement, set the gleaming sax gently within it as though it were an infant, wadded with cotton to hold it safe.

He snapped the case shut and stood with it, felt blindly with his free hand for where his fiberglass cane lay against the edge of the nearby building. His fingers closed around it with deft assurance.

Time for them each to make his own way home. Or what they called home now. Sure as hell not here.

To go while they still could.

Inigo fished in his pocket. His fingers found the coin that was always there, always newly born.

He pulled out the buffalo nickel, not knowing the source of it, at least not precisely. Dr. Sanrio, he supposed. That would be his sick idea of a joke.

The buffalo had been the first to be affected, out beyond the mountains in the federal lands, and the Indian lands, too . . . and Inigo's father had been the second.

They had left him here, his father and then his mother, and Agnes Wu, too, when the hard rain had come down.

Fortunately for Inigo, he had turned into something that could stand that hard rain, something that was pretty damn hard itself, little and wiry and tough. And although he had not been *wanted* by what remained to perceive him, It had not—fortunately, again—regarded him as sufficient of a threat to bother to dislodge him.

(And perhaps, too, some residual affection Agnes held for him—or whatever of Agnes was still left—had lent him some sort of asylum, reprieve.)

Which hadn't made the loneliness any easier . . .

Until, that was, the new arrivals made it onto the scene, these two good souls, these friends . . . and the additional interloper who was anything but Inigo's friend.

Inigo slid the coin into the breast pocket of Papa Sky's suit, just behind the white handkerchief that was always immaculately folded. He said the words he always said at this point, the ritual. It was what his father had said whenever he'd given Inigo his allowance, before Dad headed out on his rounds at the facility, or set off into the Badlands.

"Something for the ferryman."

Papa Sky nodded. "Always got to pay your own way . . ."

Inigo started off, but Papa Sky beckoned him back. He leaned down and whispered into the boy's ear, the ear that was so delicately pointed, tufted with fine, white hair.

"I had a word with the Leather Man," Papa Sky said. "He told me it's time."

Inigo drew in a tight breath of thin, chill air.

It wasn't a surprise, not really. He knew this day would come. But still, he felt far from ready.

Not that any of that mattered, though.

Yoda could be a little green dude, or he could be an old blind black man, or something with scales and wings.

There is no try, there is only do.

Inigo was the messenger.

Christina returned home as the sun was dipping below the spires of the city, the sky streaked and fiery.

Her body ached from the hours of practice at the School of the American Ballet, obeying the commands of the shade that looked and sounded like the essence of the retired prima ballerina she had so idolized and emulated in recent years, years that seemed more a dream than the dream that had awakened her this morning.

Wearily, she climbed the four flights to her flat, her book bag feeling as if weighted with stones. She fished out her key as she drew near the door—then saw that it stood half-open (and she *knew* she had locked it on leaving that morning).

With a choked cry, she dropped her bag and the key, dashing inside, the hope surging in her like a drowning man swimming for the surface that at last he had found her—the one she could almost, not quite, remember—that he had come as he had promised her, back in the place she could not summon, but that her mind told her was named Boone's Gap.

But the figure sitting in the one good chair, silhouetted against the dying embers of the day that slanted in through the window, was not the one she waited for.

From the outline of him, she knew he was wearing his manshape again. He drew on his cigarette in the darkness, and the red tip of it was a malevolent eye.

*What monstrosities would walk the world were men's faces as unfinished as their minds. . . .*

"What a day I've had," he muttered.

She settled into the rocker that her lost mother had sung lullabies and held her in; that her lost father had torn the runners off in a fit of rage, before she was born.

*Soon you'll be past the pain,* her visitor had told her long ago, on a rooftop over a thousand miles away.

She wondered when that would be.

He had never touched her in violence, never physically harmed her in any way. But he had committed horrors, and she had been the unwilling witness to much of it. Like the inhuman being in the Harrison Ford movie that was older than she was, the one who in the end found a dreadful and curious compassion.

*I have done questionable things. . . .*

She said nothing as he unburdened himself through the night, opening his dragon heart to her once more.

# FOUR

## Gateway

It took Cal and his companions nearly two hours to search out a shelter, one big enough to hold thirty road-weary travelers. In a different terrain (one with such novel variations as valleys and mountains and hillsides, not just an endless expanse of grassland), Cal would have been content securing some cave in a cliff face—ideally one with no bears, wolverines or other irritable residents, not to mention tunnels full of grunters or portals that could suddenly open onto different states.

But as Cal had learned in many a quick improvisation on this journey, you worked with what you had.

"I think this'll do," Cal said as they drew up rein and surveyed the square structure sitting smack-dab in the middle of all that grass that stretched from the horizon on the left to the horizon on the right (not to mention the horizons ahead and behind).

Goldie dismounted and strolled up to the entrance. The glass door that said IN was shattered and hanging off its hinges, while the door that said OUT was intact, if almost black with grime. Of course, no one paid the least attention to those rules anymore, not that anyone particularly ever had.

Seen from here, the interior appeared utterly dark and quiet.

Goldie turned back to the others. "The king seems to be gone from his palace."

"Palace?" Colleen asked.

"The Palace of Material Goods, the central image and shrine of all we once held dear. Or at least, *you* guys did—I myself took a path I prefer to think of as more stripped-down and Zen."

Cal thought of the vast mountain of scavenged goods Goldie had assembled in his underground home in the tunnels beneath New York, the place Goldie had led him that first night after the Change, where Cal had found his sword. *You seemed pretty damn materialistic back then,* he reflected, but said nothing; he was just glad Goldie was talking again.

The sign towered over them at the head of the vast parking lot, proclaiming GATEWAY MALL, THE FUN PLACE! But it was clear that any and all fun had long since departed; had departed in fact—if the peeling paint, ruts in the asphalt, and cracked neon were any indication—months or even years before the Change. *'Twasn't Beauty killed the Beast,* Cal thought, *it was the mercurial shift of economics and population growth and buying patterns.*

Despite this, a scattering of RVs and dusty, pitted cars dotted the parking lot. Cal knew he'd have to dispatch Colleen and Doc with a contingent to investigate these, make certain there were no surprises lurking within.

The mall was a cavernous and intimidating space, but one well out of the wind, and readily defensible.

By now, Olifiers and his group had come up beside them. The big man peered through the glass doors uneasily. He swallowed hard, looking at all that dark possibility.

His trepidation brought a recollection to Cal of a movie he'd seen ages ago when he was eight and staying overnight at Howard Turner's house. His own mother forbid having a set in their house ("it does to the brain what candy does to the teeth") and certainly would have forbid him watching a film like this, which was on the whole just exactly why he was doing it, despite the fact that it scared the crap out of him and he couldn't sleep without a night-light for months afterward.

It was the only film he'd ever seen set in a mall. A mall that was dead, literally, and overrun with the walking dead.

*The Dawn of the Dead.*

Funny, Cal realized, how since then he'd actually fought the living dead—reanimated grunters that had attacked the four of them outside the Wishart house in Boone's Gap. But that event hadn't scared him half as much; he'd just focused on the business of severing the rotted obscenities' arms and legs and getting inside that damn nightmare of a house.

But this movie, *geez* . . .

The living-dead clown, the living-dead nun. Falling all over themselves on the escalators.

Then the cycle gang showed up, and the atrocities *they* committed made the ravenous dead pale by comparison.

*Men* were the real monsters, they always had been.

Wisdom could come from such unlikely sources. . . .

"We'll bed down here for the night; post sentries," Cal told Olifiers.

"Whatever you say, Chief," Olifiers answered, and led his people inside.

As the prairie moon rose into weighted clouds and the smell of coming snow filled the air, Cal instructed Goldie to summon up his patented and reliable (one of the few tricks he could do that was) spheres of light to illumine a path into the bowels of the mall, where a safe camp could be made.

Goldie guided his charges deeper into the enormous open space. It was like an airplane hangar; their hesitant footsteps echoed into the void. He noted their open astonishment as he formed the roiling balls of light—glowing bowling balls made of fog and St. Elmo's Fire—and thought to himself, *It's a handy trick, but while their mouths say thank you their eyes definitely say creeped out.*

The Food Court on the second level—near the extinct escalators, allowing quick access to higher or lower levels on a moment's notice—proved a suitable location, if one mockingly devoid of food.

It recalled to Goldman a favorite joke he'd had as a boy—he'd pulled it a thousand times, or at least wanted to; standing midway on a stopped escalator frantically calling to the bemused shoppers below, "Help, I'm stuck on this escalator!"

Of course, he never *really* asked for help, not when he'd been a kid with those ludicrously brilliant parents, their souls like chalk and "empathy" merely a word in their universitized (hell yes, it was a word if he said it was) vocabularies, nor did he ask for help in college or when he joined the workforce or even later, when the world became more tricky and so-called reality particularly elusive.

Nowadays, reality matched what he'd sensed its hidden nature had been all along, ages before anyone else saw it—those in his immediate circle, at least (well, and anyone not in the pay of the Source Project). It gave him some small satisfaction, knowing he'd been right, and evidence that at least on certain isolated occasions he could actually trust his instincts.

*But be careful of that, Herman Goldman,* he cautioned himself, *because you know how you get.* The ever-present danger of the bipolar personality, particularly in its manic phase, that blazing conviction that one had everything well in hand . . . just before taking a magnificent half-gainer off a ledge right into the abyss.

His eyes ran along the walls, cast in the cool radiance of the globes he'd placed along the periphery. The big dusty signs were like plastic tombstones: TACO HAVEN, A TASTE OF ITALY, BURGER STATION . . . junk food for a junk culture. So much had been disposable in the world gone by, discarded without a care. Now the most disposable thing was life itself, snuffed out in an instant.

Unbidden, the face came to him, delicate and glowing, with eyes like black opal. . . .

*Magritte.*

Desolation surged up in him, fierce and remorseless, and Goldie knew if he didn't force the image away he would start screaming and not stop until the massive building came shuddering down around them, burying all thought and memory.

*Enough. Peace.*

The image of the flare faded and was gone. For now, only for now. Only until he did what he needed to do.

Sanity was a transient thing, as he himself had been transient, was transient still. But it could be held for the moment, summoned like a pale sphere of light.

Goldie helped Olifiers get a fire going, while a solid little bantam named Flo Speakman assembled a spit to cook the dressed fawn three of their band had felled with improvised bolos earlier that morning.

"We sucked at first," Steve Altman, a diminutive and hyperkinetic Long Island native, confided pridefully. "But we're making steady improvement. Hey, we actually hit something other than ourselves."

"Consistency is a talent to foster," Goldie murmured. *And overconfidence can get you killed,* he added silently to himself.

You, or someone infinitely more dear . . .

While Doc oversaw stationing lookouts from Olifiers's contingent atop the roof of the mall, Cal and Colleen backtracked two miles in the beginnings of snowfall to cover their traces. Snow would blanket the land shortly, but that might not be enough to safeguard them.

"The more people we travel with, the more visible we become," Colleen cautioned as she watched their back trail over one shoulder.

They rode abreast, both dragging heavy hunks of canvas that had once been part of a four-man tent they'd found in the remains of a camping goods store. Already the chill breeze was licking at the snowy ground in their wake, sending up little puffs of dusty snow, scattering it over their trail.

Colleen swung back around to look at him. "That's just the way it is, Cal. And no amount of Good Samaritan, hail-fellow-well-met will change that fact. It makes us targets."

"We're already targets, Colleen."

"Yeah, of course, like I don't know that. It's practically been our theme song since we crossed the Verrazano Narrows Bridge. What we're talking here is how big we want the bull's-eye."

Cal nodded as he shook the nylon rope that tethered him to his chunk of ex-tent, smoothing out a large wrinkle in the stiff fabric. "I'm planning on cutting them loose, as soon as we find a good place to set them down . . . safely."

"Now that's a tune I can dance to."

Cal hesitated, reluctant to say more of what he was thinking.

"What?" Colleen prompted. "C'mon, Griffin, I know how you are when you get that look. Give out, don't be a tease."

Hell, it had to be said sometime, didn't it? "I'm thinking of cutting you guys loose, too." Before she could counter, he added quickly, "At least, you and Doc. Goldie . . . well, he and the Source, they have a hook in each other. As for me . . ." He didn't need to finish it.

"We've been round this track before, Cal. You really think you're gonna shake us off? You get to the Source, you're gonna *need*—"

"Colleen, I don't know how to *beat* it." Cal mastered himself, continued with quiet fervor. "I've been hoping I'd find some inspiration, some guidance from on high. But I don't have a *clue* how to take on the Source—and I'm getting a real strong feeling I'm not about to." He ran a hand through his hair, blew out a frosty breath. "We *saw* what it could do in Boone's Gap, and that was just a *finger* of it, stretched taut as a rubber band, and it still wiped the floor with us."

"We beat Primal," Colleen reminded him, her voice flat, not looking at him, staring into the night.

"Yes, we beat Primal, but he had only a fraction of the power whatever is at the Source will have . . . and I don't have to remind you of the cost."

The snow was falling more heavily now, glistening in their hair and shoulders, enfolding them in its silence, its intimacy.

"I *need* Goldie, he's the only way I'm going to find it, I know that—which doesn't mean I excuse myself. But you and Doc . . ." Here his voice softened. "I've seen the two of you . . . you're right together. You deserve a life."

"Aw geez, Cal, what is this, the Lifetime Channel? No, I forgot, we don't have that anymore. Which is one of the few *good* things that's come out of all this."

"Don't joke."

"Why not? It's one of the rare things I'm good at." She looked down as Big-T's hoof connected with a hillock of snow and sent the powder flying in a wide arc into the darkness. She grew serious, was quiet a long moment that was filled only with the creak of leather and the sound of their canvas drags slithering over the rough ground.

Then finally, in a voice so low he almost didn't catch it, she said, "I'm scared, Cal."

"You?" It shocked him. Not that Colleen felt fear—after all, she was human—but that she would admit it to him.

"I don't want complications in my life," she said. "I don't want to be blindsided anymore, I don't want the unknown. I'm sick to death of not knowing what I'm gonna face around each and every corner."

"So you agree with me."

"Hell no, you idiot. I'm not talking about the Source, I'm talking about Viktor!"

Cal couldn't help but smile. "Avoiding a relationship is not a good excuse to kill yourself."

She peered again into the blackness. "This is all your fault, you know. Dragging me to hell and gone, getting me to feel all over again . . . What a friggin' mess."

For all her feigned gravity, he knew she was speaking playfully, chiding him to move him off his position, get him to yield. Another weapon in her arsenal, one she wielded as capably as all the rest. What a remarkable woman, he thought, and she had been there all along, living right on Eighty-first just down the street from him. And would he have ever noticed her if not for the Change?

No.

He'd have stayed entombed in his trivial, small life, pursuing the phantom of stability, security. Living in illusion, bracketed between interpreted past and assumed future, hardly in the present at all. Asleep to all the wondrous possibilities around him, to the miracles as well as the horrors.

How hard it was, even now, to be fully awake . . .

Yet she worked at him—they all worked at each other, the four of them, orphans and outcasts, to stay alert, to not fall into complacency, to be truly alive.

Incredibly, he realized in this moment, with the snow feathering down, the night surrounding them like a blanket, with who knew what lay ahead of them, or what pursued from behind—that he loved her; not romantically—not anymore, he had jettisoned the growing pearl of that, but intensely, deeply, gratefully.

And that, absurdly, in this fragile, transitory moment, this present—in both senses of the word—he was happy.

He leaned out of the saddle toward her, brought his lips close to her ear, nearly touching it, as if it were a kiss. "Don't be afraid to enter uncharted terrain," he said. "The past is not the future."

She let out a hard breath that might have been a laugh. "So that's my answer to you, too, Cal Griffin. And here's one other meaty little tidbit—maybe you don't need to know how to beat it . . . maybe you just need to know how to have it not beat you."

He mulled on that, both of them as quiet as the snowflakes that drifted about them.

Finally, Colleen said, "How 'bout we both find out how the story ends? . . . " She held a hand out to him.

After due consideration, he took it.

Cal and Colleen dropped the sundered tent where they hit asphalt, then guided Sooner and Big-T back through the night toward the derelict mall, the stars like glittering eyes of ghosts above them.

Colleen was relieved Cal had opened up to her, still seemed able to talk to her, even though she'd chosen Doc rather than Cal. Her family had disintegrated when she was fifteen. Her father had died physically; her mother had died emotionally, leaving Colleen an orphan and an exile.

But now Doc and Goldie were her family . . . and Cal.

She looked over at Cal, riding on his horse like a city lawyer would, sitting so badly in the saddle despite all her advice on how to ride. He caught her looking at him.

"What?" Now it was his turn to question.

"Nothing . . . only I was just wondering what sweet young thing might be waiting down the road to twist you round her little finger. . . . You smile, you think you're immune? We could take out an ad—at least, if there were still newspapers—'Wanted: single female, race not important, preferably human.'"

It felt good to laugh.

# FIVE

## The Fugitive Kind

"Man oh man, I'm tellin' you, it was just like they were this big vacuum, came down the highway just suckin' everyone up. . . ."

Mike Olifiers was hunkered around the campfire as it flickered low in the Food Court, its thin trail of smoke ascending to the skylight and out into the night. The rest of the fugitives, those who were not posting guard on the roof, sat or lay around it in a circle. The dim chiaroscuro of the firelight lent their faces a worn beauty, a wary grace.

While Colleen went off to join Doc at his station topside and Goldie dozed beside one of his glowing orbs on the periphery—a rarity for him to sleep—Cal knelt across the fire from Olifiers, drew from the ragged ones their stories, their pasts. Mechanics, teachers, physicists, all caught in the net of the slavers.

"It did not matter who you were or where you were from," Moabi, an exchange student from Botswana, told him in a sweet accent redolent of molasses and honey, shaking his dreadlocks ruefully. He had been a filmmaker and performance artist, but none of that made the least difference. "You were a pair of hands to pick, a pair of legs to walk the corn rows, the soybean fields. . . . Beyond that, you were precisely nothing."

"Sunup to sundown," added Tori Feldman, who had been a historian in a former life. "Can see to can't see."

"Did you get any sense of what authority they represented, if any?" Cal asked.

"Some were National Guard guys gone freelance, some regular army, presumably AWOL," Flo Speakman responded. "Lots of other strays and bully boys. We picked this up chiefly by osmosis—"

"The hard way," Don Anderson, an amiable guy with severe scoliosis, chimed in, rubbing a vivid welt that ran across the left side of his face. This drew murmurs of agreement from the others.

"They weren't exactly forthcoming with their resumés." That was Rafe Dahlquist, the physicist, in his late fifties but still powerful and solid.

"It wasn't like these guys were anything special," Al Watt, a little bald guy with a timid, ready smile, piped up. He'd been a researcher on the Internet before the Change—an obsolete profession, if there ever was one. "I mean, we heard about all these dudes claiming to be the government, trying to get everything nailed down, these generals on the East Coast, up around the Great Lakes. Word was they had the Speaker of the House on a leash. But then there were all these other factions claiming *they* were the real guys in charge. I mean, you just hear this stuff, pick it up along the road. Everybody fighting everybody else."

"Kinda like Yugoslavia after the USSR pulled up its tent," said Krystee Cott, a lanky brunette with a sweetness about her that all the recent hard wear had not dispelled. Cal thought Doc might have a trenchant observation or two on her comment. Before leaving the navy, Krystee had been a demolitions expert—another area of expertise rendered null and void by the new modus operandi.

"Then there was the Storm . . ." Mike Kimmel said, and everyone else grew quiet. Kimmel was "Little Mike" to Olifiers's "Big Mike," a former wrestler turned part-time actor and balloon folder ("Big Mike's the awesome behemoth," Kimmel told Cal upon their introduction. "Me, I'm just the behemoth.")

"I saw it do its handiwork on the outskirts of Philly," Kimmel continued. "These fuckin' clouds came in from the west and anyone with a glow on"—he meant the ones like Tina, the flares, fireflies, angelfire—"just got drawn up into it like it was this big magnet and they were iron filings. You shoulda heard it. I mean, I'm talkin' *thousands* of 'em, *screaming. . . .*"

"It's like that everywhere anybody seen it," Olifiers added. "It spreads like a cancer, does whatever the hell it wants—whatever the *fuck* it is. Nobody beats it, that's the rule, nobody gets out alive . . . Except where *you* been."

Cal saw now they were all looking at him with that same worshipful gaze they had given him on their first meeting. The firelight danced in their eyes, they squinted against its heat and smoke.

*Lead us,* that look said. *Take us where you're going. To salvation, to world's end, to destruction.*

A memory crashed in on Cal, of the dream he'd had the morning before the Change, where darkness surrounded him, and the hilt of the burning cold sword found his outstretched hand—the same sword he now wore in the scabbard at his belt—and the despairing, unseen multitude cried out for him to *save* them, to *act*. . . .

And he did nothing.

"I don't have the answer," Cal said.

"Yeah, we know that, Chief," Olifiers agreed. "But nobody else even seems to know the question."

That night, for the first time since before the beginning, Cal had the dream again.

He dreamed chaos.

*Darkness, blacker than anything he'd ever conceived of, center-of-the-earth black, no-universe-yet-made black, dead-a-thousand-years black. Voices shouting, so clear that he could distinguish not only male and female, but each separate human soul screaming. He could tell rage from pain from terror. In the darkness of the dream he could hear his own blood hammering in his ears.*

*The sound of blows, metal on metal—metal tearing flesh. The stink of blood and of earth soaked with blood, of smoke and of charring.*

*He stood at the black heart of the tumult as they cried their anguish, their despair, demanded, pleaded—*

*That he act.*

*A shard of light split the blackness like a razor stroke. It glanced across an immense, irregular mound that might have been the bodies of men or merely the things they had used.*

*An object gleamed atop it, brilliant in the light, and Cal saw that it was a sword. Not opulent and bejeweled but plain, the leather of the hilt palm-worn. This weapon had seen use.*

*He reached out, seized it in his hand. The grooves and creases worn into the hilt by sweaty usage fit his palm. It was his palm that had made them.*

*As he drew it out, the light danced liquid on the blade, flashed a Rorschach of half-glimpsed living things in its silver-gold. Around him, the cries rose and blended to a single keening of raw need and pain. Holding the sword high, he knew what he must do.*

*But still he hesitated.*

And here the dream added a new detail, one that tore freezing dead fingers into his heart.

In the light from the sword, Cal could make out one of the figures beside him in the darkness, a frail, delicate form with hair fine as spiderweb and eyes a scorching blue. . . .

It was his sister, it was Tina.

And others dim beyond her, among the multitude of souls, barely discernible, crying out to him, *begging* . . .

Colleen. Doc. Goldie.

Words surged from within him, a reply ripped from his throat, his soul, screaming above their screams.

"IT WILL KILL HER!"

He did nothing, knowing they would die.

All of them were torn shrieking away by the Blackness, the Dark, the Storm. . . .

Their cries were drowned in thunder that rent the universe apart.

Cal awoke to the sound of his own sobbing.

Far miles away, in the sea of mists, leaning his great pebbled arms against the railing of what some might have been deceived into calling a bridge, the distant, familiar one thought of the dream he'd had again.

*Dead-a-thousand-years black . . .*

He never saw himself in the dream, never could discern what role he might play. But he saw others there, ones he knew, enemies, those who wished him harm, never friends.

But then, he had no friends.

No, strike that. He had one.

A fragile thing to pin your hopes on, a dream of chaos and an old man blind as a stone.

Even so, he admitted, it beat getting a *real* job. . . .

His dragon's laughter, resonant and grating as a body being dragged over gravel, boomed out across the fraudulent sea and counterfeit sky . . . and was even heard by the Thing that ruled dragon, and sea, and sky.

"Penny for your thoughts."

Finishing his shift on sentry duty, Doc Lysenko found Cal Griffin sitting at the far edge of roof, peering out at the clouds, and the night, and the drifting snow.

"You've said that before," Cal said, not looking at him.

"I'm a man of simple habits, Calvin. I find what works and I repeat it."

"Not a bad trait for a doctor."

"No . . ." Doc concurred. He crouched against the raised lip at the edge and faced Cal. "'I could be bounded up in a nutshell and count myself a king of infinite space, were it not that I had bad dreams. . . .'"

"*Hamlet,* act two, scene two." Cal said.

"I'm impressed."

"Blame my mother . . . and public TV. What's your point?"

"You're a worrier."

"Shouldn't I be?"

"Oh, indeed, I would never presume to separate you from your angst. I'm merely offering a sympathetic ear."

Cal said nothing.

"You have a golden opportunity for complaining here," Doc added. "Don't waste it."

Cal smiled at that, a weary smile, the weight of the world in it. "Oh, Doc, I am so not the man I need to be."

"How many called to leadership feel they are? At least, the deserving ones? The megalomaniacs rarely have such doubts."

Doc looked into the darkness to the uncertain future, then from memory quoted, "'If only the men truly up to this challenge, the moral giants, were here to assume this mantle. But failing their appearance on the scene, we ourselves must take it up, though we are woefully inadequate to the task.' You know who said words to that effect?"

"I have a feeling you're going to tell me."

"It was John Adams, just before your country's Revolution. So I'm afraid, Calvin, that your qualms are anything but unique."

"Doc—"

"Don't 'Doc' me. You inspire others to transcend themselves. That is a rare power, Calvin, greater than parlor tricks such as passing through walls or making balls of light. The block-and-tackle doesn't question its purpose, nor the spatula nor the paper clip. But because we are conscious, we *do*, endlessly.

"Calvin, if Colleen is our rock and Goldie our erratic sage, then you are our beacon. Shine, Calvin. Just shine."

"They're looking to me to be something I'm not," Cal said. "To be this . . . *legend*. I mean, Jesus, they broke out of slavery, came on the run in search of this larger-than-life tin god."

"And that is such a bad thing?"

"If the Change brought about anything good, it's that it made me be who I *am* instead of pretending to be something I'm not."

"Calvin, six words. *The Man Who Shot Liberty Valance.*"

"For someone from Kiev, you've seen a lot of American movies."

"Five years of selling hot dogs and not going to singles bars."

"Okay, okay, I get your point. Print the Legend. If the Legend is what these people need—and what I suppose *we* need, too—then maybe I shouldn't avoid it but rather embrace it."

"I must say, Calvin, you're getting so adept at articulating what I am about to say, you really don't need me anymore. Pray continue."

"These people are looking for a cure, and I don't have one. But you'd say it's like medicine. Sometimes hope is all you can offer, and though it may seem a false hope, it can help people marshal their forces, actually get better."

"Yes," Doc replied. "Miracles *do* happen, if one comes to it with a good heart and the possibility of good actually happening."

Cal mulled it over, then said, "It's medicine, even if it's an empty black bag on one hand . . . the Storm on the other. Which is the better choice to offer?"

"And what is your answer?"

"My answer is, I'll think on it. I'm not saying yes."

"Any other reply, and I would conclude you were a spatula. But before this is over, Calvin, I suspect you will have to be our Gandhi and our Eleanor Roosevelt and our General Patton all in one. So I would advise you to get used to it."

All Cal said to that was, "Mm."

"And one thing more I might add for you to consider."

"*Another* thing?"

"We are embarked on a journey into the unknown—which, I might observe, is indeed true of life in its entirety—but even more so now. You cannot know what you will need at your ultimate moment of truth . . . nor whom. So given that, it is a good idea to bring as wide a variety of dramatis personae as possible."

Cal grinned. "Back to the theater metaphor."

"We are but players. . . ." Doc rose with a groan. "Now, I'm afraid this old man is weary. If you will excuse me . . ."

"She deserves you," Cal murmured. "Colleen."

Doc nodded, accepting Cal's acceptance. He continued on, limping slightly as he went.

"Doc?" Cal asked. Doc turned back. "What role do you play in our little band?"

"Me?" He considered it. "I am the mirror for the rest of you." He smiled. "Good night, Calvin."

Colleen and Doc bedded down in what had once been a Waldenbooks, amid the cracked vacant shelves, the discarded magazines displaying brides and movie stars and politicians. Sleep wouldn't come to Colleen, which was nothing new, merely the ongoing challenge of relaxing and letting go of vigilance. Nevertheless, she forced stillness on herself and cradled Viktor in her arms as he drifted into sleep.

She maintained the contact even when, in troubled dreams, he called out to Yelena and Nurya, his lost wife and daughter, as he often did.

Colleen envied them their eternal claim on him. He had jettisoned so much of his past, had brought along no images of them ("No photograph could adequately capture what I hold in my mind," he told her on one of the rare occasions she could coax him to speak of them). She wished she could see them just once, see what he had cherished and lost. That wound so defined him, had so charted his actions from Ukraine to Manhattan to this harsh pioneer land.

It was half-past two in the morning when Cal appeared in the shop's doorway—its metal gate forever frozen halfway up—to alert them to the fact that they had visitors.

Emerging onto the roof with Cal and Doc, Colleen found the snowstorm had intensified, the flat surface growing icy, the breaths of the lookouts misting out into the moonlit sky like the trails of lost souls. She was surprised to see that Olifiers was there, too, and that he had brought the rest of his people with him.

Cal motioned her and Doc to the forward edge, where Goldie already stood gazing out. Even with the naked eye, Colleen could make out the horsemen several miles off, bearing torches, moving deliberately in their direction.

The paddyrollers.

*How the hell did they get a line on us?* Colleen wondered. She knew she had obliterated any evidence even an astute tracker would have caught, especially at night.

"Do we pull up stakes?" she asked Cal.

"No. They could run us to ground, and out in the open we'd have a harder time making a stand."

"So what's the play?"

"We've got a few minutes. We use the time we have." He moved off to confer with Olifiers and the others.

Goldie was humming a tune Colleen at first couldn't place, then recognized as "Hail, Hail, the Gang's All Here."

"Will you quit with that?" she snapped. "Or at least hum something good."

Obligingly, he switched to "Every Breath You Take," by the Police.

Colleen didn't get the joke, until she looked through the field glasses Doc handed off to her.

In the garish light of their torches, she could see fifteen hard men riding quickly on big, powerful horses. The riders were weighted down with evil-looking knives, short swords and what looked like spearguns.

They wore body armor and police helmets.

But more striking than that—and what chilled Colleen beyond anything the white crystals flurrying around her could—were the three stunted figures scrabbling ahead of the horses, tethered to them by thick lengths of rope.

She understood now how the trackers had found them.

The posse had grunters on leashes, and were using them as bloodhounds.

# SIX

## The Paddyrollers

They stood waiting in the fresh snow outside the glass doors—one shattered, one whole—as the horses thundered to a halt in front of the mall.

Colleen had her crossbow trained on the lead horseman as he steadied his mount, holding his torch overhead in a big gloved hand. The other men were fanned out behind him on their horses, palms on their weapons. On two of the steeds were big coiled lengths of chain—shackles awaiting use.

The horses blew out steam from their nostrils, their mouths frothing from the hard ride. The trio of gray, stooped grunters were gasping, too, the vapor in the cold air wreathing them in what looked like veils. Their huge, pallid eyes stared unblinking at Colleen and Doc, Goldie and Cal.

Cal stepped forward, but said nothing. He held his sword casually, in readiness.

"I am Hector Perez," the head man said, speaking each word as if it were a command. "Lieutenant in charge of this duly deputized posse. We are currently pursuing a group of escapees from Stateville Correctional Facility in Joliet, Illinois."

"Joliet, huh? Not Unionville?" Colleen asked, with an edge.

Perez didn't move his head, but his narrowed eyes slid over to appraise her. "Sorry, ma'am, I didn't catch your name."

"I didn't give it."

Cal stepped between Perez and Colleen. "You were telling us your business," he prompted.

"We have reason to believe our fugitives are inside that building." Perez paused, then added meaningfully, "Our quarrel is not with you, unless you choose to make it one."

Cal said, "Give us a minute."

Perez nodded assent. Cal drew Colleen and the others close, none of them lowering their weapons or taking their eyes off their adversaries. They spoke in low tones.

"What do you think?" Cal asked

"I think they're full of it," said Goldie. "Olifiers and the others don't have a prison vibe—or enough homemade tattoos by half. Plus I can smell *eau de police* a mile away, and these guys ain't it. I'm telling you, they may have been regular force once upon a time, but they're independent contractors now."

"Uh-huh."

"Yeah, but what if they're not?" Colleen whispered hoarsely. "Do we really want to come down on the wrong side of this?"

Cal mulled it over, took a step back toward the grim rider. "Mr. Perez, much as we'd like to be agreeable, we aren't convinced of your jurisdiction here."

Perez grimaced, looking as if he'd just gotten a piece of nut jammed in a tooth. He shifted on his saddle and spoke solely to Cal. "Let me tell you my working philosophy. I treat everyone with respect. You can't rob a man of his respect and expect him to act rationally. But there's a hierarchy of command, and I am committed to that prevailing."

"Is that why you have been whipping these people?" Doc asked acidly.

"We have levels of escalation when we meet with failure to obey, and pain compliance is one of our tools, yes."

Recognizing he was gaining no traction, Perez sighed and again addressed them all. "I have seen enough suffering to last me a lifetime. I have seen mothers cook up their own babies in convection ovens. I have seen grown men violate boys not out of nursery school.

I'm pleased to tell you those individuals did not survive to face a jury of their peers. Do we comprehend each other?"

"I think so, yes."

"Then stand aside."

Which was when the screams started.

In later times, Goldie associated the moment he first really came into his true dark power with that night, and the smell. That terrible, irrevocable instant when the clean, crisp scent of snow was invaded by the iron tang of blood, the air hot and fresh and thick with it, and the knowledge that someone was dying or dead.

But in that moment when the screaming began, all that was immediately clear was that Perez and his men were not alone.

Miles back, Perez had divided his force—which turned out to be not fifteen men, but forty—into three contingents. The middle group, the ones with torches, the decoys, rode straight on. The others came in fast and low on foot, silently and shrouded in darkness, flanking the building.

Fortunately, as Goldie might well have observed, Cal Griffin was a lawyer, and thus well used to misdirection, treachery and betrayal.

So when these intruders came on hard and fast and furious, they discovered Cal had secreted fully half of Olifiers's thirty-three men and women in the cars and trucks and Winnebagos that had up and died in and around the parking lot that fateful day when the Storm moved in.

These ravaged men and women surged out of hiding, screaming their lungs out, armed to the teeth with the pipes and branches and stones they'd brought to the party, not to mention the knives and swords and crossbows Cal and company had picked up along the way and augmented them with.

Like a director setting up a crowd scene, Cal questioned each and every one of them beforehand, discerning their skills and temperament, giving each his or her task.

He'd requested they not harm the paddyrollers any more than they needed to.

But hell—not to put too fine a point on it—it was payback time.

The screams didn't surprise Perez. However, the sudden loud release of a very large spring from the roof of the mall building did.

Perez looked up at the sound from above, but wasn't fast enough to get out of the way.

The weighted net—Goldie's "security device," hauled all the way from New York City—was catapulted off the roof of the mall building and landed squarely atop him and his horse, snaring them both. Perez let out a curse, the horse flailed wildly and shrieked, but the strong fibers held them fast.

Perez was an old hand, however, and managed to hold on to his torch in spite of everything. The cords began to sizzle and smoke where he worked to burn through them.

The three grunters tethered to Perez's horse were clear of the net, but still bound to the steed. They pulled frantically, blindly, as if to get away but curiously did nothing to bite or tear away the ropes.

Cal cut their bonds, and they scampered away.

The other horsemen charged, and Cal, Colleen, Doc and Goldie had their hands full. But this was not the ragtag quartet that had driven a rioting mob back when Ely Stern had led it rampaging down Eighty-first. The four of them had been practicing their fighting skills every day since, and now they moved with a flow and effortless teamwork that rivaled the best basketball squad. Parry, thrust, slash, fire, fall back, regroup, attack again. And all the while Goldie dazzling the enemy with his harmless fireworks—not that *they* knew that—driving the attackers back.

Then it all went south.

Perez was nearly free of the smoldering net. He screamed at a twisted little man atop a black mare, a man who had hung back out of the action and said nothing.

*"Eddie!"*

Eddie just nodded and raised his head—which Goldie could see, even from this distance in the torchlight and moonbeams bouncing off the fresh-fallen snow, was cadaver-thin with shiny black hair pasted down like a coat of shellac. He fixed his gaze on them.

It was just as though a big invisible hand grabbed up Colleen and lifted her high into the air, flinging her toward the little man. She cried out, dropping her crossbow.

Eddie angled his head, as if drawing her toward him with an unseen tether, reeling her in. Colleen hovered ten feet away from him and ten feet up. Her arms pressed down into her sides and she grunted, as if the invisible hand was squeezing her.

"Stand down!" Perez, free of the mesh now, shouted at Cal and the others. "Stand down or she dies!"

"You do that and I will be *so* pissed!" Colleen yelled at them. But then Eddie frowned, and they could all see she was being pressed even harder, and she cried out.

And Goldie thought of Douglas Brattle, the fear caster who had attacked him and Larry Shango along that shallow creekbed in Albermarle County, and of Primal in the dark core of Chicago, who had seized Magritte—beautiful, soul-sick Magritte—and drained her of her life like a man would suck the juice out of an orange.

And the anguish and grief and rage were upon him again—and with them the screaming, cacophonous blood-choir song of the Source that was always there and not there—and this time he didn't stuff it back down and away but instead opened himself up to the tearing out of his own lungs and guts and heart.

*You open yourself to it and fall away. . . .*

In his peripheral vision, Goldie could see Cal hesitating, starting to lower his sword, and Doc his blade.

But Goldie—the pure, yes, *primal* fire that was Goldie, or what was left of his mind and self—had no such thought, no hesitance; instead, he reached out with both hands, fingers spreading like a flower blossoming to a bee.

The sheer force rippled through the night like a shock wave, you could *see* it distorting the air, pulverizing the falling snowflakes, blasting them apart and aside as it plowed ahead. It reached Eddie's steed, knocked the horse brutally back, drove it to its knees with a strangled, terrified groan.

Eddie took the brunt of the force wave. It slammed into him and hurled him back off the horse, sent him cartwheeling helplessly through the air.

The invisible cord severed, Colleen dropped onto the soft snow, the breath knocked from her but otherwise unharmed.

Not so with Eddie, who struck a big cedar with a hideous impact that shook the tree as if a rampaging bull had run full tilt into it. Then—incredibly—he was *gone*, vanished clean away. The extremities of the tree, it's bare branches, burst into flame with a sudden *whoosh* of ignition, lighter fluid on a barbecue. It blazed like a tiki torch.

Seeing this, everyone on both sides of the fray was stilled to shocked silence.

Cal recovered first, said to Goldie, "How did you do that?"

"I don't know," Goldie said, equally stunned.

"Where did he go? Did you send him away?"

A whisper now, "I don't *know*. . . ."

(But in a savage rush of emotion, Goldie realized he hungered to do *more* of this . . . and needed to learn more to be able to do so.)

"Take them!" Perez was yelling at his men. "Dammit, take them!" But they were reluctant now, all the fight drained out of them by the appalling miracle they had just witnessed.

The topmost parts of the cedar, blackened and burning furiously, cracked off the tree and fell crashing to earth, throwing angry sparks up into the night.

Goldie shot out his hands again—whether a bluff or not, no one could tell, least of all himself. The attackers wheeled their horses around and took off for the hills at a mad gallop.

Seeing he was alone against them, Perez threw aside his torch and, with an expletive, reined his horse about to race after his men.

But at the last moment, he drew the speargun from its holster on the saddle and fired one killing bolt back at Cal.

Cal had no time to even register it, for a vast figure surged up behind him from out of the doorway and threw him down into the drift. He heard the whip-crack of the spear flying above him, then the hard wet-meat noise of it connecting with the body of the one who had saved him.

There was the smell of blood, and Mike Olifiers fell beside Cal, the spear through his neck.

Cal staggered to him as Olifiers pumped out his life, red onto the snow. Doc was there, too, now, as were Colleen and Goldie, but there was nothing he could do.

Olifiers was drowning, choking on his blood, struggling to gasp something out to Cal.

"Why?" Cal asked, tortured, wanting to turn back time, to take the spear that had been meant for him, not Olifiers. "*Why did you do that?*"

"They," Olifiers gurgled, "*need* . . ." He reached up a big meaty hand, wet with blood, and grabbed Cal's shoulder hard as Cal bent over him. His eyes were fierce as they sought out the younger man.

He didn't need to say the rest.

They need *you*.

Olifiers fell back, and was gone.

Perez had followed his men—the ones who were still alive, who could still ride—away into the night, across the flatlands.

They didn't come back.

The three grunters still crouched nearby, not moving, eyes huge and wary, staring at the big dead man, and the four beside him.

"Go on," Cal told them. "Go where you like. You're free."

Two of them fled into the darkness that so suited them. But the other remained, drew timidly up to Cal.

"Want . . ." it said tentatively, "to follow you." Its eyes moved from Cal down to the body beside him, awash in its own blood, then back to Cal.

Cal weighed the offer, and then said, "What's your name?"

The grunter—whose name was Brian Forbes, and who had been a man once in Detroit—followed silently on padded feet as they carried Olifiers back into the mall.

# SEVEN

## The City and Devine

In the years to come, those who were there would tell their children and grandchildren what they saw, and call her Lady Blade. But her real name was May.

The wind off Lake Michigan was a knife that hard near-winter day, cutting through the passersby as they hurried on, driven by the cold and the fear of the streets that were a hunting ground, now that Chicago was no longer the Ruby City and Primal was dethroned and destroyed, and his palace in shambles around him.

The city had reconstituted itself, in a fashion, devolved or at least returned to something of its former power structure, the old Party Machine, in this world where machines no longer ran but power and politics and greed held the whip hand, as they always had.

May felt nothing of the wind, tuned only to the still certainty within her that she had found the terminus of a search that had drawn her across many long miles and through many black places.

She stood at the corner of Randolph and Dearborn, cloud shadows painting her light and dark as they moved, studying the twisted metal framework that speared into the sky like the flayed fingers of giants. The rubble was piled high at its base, big scorched stones, a testament to rage and chaos and, perhaps, the inevitability of ruin.

Tons of stone and insulation, wiring and furniture, pipe and cement—fifty stories' worth—thrown into a blender to spray out over the terrain. Left here to the snow and sun and rain, to wear away like a mountain of pride torn down. No one in Chicago had the equipment anymore to haul all that debris away, nor the inclination, she supposed. Better to leave it as a monument, or unmarked grave, or abandoned killing ground. She noted that the men and women hurrying by averted their eyes as they passed, shied to the other side of the street, pretended it wasn't there.

But May could look it straight in the face; it was hardly the worst she had seen, or been forced to endure.

Once the structure had been the Chicago Media Building, home to Primal Records, punching up off the pavement five hundred feet in its assurance and arrogance. Then it had transformed, mutated as so much had mutated in this spinning world, into something far grander and more terrible, into cathedral and fortress and keep, where a demigod Beast held sway, a demon who had beaten back the Storm and granted safe haven to some, the privileged, for a time.

But May knew that it had been no haven for him, whatever largesse he had bestowed, for in the secret place of his soul he was lost.

Those here who had served and feared him and lived by his whim called him Primal, but they had not known him, not like she had.

For in the time before that time, May had called him husband, and known his true name.

It was not the same as the fitting names her people gave each other, that she herself had, but it bore something of the same intimacy, the same history.

"Listen," a nervous voice beside her piped up, "it's not safe to stay here. We gotta move on."

"In a minute," she said. She looked sidewise at the one who had brought her here, whom she had found at Buddy Guy's club down on Wabash, who had been brave enough to answer her questions when no one else would meet her gaze or dare speak of the past and what had gone down.

But Gabe Cordell, with his shining black hair and broadly muscled arms, was a man with spine, even if he was in a wheelchair.

Rolling at a determined clip she'd had to walk briskly to keep pace with, Gabe had led her out into the night and brought her to a barricaded street of tenements and the home of a furtive man named Wharton, who for a time had been a follower of Primal's.

Wharton had cherished the order and safety Primal had secured him; in truth, had loved him. In this day and age, when photographs were hard to come by, Wharton understood that memory could hold only so much, an image that faded with the corrosion of time.

From its hiding place under the floorboards, he withdrew the metal toolcase that had once held other keepsakes, unlocked it and gently lifted out the plaster cast. He held it up to May, angled it to catch the light of thick candles.

He had taken the death mask of the broken, ill-used man as he'd lain abandoned and discarded among the wreckage, so much garbage in the dirt.

The plaster face revealed little of the easy intelligence, the soft sweet eyes, the compassionate, off-center grin that had made her love him. But the round face was there, the delicate features, and May had no doubt. It was Clayton.

Who had left her, because he'd had to.

So now she stood at Randolph and Dearborn, alongside Gabe, who at last had brought her the answers she had journeyed so long in search of.

May reached inside her coat of many pockets, the black leather duster, and withdrew the folded paper she'd carried across three states and nine hundred miles. The wind caught at it and made it flutter like a bird frantic for release, but she held tight to it, strode across the broad street to the pile of stone that had been the final stopping place of the one that had shared her life, in the time before this time, when he had been a man and nothing more.

She didn't read the words on the paper, didn't need to; they were written as surely on her heart, with a knife that had gone deep, the scrawl of words scar tissue within her now.

*May,* Clay had written in that queer, spidery hand of his. *Baby, I know you won't understand this, but I've gotta get out of here. It's not you or the kids.*

(How strange it seemed to May that he'd said "kids," when only their son had survived past infancy. Linda, their delicate storm child, their boy's adored younger sister, had barely lived past her first year, and then succumbed to the faulty aortic valve that had been her birthday present upon her arrival into this world. She had died literally of a broken heart. May understood broken hearts now, but incredibly, inexplicably to her at the time, she herself had continued on. Once, she recalled, she had come upon something Mark Twain had written in his autobiography. "It is one of the mysteries of our nature that a man, all unprepared, can receive a thunder-stroke like that and live." Curious, how Twain could know precisely her life when he had died almost a century before.)

*I love you. Always love you. But something's happening to me. I don't understand but it's happening and I've got to go away. They know why it's happening and I wish I could make them tell me what this is and what it means and if it's good or bad. One minute I know it's good and the next I know it's bad just as hard. It's power, May. But I don't think I'm supposed to have it. If they find out I have it I don't know what they'll do, so I've got to go away. I don't even know if I should be telling you this.*

So Clay fled east, leaving her and their boy safe behind, or so he thought.

She had thought it safe, too, and so had left their son in the keeping of her friend Agnes Wu, whom she had met through Clay's work. She and Agnes had gone to innumerable movies when Clay had pulled graveyard shift; they'd shared their unspoken stories, the wounds of their souls, long into countless nights. Like herself, Agnes felt torn from her nurturing lands, her kin, driven by duty and allegiance to this barren and secretive place. Even worse, the tight security blackout kept Agnes isolated away from the grown children in Ithaca she so loved; perhaps that's why she'd become so fond of May's boy—he'd reminded her of her own son.

A good person to leave her boy with, May reasoned, this brilliant, homesick woman, to stow her son at Agnes's spacious residence within the outer confines of the Project grounds.

May had tracked Clay from South Dakota, determined to find him, to *help* him, following clues, trying to guess just how he was thinking.

Then the Storm had come, and all bets were off . . . and she herself came to know a fair portion of what Clayton had felt.

Clay had been born here in Chicago, had grown up here until he was nine, when that drunken butcher had performed surgery on his mother and she had died drowning in her own blood, and his father, a dead man living, had drowned himself in booze. Clayton had been a castaway then, handed off to relatives in far-flung places, thrown up on barren shores, homeless until he had found a home with her.

So perhaps he had come to this city because it had once meant security to him, and sanity. He had tried to re-create that sanity, had failed, had died.

May drew alongside the towering pile of stone, lifted one of the smaller pieces, slid the note into the recess within. She touched a finger to her lips, then to the cold rock. *Rest in peace.*

"Okay," she said, turning back to Gabriel. Time to go home now, back to her son. Then try to catch the trail of the one who had done this, to find his reasons, to bring him to justice, if she could.

And having come to know a good deal of her nature by now, May felt reasonably certain that she could.

A rough clatter down the street seized her attention.

"Uh-oh," Gabe said. "Outta time."

May could see them now, sliding out of windows, oozing out of doorways, coming up from holes in the pavement like angry ghosts.

"Wreckin' crew," said Gabe. "I warned ya about this."

The scuzzy men and women were walking junkyards, armed to the teeth with chains, clubs, saws, knives, you name it, and armored with essentially anything that could be bent to that purpose. They were closing in from all sides, and to the silent observers who watched from behind their curtains and window shades it looked like the lady in the long leatherpiece and the guy in the chair—unless they could suddenly levitate—were pretty much toast.

"Not that I hold a grudge," Gabe said, "but if you'd like your last words to be an apology, I wouldn't say no."

"In a minute," May said for the second time, just as the mob let out a hair-raising cry and charged.

Now, Gabe was a pretty cool customer when it came down to it, and in the moment before they rushed him, he'd locked his chair and gripped taut in his gloved hands the length of razor wire he'd brought along for just such eventualities. But he had to admit he was pretty well flummoxed that Little Mrs. Primal didn't even bat an eye.

She just stood her ground as they came on, noisy as a parade of drunken Shriners, and then she went to work. Spinning, rolling, slashing, throwing—a knife came from every one of those million pockets in her long coat, and she put every one of those gleaming beauties to best use.

It seemed like forever and no time at all, blood everywhere but amazingly not one of those bastards was killed nor even particularly amputated. They took off screaming, with a good number of new beauty marks to show off to the folks, and before you knew it there were just the two of them, May and Gabe—without a mark on them, except maybe a little sweat from exertion—out there on the street.

But not for long. The whole neighborhood came pouring out of their makeshift homes and storefronts and businesses cheering, everyone wanting to make them kielbasa.

May was gracious, but as soon as she could she extricated herself and set off west, leaving behind only a multitude of witnesses to spin the story, and one of her best throwing knives as a thank-you present for Gabe.

She wasn't the showy type.

Just as she was on the outskirts of town, however, Gabriel caught up with her, rolling fast. "You don't get off that easy, not without you telling me how you pulled that stunt."

It was a fair question, he had earned it.

So May showed him the finely worked necklace of porcupine quills, of eagle talon and bear claw, passed down to her from her mother's mother, who in turn got it from her own father, who had ridden with and been kin to the one known sometimes as Curly, or Our Strange Man, or Crazy Horse. May had always been pretty fast and alert, but since the coming of the Storm, the attributes had soaked down through her skin, and now she could move and sting and tear like nobody's business.

Gabriel listened in quiet solemnity, then she told him her fitting name.

In the years to come, those who were there told their children and grandchildren what they saw, and called her Lady Blade. But her real name was May, and for a time she wore the name her husband had borne, which was Devine.

But she had another name, handed down by her people. In the

generations since her great-grandfather had been forced to go to the white boarding school and truncate his name, it had been Catches.

But in this free and terrible time, May saw that it could at last return it to its full and fitting truth, and so she wore it along with her necklace of porcupine and eagle and bear.

They called her Lady Blade. But her real name was May Catches the Enemy.

# EIGHT

## Leaving Burnt Stick

Mama Diamond woke up in bed with her boots on.

She didn't recall falling asleep. Didn't recall anything past her meeting with the dark-skinned federal agent, what was his name? Shango. Larry Shango.

She recalled all too vividly her encounter with the dragon Ely Stern and the loss of her gems. The memory made her want to close her eyes and fade back into unconsciousness. It felt like a death, although she knew it wasn't one, not really. Not like when Katy had nearly lost Samantha in '73, and Mama Diamond had flown out to be with them, and she and Katy had spent three sleepless days and nights by the infant's bedside in the ICU at Good Samaritan, listening to the hiss of oxygen and the child's wet, tortured breaths. Nor even that moment when Mama Diamond thought she'd heard the whisper of the scythe coming for her, when Stern had threatened to take her own cantankerous life—and would have, too, had she given him the least excuse, she felt sure of it; there was the scent of murder in that leathered monstrosity.

Still, the loss of what she'd thought of as her treasure weakened her.

In recent times, even before the Change, Mama Diamond had found herself increasingly choosing isolation, withdrawing from the world of men, insulating herself with inanimate belongings, the glittering offspring of leveled mountain and evaporated sea.

People could leave you, but not possessions; those were truly yours.

And no, Mama Diamond lied to herself, she wasn't thinking of Danny, who had fleetingly called himself her fiancé once in a century gone, when promises were something to be believed and credit given not just to customers but to lovers. Only a memory on the wind now, a faded snapshot locked in the depths of mind and heart.

People left you.

But now her possessions had, too.

And what remained? Only the grinning skulls of Cretaceous and Jurassic dragons, seeming to mock her from their stone matrices in the walls of her home.

She turned her head against the yellowed pillowcase and sighed.

But she couldn't sleep anymore. She stank of her own sweat. She ached in every part of herself—physical and spiritual.

Besides, she could hear someone moving downstairs, in the shop, what was left of it.

Climbing out of bed was an adventure. What was a body, that it should protest so vigorously a simple motion? *Quiet, you bones, you sinews.*

Mama Diamond slept above the shop in the same room that housed her antique sofa, her rolltop desk, and a wood-burning stove that vented through the ceiling. Nothing but ashes remained in the stove. The chill of the night lingered. She was glad that whoever had put her to bed—could it have been that stiff-looking Shango?—had been generous with blankets. But it was morning now, the pale November sun glancing through the ivoried roll blinds.

More bumping downstairs. Face the music and dance, Mama Diamond told herself.

She took the stairs slowly, came into the body of the store and was greeted by the smell of hot coffee. It almost took the pain away.

"You're awake," Shango said, entering from the back room where Mama Diamond kept her coal stove for cooking.

"And you're using my kitchen."

"You mind? You were asleep."

"I'm often asleep. It's not an invitation to raid the pantry. But I guess I don't mind . . . if you have a cup of java for me."

"You take it black?"

"As God intended."

Mama Diamond had lived in and over this shop for thirty years. She had a fully equipped kitchen upstairs, gas stove, refrigerator, microwave, the works. Nothing fancy, but it had more than suited her. All useless, of course, when the natural gas ceased to flow and the AC outlets turned into holes in the wall. Since then, she had fixed most of her meals on this coal stove salvaged from Old West Antiques across the street. She had even set up this little back room with a Formica table and a couple of tattered pipe-and-vinyl chairs. One to sit in, one to put her feet on. She hadn't expected company.

She eased into the nearest chair while Shango poured coffee.

"There are eggs in the cold corner of the cellar," she said, "if you're ambitious."

Shango looked surprised and more than a little tempted. "You have eggs?"

"Didn't I just say that? I used to keep chickens, up until a week or so ago. Henhouse out back."

"What happened?"

"Something broke in and ate the brooders."

Shango retrieved the eggs and cracked three of them into an iron skillet. Mama Diamond didn't care for people who intruded on her privacy, but yesterday's encounter with Ely Stern made Shango's sleepover seem like a courtesy call. Why should she trust Shango? *Did* she trust Shango? Mama Diamond didn't share the grudge so many of her neighbors had seemed to hold against Washington, D.C.—perhaps because her taxes had never been audited—but neither did a federal ID card render a person automatically trustworthy.

Still, there was something to be said for a man who would fry her an egg when she ached in every joint and ligature.

Shango looked hungry but waited for Mama Diamond's invitation before he added a couple of eggs for himself. Mama Diamond let the inevitable questions wait until breakfast was finished. Then, over a second cup of coffee, she cleared her throat. "I hope it won't offend you if I find it hard to believe that the U.S. government is still in business, much less that you're interested in preventing petty burglary. I expect, over much of this great land of ours, petty theft has become a fairly common pastime."

"I don't know about the government," Shango said. "I hope there are enough good people left that our government may yet recover itself, when this is finished."

"When what's finished?"

"The Change, I've heard it called. The Storm, as well."

"You see that coming to an end soon?"

Shango's mouth tightened and something roiled around in his eyes, but he said nothing.

"Is that the business you're about?"

Again, nothing.

Mama Diamond sighed. She understood how a man might be reluctant to talk about himself in this day and age. But, dammit, those eggs should have earned her at least a little conversation.

She tried a different approach. "You seem to understand what happened here."

Nothing.

"So is it the dragon you're after, or me?"

"The dragon," Shango ventured at last. "But I know a little bit about you, too." He pulled a tattered blue notebook from the weathered backpack stowed in the corner. He found a page and read from it: "The Stone and Bone. Judith Kuriyama, AKA Mama Diamond, proprietor."

"Uh-huh," Mama Diamond said, unenlightened and a little miffed to hear her old name from this man's mouth.

Shango said, "I'm sorry. I'm not trying to be obtuse. But maybe if I could ask *you* a couple of questions, it'll be easier when I try to explain why I'm here. How's that sound?"

"All right, I suppose." *If you're a man of your word.*

"Okay. Miss Kuriyama—"

"Might as well just call me Mama Diamond." That other name was long ago, far away.

"Mama Diamond, you're obviously a gem merchant."

"Semiprecious stones and minerals." Not to mention fossils from the Devonian to the most recent Ice Age, but that wasn't what this was about, what it had ever been about.

"Right. When you were in business, did you keep records?"

"My Christ, this is an audit!"

"Obviously not."

"Is anything obvious anymore? Yeah, I kept business records."

"On paper or computer?"

"You'd think an old bone like me would be ignorant of computers, wouldn't you? Well, that's not strictly the case. I had a very fine IBM machine only a little out of date when the electricity stopped. Had my own website. Doubled my business over the old mail-order catalogue, too. Orders in and out the same day, MasterCard, Visa, PayPal . . . Did I keep the books on the computer, too? Yeah, but I printed copies of everything just in case the IRS came calling. Are you sure you're *not* the IRS?"

"Not even close. You still have those records in your possession?"

"I believe so."

"May I look at them? I need customer transactions, mail orders in the last twelve months before the Change, especially any large-value orders that might have come through, or big repeat orders."

"I don't deal in large volumes but I guess you can see the records. Lucky I didn't burn 'em for heat. Will this get me my stock back?"

"In all likelihood, no."

"Well," Mama Diamond said, "at least the man is honest."

It pained her, and not just physically, to walk through the emptied store. Without its mineral cargo, the Stone and Bone was just one more looted storefront. She led Shango upstairs to the room Mama Diamond had once called her office.

"I keep my sale records in chronological order here," she said, indicating a battered file drawer, "most recent at the front."

Shango opened the drawer, surveyed the contents, then began to page through the files systematically.

Soon enough, he found the invoices with the familiar place names, the Xeroxes of checks that could be cashed just as readily as if the signatures on them belonged to people who had actually existed. There were twelve different shell companies named (elsewhere, Shango had found as many as thirty), but most of the bulk of them were from a location in New Jersey.

"Tell me about these," Shango asked Mama Diamond, although he already knew the answer.

Mama Diamond remembered this group of orders because of the cryptic letters and the extravagant offers they had contained.

The first one—she found it for Shango—had been innocuous enough, an order form printed from her website requesting a number of fine garnets and inquiring about volume orders and discounts.

"Signed by Anthony St. Rivers," Shango observed, as if this were significant.

Mama Diamond filled the order and wrote to Mr. St. Rivers advising him that she didn't ordinarily fill high-volume orders—she was a retailer, not a distributor; her stock was carefully assembled to meet the average needs of her typical customers, and she was reluctant to draw down too much inventory for fear of disappointing her regulars. (She could, of course, have accepted St. Rivers's orders and simply filled them through a distributor at some extraordinary markup and after a long delay . . .but that didn't seem quite honest.)

She had gotten back a nice note from St. Rivers, mentioning he would refer her to his other friends and compatriots across the country. St. Rivers had further ordered a modest selection of raw and cut stones—opals, tourmalines, more garnets—and thanked Mama Diamond in a courteous fashion.

The orders continued to arrive with some regularity from St. Rivers and his well-heeled friends. Mama Diamond was intrigued enough that she'd mentioned St. Rivers to an importer, Bob Skarrow, at a gem-and-mineral trade show in Phoenix.

Skarrow rolled his eyes at the mention of the name. St. Rivers had contacted him, too, and when he couldn't fill his entire order—"It was frickin' ridiculous in volume alone"—St. Rivers and company had gone in turn to Skarrow's sources, and it was skewing the entire market in semiprecious stones, driving up prices and creating spot shortages.

"What do they do with all these stones?" Mama Diamond had asked.

But Skarrow didn't know. He'd had a couple of phone conversations with this St. Rivers (always with St. Rivers, not Skarrow, placing the call, the number invariably blocked), but St. Rivers wouldn't say anything about that.

Skarrow said the man's voice was papery thin and cultured, an old man's voice, with the faintest wisp of an accent, Spanish maybe or Mexican or Cuban, as if he'd planted roots here a long time but had hailed once from an alien land.

"Best guess in the trade is, they're working on some kind of optical device," Skarrow had concluded. "Like they used to use rubies for lasers. But that's just speculation."

Mama Diamond had let it go at that. Shortages, price-gouging, and overblown crises were an unavoidable part of the gem trade. "Apart from regular small orders from St. Rivers," she told Shango, "that's the whole story."

Shango nodded thoughtfully.

"Now," Mama Diamond said, "suppose you answer *me* some questions."

Shango asked Mama Diamond if she would be willing to walk with him to the train depot—if she felt well enough.

Oddly enough, she did feel well enough. She had this hazy, dreamlike memory that Stern had press-ganged her into a great deal of unwilling physical labor alongside the corpse-gray, distorted little men who made up his work crew. The pain was still there, throbbing in every joint. But she felt a peculiar energy, too. All that adrenaline flowing in her veins, she supposed. The giddy aftermath of fear.

And at the very last, amidst the steam hiss of the soul-damned train firing up again, Stern's words coming distant and watery to Mama Diamond in memory or imagination.

"Home . . . then Atherton."

Emerging with Shango from her dinosaur-bone house onto the porch, Mama Diamond spied her bent-birch rocker, the Tom Clancy novel still there under the canteen, pages restless in a dry wind. *It can stay where it is,* Mama Diamond thought. *I'm through with that book.*

They walked together slowly on the unshaded side of the street. The wind was brutal again today, bulling down the cross lanes like the propwash from an old DC-3. Mama Diamond wore her old slouch hat to keep her head warm, atop the pageboy she had affected since she was five (hell, one hairstyle should last a lifetime). Shango, God bless him, wore a fedora.

"Suppose you start," Mama Diamond suggested, "by telling me how you came to be here."

"That's a long story."

"I have time on my hands."

Shango began with stark simplicity: how he had come out of the navy to work for the Secret Service; his role at the White House before the Change; how President McKay had confided to him the likelihood that the clandestine Source Project was the root and center of the Change; how McKay had sent Shango along with Deputy Chief of Staff Steve Czernas to find the lost agent Jeri Bilmer, who might just have had the key to it all.

Then things got really interesting.

Later, upon reflection, Shango told himself it was because Mama Diamond comported herself like a woman who'd had no company but her own for far too long. Shango understood about that. He'd had more experience with loneliness than most folks.

But he had unburdened himself like a Mafia don at last confession.

Before his return to Washington, Shango told Mama, he had found the pitiful remains of Jeri Bilmer and her even more pitiful list, the roster that told nothing more than the names and former addresses of the scientists at the Source Project—perhaps complete, probably not, certainly not including the support personnel who might or might not have been dead by that time.

Shango had not succeeded on his own in achieving this objective. He had been helped at the end by the odd quartet of travelers from New York whom he had chanced upon when he had helped save the most erratic of the four from murderous attack. Herman Goldman, whom Shango had rescued and who in turn had used his remarkable powers to help Shango locate Bilmer's remains . . . and then reveal to him that President McKay was dead.

Was it that knowledge that finally coaxed Shango to violate his oath of office, to reveal what he had sworn only to share with McKay? Or was it rather a growing empathy with the band's leader, Cal Griffin, on his quixotic mission to save his abducted sister and challenge a force that had only overturned an entire planet?

Fools' errands were something Shango understood, too.

Whatever the motive, Shango had shared all he knew about the Source Project with them, in the hope—probably equally foolish—that it might turn the tables just enough to save their lives.

Shango knew full well he had come to the crossroads and chosen. To turn his back on what he had been, what he had prided himself on being. To become visible again.

For eight years, Shango had worn a black suit like his personal armor, earpiece wire coiling off into his collar, wrist handcuffed to the briefcase that would fall away to an Uzi at a moment's notice.

But most of all, he remembered that *feeling*. . . .

Unseen, unobserved, unremarked upon.

*Clouding men's minds.*

One time, when Shango was just a beanpole of a kid in a tumbledown, squalid neighborhood of New Orleans where no Nielsen company or Harris Poll ever asked anyone's opinion, his father had brought home some beaten-up cassettes he'd scored at a swap meet—odd behavior, to be sure, for the old bastard usually hoarded every penny for beer and escape. But it turned out this was release of a different kind, for when Dad himself had been a kid he had fled not into liquor and a feigned, desperate gaiety but rather the deco dreams issuing from the hand-tooled fine oak cabinet and glowing amber eye of the Atwater Kent. Now he wanted to relive it and—incredibly, uniquely—share it with his children.

The tapes were of an old radio show, ancient even then, from the thirties. Shango had recognized the voice emanating from the cassette player—it was that old fat dude from the commercials ("No wine before its time . . ."). But this wasn't hokey or a fast hustle. It was simply *wonderful.*

*Who knows what evil lurks in the hearts of men . . .*

The Shadow knows.

A man who could not be bought or swayed or corrupted, who stood for one pure, clear ideal, who could go anywhere, do anything . . .

Because he could cloud men's minds.

So they couldn't see him, didn't know he was even there. Until he struck and struck hard, setting everything right.

Sometimes it's just like a penny dropping into a slot, a lightbulb going on . . . and you know you've found that one right thing to give your life over to.

Shango studied and trained, entered the Naval Academy on an athletic scholarship, busted his ass getting his grades into the stratosphere, spent four years in Naval Intelligence working up to lieutenant commander, brushing up against all manner of government operatives.

All preamble, so he could apply to the one organization where he truly belonged.

*Why do you want to join the Secret Service?* the form had asked. And of course he had not said, *Because I want to be the Shadow, stupid.*

What followed had been a grueling year at the Federal Law Enforcement Training Center in Brunswick, Georgia, augmented by specialized training in Beltsville, Maryland. After that, five years' duty in the New Orleans and Chicago field offices, working criminal investigations, identity theft, protective intelligence, proving himself outstanding, exemplary, without error or peer.

Until finally, he was selected for the elite, the Presidential Protection Division.

Where at last Larry Shango could fully become the Shadow.

The invisible man, the one no one saw, silent as a radio switched off, always—literally—shadowing the Big Man, *numero uno,* President of what was once laughingly called the United States.

Not so United anymore, and as for the President, well . . . if there was a heaven—a belief Shango's mother had so fervently believed and Shango himself so fervently fled—McKay was there. And if not, at least McKay's worries were over.

Which was hardly the case with Larry Shango. Since his moment of decision around the campfire with Cal Griffin and friends, Shango had been visible indeed on his rambling See the USA sojourn, more often than not in someone's crosshairs. The long highway might as well have been paved with broken bones for all the damage he'd been forced to inflict with that ten-pound sledgehammer slung across his back.

It was a way to fill the time at least, to sometimes actually convince himself his life had a purpose . . . or at least hadn't run out of steam.

But at night, camped in some high redoubt, his back to the rock-face, carefully calculated to be secure against attack, he'd long for even a brief return to what he used to think of (though naturally never actually *said*) as *his Power*. . . .

Funny, because now all sorts of people had all kinds of power, way beyond what that funky old Shadow could ever have cooked up.

But Shango had stayed achingly unchanged—human, mortal, ordinary. As ordinary as any man who had walked his path and seen what he'd seen.

Griffin and his companions were probably dead by now, having gotten nowhere near the Source.

As Shango himself had failed.

But that was long after their meeting around the campfire. Initially, Shango had ignored Goldman's warnings. He'd had an obligation—and more than that, a personal need—to verify that his Commander was indeed dead, that Shango had in fact deserted and condemned him (even if McKay himself had ordered Shango away).

On the grounds of the White House, beside the fountain and rose beds as Goldman had predicted, Shango verified that General Christiansen of the Joint Chiefs had seized power, and that McKay and his wife, Jan, and even their dog, Jimmy, were dead, murdered.

That had been the second crossroads, as Shango had been forced to choose—vengeance, or some other engine to drive his life. He chose the one remaining task he knew McKay would want him to fulfill—to find and safeguard the life of their son, Evan, if he could.

So Shango set off for Bar Harbor, Maine, where the boy had been vacationing with his uncle and cousins and a detachment of Secret Service agents. That had been one hairy journey, traveling overland through some of the densest and most desperate regions of the eastern seaboard. Factionalism had run riot. Rumors abounded that the President was dead, and it really hadn't been possible to keep *that* soundbite a dirty little secret (even in a world that no longer had soundbites). No one seemed to know the whereabouts and condition above- or belowground of the Vice President, so the position of head of state devolved to the Speaker of the House. Christiansen had somehow managed to sew up—or lock down—Senator Mader's allegiance, or at least compliance, and thus declare martial law. But it was hotly disputed, and various National Guard units recognized widely divergent authority—if any at all. Pockets of civil war, civil disobedience and uncivil acts of every stripe were the order of the day.

The only thing to be thankful for—and it was precious little—was that munitions no longer worked.

But on the other hand, dragons flew and could shoot fire.

Shango arrived at Bar Harbor ten days late, to find that a contingent of Christiansen's men had already tried to kill the boy there, as if he were the lost Dauphin or Anastasia or Bonnie Prince Charlie. The team of Special Forces assassins had overpowered and dispatched Jan McKay's brother, her nieces and nephew, and all but one of the Secret Service agents.

Although bleeding her life out from internal injuries, agent Jaime Mintun had gotten the boy as far as Bangor, where a sympathetic older man and his wife had kept the boy hidden in a big sprawling mansion behind a spiderweb iron gate until Shango had arrived and convinced them of his friendly intentions.

Mama Diamond and Shango came to the decaying railway depot, and she led him into the equally decrepit cafeteria—refurbished for tourists once long ago—where they sat at a dusty table.

Mama Diamond had cleaned out the kitchen here shortly after the Change, had dumped the rotting perishables into an arroyo well out of town and swabbed the floors and walls with ammonia to kill the stench. With the doors closed against the breeze, it was another pleasant place to spend time. Or at least it had been. The black train, the dragon, had tainted it.

"Where's the boy now?" asked Mama Diamond.

"With my aunts and sisters and cousins outside New Orleans," Shango replied. "Oh, he's got a different name now and looks a whole lot different. If any of Christiansen's men decide to come after him, well, those old swamp-rat relations of mine know how to vanish into the bayou. And I suspect not even black-op hit men—or dragons themselves, come to mention it—would go in there without considerable trepidation."

"But that put you back at square one," Mama Diamond noted.

Shango nodded. "I could wall myself behind some fortress and spend the rest of my days raising turnips and fighting off monsters. Or I could put myself in the middle of it, like those folks I met, Griffin and the rest. Head for the Source and see if I could undo some of the badness . . . or at least learn if McKay's suspicions were right, if it really was the origin of all this misery and upheaval."

Shango was looking straight ahead, talking to himself as much as to Mama Diamond. "All I had was that rain-spoiled list of scientists' names. . . ."

But it was a start.

At the Latter Memorial Library on St. Charles in New Orleans, remarkably still intact and in full operation, Shango researched the names. He discovered that a preponderance of them were in allied fields of chemistry, molecular engineering and—most particularly—analysis and application of gemstones for use in laser technology and quantum physics research.

Specifically, Shango found that a number of the Source scientists were previously engaged in studies utilizing a variety of gemstones to focus energy and alter its proton and electron signatures, with the aim of splitting and recombining it in fierce new forms. One obscure article even hinted at the theoretical notion of exploiting these properties to harness great amorphous energies from other dimensions in space-time.

What enormous quantity of gems—and what bottomless purchasing power—might it have taken to accomplish this, Shango wondered, if indeed those at the Source Project were responsible for summoning the raging forces that had punched into this world and overwhelmed the planet?

McKay, in the brief interview by the fountain that sweltering summer day right after the Change, mentioned that the Source Project had been kept hidden even from him, a black box operation whose existence and funding were squirreled away in any number of secret cubbyholes, spread out between CIA, DoD, NSA. . . .

Returning to the environs of D.C.—or what was left of it—Shango paid a call on Reynolds Darden, an old friend in accounts receivable at the sprawling National Security Agency complex at Fort George

Meade, Maryland. Childhood friends since the frenetic days in the New Orleans projects, Shango had done him a favor once, engaging in a brief conversation with a boyfriend of Darden's sister, a man with a past full of wreckage and excuses. After that little talk with Shango, Mr. Significant Other booked a flight to Adelaide and didn't come back.

"What're you looking for?" Darden asked, eyes glinting behind owlish bifocals.

"I'll know it when I see it," Shango said. But he knew where to start—with any purchase order that bore the name—or anagram of the name, or false name derived from some biographical detail—of any of the Source Project scientists.

It had taken weeks of grueling, tedious effort, but at long last Shango found it: a list of purchase orders from a number of gem shops scattered across the middle of the country. No single quantity large enough to raise eyebrows, but in the aggregate one shitload of semiprecious stones . . .

The majority of the orders were from Anthony St. Rivers, who naturally proved not to be on any department's payroll records. But applying certain historical allusions and a little creative translation, Shango found he could resolve the name readily enough into . . .

Marcus Sanrio.

Of course, he knew that didn't make it so.

In the old world, the one with the Internet and cordless phones, the next step would have been a snap. But in the new one . . .

Shango hit the road again to talk to the rock hounds, find where they had shipped the purchases. When he found the shops still standing, their owners in residence, he perused their files, and learned that most of the purchases were sent to various letter drops, P.O. boxes, elusory safe houses designed to make the path circuitous, impossible to trace.

And none on any flight path Bilmer had flown.

But in a scrubby little shop outside Middleburg Heights, Ohio, Shango found one scrap that somehow had missed the cloaking device of smoke and mirrors the Source Project was so adept at erecting.

It was a note that read in a scraggly hand, "Time is of the essence. Send shipment direct." A return address was printed at the bottom. And the page was signed, "Marcus Sanrio."

There was no objective way Shango could be certain that this was the information he had traveled so long and hard for, that his friend and fellow agent Jeri Bilmer had died trying to convey. But even so, in his heart, he *knew*.

He had found the location of the Source Project, the dark core of it.

He didn't even wait for sunup. He left immediately.

"Not an easy trip," Shango told Mama Diamond. "And fifty-three miles from it . . ." Here his face clouded, and a violent shiver coursed through him like a current. "I was turned away."

What had it taken, Mama Diamond wondered, to frighten a man like this so badly?

He wouldn't elaborate.

"But I still had my notebooks. So I tracked the remaining shops, figuring I just might find a back door in. . . ."

Which made him, Mama Diamond thought, not just brave but a very stubborn man.

Shango carried his canvas pack, and he took a bottle of water from it and drank deeply. "There were four addresses left," he said, "you being the last."

"Uh-huh."

"The first retailer had been stripped clean. I didn't think too much about that at first. Lots of places were looted early on after the Change, and people would steal the damnedest things."

"Money's not too useful these days."

"No, but there was a jewelry store with most of its stock still in place. I can picture somebody wanting a more solid commodity than cash, maybe for trade—but why take garnets and leave diamond rings behind?"

Mama Diamond shrugged. "Like you said, people steal the damnedest things."

"Still, it struck me as odd. The next place—"

"What place would that be?"

Shango fished his notebook out of his pack and leafed through it. "Corky's Stones and Minerals, on the North Platte."

"Corky Foxe's store. He's a tightfisted SOB I know him a little."

"The shop had been burned, but it was obvious it had also been raided. I can't tell you what happened to Corky. Next, Lightfoot Novelty Imports, Vernal, Utah. Empty. Proprietor MIA." He glanced again at Mama Diamond.

"It's okay, I didn't know the man."

Shango told her that locals, mostly squatters and scavengers, described a group of crouched, darting figures who had arrived aboard a pitch-black train on abandoned rails—figures glimpsed fleetingly in the darkness, moving certainly, emptying the place without benefit of even moonlight—and the lone eminence that towered over them like a dark god.

"Stern," said Mama Diamond.

Shango nodded. But was the dragon working for the Source Project? Was his theft of Mama Diamond's stones part of the larger picture? And if it *was* the Source, did that mean that whatever lurked at its heart was still accruing gems, still had the continuing need of them . . . or perhaps some new need?

"I don't know," Shango said. "All I know is, unless you or your files have something new to tell me, it's the end of the line."

Mama Diamond stepped to the cafeteria door, cracked it open. Outside, the wind was buffeting a tattered old newspaper against the rusted iron track. She took a deep breath of the air that was as familiar to her as her own constant, fluttering heartbeat, the ache of years in her bones. The dry sharp cold dried up the mucous membranes in her nose, and the smell of coming snow was clear as a telegram. Maybe not today, but almost certainly tomorrow.

And if she let this man, hard as a piece of volcanic rock, face the blizzard, track that hell-black train into the jaws of night . . . ?

Sometimes you reach the crossroads, Mama Diamond thought, and sometimes it reaches you.

"There's something I may have heard in a dream," she told Shango.

Mama Diamond was glad she hadn't hauled just that heavy bitch of a coal stove from Old West Antiques, but also the dusty framed map of the forty-eight states. As she and Shango scrutinized it on the wall of her back room—with Mama surprised that her creaky old bad eye on the left somehow seemed to be seeing just fine now—it hadn't taken long to find the eight tiny letters right there in Iowa.

Atherton. Smack dab alongside the black lines that indicated railroad tracks.

"College town, I've heard of it," Shango told Mama Diamond. "Small, but it has one of the best research institutes in the country, or at least it did."

"If that's what Stern was talking about," Mama countered. "And not some drinking buddy he likes to hang with after raiding folk's back stock."

Shango shrugged. "I'll take my chances." No surprise there, given all he'd said and done.

Shango went off to gather supplies for the journey, leaving Mama Diamond to the privacy of her thoughts.

It had been a busy twenty-four hours, that it had, with many a curious visitor. Soon enough, Shango would be gone and the ghost town would settle back around Mama Diamond like a shroud, with even less in it to remind her she was any different from the parched wood and the dead earth.

Would she ever know what end of the line Shango reached, what conclusion he arrived at? Probably not.

*People leave you, and possessions, too.*

Mama Diamond walked stiffly to the front of her shop, the lowering sun casting hall-of-mirror reflections off the mostly empty cases. Her fingers trailed the cracked ivory of the mammoth tusk atop the counter.

She had armored herself against the world in tourmaline and agate, morganite and black opal, just as Shango had once armored himself in a black suit and coiled earpiece. But it was the same difference, really. The world stripped away your armor, that was just how life ran . . . until it ran out.

And whether that whisper came here in Burnt Stick or somewhere else along the tracks was not for Mama Diamond to say. It was just for her to say with whom she might be.

*Sometimes you reach the crossroads. . . .*

She mulled over these thoughts until Shango reappeared, lugging cans of vegetables and beans, and more bottled water.

"You have transportation?" Mama Diamond asked.

Shango nodded. "Rail bike."

"Rail *what*?"

"Come on. I'll show you."

Rail bikes, Shango explained, were an obscure form of sporting bicycle, used by hobbyists in Europe and America where abandoned railways lines remained in place. The bike's modified wheels sat on one rail; an outrigger supported two more passive wheels against the opposite rail. A bicycle modified to fit a railway track, basically. He had not been able to scavenge a true rail bike, but had modified a quality mountain bike in a metalwork shop.

He had ridden this device up to the depot last night, after Stern had gone and while Mama Diamond was sleeping, and concealed it north of town. The bike was an ugly assemblage of aluminum tubes, ungainly seeming.

"Going over those hills, you have some pretty steep grades ahead of you," Mama Diamond said. "Then you'll hit the Laramie Range."

Shango shrugged.

"And no potable water for a long way. Nor food."

"I'll manage."

"You want company?"

That provoked a surprised look. "Ma'am, much as I appreciate—"

"I'm serious. If there's a chance of getting back my property . . ." Without benefit of a vocabulary of feelings for a good many years, Mama Diamond thought it best to leave it at that.

"I'm sorry," Shango said, "I don't mean to be rude, but at your age—"

"I thought maybe I could help. Well, never mind. You heading up into the hills tonight?"

"Yes."

"We'll see how far you get."

"What?"

"I mean, good luck."

"Right. Thank you," Shango said. "I don't meet a lot of decent people, not these days, not since . . ."

He trailed off.

"Since the world ended," Mama Diamond supplied.

At dusk, while the sky was still a vivid and radiant blue, Mama Diamond watched Shango peddle away from Burnt Stick on his ridiculous rail bike. He looked, Mama Diamond thought, like one of those shabby bicycle-riding bears out of some Eastern European circus.

Mama Diamond suppressed a smile.

Then she walked back to her shop—to the makeshift stalls behind the shop, in back of the empty chicken coops.

Achy as she was, exhausted as she was, she knew it would take her some time to saddle and pack the horses. They needed to be fed and watered, too. She had neglected them today. "Settle down, Marsh," she told the black stallion. "Settle down, Cope," she told the mare.

Stars filled the sky, gemlike in their indifferent glitter, and the still air grew colder around her.

# NINE

## Inigo on the Train

A *guy could get killed this way,* Inigo thought, and actually laughed out loud. Not that anyone could hear him over the lunatic shriek of that whistle.

But then a guy—a completely human one, at least—could never have done this at all.

The blasted-rock tunnel walls were twisting serpentine now and rushing at Inigo with alarming speed; in this center-of-the-earth blackness, a normal kid wouldn't even have been able to *see* them, let alone press his funky-ass self tight to the cold metal of this impossible train.

The night train, speeding straight out of hell.

Inigo flattened himself along the surface of the roof as the car banged and rattled in its headlong flight, his big, bony fingers with their huge knuckles gripping onto the front edge of the car with all the strength and determination he could muster.

A sudden sharp curve hit him with centrifugal force like a blow and he was nearly thrown clear off. He clutched wildly and managed to pull himself back on top, gasping as the numbing chill air pummeled him.

Trust the Leather Man to come up with a thing like this. He was always full of surprises, and pure mean dangerous, too. You had to do your damnedest to keep on his good side (not that there really *was* one . . .). But Papa Sky tried his level best to keep the big cat honest, if such a concept truly existed anymore in this topsy-turvy life.

Still, as Inigo's dear departed dad always said, *When someone offers you work, you take it.*

Of course, his mother had always said wear your rubbers, and look both ways before you cross the street, and don't *ever* do anything that might cause you to wake up one morning seriously stone-cold dead.

But then, she was gone, and this freaky world was here, and he was forced to do a lot of things differently.

His teeth chattered from the cold and the vibration, and he fought to still them. To distract himself, he ruminated on what function this channel through the rock must have held before the Storm—certainly not a subway tunnel, not in this part of the country. No, it must've been a mine, and the narrow tracks sliding beneath laid for ore cars years and years back, maybe even when Custer and his marauding blue boys came whooping through these parts.

Papa Sky had told him true: The hell train was an adaptable beast, able to negotiate narrow gauge and wide, gobbling up the miles as it drove through the belly of the earth. Because not every place could be gotten to via the shortcut portals that some could open between here and there; sometimes you could only get *approximately* from one place to another, and then you had to cover ground the old-fashioned way, foot by foot and yard by yard, and so you needed freight cars to haul the cargo . . . and carry the crew to load it.

Hanging on for dear life, his long, wiry arms aching like a sonofabitch from the effort and the cold, Inigo could feel the skin of the train under him vibrate from more than its furious speed. It pulsed and moved as if alive, with a creepy, itchy feeling he could discern even through thick layers of jacket and sweatshirt and pants. Like black beetles surging over each other in their insatiable, endless combinations.

Shuddering and groaning like an irritated sandworm, the train canted upward as the tunnel began a steep climb under the pitiless miles of rock. The air was rank, and Inigo coughed raggedly, his throat burning from the raw smoky fumes roiling at him from the front of the train. He spat aside a phlegmy mass, intently determined not to have it blow back in his face. The train bounced abruptly and he bit his tongue, cried out in surprise and tasted blood.

*I don't need this shit,* he thought fiercely. But then in his mind's eye he saw the Girl in her glowing solemnity, the dancer, Christina, and his rage quieted.

*Even so, to be able to ride inside like a regular person, to sink into plush seats, or belly up to some nachos in the dining car . . .*

But those inside *this* train were far from regular.

Which was the whole point of his riding on the outside.

It was the only way he wouldn't be detected by his tweaked brothers within, the ones so like him in appearance but so alien in mind, with their white Necco-wafer eyes, gray grub skin, needle teeth . . . and major Bad Attitude.

He'd seen a pack of them let loose on a bull once, and they'd enveloped it like a school of piranha, slashing it to pieces as it screamed, devouring it before it was dead.

That little Viewmaster reel of 3D images in his mind had given him nightmares for weeks.

And he looked just like one of them.

So why was *he* different? Because he was twelve, not fully grown? No, that couldn't be all of it.

Maybe it was because there were variations in the breed; though, clearly, you still needed to be some kind of weirdo outsider to become one in the first place. Inigo knew he'd always been most comfortable keeping more or less to himself; he'd never fitted in, never felt like other folks.

And so now he wasn't. It was some cosmic kind of justice, or at least a rebalancing. Assuming that there *were* others like him, that not every other grunter in the universe was a ravening SOB.

He'd sure like to meet those guys, if only for variety. . . .

But regardless of that, he knew down to his gnarly gray toes that if his fellow grunters on the Midnight Special realized he was there, they'd tear him up just like that bull. It got into their minds, the Big Bad Thing, did stuff there, twisted them to its will, made the nasty ones even nastier.

It hadn't gotten into *his* mind, though, maybe because of the Leather Man, or Papa Sky, or the Dancer Girl. Because maybe he was under their protection . . .

Abruptly, the train *rippled* like muscles on a big cat stretching, and it began to shift, to take on a more complicated shape, with all sorts of black protrusions. His fingers felt the front of the roof edge rise up into an ornate lip ahead of him.

The train was picking up speed now, a holy terror. The inhuman screech of the whistle changed timber, not echoing in the open passage anymore, but flattening out as if screaming toward a hard, blank wall.

Papa Sky had told him of this, had warned it would be the worst part, and Inigo scrunched down further, pressed his head behind the lip of the car, exhaling every last bit of breath and holding it.

The whistle howled its rage at the universe, shrieked louder and louder until it seemed it had leeched every sound out of the entire planet.

There was an impact like nothing Inigo had ever known. Big clots of earth blasted back at him, bouncing off the lip, smashing like rocks caroming off each other in an asteroid belt.

It took every ounce of his will to hold on, to not be swept away. He gritted his teeth and closed his eyes and focused every bit of attention on his fingertips, on keeping his hands tight to the shifting black metal.

*The train was actually erupting from the earth.*

Then Inigo felt the kiss of the cold night air, and the train came down flat and hard on wide rusty tracks and kept right on going, screaming like a banshee through the night and over the flat prairie land.

"Welcome to Iowa," the boy said to nothing and no one in particular—blessedly still alive, even if he wasn't normal or regular or human.

And he laughed out loud for the second time that night.

Jeffrey Arcott walked westward, away from the town and up toward the lip of the valley and the flatland beyond the highway, where a subdivision had been under construction when the Change came. He followed a dead-end crescent, the half-built houses on each side of him skeletal and black in the light of a rising moon. Beyond the skeleton houses there was a stand of scrub woods grown back since the fires of 1978, low and patchy wild oaks and knee-deep brambles. In the summer you could find wild mulberries here, but the vines had withered with the hard onset of coming winter.

Near the top of the slope, in the clearance under an unused microwave relay tower, he paused and looked back at the town.

The frigid wind bit through his jeans, curled in along the neck of his leather jacket, but he felt powerful here, invisible in the shadows, gazing from a height at the town he had almost single-handedly resurrected from the nightmare of the Change.

He checked his watch, a retro Hamilton Futura with cut garnets set into the rim at precise intervals. It was nearly ten o'clock, almost curfew, power-saving time. He wrapped his arms around himself, cold, waiting.

Time. He imagined generators—*his* generators, inlaid with quartzite dodecahedrons, coils wrapped on ruby cores—slowing, stopping, their hum diminishing to silence. Bedtime for the dynamos. Ah: *there.*

The grid of streetlights, the whole valley full of fairy-light, gave way to darkness.

Darkness and moonlight and bitter, unseasonable cold. Last year at this time, he had walked the hills in the kind of cool his mom had called "sweater weather," listening to the clicking of autumn insects. They were silent now, pounced upon by this stealthy, unnatural winter.

The moon and stars took charge of the sky as Arcott turned away, toward the greater darkness beyond this low ridge. To the old railway tracks alongside Willow Neck Creek, where there should have been nothing at all; but where, just now, he anticipated—or could he actually hear?—the ancient tracks rattling to an unaccustomed presence.

His own private special delivery was out there, hurtling through the night, off in the darkness, still unseen.

He had stepped into the shadow of the trees along Philosopher's Walk to avoid being seen on the way here. "Keeping himself to himself," as his father might have said.

Because he was ashamed?

No. Because there were some things that could not yet be divulged, even to Siegel, even to Wade, his confidants, his lieutenants, his good hands right and left.

Sometimes research had to proceed in secret, or at least with due regard for security. They could know everything else about the operation, but people couldn't always interpret certain facts correctly.

At least for now, at least until the Radio was on the air . . .

He followed a footpath to the old concrete railway piers. The trees here were bare of leaves. The railroad stretched toward the dark west like a dry river. Moonlight glinted fitfully on the rust-eaten rails.

He caught himself whistling a tune, something from his father's jazz collection, a half-forgotten Chet Baker song. Bad idea. The sound would draw attention to himself. Better to remain anonymous, even in the empty night.

The cracked concrete piers stood canted at the trackside. These had been loading bays for the gypsum plant that had been abandoned and torn down forty years ago. The slabs, ten feet by fifteen and half as tall as a man, must have been too massive to cart away. Arcott selected the nearest one, hauled himself up onto its abrasive surface, brushed away a layer of fallen leaves, and sat cross-legged. He shivered. His denim pants and cowhide jacket were feeble armor against this graveyard chill.

He saw the train far out on the flatlands. It seemed to grow more substantial, more *material*, as it approached. Such was the nature of things.

Arcott stood up. He hated these encounters. They were unavoidable, obligations of iron necessity, like the church services his father had dragged him to every week, fundamentally unpleasant.

The train was black as night. Blacker. He watched it come, mesmerized. Soon it would glide silently to a stop, and Arcott would scramble toward it, a little afraid as always, but also trembling with anticipation, imagining the weight of treasure that would soon be his, the cold beauty and clean utility of the stones, raw and cut, all the angles of symmetry, indices of refraction, directions of cleavage, the semiprecious stones gathered from a thousand places. . . .

The gift from the west, from the Ghostlands.

In due time, the train passed through a wavering mist like a night mirage and drew to a stop on the outskirts of a slumbering town. Steam hissed from the locomotive's ribs like a foul breath, like a killing fog.

(Inigo recalled the fog in London that had killed all those people on a bleak day in the previous century, in the 1950s; his father had related it to him like a fairy tale, stressing the imperative moral of the story—that the world can turn hostile in a moment, that it can kill you.)

From his perch atop the passenger car where he lay silent and still, Inigo watched the man in the long black coat emerge from the front of the train. The other man was waiting for him beside the tracks, younger, with wavy dark hair and bright blue eyes, and the overalertness of the scholar, the intellectual.

Without his heightened senses, Inigo wouldn't have been able to see him clearly, to make out his smooth olive skin, the faded bomber jacket that gave little protection against the brittle night.

Or to smell the fear and eagerness radiating off him like sweat on a hot summer day.

The man in black strode toward him, and as he crossed the headlight beam of the locomotive like a hellish eye, Inigo saw the man's silhouette change like a gargantuan black umbrella unfurling. Then he was through the searchlight and his outline was a man again.

Bomber Jacket had seen it, too, and grown pale, taken a shaky step back.

"Jesus, I hope they grade you on a curve," the man in black said contemptuously, and he laughed.

It made Inigo's skin crawl even more than the insect feel on the skin of the train.

The man in black canted his head back toward the train, murmured something Inigo couldn't hear over the hiss of steam.

The big doors on the black passenger cars slid back, and the twisted forms so like Inigo in shape and unlike him in soul began unloading the shipment, the precious cargo Bomber Jacket craved so much that it held him there despite his fear.

The man in black leaned idly against a pillar, lit up a cigarette and stood inhaling the frosty blue smoke, stirring it about on his tongue, then lazily exhaling it. Inigo caught a dusky whiff of the exotic tobacco and was impressed, for he knew despite all appearances that the dread visitor's smoke was not tobacco, and its source not the illusory "cigarette" but rather the visitor himself.

Bomber Jacket worked up his courage, and hesitantly approached his deliverer.

"Something to add?" the man that was not a man asked, and in his casualness sounded oh-so-threatening.

"Um, the schematics . . . they're clear, but . . . challenging."

Smoke eddied about the visitor, the wind whipping it into mist devils, enshrouding him as though he were a phantom paying a call, death on vacation.

"It's not anything I can't do—in *time*." Fear and nervousness made Bomber Jacket gabble in relentless staccato, machine-gun bursts of words. "But an *assistant*, a Pretorius, if you will, if one of them could just come out for a day or two, not more, surely not more, to provide some guidance, I mean, just to elucidate some of the physics, untangle a cat's cradle, a string or two—"

Bomber Jacket stopped abruptly as he caught the low sound coming from the other.

He was chuckling.

The man in black extended a hand palm up and affected a quavering voice that was an obscene mockery of a child's. "*Please, sir, can I have some more?*"

Then he dropped the hand, and his voice was his own again. "They could send someone but, trust me, you wouldn't have the furniture."

He stepped through his curtain of smoke, brushing it aside, glowering down at the trembling young man. "Hit your mark, say your lines, get off the stage. Now, is that so hard to do?"

"N—no," Bomber Jacket blurted, backing away. Inigo could tell he didn't have the foggiest notion what the man in black was talking about.

But then, Leather Man's message hadn't been for *him*.

Unobserved, Inigo slipped off into the night and, within minutes, was miles away.

# TEN

## Griffin Before Dawn

The snow no longer falling, Cal sought out a spot thirty yards behind the Sears Automotive Center, given over now to the wind and a solitary gray owl circling overhead in a last foray as the night wore down. Big stacks of worn-out truck tires provided a windbreak there, and the ground was soft enough to bury Big Mike deep and away from the predations of men or beasts. Doc expertly closed the dead man's wound, then Mike Kimmel and Flo Speakman washed the body and found enough discarded garments left in the Big and Tall Men's Shop to lay Olifiers out in fresh, if musty, new clothes.

*From Manhattan to Boone's Gap to Chicago to the Fun Place in Iowa,* Cal thought. Another Kodak moment. Another funeral.

As he helped Kimmel and Doc and Colleen enfold the body in a king-size silk sheet recovered from Macy's (in their travels, it always surprised Cal the incongruity and illogic of which items were scavenged and which remained), Cal surveyed Olifiers's beefy, innocent face, saw the release, the look of serenity there.

Big Mike had paid his life out, sacrificed it in a moment, for him, for Cal.

And why?

*They need you,* he had said, or tried to, in his last dying moments.

"I don't have the answer," Cal had pleaded with him earlier that night.

And unshaken, Olifiers had simply replied, "Nobody else even seems to know the question."

No more running for Olifiers, no more fear. Just, at the end of the road, certainty.

The moon dipped low over the powdered earth as the long night waned, and they lowered Big Mike into the ground by the light of Goldie's spheres, lowered him with the lengths of chain their attackers had brought to drag Big Mike and his kindred back to slavery.

Free now.

All of them stood along the gravesite, Al Watt and Krystee Cott and Rafe Dahlquist and the others, and they looked to Cal to say something.

But what was there to say?

*The man with the question . . .*

Unfortunately, Olifiers had never gotten around to discussing with Cal just what that question might *be*. Certainly there were any number of tantalizing items on the menu, mouthwatering delicacies laced with cyanide. . . .

What dark mentality lay at the heart of the Source? What was stealing away flares? *Why* was it stealing them away? What integral piece was Fred Wishart in that equation, or the other scientists on the list Agent Shango had given Cal in the woods of Albermarle County—Marcus Sanrio or Agnes Wu or Pollard or Sakamoto or any of the rest?

*I don't know how to beat it,* Cal had told Colleen.

But standing in the fierce November wind looking down at the hole gouged in the earth like a bloody wound, Cal knew the question the currency of Olifiers's death had purchased him.

*How* do we beat it?

Cal's eyes moved along the somber, calm faces of Olifiers's mourners. The fact of any of their deaths was no surprise to them, given the lives they'd been living, only the specific time and place of it.

Rafe Dahlquist, the physicist; Krystee Cott, who had been a soldier; Al Watt, who knew how to find information; so very many of them . . .

With the skills he would need.

Not to mention Goldie and Doc and Colleen.

Cal had been laboring so hard to find excuses to jettison those traveling with him, to safeguard them, to shield himself from responsibility and guilt and loss.

But if he was going to accomplish anything, if Olifiers's life and death were going to have any meaning at all, Cal wouldn't have time for such luxuries.

The one he needed to jettison was himself.

*Print the Legend. . . .*

He saw that Colleen was watching him intently, almost as though she could read his mind. And why not? She had been the first to throw in her lot with him, before Goldie, before Doc. Before any of the warriors and wayfarers and holy fools that had accompanied them for a time.

He realized he would need many of them back again before this was done.

"Big Mike was the first of you to die," Cal said, by way of eulogy. "But if you follow me, he won't be the last."

Then he told them everything he knew about the Source.

Cal found Goldie in the heart of the mall, squatting at the top of the escalator, peering into the darkness, the nothingness of the vast, brooding space. Since he had dispatched Perez's magic man, pulverized or transported him to parts unknown, killed or banished him, Goldie had said little, done what was asked of him, kept his distance, deeply shaken and withdrawn, and folded in on himself.

"'Your old men will see visions . . .'" Cal intoned softly, climbing the stilled metal steps until he stood just below him, his face level with Goldie as he crouched.

"'Your young men will dream dreams,'" Goldie completed the quotation. *Revelation,* what Goldie had said to him on that day of days, just before the world had come spinning to a halt and they had been thrown together, launched on this mad, uncertain trajectory.

"It's a bitch to be lead dog," Cal said.

Goldie nodded. "Canary in a coal mine's no Swiss picnic, either."

"Got any line on what you did with Eddie back there?"

"Nope. Just did it."

"Are you getting better at this, Goldie . . . or is it getting the better of you?"

"This multiple choice?"

"I've got this twitchy feeling we're getting close real soon, ready or not."

"Yeah, I've got that feeling, too."

"We'll need every trick we can muster, every reinforcement along the way."

"Portals aren't a snap to open, Cal; it's not like making a call. Correction, like making a call—"

"Used to be, I know." Cal sighed. So much of their associations were what *used* to be, as if they themselves were lingering ghosts who didn't know when to depart. "Look, I'm not asking for miracles . . . okay, I guess I am. Get as good as you can, as fast as you can. Ask for what you need. Don't be a solo act."

Goldie was staring off into the darkness again, enclosed in solitude. Cal grabbed his shoulder, forced his attention. "We're family here, Goldie," he said, and meant it.

"I've done family," Goldie replied darkly, in his unshared, black memories. He turned to Cal at last, and smiled wanly. "What you've worked up here trumps it, believe me."

Then he added, "I'll do my best, Cal, really and truly. But take some advice from the unsettled set—have a fallback plan. . . . And if you need at any propitious moment to ditch me as thoroughly as Jerry Lewis dumped Dino, then you do it, and do not look back. You got that?"

Cal nodded, hoping he wouldn't need to, not knowing if he could.

They sat a long time in the dark, sharing the silence.

While Colleen and Doc took morning watch, Cal returned to the gutted Waldenbooks with the torch Perez had discarded. What remained of the stock was patchy, but sufficient to Cal's purpose.

Extinguishing the flame, he settled himself beside a crack in the wall where a shaft of dawnlight filtered through, and began to read.

He started with Martin Luther King, Jr.'s *A Call to Conscience*.

Soon enough, he would move on to Sun-Tzu's *The Art of War*.

Cal didn't realize he'd fallen asleep until an awareness of a nearby presence startled him awake, adrenaline surging in him. He threw himself back and grabbed for the sword at his hip. But the misshapen figure didn't move.

It stood watching him silently in the shadowed part of the room, away from the shaft of daylight, the dust motes dancing in the air.

From its shape, Cal could tell the creature was a grunter, and for an instant he thought it was Brian Forbes, the one he had liberated from Perez, and who had asked to join him. (Curious how a small minority of the grunters, like Howard Russo and Forbes, lacked the viciousness of their brethren, sharing only the same air of forlornness and pain.)

But then Cal saw that this grunter was smaller. And even though he *was* smaller, even in the dimness, Cal could glean from his body language and the expression on his face and a thousand subtle other things that he was far more formidable than either Russo or Forbes.

"My name is Inigo," the grunter boy said.

Having seen *The Princess Bride* on countless occasions—it was a ritual with Cal and Tina to watch it together on her rare sick days, in the close times before her life had been consumed by ballet and his by law—Cal half expected him to complete the statement with, "My name is Inigo Montoya. You killed my father. Prepare to die."

But thanks to the deeper education his mother had given him before her death, Cal also knew of another Inigo, Inigo Jones, a renowned British architect of the Renaissance, who had studded the realm with glorious palaces, churches and halls.

So which Inigo's spirit would this inhuman boy embody—the builder . . . or the destroyer?

"There's somewhere you need to go," he told Cal.

# ELEVEN

## Diamond Dogs

Familiar as these ancient hills were to Mama Diamond, even they had changed some since the world lost its way in recent days.

Physically they were the same: the expelled marrow of volcanoes a million years extinct, the compressed effluvia of what must once have been the floor of a primordial sea . . . and couldn't you just feel it here, the weight of those centuries stacked one atop another like the laminar striations in a canyon wall?

*I'm just one more fossil now,* Mama Diamond thought. *The difference is, I happen to be breathing.*

A half-moon lit the chilly sky. She understood that she would have to find a place to make camp before moonset. Cope and Marsh, her horses, stepped lightly and a little nervously along a trail Mama Diamond had first explored thirty years ago. The train tracks were periodically visible, looping up a gentle incline from the east and crossing a canyon on a steel trestle. Mama Diamond had followed the tracks most of the way from Burnt Stick. But the horses disliked that high trestle and she had accommodated them with this back route.

In the distance she heard the howling of wolves—a great many of them, it seemed to her. That tribe had prospered since the collapse of technology drove human beings out of these hard lands. They feasted, she thought, on our leavings. Now they were getting hungry again.

It was late, but Mama Diamond felt remarkably fresh. She wondered how that could be. The encounter with that dragon, with Stern, had left her sore and dispirited . . .but life had crept back into her over the course of the day, maybe *too much* life, a strange euphoria.

Why did she feel stronger rather than weaker? Was it possible the Change had not left her untouched after all? But Mama Diamond disliked that thought and dismissed it from her mind.

She was able to avoid the trestle because she knew these hills, knew them perhaps even more intimately than the surveyors who had laid down the rail routes way back when. And she doubted the extra time would put her far behind Federal Agent Larry Shango, who was depending on pedal power and force of will to carry him up the incline. But some difficulties she could not avoid . . . such as the upcoming tunnel that was blasted through the most difficult rock face these eroded hills had to offer. A half mile of darkness by day or night.

Mama Diamond considered making camp this side of the tunnel, but she didn't want to lose the time or make a habit of postponing unpleasant obstacles, particularly when she felt so well. This was why she had packed a quality oil lamp. She had anticipated this passage.

Still, the sight of the tunnel mouth with its stained concrete lintels, like the entrance to a demonic temple, was disheartening. "Not everything is easy," she whispered to the horses. Marsh sidled uneasily. Cope blew a gust of breath through flaring nostrils.

Mama Diamond lit the lantern, closed its mantle, and tried to draw some confidence from the flickering light. After all, Shango must have come this way already. And come out the other side . . .unless, of course, Shango was lying dead in the darkness next to his ridiculous rail bike, an image on which Mama Diamond preferred not to dwell.

The moon hovered just beyond the near peaks of the Laramie Range, watchful.

"Hey-up, Marsh," Mama Diamond said, and the animal stepped into the shadows with an almost palpable reluctance, Cope hanging behind at the end of his rope like a counterweight.

Ambient light faded instantly. Mama Diamond's lantern was too feeble to cast more than a narrow circle of illumination around her. Darkness enfolded her like a blanket. But she could see the tracks well enough to follow.

She disliked the smell of the tunnel. The tunnel stank of damp stone and rusting iron and cold cinders and limestone. And animals had been here—were still here, perhaps.

Were *definitely* still here, she decided a few moments later.

More wolves, most likely. They kept out of her circle of light, but she smelled them and heard them moving parallel to the tracks, keeping pace; heard their wet tongues slopping out of their mouths.

Marsh and Cope sensed them, too, probably more acutely than Mama Diamond did, and she had to speak to the horses to soothe them, faking a confidence she didn't feel. Had it been a mistake to attempt this crossing tonight? But when would have been better? Daylight? There was never daylight in here.

Canine eyes peered out of the darkness, almost comically like a cut-rate special effect or a carnival-ride illusion, a Saturday matinee recalled in a nightmare.

But there was light ahead now, the faint but welcoming moonbright oval of the tunnel's far end. She trotted Marsh toward it.

However—

However, parked in that slat of moonlight was a single old gray wolf, a big gap-eared beast missing patches of fur, smiling its perpetual canine smile, black lips pulled back over yellow spearpoint teeth. It sat in Mama Diamond's path coolly watching as she approached.

Mama Diamond rode until Marsh would go no farther. The horse simply stopped and stared, trembling, as if the motionless wolf were a writhing nest of snakes.

Mama Diamond spoke, meaning to reassure the horses, but she found herself addressing the wolf instead:

"Ho there, Old Dog. One old dog to another."

The wolf seemed surprised, but it didn't budge.

"What do you want from me, then, Old Dog? Do you plan to eat me? Well, that's not in the cards—not tonight, anyhow. I'm feeling brisk and I'm feeling mean. Fair warning."

And how powerful and assured her words sounded, even to herself! What made her speak so masterfully to a low animal like this one?

The wolf seemed abruptly uncertain of its intentions. It looked from side to side, licking its dark cracked lips.

"Oh, I know you have your tribe here with you. But they can't protect you, Old Dog, nor you them. Not from me." She raised her hand and her garnet rings glittered in the moonlight. More words spilled from Mama Diamond's mouth: "But you're not the boss, are you, Old Dog? You're in charge for the moment, but the Big Boss isn't here."

The wolf whined and snapped its jaws.

"Well, Old Dog? What will it be? Fight or get out of my path?"

The wolf emitted a series of breathy barks, smacked its lips and drooled a string of spittle. But what Mama Diamond heard was:

*You have no place here.*

"Don't tell me where I belong, Old Dog! Now stand back, or my horses will trample you."

The animal rose uncertainly.

"*Move,* I tell you! Out of my path, Low Thing! Carrion-Eater! Haul your stinking carcass aside and tell your boss I said so!"

The wolf yipped and scuttled into the cavernous dark.

Mama Diamond led her horses from the mouth of the tunnel into moonlight and cold, clean air.

Now *that* was strange, she thought.

She caught up with Larry Shango a day later.

As she rode up, the government man squatted by the side of the tracks where the railroad divided a weedy meadow. Shango was striking matches into a loose assortment of cottonwood kindling—more hoping for a fire than making one, Mama Diamond thought.

So intent was Shango on this task that he was visibly startled to see Mama Diamond and Marsh and Cope practically on top of him.

"Not very vigilant," Mama Diamond observed, "for a government agent."

"I made a career out of vigilance. Jesus! Those horses must have rubber-soled shoes."

It did seem to Mama Diamond that she and her mounts had been moving with a certain stealth ever since their encounter with the gatekeeping wolf. Maybe that wasn't just wishful thinking.

"I can help you with that fire," Mama Diamond said. "You're wasting matches. And unless you clear a break, you're liable to start a brushfire while you're at it."

Shango stood up to his considerable full height. "Thank you, but may I ask what you're doing here?"

The sun was low but the merest whisper of afternoon warmth lingered like an uncertain ghost. It would be a cold night. And a starry one, the air as clear as it was.

"There's not much left for me back in Burnt Stick, you know. Not with my treasure stolen. Thought I might come along and keep you out of trouble."

Shango's expression remained stony. "You're welcome to stay the night, ma'am. But I'm afraid I can't let you travel with me. No offense, but I don't need that kind of liability."

"Of course not. All you need is some help with the fire. Oh, and I brought a rabbit we can cook, unless you have some game of your own. No? Well, then."

The government agent sighed, looking at the rabbit with real longing.

They talked amicably enough over dinner, but not about anything substantial—jewel-thieving dragons, for instance, or the so-called Source Project. Mostly they talked about the journey through the Shirleys and the difficult road yet to follow, though Shango was cagey on that topic, too.

It didn't matter. They retired peacefully to their respective sleeping bags. The night was as starry as Mama Diamond had hoped, stars and planets so bright and crisp they showed their colors, Mars like a little pale ruby on the smoky throat of the sky. The air was cold, though. She tucked her knees up beside her and fell asleep listening to the small restless noises of Cope and Marsh and the rustling of wind in the weeds.

She was unsurprised, when she woke in the morning, to find Shango and all of Shango's baggage already gone. She imagined she could hear the faint squeal of Shango's lunatic rail bike somewhere down beyond the thin line of the horizon.

She could have caught up easily if she had saddled the horses then and there. But she didn't. She tidied up the campsite, made sure the fire was thoroughly doused, packed her saddlebags equitably and at last rode north at an easy trot. There was no talking Shango into this deal, Mama Diamond realized. Larry Shango would have to come to certain conclusions in his own way and on his own time.

For two more days she followed the government agent as the land rose and fell and the temperatures just fell. Both nights she showed up at Shango's campfire with game she had trapped or shot with her Indian bow. Shango accepted the food and seemed not to object to the company—Mama Diamond learned a little about Shango's childhood in the New Orleans projects, and shared some stories of her own—but he was adamantly silent about his long-term goals. Shango traveled alone. That was nonnegotiable.

He was a stubborn man. Well, Mama Diamond thought, that figured. Shango was a man on a quest, stubborn almost by definition.

Her fourth day out, Mama Diamond spent too much time stalking an elusive antelope. In the end the animal outmaneuvered her and she wasted an arrow on the prairie grass. By the time she had ranged back to the railway tracks, night had fallen. A fingernail moon shimmered through faint, high clouds. The old moon in the arms of the new, she had heard it called.

Missed dinner, she thought, riding alongside the moon-silvered rails, and the night was darker than she would have preferred for this kind of traveling. She didn't want Marsh or Cope to step in a gopher hole and break a leg. She would have preferred to have them watered and resting by now. Stupid old woman, she had miscalculated the time. . . .

But at the next turn of the breeze, she smelled dinner ahead. Pork and beans, wafted on a southerly wind. She was surprisingly hungry. She had not had an appetite so voracious since she was a much younger woman—Mama Diamond had been a picky eater for at least a decade. Her appetite had come back to her on this trip like a welcome if demanding guest.

Then she saw Shango's campfire flickering ahead of her, and she smelled something new, something she didn't like, something akin to the reek of burning hair.

Distantly, she heard Larry Shango shouting. Mama Diamond

urged Marsh to a trot, pulled her bow from her shoulder and nocked an arrow. A gust of howling and barking came to her on the wind.

*The wolf*, Mama Diamond thought. That damned Old Dog!

The rank smell was the stink of singed fur.

Closer now, she saw that Shango, under siege, had thrown one animal into the fire. The government man circled the campfire warily, as if waiting for the next attack. He carried a weapon: a huge hammer, presumably liberated from his travel gear.

The burned wolf had escaped the flames and rolled in a patch of dust outside the circle of firelight. It howled its pain. The boss wolf—and it was indeed the Old Dog she had met in the train tunnel—stood bristling but silent at the front of a pack of some ten or fifteen other animals.

That wasn't the whole story, however. The Old Dog wasn't in charge tonight. Something else prowled the shadows, half seen, silkily invisible except for its motion. Something large, sleek and self-confident. Something that made the horses tremble and dance. Mama Diamond climbed down from the saddle feeling frightened but oddly elated, energy coursing through her from her fingertips to the sockets of her eyes. She planted her feet firmly and said, "Stand back, you Beast!"

Her voiced boomed out of her, so loud and so resonant that it sounded alien even to her own ears. All that air, she thought; how had she drawn all that air into the leathery old marble-sacks that passed for her lungs?

The pack turned toward her, dozens of glowing yellow eyes. Shango, gap-jawed, also stared.

But in the shadows the Boss Beast prowled on, unimpressed.

Mama Diamond strode forward, fearless and ecstatic. Wolves fell back from her heels. She said:

"Carrion eaters, you! Kitten stealers! Leave this man alone! He's a *good* man! Back away, mouse biters! Stand down, you louse-furred scavengers!"

The wolves whimpered and backed away.

"Good God," Shango whispered, "is that *you?*"

His speech was nearly unintelligible to Mama Diamond's ears.

Even the alpha wolf, Old Dog, ducked and drooled and moved muttering from her path. That prowling, pacing shadow, however—

"Behind you," Shango said.

Mama Diamond turned.

This was no wolf.

This one was—a cat. A big one.

A black one.

"You're not native to these parts," Mama Diamond said, her confidence flagging at the sight of bared, bright teeth. The big cat stepped into the firelight, its eyes giving back the fire, its coat as black as a starless night.

A panther.

Escaped from some zoo? Liberated by the Change? Liberated and, worse, somehow *altered*? Those eyes were not merely bright. They were intelligent, uncanny.

"So you're the one behind this," Mama Diamond said.

*Give us your friend,* the panther said. *Give us your friend, or be our dinner with him.*

"I'm no dinner for the likes of you, Shiny Flanks. Nor is my friend."

*We don't care. He was given to us.*

"Given? By whom?" The panther blinked but did not answer. Its muscles, Mama Diamond saw, were tight as steel springs. "What makes a big cat like you travel with a pack of stinking dogs? Who is it that gives you men to eat? It wouldn't be some dragon, would it? Some big smelly red-eyed batwing dragon?"

Stern, she thought. But she detected something fleeting in the big cat's eye—lack of recognition?—then it was gone, replaced by naked, brute ferocity.

*Stand out of our way.*

"I will *not*! You heed *me*, you Barnum and Bailey castoff!"

The panther pounced.

Mama Diamond ducked aside, faster than she had imagined possible. Nonetheless she felt hot air as the cat flashed past her face, smelled the burnt-wood smell of its fur a fraction of a second before it landed foursquare, beyond the campfire, and swiveled to face her once more, eyes glittering like furious opals.

Reflexively, Mama Diamond snatched up a cottonwood branch from the perimeter of Shango's crude fire. The stick was not alight, merely smoldering at the far end. She brandished it at the monstrous cat, feeling the ludicrous inadequacy of it.

But then a word formed on her lips, and Mama Diamond couldn't say that she intended it before it was said.

*"Fire."*

Nothing changed, really, not that she or Shango could observe. Looking down at her arm, she saw that the blackened branch remained the same.

But in the huge eyes of the cat, her reflection told a different story. There, the branch burst instantly alight. Blue flame, like the subtle fire of an alcohol lamp, scuttled up the branch to the mirrored image of Mama Diamond's hand, then her arm, then all of her.

It occurred to Mama Diamond that this must be something akin to the trick Stern had first played on her when he had emerged from the death-black train, when he had appeared human for a moment.

*I couldn't decide what to wear . . . so I thought I'd give you a choice.*

A trick of the eye. Or, more appropriately in this case, the voice.

Mama Diamond suddenly remembered that moment in her shop, when Stern reached out to her and that spark of blue devil flame leapt from his hand to her shoulder and filled her with renegade lightning. Just what in the name of creation had happened there?

Creation, indeed. It seemed to shock them both, most particularly because it suggested a kinship, an intimacy that neither courted. Could it be, Mama wondered, that the calling she had recognized long ago within her, the humming resonance in her core that had drawn her across the world in search of those ancient, thundering bones . . .

Was her dragon soul.

It was as if Mama Diamond had opened a door in a familiar house only to discover a whole new room beyond it. Known, yet not known.

The cat's eyes narrowed against the incandescent holy glare of her. It backed up a pace, and then another.

Mama Diamond began to feel her powers draining from the exertion, the way the last water drains from an emptying cup, exhaustion rising from the marrow of her bones.

*Just a bit longer,* Mama Diamond willed.

The wolves turned tail and scattered. They must see the same heat mirage, Mama Diamond thought, these dark hunters, these predators.

"That's right," she said, "back off, Black Cat. You're in over your head, you Night Animal. Look at me and go blind."

The panther stood a moment—displaying a courage Mama Diamond was forced to admire—then howled and bounded into the darkness.

The wolves took their cue and ran like the dogs they were, tails tucked behind them.

Mama Diamond exhaled (had she been holding her breath?) and felt the power of illusion fade from her. The sensation was like stepping out of a warm shower into a chilly bathroom. She was suddenly cold and vulnerable. She shivered.

She looked down at her body with sudden fear, abruptly unsure that what she had seen in the cat's looking-glass eyes was only an illusion and not the reality. But she wasn't burned. She wasn't hurt. She was only, suddenly, quite tired.

"I think I have to sit down," she told Shango.

Shango struggled with words but finally managed, "Be my guest."

"I'm sorry to disturb your meal," Mama Diamond said, knowing even as she said it the absurdity of it, knowing it showed how rattled she was.

"Think, uh, nothing of it." Still staring, the federal agent added, "You want something to eat? I kind of lost my appetite, myself."

"Thank you, but I think what I really need is to sleep. Will you still be here in the morning?"

"Yes—I believe I will."

"You're willing to let me travel with you?"

"I have a feeling I'd be stupid to say no."

"You were stupid the first time you said no. Will you fetch me my sleeping bag, Mr. Shango? My legs don't want to carry me right now."

# TWELVE

## Plague Town

"This can't be right," Cal Griffin said. The stench wafting off the valley was the worst he'd ever smelled. And that was saying a lot, considering all the dark places he'd been.

The snow on the ground wasn't yet thick enough to hide the evidence of what must have happened here. But clearly, the cold weather had preserved it a lot longer than if it were the summer months.

Cal was glad he had instructed Flo Speakman and the rest of her group to stay sheltered in the abandoned grain silo they had encountered three miles back, just off the 113 toward Des Moines. After all they'd been through, they didn't need more nightmares.

Not that he particularly did, either. But a leader leads . . . and a lawyer searches for expedience and loopholes. He had been the latter in his old life, a reluctant if effective one, serving Ely Stern's cold-eyed "pragmatism"—nothing more than an excuse for heartlessness and moral absenteeism, really. Now he was trying to be the former, to rise to the challenges so evident before him, to get good enough at it to be of some earthly use in the time they had left. . . .

And also just maybe to utilize some of what he'd learned under Stern, to turn it at last to good use.

He'd made the choice to trust this grunter boy—so unlike the others of his kind Cal had met, so keen and articulate, if evasive—and had led those who followed him to this detour, this frigid place that might avail them of information or resources or . . . something.

Still, what benefit could they possibly glean from this scene of horror?

"It's not what you think," the grunter boy Inigo said, trying to sound confident but uneasiness leeching it away. It was the first time he'd seen it, too, at least in the day. And it *was* truly awful . . . which of course was the whole point.

"Yeah?" Colleen shot back. "So what would you call it? Hitler's birthday party?"

From where the five of them stood on the lip of the valley, they could see the town hadn't been particularly large, but it had held thousands, before it had been broken and burned and razed, not one of its modest buildings left standing.

It looked like most of the residents were still there, however, right out in the open, strewn about like so many dead Dorothy Gales deposited by a cyclone, or piled high in massive heaps of rotted flesh and sad, ragged clothing.

Something had been at them afterward, too—a lot of somethings, if the scraped bones and torn meat of the bodies were any indication.

Cal turned his face away from the wind that blew up from the valley floor. The stink was the pungence of death he had come to know in those black, appalling days after the Change in New York and the journey down the eastern arm of the country to Boone's Gap. And, most particularly, in the fetid breath of the grunters who had cashed out their lives flinging themselves futilely at the Wishart house, then—still driven by the merciless will of the Source Consciousness—had risen dead to attack Cal and his friends.

The smell of blood and fat and excrement, a smell that you couldn't get out of your nostrils, that settled into your skin and hair, that you couldn't wash away.

That was the stench coming off this dreadful valley now, that and the gritty smell of burnt wood and meat and plastic. . . .

And something else, an even more frightful reek that drove sharp claws into Cal's gut, that wanted to make him run screaming back the way they'd come and never venture here again.

The horses caught it, too, whinnied nervously, tried to shy away. Cal held Sooner's reins tightly, and he could hear Colleen whispering reassurance to Big-T.

Decay, and *sickness* . . .

Doc was squinting down at the valley through the field glasses he'd taken from his pack. He handed them off to Cal.

"Observe on some of them, Calvin, the growths under the arms and at the neck and groin, the black and purple eruptions. . . ."

Doc was silent for a time, considering, then shook his head grimly. "I would need closer inspection to absolutely verify it, but I don't think there can really be doubt. It's bubonic plague."

Colleen sighed. "You know, what with all we've been through, our stress level was getting kind of high, I was thinking maybe a cruise. But this is so much better."

"You just gotta go down there," Inigo said. "Believe me, you won't regret it."

"I regret it already," Colleen replied.

Cal turned to the grunter. "I don't think you'd have gone to the trouble to lead us all the way here just to give us the plague. So what's waiting down there for us?"

Inigo hesitated a long moment, hunched his shoulders, his eyes darting furtively to the west. He had been warned before his long journey not to talk too specifically, too overtly. The Big Bad Thing had long ears and long eyes—and a long reach, too, for that matter, how well he knew that. But even if he were free to tell every single damn part of it, what would make them believe him?

At last, he said, "I . . . can't say."

"You don't know, or you can't tell?" Cal asked, and Inigo was surprised at how kindly his tone was, how patient and sympathetic. He saw Christina's intelligence and endurance in this young man, but seasoned and even stronger, and he liked him for it.

Still, he said nothing.

"Okay, blue boy," Colleen was grabbing him by the front of his baggy jacket, yanking him off his feet. "Enough fun and games—"

Cal stepped between them and extricated Inigo. From past run-ins with the wiry but massively strong creatures, Cal knew the boy could've lifted Colleen and flipped her careening into the valley without breaking a sweat—and he'd spied the quick flash of rage in the boy's eyes.

Fear or restraint held him, and Cal wasn't inclined to discover which.

"Brute force won't solve anything," Cal said evenly, aiming it at both of them.

"Yeah," Colleen responded, "but it gives you such a warm, fuzzy feeling."

Cal didn't rise to it. "Let's look at our options—"

"Okay, sure," Colleen cut in. "Way I see it, we backtrack and try to make up for lost time, heading wherever the hell it is we're heading. Or we mosey on down into Hidden Plague Valley—which somehow I don't think is going to make it as the name of a salad dressing."

"Colleen," Doc tried to mollify. "There's a Russian saying—"

"There's always a Russian saying, Viktor. Geez, didn't you guys do anything but sit around making up sayings?" She pointed an accusing finger at Inigo. "I don't think we should have trusted this little rat bastard in the first place."

"We've all had experiences with grunters, good and bad," Cal said (not adding that it had been mostly bad).

"Yeah, but I'm the only one who's slept with one." She meant Rory, naturally, her old boyfriend. He hadn't been a grunter at the time, but why split hairs?

"One of you has something . . ." Inigo began softly.

"Yeah, yeah, yeah," Colleen snapped. "Why don't you quit with the elliptical bullshit, okay?" She wheeled on the others. "And yes, I know you're astonished I said 'elliptical,' but hey, I read a book once."

"Let him speak, Colleen," Cal said, and the look he gave her and the firmness under his words finally quieted her.

"Go on," he told Inigo.

"There's something someone gave you, in Chicago. . . ."

"What do you know of Chicago?" said Doc, but Cal silenced him with a gesture.

"You weren't expecting it," Inigo said with deliberation, as if coached to speak these words precisely. "But it saved you."

Colleen's face betrayed surprise. Then she pulled the chain from around her neck, revealing again the dog tags from her dead father, the Russian Orthodox cross from Doc . . . and the iridescent black scale, the charm that had saved her, had saved them all, from Primal.

She held the piece between thumb and forefinger, waved it in

Inigo's face. "You mean this, kid?" Then she glanced out at the valley, and her jaw dropped.

"Oh. My. God."

"What? What is it?" Cal asked.

"They're gone, they're all gone. The bodies. And—and—" Words failed her.

It was fucking impossible.

(Watching this, Inigo nodded to himself. Papa Sky had known what he was talking about telling him to mention that charm, that blade of leather. But then, he always did.)

"I—I see the town completely undamaged," said Colleen.

"Curioser and curioser," muttered Doc.

"Choose one from column A or one from column B," said Cal. "Goldie, what's your—"

And for the first time since they'd reached the valley, Cal and Doc and Colleen realized Goldie had said nothing all the time they'd been there.

He stood transfixed staring down at the town, pure terror on his face.

*Raging, red turmoil, something monstrous waiting. Thunder smashing. Blurred streaks like blood smeared on a mirror. Sparks pinwheeling. Slashing into all colors and none, a whirlpool blazing of pure, savage power, screaming, screaming,* SCREAMING.

It went on forever. And that was just the least of it.

It wasn't here yet, not yet, not completely or even at all—hey, it was Paradoxes R Us. But it was coming fast down the tracks. And Herman Goldman knew he was not ready for it, not one teeny-weeny bit. If he was a Lincoln penny, this Big Enchilada was *mucho dinero*.

And opening to it was like what had happened when he was twenty-three and the Devil had come calling, literally. He'd never told anyone about that—hell, they'd think he was crazy—but he had swooned into that place of insanity and assurance, had lost the world and himself, had become a universe and a god of one.

That was what this fucker thought *It* was.

And Goldie knew that it was what he himself would need to become, that and more, if he was to get justice or vengeance or whatever it was his eviscerated soul cried out for.

Save your hate for the Source, his love had told him.

*Oh, Magritte . . .*

Could she have saved him from the Source, from himself?

It really didn't matter anymore.

Herman Goldman was saving up his pennies.

Now all he had to do find was the right bank.

"Not good, way not good," Goldie said, when he finally roused himself to answer their concern, their questions as to what he saw. "Cal, I can't go down there, at least not right now."

"Okay," Cal said. "Go back and join the others. We'll see what we can suss out."

But before Goldie could mount Later and turn his buckskin back along the road, away from this place of phantoms, of repulsion and beckoning, there was a soft rustle of footsteps behind them.

They had company.

# THIRTEEN

## Sky and Grass and Highway

"These friends of yours?" Cal asked Inigo.

The tweaked boy slowly shook his head, never taking his creamy huge eyes off the visitors. If anything, he seemed even more disquieted by their arrival than did Cal and the others.

*Grunters.*

Cal wondered where they'd come from on this flat plain with its cracked asphalt highway an enormous arrow pointing clear to the horizon. Certainly not out of the valley; all of them had been looking that way.

In the fading light of sunset, the clump of huddled figures with their bandy legs, their long bony arms, advanced with seeming timidity, like whipped strays drawn back to the company of men but sorely afraid of it. All were small compared to grown humans, of varying heights, none more than five feet. Cal could see that they had once been women and men, and a few of the shorter ones had a hyper quality that made him think they might have been—might still be—children.

In his travels, Cal learned that family members never all transformed into one kind of changeling, but that often the altered outcasts and abandoned ones found companions of like mind and form.

And although these eight twisted beings—with rapper caps pulled tight over bulbous gray heads (either wholly bald or with strands of wispy hair like chick fluff escaping out from under them), capacious Salvation Army jackets and jeans and long, thick-knuckled feet—had no doubt started life with no relationship to one another, now they were family.

Or at least, a crew, a posse. A pack.

Cal had seen other grunter packs in a proximity he'd sooner have avoided, been cornered by them in the bleak tunnels under New York and diverse spots along the map, fought tooth and claw to survive. In groups, they were invariably frightful, ravening homunculi with a wild, lithe ferocity.

But this gathering before him seemed of a wholly different cast, even if in the dimming light he could see they bore the same serrated teeth, the same yellow dirk nails.

There was none of the cunning, the calculation about them. Nor even the wary alertness of this boy who stood breathing fast beside him.

Colleen had whipped her crossbow off her back and leveled it. Doc held his machete. But Cal shook his head, motioned their weapons down. He moved toward the group slowly, with a show of calm he hoped was more convincing than he felt (because—despite all this talk about his great instincts as a leader—if he was *wrong* about these guys . . .)

The lead grunter stepped closer, eyeing Cal.

Cal addressed the newcomer. "My name is Cal Griffin. This is Colleen, Goldie, Doc. And that's Inigo. What's your name?"

The creature frowned spectacularly, and when he spoke, his voice was cracked and high-pitched—he sounded like Andy Devine in one of those ancient Westerns. "My name," he said, "is Tom."

"Just Tom?" Doc asked.

Tom shrugged, as if at an irrelevancy.

Doc leaned in close to Cal, whispered, "Even for a grunter, he appears rather—"

"Dim?" Cal finished in a whisper.

"Let's just say I would not hold out for an Ivy League college if I were him."

"What's your take on this?" Cal asked Inigo, who continued to stare at his fellow trogs perplexedly. But the boy had nothing to offer; he'd never seen anything quite like them, either.

"Guys," Colleen put in, "we don't have time for this."

But Cal had a feeling it was all connected somehow, that this was in some way a part of the larger mystery.

"It's like a tumor," Goldie suggested at last. "You know, some are malignant, some are benign." Then he added, to Inigo, "No offense, my man. I'm talking groups larger than one, when that utterly delovely mob mentality kicks in." And the way he said it brought home freshly to Cal that Goldie had seen in his desultory ramblings the worst the world had to offer . . . and not just from grunters.

Tom regarded them indifferently during this exchange, and then croaked, "You brought us food? You brought us blankets?"

"Well," Cal said, surprised, "we have very little of those things ourselves."

Tom looked suddenly, grievously disappointed. Cal wondered whether the creature might actually begin to weep.

"No blankets to spare," Cal hurried on. "As for food—"

He walked to Sooner's saddlebag, pulled out a can of creamed corn. "You can have this, if you like."

Tom apparently did like, very much; he scuttled over to Cal and snatched the heavy can from him with the cupidity of a hungry goat in a petting zoo.

Cal stepped back, appalled by the smell of the creature, which cut through the horrendous stench of the valley like a knife blade. While Inigo had a smell like damp soil, earthy but not unpleasing, Tom reeked like a wet dog that had rolled in something, or an unwashed stable, or rotting hay—or some combination of all three. Tom grinned, bearing his big prognathous teeth. His breath was bad, too.

"It's as if he expects it," Doc said. "As if he's done this before."

"So?" Colleen added. "Any beggar in Times Square has done the same thing. And they have better patter."

Tom blinked at this exchange—maybe confused, Cal thought, but essentially indifferent.

Cal said, "Is it true, Tom? Have you done this before? Have other people given you food?"

"People from the lights," Tom said. His speech was obviously painful and truncated, but there was nothing unusual about his accent, Cal thought. When he squeaked *People from the lights,* he squeaked it with a hint of a broad Midwestern twang. What had this man been before the Change overtook him? A counter clerk, a plumber, a computer programmer? Someone you'd pass in the street without looking twice.

Now he was bent and malformed and had difficulty mustering the intricacies of a simple declarative sentence.

"People from the lights?" Cal asked.

Tom seemed to reconsider his position, began to look vaguely frightened. He clasped the can of creamed corn to his chest and backed away a step.

"Hang on," Cal said.

"No . . ." Goldie said faintly. Cal glanced over to him. His expression had gone vague, eyes wide and distant, and Cal understood with a sudden quickening of the pulse that Goldie wasn't referring to the grunters.

Inigo caught the vibe, too, on the air, the night wind. "Something's coming," he murmured.

Reflexively, Cal shot a hand to the hilt of his sword.

Now the rest of his brood noticed it, too. They stood upright, turned their heads to the south.

A distant drone, achingly familiar, resolving as it drew rapidly closer into—

The rattle and sigh of leather stretched by wind.

"Shit!" Colleen cried out, dropping down, swiveling her crossbow up high.

The dragon came low out of the setting sun, out of the flame-streaked clouds.

Hunting.

With a cry, Tom and his brood took off at a wild, loping run, back the way they'd come, in a desperate attempt perhaps to reach whatever hidey-hole they'd emerged from.

But the dragon swooped down on them, big jaws snapping, missing one by inches. The grunters screamed and scattered, a number of them falling aside roughly and rolling, crab-crawling into the tall grass in an attempt to hide.

But the smallest of the bunch, one Cal thought to be a child, bolted away from the others in blind terror, shrieking, toward a bare patch of earth with no hint of cover.

Cal saw the dragon wasn't Stern but rather another grotesque, bands of green and red rippling along its rough, scarred body. It hovered at the apogee of its ascent, huge wings angling against the wind, ridged head swiveling as it scanned the ground with eager, fierce eyes. In the fiery dark sky, its outstretched wings were almost translucent, the color of port wine.

Its eyes fixed on the grunter child.

With its wings drawn up behind it like lateen sails, it arrowed down some invisible arc of the wind.

Cal raised his sword and darted forward, Doc close behind, running hard. But it was futile—the grunter child was a dozen yards away.

Cal glanced back and saw Colleen fighting the bolt that had become jammed in the cradle of her crossbow. Goldie—

Goldie stood upright and raised his hands. Balls of fierce turquoise light arced from his palms and flew toward the plunging dragon.

The light was brighter than the glare of the setting sun, and the grunter child looked back to see the source of these sudden shadows. When he saw the dragon dropping toward him, he stumbled and fell—which might have saved his life, Cal thought. The dragon overshot its prey. Goldie's fireballs overshot their target, too, but the dragon was forced to curve low to avoid them. It folded its wings and struck the tarmac of the highway, rolled a few times before it stood upright.

"Motherfucker!" the dragon howled, its voice like stone grinding stone in some fetid cavern. "I'm gonna fuck you up, you fucking fucks!"

"Aw, geez," Colleen muttered to herself. "White-trash dragons, yet."

The dragon on the ground was no less threatening, no less lethal, than it had been in the air. At its full height it towered over the grunter child. For that matter, it towered over Cal, who arrived between the child and the dragon and held his sword at point.

"Run!" he told the child. "Get out of here, find a place to hide." But the grunter only stared at him, paralyzed.

The dragon grinned.

The dragon's grin was terrible, resplendent with tooth and fang. Cal raised his sword. The dragon's eyes followed the bright steel.

Colleen chose that moment to fire her crossbow. The bolt sped past Cal and embedded itself in the dragon's shoulder—not deeply, because the dragon's pebbled skin was as dense as leather. But deep enough that the dragon screamed.

The scream—an eardrum-rattling roar, animal pain aligned with human rage—seemed to set the grunter child free. He turned and ran for the tall grass while Colleen nocked another bolt. Cal steadied himself in case the dragon leapt at him. And the dragon did leap, but directly upward, rowing the air in an effort to heave himself aloft. Cal was thrown to the ground by the wind rush and almost deafened by the kettledrum beat of the vast black-red wings. The dragon flashed over his head, diving once more toward the grunter child. The child had begun to scream, long hooting screams that erupted from his larynx like hiccups. And there was another sound—

Another sound, familiar and yet exotic.

The rumble of an automobile engine, the grinding of tires on gritty tarmac.

Which was, of course, impossible.

Colleen was distracted by the arrival of the vehicle. Her second shot went wide, the bolt passing the dragon's left wing like an errant torpedo.

The child continued to scream. But even the dragon seemed to hesitate in the air at the sight of this new arrival.

Here was a miracle.

It didn't look much like a miracle. It looked like an old Cadillac El Dorado, dusty black, with a cracked windshield and a rust-spattered scratch running down the passenger door like a lightning bolt. But it was moving under its own power.

Everything Cal had learned since the Change made this a miracle. Automobiles were useless; engines were useless. Since that watershed day in July, no one on earth—to Cal's knowledge—had been able to run a motor or plug in an appliance. That was the essence of the Change. There was no clause exempting late-model Caddies. It was as if a living mastodon had wandered down the road—more surprising in fact; the Change might well have revived a few mastodons, but the automobile should have been irrevocably extinct.

The dragon lost interest in the grunter child and spiraled upward, sculling for altitude.

Tom came running out of the high grass, grabbed the child up in his arms and dashed back to hiding.

The automobile crunched to a stop. The driver's door flew open and a young man stepped out.

The driver appeared to be in his twenties, a short, amiable-looking guy with glasses, thinning black hair and a bristle-length goatee framing his mouth. He wore a black T-shirt under a Day-Glo orange vest. At the sight of the dragon, his expression betrayed shock and surprise. Whatever he'd come here for, it wasn't this.

He reached into the car, grabbed up something from the backseat.

He pulled it out, wheeled around with it, braced himself against the roof of the El Dorado.

The dragon screeched and whirled, red eyes flashing.

The newcomer fired his rifle—

And that was impossible, too. Cal had seen people attempting to use firearms in the immediate aftermath of the Change. The result was a slow fizzle at best, as if the gunpowder were burning at an inhibited speed. No bang, no bullet.

But the stranger's rifle—which was decorated, oddly, with what looked like garnets or rubies—barked and kicked.

The bullet went wide.

"You son-of-a-fuckin' bitch!" Enraged, the dragon dove at the stranger, batted the gun aside. It seized him by the shoulders, thorny yellow claws digging deep into his nylon vest, clenching the muscles beneath so tightly that the young man's arms involuntarily stuck out from his sides. His eyes rolled with pain, and he screamed as the dragon flew up with him into the dazzling sky.

It hovered there, clutching him tightly—and drew the knife-blade talons of its free paw forward to eviscerate him.

But by now Cal had reached the car and grabbed up the rifle. He pumped another shell into the chamber. *God, let this miracle work again.* He aimed and fired.

The dragon screamed, dropping its captive, who fell the dozen or so feet to the ground, landing with a cushioned *whoomph* in the high grass.

Its enormous wings reduced to limp fabric on a sagging frame, the dragon plummeted to earth, hitting the highway with a satisfying thud.

Its body twitched once and fell silent, conspicuously dead, the iron stench of its blood thick on the air.

The grunters, terrified, had vanished.

Cal lowered the still-smoking gun. The acrid tang of gunpowder was in the air; Cal loved that smell, had loved it since he'd been a kid with cap guns.

Colleen sidled up alongside him, impressed. "Pretty slick shooting, ace."

"Yeah, well, my dad made me go to firing ranges when I was a kid." How Cal had hated those excursions, his father's attempts to make him a "real man"—when Dad hadn't the least notion that being a real man had nothing to do with the way one handled a gun and everything to do with the way one handled life. "Turns out I had a knack."

"I'll keep that in mind, next time we have the need."

By now, Doc was crouching beside the fallen newcomer. Cal and Colleen joined him. The stranger moaned, half conscious.

"No obvious broken bones," Doc remarked. "Under ideal conditions, I wouldn't think of moving him." He cast a glance at the dragon carcass in the tall grass, and at the sky. "But getting him to his people would not be inadvisable."

Inigo spoke from behind him. "He came from back there."

Cal saw he was gesturing toward the valley. And the town.

"What do you want to do, Cal?" Colleen asked.

Cal took a deep breath, and the icy air filled him. They were looking to him, it was his call. They, along with the strangers back at the grain silo who now folded their lives in with him, would follow wherever he might lead. He looked at the dead thing in the grass, this thing that had been a man once (though, if Stern was any indication, not a very estimable one), then turned to look at the way they had come, the long, shadowed land behind them and then the valley ahead, with its hideous phantom of plague and decay—if Colleen's talisman could be trusted.

The talisman the enigmatic old black man Papa Sky had given them in Chicago, the talisman that had saved them from Primal when the chips were down.

Then he looked at the boy, the grunter boy who had brought them here, to this place of faux plague and real dragons and jeweled guns that worked.

Inigo.

*My name is Inigo Montoya. . . . Prepare to die.*

*Real or Memorex?*

You go with what you know.

And when you don't know, you go with your gut.

A leader leads, and a lawyer searches for expedience and loopholes. He figured this was as good a time as any to be both.

"Let's take him home," Cal said.

# II

# Diamond and Sky

*It is in the darkness of their eyes that men get lost.*

—Black Elk

# FOURTEEN

## The Zen of Horses

Mama Diamond was quiet for the next couple of days' traveling, riding one horse and leading the other as Shango pedaled his ridiculous rail bike. The land was flat now, scrub prairie, the skies by daylight as blue as Dresden china. It was brutally cold, though, as they tended east. Mama Diamond had unpacked a fleece vest and wore it over her flannel shirt and under her leather overcoat with the elk buttons and rabbit lining. She wore a woolen cap to keep the breeze from biting at her ears.

The animal encounters had left her puzzled and disturbed, and she spent much of this time in profound thought.

Stern, it seemed, had taken something . . . and left something behind. Something more than the life—her life—he had promised to spare.

But exactly how had this happened, and why? Stern seemed like a man—a creature—*an individual*—that rarely if ever did anything by accident; beyond the huge joke-of-fate accident of his own transformation, an event which Mama Diamond felt certain he'd had absolutely no say or choice in.

As was the case by and large with everyone who had changed or gained some weird power or discovered some uncanny new talent.

Which now, surprisingly, unexpectedly, included Mama Diamond herself.

Someone or something—maybe God His Own Self—had rolled the dice with the whole damn world.

Not that she believed in God, at least not some old white dude with a beard. She wondered what her dead and buried Buddhist parents might have said about all this. Some creaky old Zen parable, undoubtedly. She could never make heads or tails of those. They weren't like a gemstone or a fossil bone you could hold in your hands, solid, real, undeniable.

But now so was the fact that Mama Diamond was possessed of a truly distinctive new social skill.

Not *possessed* in the Salem inquisitor's sense of the word. No, when she spoke to the animals, it was she, Mama Diamond, who had done the talking. She felt—*knew*—that she had spoken from the deepest and truest core of herself, the most authentic part of her, and that was the most unsettling thing.

Because, if that was the case, Stern hadn't actually *given* her this power. It had merely been dormant and, deliberately or inadvertently, he had simply awakened it.

Sleeping Beauty waiting for her kiss.

And Stern was the handsome prince? No way, José. Mama Diamond shuddered at the thought. She had sworn off men since Danny, her fiancé of fifteen minutes back in '62, and at this late date (when, if she was going to be a pinup girl for anything, it would be arthritis) Mama Diamond sure as little green apples wasn't going to be spliced to some hell-spawned T. rex imitator.

Still, Mama Diamond didn't get the feeling she could reject this wild Dr. Doolittle, talk-to-the-animals (or more like screw-with-the animals'-ability-to-discern-reality) facility within her so readily.

She pondered once more what her parents might have made of this, and it occurred to her it would have astonished them at least as much as it astonished her. Not for what it *did*, but that Mama Diamond, known to them only as Judy Kuriyama out of San Berdoo, their rebel-without-a-cause tomboy of a little girl, had manifested it.

This was the kind of spooky crud only a Zen master might pull.

Did that make her a Zen master?

*Hoo boy, don't go there, Mama*. You get cocky, you end up stepping on the wrong stone and sliding right down that cliff face into an arroyo. End of story. This newfound capacity guaranteed her *nada*, it was no get-out-of-jail-free card.

She learned that in a train yard at a junction town outside Sioux Falls, just across the border into Iowa.

The brittle, clear skies had given way to a raft of cloud, which yielded up, at dusk, a cold and dispiriting drizzle. Shango had told her the name of this town but Mama Diamond had already forgotten it—some largely abandoned town skirting a quartzite quarry, as bleak in the rain as a rusted automobile.

They camped in the train yard under a tin-roofed shed, the smoke from their campfire rising through a broken skylight to hang in the damp, still air. Marsh and Cope stood tethered in a far corner, restless in the shadows.

Mama Diamond was restless, too. She had noticed a sooty gas station–cum–general store on the ride in, and she offered to walk there now, maybe scavenge something interesting for dinner.

Shango agreed. "But be back before dark," the federal agent admonished, gathering more scrap lumber to feed the fire.

Of course, the tiny shop had already been looted. All that remained of any interest was a single can of vegetarian chili half hidden under a stockroom shelf. Slim pickings. But Mama Diamond dutifully picked up the can and dusted it off and carried it back through the wet grit and gravel to the train shed.

She heard voices before she entered and was wise enough to stand a moment in the shadows, icy rain trickling down her collar. Voices. Strangers. Perhaps not friendly.

She didn't feel much like a Zen master just now. She felt old and wet and a little bit frightened.

One harsh voice ordered Shango to stand aside and keep his hands away from his body.

Mama Diamond quietly maneuvered herself to a place where she could see into the enclosure. Three men had gathered around Shango. A fourth stood by the horses and was rummaging through the saddlebags—looking for food and dry goods, probably. He discovered Mama Diamond's tube of Polident and threw it aside with a snort of disgust.

The men were seedy-looking, drifter types. Such scavengers had had a relatively easy time of it after the Change, living off the stored fat of civilization. But times were leaner now. Most scavengers had learned to trade for food. Some had resorted to raiding and stealing.

The three men around Shango, two of them armed with baseball bats, were demanding to know where Shango's partner had gone.

"I don't have a partner," the federal agent said coolly.

"So? That's your fuckin' Polident, I suppose?"

"I trade in small goods," Shango said. "Amazing what people will barter for denture cream, toothpaste, aspirin, hemorrhoid ointment—"

This was not a cooperative answer. The questioner jabbed Shango's belly with the handle of his bat. Mama Diamond saw real pain on the government man's face.

Enough is enough, Mama Diamond thought. She tried to recall the energy that had risen in her veins back at the wolf encounter. That sense of *command.* Of seniority, power, wisdom—whatever you wanted to call it.

How do you summon such a thing?

She tried. It even seemed to her that she succeeded. But was she truly *feeling* the energy or just *remembering* it? Elusive, this skill.

Nevertheless she stepped forward, until the light of the fire made her plainly visible. "Stop that," she said.

It didn't sound like the voice of command. It sounded like her own customary croak. Worse, it sounded almost timid.

The thugs looked at her for a long, startled moment. Then the vocal one laughed out loud. "Calm down there, Grandma," he said. "You'll pop your dentures."

This was not a token of success, but Mama Diamond resolved to keep trying. "Don't get smart with me," she said. "If you know what's good for you—"

She wasn't allowed to finish. The scavenger who had been looting her saddlebags took a couple of steps closer and swung at Mama Diamond with a wooden billy club that had been strapped to his belt.

Mama Diamond took the blow in the ribs. The pain was agonizing. All her breath went out of her at once, and she fell to the grimy floor like a bag of rocks.

"There's no need for that," Shango said immediately.

"He speaks," the chief thug remarked.

At which his two buddies held Shango's arms behind him and the chief began to beat him with his fists. Mama Diamond, writhing on the floor, wondered whether all this might be a dream . . . or whether she had dreamed her conversation with the wolf and the panther.

Or maybe her skills only worked on animals.

The scavenger who had clubbed her went back to the saddlebags. He pulled out a pair of Mama Diamond's long johns and held them up. "Winter drawers," he remarked. "Shit, I thought these went out with black-and-white TV."

Nearer the fire, the beating of Shango continued methodically.

"Marsh," Mama Diamond groaned. "Cope."

The horses regarded her with rolling, fearful eyes.

"Help," she said.

Cope let out a trumpeting cry—in seeming acknowledgment, or was that wishful thinking?—then lashed out with his rear legs. Both hooves hammered the small of the unsuspecting vandal's back, propelling him several feet through the air. He landed on his face in an ungraceful sprawl and lay motionless, but still drawing breath.

He was lucky, Mama Diamond thought. Lucky to be merely unconscious. Lucky to have been standing so near the big horse that the beast's powerful hind legs hadn't gotten fully extended.

It was all the opening the government man needed. Shango did something Mama Diamond could not quite follow—bent and twisted himself free of the men who held him—and delivered two or three kicks of his own, barely less powerful than Cope's.

The horses yanked and fought their tethers. "Calm down," Mama Diamond whispered, struggling to her feet. Her upper body burned like fire, but she didn't believe any ribs had been broken. That was a mercy.

One of the thugs fled past her, out into the drizzling rain and the dark of the rail yard. The thugs who remained were unconscious on the ground. Shango took a length of rope and bound them methodically to a standpipe. Then he helped Mama Diamond closer to the fire.

"I doubt we'll have any more trouble tonight," Shango said.

"These types tend not to have a whole lot of friends. But we should move out pretty hastily come dawn. And keep watch till then."

"I could have used the sleep."

"So could I," Shango admitted. He was bleeding from a cut beside his right eye, dark blood on dark skin. He winced when he smiled ruefully.

Mama Diamond took a fresh handkerchief from her saddlebag, cleaned out the cut with a little water and taped it shut with a Band-Aid. She cast a satisfied glance at the unconscious men—the one Cope had dispatched at her bidding, the other two the result of Shango's efficient handiwork.

"Well, Mr. Shango," Mama Diamond said, "it appears I have a way with animals . . . and you have one with men."

Come morning, the air was cold but the rain of the night had gone. Sunlight came through the cluttered junk of the train yard at slants and angles like the strings of a cast-off harp.

Mama Diamond had hardly slept, even during her off-shift. Her eyes were raw and her chest ached dully. Stubbornly, she refused Shango's offer of aspirin. This pain had come hard-won; hell, she might as well feel it.

The three captive vandals continued to moan against their gags—Shango had gagged them around midnight, when they took to emitting loud verbal obscenities—and squirmed against their restraints. Mama Diamond said, "We just leave them?"

"Their buddy might come back. Even if not—you know how hard it is to tie a man up so effectively he can't work himself free? If we're not here to kick 'em when they wiggle, they'll soon enough be undone."

"I don't want their lives on my conscience," Mama Diamond said.

"Neither do I," said Shango, "though it wouldn't be such a heavy burden, would it?"

"I suppose not," Mama Diamond said. But she was relieved it was a subject she didn't have to fret over.

❦

Shango rigged a device whereby the horses could be harnessed to the rail bike, one rider per horse, and supplies strapped to the bike itself. It worked well enough that Shango was able to learn the basics of riding, and it seemed like an economical division of labor, at least where the land was level, the berms not too high, the rails unobstructed.

As the day's ride dragged on, Mama Diamond smiled to herself as the thought occurred what some passing stranger might remark upon seeing their passing parade, this weird assemblage like a land catamaran with horses instead of pontoons.

*"Well, that's certainly different."*

*I know what it's like to be different*, Mama Diamond thought, glancing over at Shango as he rode atop Marsh, his solemn level gaze on points east, the destination ahead. Even as a child, Mama Diamond had been alone more often than not, secretive and self-absorbed, an outsider. The camps did that to you, even if you were a kid; you'd listen to *Fibber McGee and Molly* on the radio, *One Man's Family*. All those normal folks who were able to go where they wanted, do whatever they chose, just get in a car and *drive* . . .

But there you and your folks were, and all those thousands of people who looked just like you, locked up in an internment camp in the middle of nowhere, a hot flat desert ringed by glowering, unsympathetic mountains. An *alien*.

Her mother told her the authorities said it was for their own protection. But if that was so, then why were the machine guns in the guard towers pointed *in* rather than *out*?

Mama Diamond remembered the baking summer night—she couldn't have been more than seven, if that—when she'd fired an improvised arrow out of her homemade toy bow up and up into tower number three. Boy howdy, she'd set those alarms *yowling*!

So Mama Diamond well knew that inside every quiet, self-sufficient loner was one hell-raiser just waiting for an excuse to bust out.

Shango shifted in the saddle, gave a low grunt. The tenderfoot way he was riding, Mama Diamond could tell he'd be plenty sore tonight. Not that he'd complain . . .

She knew he'd been different, too; it hadn't taken a Change to make him the Cat Who Walked Alone. She wondered what message the Cold Old World had sent him as a kid to cut him away from the herd.

Now here they were, the two of them, two loners spliced together on the road, on a treasure hunt—and who could say whether the treasure they'd find would be Mama Diamond's gemstones or the dark new heart of the planet?

Certainly not Mama Diamond. Nor could she say, if two loners were together, that they could truthfully be called loners anymore.

Mama Diamond felt the music of the power within her, felt her strange new talent—and this other thing, this new good feeling she could not name.

It made her uneasy, this feeling, this new situation, all of it. As a rule, she distrusted the good even more than the bad; after all, as she'd told her old friend Arnie Sproule on many a starless night, happiness was dangerous . . . while *misery*, well, they never could take *that* away from you.

Still, for all its danger and its newness, Mama Diamond thought she'd work on standing this good patch a while longer, trying it on for size.

Because even if she knew what it was like to be different, Mama thought as a few bright clouds rolled high and far through the frozen blue of the sky . . .

She didn't know what it was like to be this.

# FIFTEEN

## The Valley and the Stars

Grunters, dragons, piles of plague victims that appeared and vanished, guns and cars and everything stinking to high heaven.

It had been one cocked-up day, Colleen Brooks told herself, and it was shaping up to be an equally charming night.

At least it wasn't snowing anymore, and the evening had turned surprisingly mild. But it was small comfort, considering.

The five of them stood edgeways to the Valley of Mystery, the rotting dragon corpse not fifty feet off, the sun sunk beneath the horizon and the moon not yet high enough to be much help.

Colleen had asked that friggin' undependable Herman Goldman to whistle up some of his glowing blue balls (and no wisecracks here, please) to shed a little light on the situation. But all he'd done was stood staring freakily off down into the valley, even though now you couldn't see any of the bodies, just still smell them.

So Colleen fetched the ready-made torch from Big-T's saddleback and fired it up with her Bic. They were still dependable when you could find them, thank the Lord for small favors.

She jammed the torch into the snowy ground beside the dusty El Dorado convertible, where Doc and Cal were loading the groaning newcomer—just now starting to come around—into the backseat.

The grunters they'd saved from that white-trash dragon had all hightailed it into the tall grass—or wherever the hell they came from. But that snarky little tweak Inigo remained.

"I can't go into town with you," Inigo told Cal. "I mean, maybe eventually, but not right now. It should be safe, like I told you. Only don't mention I sent you."

"Now, that's a trustworthy statement, if I ever heard one," Colleen observed acidly. She had the hood open and was inspecting this golden oldie. Internal combustion engine, eight valve-and-piston job, no surprises—if you ignored the big red, green and blue gemstones running along both sides and atop the engine block, solidly bolted to it.

Oh, mama, but did she have a million and one questions . . .

Cal grabbed the rifle from where he'd cast it aside in the fresh snow. He looked it over, turning it in his hands.

Colleen came up alongside him, studied it more closely. She could see that it was a stock Remington hunting rifle, but one that had been curiously ornamented. The grip was inlaid with what looked like chips of quartz. The area around the firing mechanism was encrusted with beryl and agate; a line of garnets ran up the barrel, and the gunsight had been replaced with a sliver of gleaming opal.

Cal tossed it onto the passenger seat. He fished out the injured guy's battered wallet, thumbed through the cards.

"Driver's license . . . college ID . . . Domino's Pizza buy-ten-get-one-free card . . ."

"Is this guy an optimist or what?" Colleen asked, slamming the hood.

She noticed now that Cal had pulled a folded paper from within some hidden pocket inside the wallet. He opened it to reveal a creased snapshot of a pretty girl with caramel skin and cascading hair the shade of autumn leaves, her brilliant dark eyes guarded but not unfriendly; wounded, perhaps.

The image was arresting, enigmatic, and—given where he had stashed it—something this young man undoubtedly didn't want to share.

"His name's Theodore Siegel," Cal added, slipping the photo back into the wallet, and the wallet into Siegel's pocket.

"Ring a bell?" Colleen asked Inigo.

Inigo shrugged. "I'm not from around here."

"Really? And would you care to impart precisely where you are from?"

Inigo was a sphinx.

Cal turned toward Doc. "Care to ride shotgun?"

"When for once it's actually literal? Certainly, Calvin . . . Er, in just one moment." He hotfooted it over to where the dragon carcass lay crumpled in the grass.

Colleen caught the flash of Doc's lighter flaring up. He held it over the dragon's body, squinting closely at it. Then she saw the dancing flame glint off the metal blade as Doc pulled out his scaling knife and sawed at the beast's dead shoulder a moment.

*What the flaming blue hell . . . ?* Colleen thought.

Doc pulled something free, held it briefly in his palm, then pocketed it. Killing the light, he sidled back.

"Got something for show-and-tell, Viktor?" Colleen asked.

"Question me no questions, *Boi Baba*," he said airily.

"All I can say is, it's a good thing Mr. Pottymouth Lizard's gone and joined his trailer-park ancestors in the Happy Hunting Ground or you might be in the market for a replacement head, *mi amigo*."

"I am the soul of caution, Colleen."

Colleen snorted so loudly the two of them nearly missed Cal loudly and pointedly clearing his throat.

Doc got the message. He slid in on the passenger side of the El Dorado, resting the rifle on his lap.

Goldman was still staring down into the valley, not moving a muscle, as if waiting to see who would blink first (and it sure as hell wouldn't be him). Colleen nudged him in the ribs. "Wake up, Sleeping Beauty. Into the Valley of—"

"No, Colleen," Cal said. "You two go back to the silo, see how the others are doing."

"In a pig's knuckle, Cal."

"I mean it. We don't want to go down there en masse and be perceived as a threat."

"Oh, I think we very much want to be perceived as a threat." She thought of the late, definitely-not-lamented reptile on the wing they had just recently dispatched. *Better than being perceived as an in-flight snack.*

Cal unbuckled his sword and laid it in the passenger well beside

Doc. He climbed in behind the wheel, nodded toward the folded, nearly spindled and somewhat mutilated Mr. Siegel. "We just saved their homeboy here. Hopefully they'll see us as allies."

"And if they don't?" Colleen asked. "Are we supposed to bake a file into a cake? Or maybe just carve the headstone?"

And just what would that tombstone say? *I'd rather be in Philadelphia?* They'd passed by Philadelphia, and it was *definitely* a place you wouldn't rather be.

She shot Doc an imploring look—*C'mon, Viktor, don't be the stalwart physician here, come down on my side, for God's sake.* But he was tending to Siegel, murmuring low words, urging him to stay awake.

"Hey, when the man's right, he's right, Colleen," Goldman said. He had snapped out of his swami trance just at this inopportune moment, darn his big brown eyes. "Two's company, four's a convention. We'd just futz things up."

"And what about Haley Joel grunter here?" Colleen snapped. She meant Inigo, but he had that spooky look that kid from *The Sixth Sense* had, when he was lit from beneath and the frosty breath was curling out of his mouth, right before the ghosts came by.

"You'll go back with them and stick around till we return, right?" Cal asked Inigo.

"Sure," the boy assured him, but Colleen could tell by the way his eyes avoided Cal's that he was lying his little gray ass off.

She was gonna stick to him like leeches to Bogart in that movie with the African boat, like something superglued to a finger that you had to make a trip to the emergency room to separate.

*And if anything happens to Cal or Viktor . . .* She fingered the hilt of the brass-knuckle-grip, Eviscerator Three Special Superknife that Rory had bought at Hunter's Heaven in Greenwich Village back in the life before, and which she had brought along and worn at her belt in her travels since—figuring now that Rory was MIA and not quite human anymore, he wouldn't exactly be needing it. Whereas Colleen had had to protect a man or two that she'd grown particularly fond of lately. And yeah, dammit, all right, she'd admit it, Goldman, too.

Inigo was watching her intently, caught the motion with the knife. He swallowed hard.

Good, the duplicitous puny little tweak was nervous. She'd keep him that way.

"Here goes nothing," Cal said, and turned the key in the ignition. The big V-8 engine roared to life like a dinosaur in the jungle. Now, wasn't *that* an amazing sound?

On sudden impulse, Colleen ran around to the passenger side, leaned in through the open window and kissed Doc. "Don't do anything stupid," she said.

He opened his mouth to make a joke, then thought better of it. "I'll endeavor not to." They looked deeply into each other's eyes; she found some comfort there, a fact that no longer made her feel screechingly vulnerable.

He reached out and withdrew the chain from its place beneath her shirt, fingered the leather charm.

"If I may borrow this, for a short while. It may prove of use."

"If you think so," she responded, taking the length from around her neck.

"I think so." Delicately, he unhooked the charm, removed the rough triangle of iridescent leather, then returned the chain with its Russian cross and dog tags to her.

Cal gave them their moment, let the engine idle, warming up. Inigo sidled up alongside the driver's window.

"When you get down there, don't believe everything they say," he advised Cal. "And don't let 'em dazzle you. Just keep an eye out for what you really need."

"That your shopper's tip for the day?" Cal asked.

"Nah, not mine," Inigo murmured, and from the way he said it, Cal understood he could have added, *It's what I've been told to say.*

Inigo bent his oversized head in the direction of the dead dragon. "You did good back there. You have a knack for saving people."

"Thanks," Cal said.

And though neither of them knew it, or truly knew each other yet, in that moment they had an identical hope, and the same thought.

Of Tina.

The road started out lousy, full of ruts and fissures Cal had to swerve wide to avoid. But as they continued down into the valley, it got better tended.

The bloated dead lay directly in their path. And by God, they looked real.

*I see the town completely undamaged,* Colleen had said. Well, there was only one way to really test that theory.

"Buckle your seat belts," Cal said. Doc pulled his shoulder belt and snapped it in, then helped Siegel with his.

Cal floored it. With a roar, the El Dorado's big tires shimmied laterally, then gained traction, screeching. The car surged forward.

They sped toward the grotesque heaped bodies of men, women, children. And then . . .

Nothing.

It was like passing through the surface of a mirror, if the mirror were insubstantial as smoke, and suddenly seeing the reflection wasn't real at all.

"*Bozhyeh moy,*" Doc muttered under his breath.

"You can say that again," said Cal.

For in the valley spread out ahead of them, the cloudwrack opened and the pale moon raked cleared, pristine fields of what might recently have been rows of wheat and corn. The adjacent farmhouse had smoke curling complacently up out of the chimney, and brilliant, unwavering lights blazing within. Sound echoed from inside, vibrating through the keen night air toward them, lush orchestrations, and *words,* impossible words, and familiar.

"*Hide the ring, Frodo. Keep it safe!*"

"Jesus H. Christ," Cal whispered. There were only two possibilities: either Sir Ian McKellen himself had dropped by and was reciting his number one hits . . .

Or someone was watching *The Lord of the Rings.*

A *working* television, *working* VCR or DVD player, and *electric* lights.

Beyond the farmhouse was the town itself, the buildings upright and intact, night settling down snug around a scattering of lights, amber streetlamps, astonishing dependable current humming through them, a carpet of them tucked into the gentle river valley, twinkling. People strolled the main street and lingered in the gazeboed park as if they hadn't a care in the world, as if there had never been a Change or a Storm or a Darkness to make them shed a single tear.

Cal understood now just what the people here had to protect.

A safe haven, a hiding place . . .

*Sanctuary.*

The first such town Cal and his companions had come to on their winding pilgrimage was Stansbury, near the banks of the Patuxent, where Lola Johnson, that laughing, wise Earth Mother, somehow managed to plant the suggestion to marauding passersby that they not see the town at all.

Mary McCrae used concealing fog and portals only a very few could open to keep her Preserve enclosed.

Fred Wishart had done the same with Boone's Gap for a time, and conjured monsters.

The folks here used plague, the illusion of it, to summon up terror and keep visitors away.

"Where should we drop you, Mr. Siegel?" Cal asked their passenger.

"Call me Theo." He was sitting up straighter now, propping himself up with a hand on the back of Doc's bucket seat. "Left at the stoplight, it's the only one."

Cal made the turn and saw that laid out ahead of them were the homey brick structures of a college. A row of wire-strung power poles stood evenly spaced on either side of the street, fanning out from the campus to the rest of the town. Closer now, Cal could see that each of the poles was arrayed—like the rifle Theo had wielded, like the engine of the El Dorado—with gleaming bright gemstones. They glimmered in the illumination from the lamps overhead, and cast multihued refractions.

Cal pulled up to the Student Union.

"Thanks," Theo said. "Hey, listen, how 'bout you come in a minute? There's a couple friends I'd like you to meet."

Doc shot Cal a questioning look. Cal nodded confirmation. The two of them climbed out of the big boat of a car and helped the pale young man shakily to his feet. Cal's hand brushed the back of Theo's neck, and he was surprised to feel a hard bump under the skin.

It was just about exactly the size and shape of one of those stones lining the streetlamps.

Theo, trying to put weight on his left leg, cried out in pain.

"Broken, in all possibility, or badly sprained," Doc said. "What I would give for a—" Then a remarkable look dawned on his face, as he cast his eyes on all the streetlights ablaze.

"You would not by chance have a medical center?" Doc asked, and Cal caught the tentative eagerness under the words.

Supported by them on either side, hobbling all the way, Theo led them there. But not before Cal retrieved his sword from the Cadillac, buckled it around his waist, and handed Doc the rifle.

# SIXTEEN

## Silo

It made Inigo's stomach hurt having to lie to Christina's brother. But if he hadn't, Cal Griffin would never have left him to go into town.

Still, Inigo's mother had told him never to lie. But then, she had said she was only leaving him for a week or two, that he would be perfectly safe with Agnes Wu (make that *Dr.* Wu, if you please, though it had always seemed odd to Inigo that someone who pushed elemental particles around had the same title as a guy who gave you a tetanus shot), that she would be back before he knew she was gone.

And that had all been a lie.

So where did that leave him?

Telling Cal Griffin he would stay put, when that would be the most dangerous thing he could do for any of them.

No, he had to be in and out, before the Big Bad Thing got a whiff of it, in plenty of time to watch Christina dance on the corner again, to listen to Papa Sky belt out those mournful blues, to have the Leather Man not say a word or bat an eye.

Because shit, if you crossed that crazy dude, he'd say more than a word and bat more than an eye.

That scary lady with the crossbow and the knives hauled him up on her horse—Big-T it was named, was that some kinda joke, like Tyrannosaurus or what?—and held tight to him all the way to the towering grain silo where the other happy campers were stowed. That funny, schizzy guy with the black curls rode alongside them on his buckskin horse, staring at him all the way, without ever looking directly at him.

Creepy, that.

Even when they got to the silo, Xena Warrior Princess kept him walking ahead of her, breathing down his neck, never letting him get so much as a yard away.

*Oh brother, they were making him work. . . .*

Once inside, though, things took a serious upswing. Biker Girl and Hippie started talking to the rest of the gang, making sure they were warm, the fires well stoked, everybody with enough food in their gut and no grumbling from anybody. Plus they had to hip them to what Cal and Dr. Russian were up to.

A lot of ground to cover, chores to attend to. And finally, *finally* neither Goldie nor Colleen was watching him, and Inigo was able to slip out the door and into the night.

To where the other silo was waiting.

Since his transformation—and long before that, actually—Inigo could move on swift cat feet, covering a ton of ground making no sound at all, like wind rippling on the air, and nobody, not even an owl or a wood mouse, getting the least hint he was there.

He was a good way from the grain silo now; it was the barest silhouette against the night sky. The terrain spread out before him was a featureless expanse of mottled snow and high grass.

In the normal scheme of things, he wouldn't have been able to see anything at all, wouldn't have been able to find the hatch set flat in the ground. But this was far from the normal scheme of things, and he wasn't a normal anything anymore.

Generally, he hated being the stunted, twisted freak he was—the bonsai distortions the Storm had laid on him made him studiously avoid mirrors. But for once, he was thankful for the milky, big, egg-membrane eyes of his that could pierce the darkness like a night-vision scope and better. It was a snap finding the big steel hatch, lifting it effortlessly with those long, lean superhuman arm muscles of his.

He peered into the deep, black hole. Hot air rushed up out of it like the exhalation of the biggest junkyard dog in the world. Cloaked in the night, Inigo could spy downward with perfect assurance, see the dead elevators, the emergency handholds set at regular intervals in the wall down the endless length of the shaft.

This would be the hardest part of all, harder even than hanging on to that shrieking hell-train as it screamed underground and punched up into the air like the Devil himself being born. But Leather Man had coached Inigo thoroughly, given explicit directions. There'd be a lot of hard traveling, and he'd have to move fast, but if he was really on his toes, kept a sharp lookout, he could find shortcuts, doorways on the fade that hadn't winked out yet, that he could still squeeze through.

And, of course, he'd have to keep clear of the lurkers in the dark, the smilers with the knives, the dark little men who would cut him open and eat him raw without the least hesitation. . . .

Man, he hated being one of them.

Leather Man would leave that last back door open for him, or else he'd never get back, not in a million years of Sundays—the door that almost nobody else could get through, certainly no human, certainly not Cal Griffin. The Big Bad Thing would sense a thing like that for sure, and crush anyone flat before he so much as drew a breath.

But a little gray guy, particularly under just the right protection and at the right moment, might just slip on by, be taken for one of the ground crew, one of the staff.

Because as Leather Man and Papa Sky had drilled into him and into him . . .

Grunters It drove crazy (except for him, for the time being), flares It swallowed whole to fuel the furnace, and dragons—

Well, dragons were another thing entirely.

Time to go home. Or at least what had once been home, and now was—

"Hold it right there, you lying little creep."

The voice came from behind him, stunningly close. Inigo turned around slowly.

Colleen Brooks stood there, not ten feet off, her crossbow aimed right at him.

He hadn't heard her coming at all.

Damn, she was good . . . for a human.

"You wanna talk about it?" Colleen glared at him. "No? Suits me just fine, because most sphincters I run into just want to yak and yak. C'mon, we're heading back."

Busted. He took just one step toward her, when abruptly someone dashed up from behind and to the right of him, grabbed him hard and threw him down into the snow.

Which was the only thing that saved him, or his hypersensitive sight at least, because right then there was this explosion of light around him, and Colleen Brooks screamed.

When the light cleared enough for him to look up, Inigo thought for one terrible instant that she had been melted to nothing right there on the spot. Then he saw to his relief that she had just dropped to the ground and was rolling around in pain, holding her eyes and cursing, blinded—temporarily, he hoped.

Then whoever it was behind him grabbed him again.

"Move," the voice said, and shoved him toward the open shaft. The two of them crawled in quickly, hanging from the handholds.

"The hatch, grab the hatch," the voice commanded.

Inigo grabbed the heavy iron door by its inner wheel, pulled it down secure.

"Now dog it. Hard."

Inigo twisted it, then gave it an extra turn no ordinary mortal could undo.

The two of them slid down the walls of the shaft like lizards, like the geckos Inigo had seen on Kauai when his folks had taken him on vacation, in the good time before his dad had gotten the security job at the Project.

It seemed to take forever, the two of them descending in silence, but finally they reached bottom. Breathing hard in the echoing blackness, Inigo faced the one who had saved him.

The man reached out a hand palm-up, and a glowing ball appeared in it, a flawless globe of shimmering blue fog. Inigo squinted painfully against the light.

The figure adjusted his straw cowboy hat with the five aces, set it right.

"Now you're gonna tell me a thing or two," Goldie said, neither his eyes nor his mouth smiling, in his own way every bit as terrifying as Leather Man could be.

There was nothing funny about him at all.

# SEVENTEEN

## The Triangle and the Stones

Back in the good old twentieth century when Einstein was the latest word in all things physical, the Astronomy Department had set up this telescope—a Meade Starfinder situated in the cupola atop what had once been the Atherton Agricultural College, next to the newer Physical Sciences Building—for long-term use by its faculty and student body.

But Melissa Wade was the only person who came here anymore.

The retractable domed roof of the cupola had been donated by a wealthy alumnus, a tool-and-dye tycoon with a stargazing fetish. Melissa hadn't expected a clear night, considering the long snowy day. But the sky had opened like a treasure box just after dark. And so, alone between dinner call and lights-out, she had come here and cranked back the roof.

The room was stocked with scope accessories—digital imagers and trackers—but Melissa left these alone. They were an unnecessary draw on the community current, for one thing; moreover, Melissa wasn't here to do research or even serious observing. She just liked the place. It was conducive to thought. It was her aerie. Crossing the night-lit room, she caught her reflection in the curved glass of the dead monitors, and quickly looked away. Not that she was unattractive; quite the reverse. She got her curves from her mom; her wide, radiant smile from her dad; and that glowing, perpetual-tan skin from the mixture of both, the sweet gift of having one parent white, one black. Whenever she traversed the quad, she was aware of heads turning to watch her; the men, and women, too, as if she was something quite extraordinary.

But she wasn't, she knew; at least, not that aspect of her. It was merely something she'd been given, not something she'd earned. And so she chose not to dwell on it, not even in reflection.

And anyway, her looks had no effect on Jeff.

Melissa plopped herself down in the plush leather chair and stared up at the expanse of stars through the open dome, gemstones scattered across black velvet. She put her eye to the viewfinder, and the scene leapt to dazzling intensity.

Some astronomy plebe might look at that array and see only constellations and nomenclature; man imposing his arbitrary meaning on nature, and rendering himself blind.

But Melissa's focus of study had never been astronomy, and what she'd learned by rote in those required classes she'd mostly forgotten. Of all the celestial bodies in the night sky, she could still identify only the moon, Venus and Mars, the Big Dipper, Polaris the North Star and a smattering of others.

But none of that mattered. She didn't have to name them. She loved them much more simply than that.

With all its optical gear and tracking equipment disengaged, the Meade was little more than an expensive amateur scope. What was different since the Change was the sky. Less pollution to block the view. No competing light from automobiles or cities or towns (except here in Atherton, and then only before curfew). Melissa had grown up in Los Angeles, where the night sky was generally blank as slate. Out here in the boonies—and since the Change—the sky was a river of stars.

She bathed in it.

Stars were suns, very far away. The fuzzy ones were galaxies—whole clusters of stars. And even after the Change they had not varied in their courses. Maybe that was what she found so reassuring in this immensity, the fact that all this scary terrestrial stuff was less than a fleabite against the somber rotations of the sky.

Still, it didn't change the fact that the natural laws—at least locally, in galactic terms—had become a whole 'nother ball game.

Melissa had been a physics major, specializing in quantum mechanics, but had soon found that her real skill was as a grease monkey. She'd always messed around with motors and engines. Her dad had been a first-rate mechanic—a weekend hobbyist mainly, but a good one—and he'd let her fool around with tools and equipment from before she was riding a bike minus the training wheels.

So when she joined the Atherton lab as a grad student import from UCLA's Large Plasma Device facility, she'd just naturally fallen into being the pair of hands supervising the building of Jeff Arcott's own radically original version of the plasma zapper, hand-tooling the steel housings and mounting the big water-cooled bus bars, pumping all the air out of the hundred-yard cylindrical chamber until you had a near-perfect vacuum at barely a billionth of an atmosphere, then introducing argon into the mix. Theo Siegel had taken the lion's share of fine-tuning the lasers and doing the other minute calibrations. And Jeff Arcott was the designer on high, the lord of creation, the big brain in a globe the mutants carried around.

Nowadays, of course, the plasma zapper was just so much rusting junk; there were bigger fish to fry. Oh, she supposed they could summon up the raw energy to get it all sparking again. But the elusive Holy Grail quest for fusion power was Old Physics thinking now, when there was so much more of a pot of gold at the end of the rainbow if you started pursuing new lines of inquiry.

At least, that was Jeff's point of view.

Sometimes—quite often, actually—Melissa felt like someone standing halfway up a mountain, unable to see anything over the top, while Jeff stood on the summit, gazing out onto immensity and rhapsodizing over what he saw.

She just had to trust that what Jeff reported was what was actually there.

And why should she doubt it? Why should she listen to the queasy, whispering little voices within her?

Not long ago, she and Theo had discussed this topic, for he shared her—all right, call it *disquiet;* she was alone and, in this moment at least, could be candid with herself.

What if Jeff was mistaken, what if he was drawing all of them into the darkness rather than the light? There was no evidence of that so far, given his triumphs here in town.

And yet, there were still those whispers. . . .

In conversation with Theo, she'd betrayed none of these doubts, had instead hotly defended Jeff. "He's doing something incredible," she'd said, "and we can help make that happen. What's this stupid life for anyway? You only have the people you care about, and if you're not loyal to him"—she quickly amended it—"to *them*, then what do you have?"

Theo had said nothing in response, had only grown abashed, and retreated.

Which had been no mystery, for although by mutual unspoken consent they had never discussed it openly, had in fact barely alluded to it, Melissa was aware of how Theo felt about her, and equally aware of how nothing could come of it.

Melissa knew herself well, knew the recurring patterns of her life. Every man that had held center stage in her life, from her professorial father on down, had been a distant star retreating, as cold and unreachable as the ones in the firmament, the ones she could spy through the opening in the cupola above.

And Jeff, with his immense charm and charisma, that incredibly sexy air of assured genius (in her lighter moments, Melissa liked to fantasize about an infomercial for a videotape called *Scientists Gone Wild*), was merely the latest and greatest, the most brilliant and rejecting of all.

And she cherished him more than the gems he had studded Atherton with, the treasures that had restored sanity to the town.

Even now after so much had happened, when Jeff entered a room, Melissa still felt weightless.

Which—as her father liked to say in his favorite colloquialism—was to laugh, because the only thing that made Jeff Arcott's head turn, the only thing he had ever truly loved, was the quest for pure knowledge.

So she mooned over Jeff, while Theo mooned over her. At present, she suspected Jeff held much the same affection for her that she held for Theo; if that wasn't her projecting emotions onto Jeff, filling in the blanks. She could hope at least, knowing that sometimes affection bloomed into more, a great deal more. She'd seen that happen on numerous occasions . . . and not all of them just in movies and TV.

Normally about this time of night, Theo would be seeking her out, asking if she might like some peach tea, or offering up a day-old Danish from the bakery the campus cooks still maintained despite all that had happened. He was as solicitous as a little brother, as kin, and she supposed in some odd way he was . . . given the nifty hand-tooled item just the two of them shared under the skin.

Through the open cupola, Melissa heard footsteps and voices echoing from the sidewalk outside. Two of the voices she didn't recognize, but the third she knew as Theo's, though laced with a tension she thought sounded like pain.

Theo cried out as he took a misstep, verifying her suspicion. Melissa looked away from the eyepiece and closed up the cupola.

She found Theo standing one-footed stork-like on the pavement outside, flanked by two strangers who introduced themselves as Cal Griffin and Dr. Viktor Lysenko.

Strangers, here in town. Incredible.

Jeff would certainly have a word or two about that. And more than a word. As she was sure Theo knew every bit as well as she did.

Melissa clucked her tongue in mock disapproval. "My goodness, Theo, what have you been up to?"

Theo shrugged and smiled haplessly. Shaking her head, Melissa couldn't help but smile back, feeling a warmth surge up in her that was far from being in love.

Telling them nothing, she helped them get Theo to the Med Center.

Watching the MRI tech and the night nurse load Theo Siegel into the big magnetic resonance chamber, Doc Lysenko seemed moved almost to tears.

"I didn't believe I would see equipment like this up and running for many years," he told Cal, who stood alongside him in the waiting room just outside. "Truly, this town has accomplished the miraculous."

Yes, Cal acknowledged silently to himself, but at what price? His hand rested on the hilt of his sword and he noticed that, despite his words, Doc kept a close grip on the rifle.

*Miles to go before we sleep . . .*

Cal glanced over to where the young woman who had introduced herself as Melissa Wade sat waiting nearby, idly flipping through an old magazine—what other kind were there now? The photo he'd seen in Theo's wallet hadn't done her justice. She was breathtaking, and not flashy about it. In fact, dressed casually in jeans and an oversized man's work shirt, it was obvious she was trying to downplay it.

Still sitting, Melissa stretched, one hand sweeping the hair up off her graceful neck, craning her neck against the kinks.

Cal felt a chill—*on the back of her neck was a bump seemingly identical to the one he'd felt on Theo when helping him out of the El Dorado.*

When they were alone again, he would mention this to Doc. He felt certain Doc would be equally intrigued; perhaps the two of them might prevail on the medical staff to later run an additional MRI on Theo Siegel's neck.

*Just keep an eye out for what you really need,* the grunter boy Inigo had told Cal. But were these mysterious bumps part of what Cal needed or merely yet another of an endless series of distractions, delays from getting what he needed, to get where he had to go?

Spying an intern passing by in the hallway, Doc exited quickly and collared the man. Through the door, Cal could hear Doc requesting access to a microscope.

He watched as the intern led Doc away, and made no move to intercede.

Half an hour later, Doc returned and took him aside, out of earshot of Melissa Wade. The young woman continued to read her magazine, seemingly unconcerned with them.

"I needed to verify a suspicion, Calvin," Doc said. He held up Colleen's amulet, the one Papa Sky had given her in Chicago, the one that had saved them from Primal. Then he showed Cal the ragged piece of hide he had sawed off the dead dragon outside of town. "This and this, the *same.* At least, the same species, but not the same individual. They're dragon scales."

*Incredible.* To date, Cal had seen only two dragons up close, Ely Stern and the one he had killed today. It was hard to imagine that Papa Sky, aging and blind, had had a run-in with a dragon and lived to tell about it. He'd said the scale had been given to him by some unseen "friend." Supposing Papa Sky's mystery man really existed, how had he come into possession of something like this? And how had he known what powers it possessed—how vital it would be to their survival?

Perhaps an even bigger question was *why*.

Every answer only raised more questions. . . .

Cal took the scale Doc had cut off the dragon carcass. "Do you think this might have the same properties as the other one?"

"I don't know," Doc answered. "But I think it would certainly be advisable to find out."

The door to the MRI room opened and Theo Siegel emerged on crutches, his leg securely taped at the ankle with a surgical bandage, followed by the night nurse and the emergency room MD who had first examined him. Cal handed the scale back to Doc, who quickly stowed both in his pocket.

Cal stepped forward concernedly, Doc beside him, while Melissa Wade rose and followed them. Cal saw that Doc still held the gem-worked rifle loosely at his side. Cal himself kept a close hand on the hilt of his sword.

Cal positioned himself with his back to the wall, the entrance to the room in his line of vision. He saw Doc casually do the same.

"Nothing broken," the doctor, whose name was Asher Waxman, assured them. "Just a bad sprain."

"It's a good thing you're sturdier than you look," Melissa admonished Theo, leavening it with a smile. Cal could readily see the fondness there—and read a good deal more in Theo's shy glance back at her.

There was a knock at the waiting-room door, which seemed a curious formality to Cal. Through its small window, he could see a young man with blazing blue eyes and a broad forehead crowned by wavy black hair. He wore the faintest hint of a smile—not mockery; Cal had the impression it reflected a permanent air of ironic bemusement.

"That's, um, Jeff. Jeff Arcott," said Theo, ducking his head with reflexive subservience.

Cal saw Melissa's eyes light up at the sight of Arcott, saw her draw in a quick breath, could almost hear her heart pick up its pace.

The doctor opened the door and Arcott sauntered in, hands hooked lightly in the pockets of his faded bomber jacket. Two uniformed sheriff's deputies entered behind him and took flanking positions opposite Cal and Doc. Cal noted that each had a hand on a holstered nine-millimeter pistol—guns that, like the rifle, had gemstones worked into them.

Arcott gave Melissa the barest nod then appraised Theo dourly, neither acknowledging nor overtly ignoring Cal and Doc. "My my, Theodore . . ."

The way he said "Theodore" made Cal think of the condescending, smart-ass way that guy on *Leave it to Beaver* referred to the little kid who starred in the show. *I'm smarter than you,* it said. *Way smarter.*

"I got a call you'd had a bit of a party tonight," Arcott continued, "complete with piñata . . . only it seems *you* were the piñata." Now at last his eyes came to rest on Cal and Doc. "Brought home a few new friends, too."

Melissa stepped between Arcott and Siegel. "They helped him back to town, Jeff. Drove the car back, too." Her tone was ameliorating, her voice, as ever, musical. Cal sensed she was trying to protect Theo, to intercede for him.

Siegel worked the crutches laboriously, drew up to Arcott. "They're okay, Jeff, really. They saved my ass."

"Said ass shouldn't have ventured outside the town limits, Theodore." That strange formality again, that presentational style with its feigned lightness, its considered air of playfulness a thin coating over dead seriousness.

And through it all, the easy air of authority—and implication of threat.

"The coffee here is appalling." Arcott addressed Cal now, and Doc. "There's a *boulangerie* around the corner that should be open awhile and serves up something considerably more serviceable. Let's talk . . . and see what we will be to each other."

Doc glanced at Cal, who nodded agreement. Letting Arcott lead the way—and never allowing his security goons to position themselves behind them—they emerged out into the night, Theo Siegel struggling alongside on his crutches and Melissa Wade bringing up the rear.

The vapor lamps of the town hissed and blazed from on high, as they prepared to learn just precisely what Jeff Arcott had in mind for them.

# EIGHTEEN

## Goldman in the Kingdom

Underground, in the dark, untenanted and unrecalled, the cavernous space held the smell of the earth, of only the soil now, no air handlers processing it, sanitizing it to nullity. To one of the intruders, the dead controls and silent alarms, the corridors snaking off to infinity, presented themselves as clearly lit as if by a camera flash. To the other, the darkness beyond the periphery of the musty blue light was total.

But it still felt like home.

After all, Herman Goldman reflected, there wasn't a whole hell of a lot of difference between the tunnels under New York and a missile silo beneath the Iowa sod, other than that one tended to the horizontal, the other to the vertical—once the subway trains and nuclear missiles were rendered a historical footnote.

Inigo stood staring quizzically at him in the pale light of the roiling sphere, and Goldie knew the inhuman little Caliban would just as soon sprint off into the blackness as give him the time of day—but that fear and curiosity held him rooted there.

"Why'd you do that?" Inigo asked, with a quaver of uncertainty, like his voice was about to crack. "Up there. I thought she was your friend." He meant Colleen, whom Goldie had left rolling on the ground as if trying to dig a hole to China, temporarily blinded and helpless when (to mangle unapologetically "The Battle Hymn of the Republic") he had loosed the terrible swift sword of his lightning against her.

"Hey, I'm from New York, we don't have friends."

Which got exactly the look from the pint-size gnome it deserved. Goldie grew serious. "Colleen Brooks is altogether too formidable for me to give her half a chance to work up a good head of steam. She'd wipe the floor with me, not to mention the windows and baseboards."

He knew that didn't answer the question, not at all, not really. It was merely the *what*, not the *why* of the act. But how could he answer that, even to himself, measure out the dimensions of ambush and betrayal, when he had no clear notion, no answer other than that he had acted wholly upon impulse?

And that it was only the beginning. . . .

"So how 'bout you riddle *me* a thing or two, eh, little buddy?" Goldie went on. "Like why you were making such a beeline for this retro artifact of what was once laughingly referred to as the Balance of Terror? Not for its piquant charm, certainly. And don't say you were intent on homesteading."

Inigo hesitated, debating his answer. Then he said quietly, "You want to let me go."

"Aw no, I don't think that's the *sine qua non* of the ideal answer, pardon my French. Two more to go."

Inigo looked at his feet.

"And while you're ruminating on a verb or two, let me just add an inquiry as to precisely how you knew to lead us to the delightful hamlet of Imaginary Corpse Town. Or for that matter, how you grokked what went down in Wind City, and the enigmatic little *tchotchke* Colleen laid with such refreshing venom on Primal. Why, you're just a walking yellow pages of mysteries and miracles, you are, Boy Wonder."

The babbling, effervescent torrent of words warned Goldie that he was inching way over into the red zone, majorly in danger of full-tilt out-of-control-dom.

*And didn't this infuriating, distorted, stunted, sad little boy only know he was throwing fuel on the fire by pulling this wordless Jesus-before-Herod crap?*

"Okay," Goldie sighed. "I'm gonna turn over all the cards."

He reached out his hands, and crazy energy bubbled out of them, building in intensity.

Soon, he knew, Inigo would begin to scream.

*I don't want to do this,* the tiny soft voice inside Goldie said.

But then came the answering self, the grim, dark presence that was increasingly finding purchase in the desolate stone landscape within him.

*You ain't got a choice, Jack.* Not and get to the church on time.

On other occasions, he had heard the murmuring voices in his head, the iron railroad spikes driven deep into his mind, had known them for the dissonant thrum of the Storm, the Source like the ultimate Benzedrine-mainlining Stravinsky chorus, the distant chaos land of power and enslavement and release. He had scuttled frantically away then, pushed his consciousness far from them to survive, to salvage some distinct notion of himself, of who he was and (here he had to force himself not to laugh) what he stood for.

*Get thee behind me, Satan . . . and don't push.*

For Herman Goldman, this was anything but academic.

For long ago, in a galaxy far, far away known as Manhattan, New York, he had met the gentleman with the inimitable headgear and sunburn to die for.

And wasn't *that* a topic for casual after-dinner conversation. . . .

He had been a grad student in his penultimate year, teaching—and please stifle your guffaws, ladies and germs—a course at NYU in Beginning Psych (having by then jettisoned his equally laughable pursuit of law) for the third dismal semester in a row, spewing it out by rote, no improvisation allowed, please, he had the patter down cold. Transference, anima and animus, borderline personality disorder, chronic narcissism, you name it, A to Z in the DSM-IV.

Droning on to the bored undergrads with their butts planted in those uncomfortable wooden amphitheatre seats because they'd rather have a marginal shot at a future than just eat the damn twelve-gauge now. Herman (he was called Herman then, not yet Goldie) smiled again at the cute Anorexia Lite girl in the third row like Feiffer's Dance to Spring, when he suddenly noticed—

The Devil, sitting right there in the front row, grinning at him like . . . well, like the Devil.

Herman blinked his eyes, hard, then blinked them again.

But the sonofabitch was still there.

Not such a bad-looking guy, actually. But then Satan began to needle him, really get his goat, heckle the hell out of him. It took all of Herman's concentration to keep lecturing, to act like he was ignoring the bastard.

Didn't the freak with the wings have any better place to be?

At which point, the Dark Angel pulled his trump card, levitated the whole damn class right up to the ceiling and held them there.

So Herman kept lecturing up at them where they floated. In due time, they settled back down en masse into their seats, still as shit-ass bored-looking as ever, and the bell rang.

One of them, a pimply sophomore named Lenny Hoffmayer, sidled up to him at the lectern. "'Scuse me, Mr. Goldman, um, why were you talking up at the ceiling for a while there?"

"Well, because that's where you *were*," Herman shot back, offended.

Lenny didn't stick around. The rest of the students had filed out, too. Only the Devil remained.

In fact, he stuck around for days. Going everywhere Herman went, engaging him in long philosophical debates. Herman was surprised to find out the guy was actually more optimistic than he was himself.

And because Herman Goldman had his line of patter, his syllabus, so stone-cold down, he found he could continue his lecture schedule without breaking a sweat, punch his clock same as regular, in essence pull the wool over everyone's eyes.

After that first class, no one tumbled to the fact that Herman Goldman had an extra passenger aboard.

Then, after a few days, he clicked back to normal like the reset button had been pushed, and realized he'd been hallucinating. Which surprisingly, rather than filling him with dread, gave him an odd sense of security.

He'd always feared that if he ever went crazy, he'd *stay* that way.

But some inner equilibrium had kicked in, brought him back to the air-bubble-smack-dab-in-the-center-of-the-liquid level of sanity.

And here was the key thing, the relevant part—he realized that Satan had not been anything other than . . . himself.

Just as in this breathless moment, in the flat heart of the country a thousand feet down, in the vast, dead home that had ever-so-recently housed a chummy nuclear family of MIRVs, the implacable voice telling him to torture this helpless Changed boy was none other than—

Himself.

And he had no idea, no idea at all, if this time he could reel it back in.

On the road to Atherton, the new recruit to the fold, the little gray brother named Brian Forbes, had told Inigo everything Herman Goldman had done to the fake policeman in the snowstorm night outside the Gateway Mall.

Standing now in the missile silo, his stunted back to the gunmetal wall, with absolutely nowhere to run and Goldie staring at him with an intense, anguished expression while his open hands erupted hot radiance like a pair of Fourth of July sparklers on steroids, young Master Inigo Devine had a nasty feeling he was about to be on the receiving end of a sensation a whole hell of a lot like it.

He screwed his eyes tight, tried to brace himself for what was coming, something far worse than riding a hell-bound train, or climbing down a freakin' missile silo. . . .

But then there was a cry that came, not from Inigo, but from nearby, and went echoing off into the void. Inigo opened his eyes in time to see Goldie collapse onto his knees, see the light from his hands flicker out.

"I'm sorry, oh God, I'm *sorry*. . . ." Goldman reached out to him in supplication and shame—although, Inigo realized, Goldie had stopped himself, had not done anything (short of scaring the shit out of him).

Which was when the Big Zap happened.

It was like Inigo's mind was a battery suddenly discharging, shooting a flood of raw images into Goldie's mind, one huge, mentally migraining mindburst, a zillion-mile-an-hour blur made up of bits and pieces that might (or might not) be Tina, Papa Sky, New York or something like it, and . . . and . . .

"The Source." Goldie was gasping, dry-mouthed. "You came from the Source."

Inigo didn't need to say anything. Goldie *knew*. At least, that much of it.

And Judas Priest, this was dangerous, because now that it was out of his mind and into Goldie's, it was way possible—

You Know Who might be able to hear it.

"*Quiet*," Inigo hissed, sitting up now, every nerve like burnt insulation and sizzling wire. "The Big Bad Thing—"

But he shouldn't even say that, shouldn't *name* It. Goldman shot him a wide-eyed, questioning look, but didn't press it.

"You're going back there," Goldie said instead. "You know where it is." He grabbed Inigo by the shoulders, crouching there at his level as the globe started to gutter and long fingers of darkness enfolded them. "*Take me with you.*"

Inigo shook his head slowly. "It would burn you up in the turnstile, It *does* that."

Goldie nodded solemnly, fortunately accepting (maybe thanks to the connection they'd just had) that he was telling the truth. No way in, no argument, and no talking about it, either.

*It would burn you up.*

Suddenly, from far down one of the corridors, came a sound like a marathon of barefoot runners, moving fast, growing in volume and then diminishing again, passing them by.

Inigo gave it all a furtive look.

"That something you can talk about?" Goldie asked him.

And fuck it, they were so worn out, and both oddly thrown together in this brutal journey neither had invited nor relished, that Inigo told him.

"Little gray brothers, I guess you call 'em—us—grunters . . ." He shrugged, and said simply, "They're digging across the country."

Goldie looked like Charlie Brown after Lucy yanked away the football, agape.

"Old mines," Inigo continued. "Subway tunnels, storage facilities, caverns, anything underground basically. They're connecting them all up, so they don't have to go out in the air much, where there's sun and stuff."

Goldie, who'd had diarrhea of the mouth only moments before, was speechless. Then he rallied. "That's nuts. I mean, Buddha on a Popsicle stick, do you know how many homunculi a stunt like that would *take*?"

"A friend of mine"—Inigo studiously avoided naming Papa Sky—"says maybe one in seventy-five turned into gray guys, maybe one in fifty. That makes somethin' like two, three million of us, just here in the States alone."

"Yeah, but not every one of you—"

"More and more of 'em diggin' in every day, least that's what I hear. I mean, I'll tell ya, that UV's a bitch."

"It's not possible. The *whole* country?"

"Well . . ." Inigo hesitated. "When they hit something they can't go though, they find a way . . . around. There's guys like you."

Goldie's eyes flashed, and there was that crazy scary determination again. "Guys like me. You mean, who can do some of the stuff I can do?"

Inigo nodded. On the road to Atherton, he had heard of Goldie's knack with portals. And while portals could be finicky and selective—the more so depending on who wielded the power—they certainly cut down on travel time.

"Some are volunteers, some are drafted," Inigo said of those with the gift. Captured he meant, held as slaves, like Olifiers and his group, but with different masters, to a different purpose.

Goldie was squeezing Inigo's shoulder again, hard now. "Who's the best you know?"

Inigo couldn't tell him the best he knew, not personally. But he could tell him the best he'd heard of.

And fearing that Goldie—or the part of Goldie that was nothing like the rest of him—might change his mind and turn the juice on, Inigo showed him how to get there.

Moving quickly through dark passages, Goldie could sense the telltale membranes, the fading shut doorways where the connective tissues of the world were particularly permeable. For a time after they were opened, even those without the special gift, without the power to make things part, might still be able to pass through the doors.

Inigo led him to exactly the right spot, where the wall glowed in just exactly the right way. The boy was too terrified to pass through, but Goldie still had that strange connectedness to him, the vibe that let him know the boy had led him true, was pulling no shell game of bait and switch.

He let the boy go, and Inigo took off running full-out, back the way he came, all too glad to be let off the hook.

Goldman, however, pressed on.

He passed through the shimmering portal to parts unknown, felt the queasy, familiar sensation of being transported to someplace far from the point of origin, hundreds, perhaps thousands of miles away.

*The best you know . . .*

The Man with the Power. And Goldie would need that power, would need every trick he could glean, every skill and talent he might derive.

Emerging through onto the other side, he found himself in a dark corridor, the only sound the mausoleum-knock of his footsteps. He willed another globe rolling brilliant onto his hand and crept forward.

Then froze in his tracks.

Ahead of him, as far as the eye could see, metal spikes projected diagonally up out of the wall.

*With heads stuck on them.*

*Big* heads, far larger than any human would have—any normal human, at least.

His stomach lurching, throat in his mouth, Goldie forced his feet to move, forced himself to approach the nearest of the hideous trophies. He reached out and felt it, found to his relief and amazement that it was *not* flesh but rubber instead.

The heads, the heads were all *masks*, huge and grotesque, of mice and dogs and tigers and bears, of dwarfs and a rootless boy who led other Lost Boys.

Incredibly, he *knew* them, or at least recognized them from childhood years sitting planted in front of the TV screen. With a sense of disorientation and homecoming, he began to suspect just where he might be.

Continuing on, he discovered a stairway that led up to a closed metal door. He opened it, and it swung outward, surprisingly silent.

A balmy night wind met him as he stepped onto level ground, with no hint of Midwestern chill.

Everything was dark, of course, and some of it was far different than he remembered it from long ago, when he had come here with his parents.

There was no Skyway, no Rocket to the Moon.

And, most significantly, no people.

At least, none of the human variety . . .

The puny, gnarled creatures scurried this way and that in their huddled groups, muttering nastily to themselves, one group chasing down a rat, pouncing on it with teeth and claws, consuming it alive.

Sounds like needle jabs drew Goldie's attention, and he realized that it was demented, high laughter. He spied a bunch of the loathsome little curs swinging on the unmoving arms of the familiar framework he recalled from his youth. They clambered up into the fiberglass cars so artfully formed into the shape of grinning, flying elephants.

They were everywhere, had overrun the place, claimed it as their own.

*A real E-ticket ride . . .*

The grunters in the Magic Kingdom.

# NINETEEN

## The New Physics

Arcott called the place a *boulangerie*, but Cal discovered in reality it was nothing more than a funky new-old coffeehouse named Insomnia, crammed with thrift-store sofas and sagging bookshelves, stained oak tables with irregular legs, and scruffy college types poring over dog-eared texts.

And oh yeah, John Lennon and Bob Dylan blaring out of the speakers, laptops blazing atop every surface, and the microwave heating croissants to buttery perfection.

Nothing out of the ordinary.

For last year, that was. But for right now, a drop-jawed astonishment, as with everything else he and Doc had seen since crossing the city limits.

Not to mention why these students would be so casually bothering to study instead of scattering to the four winds in search of kin, or taking up a useful trade such as farming or necromancy or wandering samurai-for-hire.

A Cheshire Cat, Arcott settled himself into a scuffed leather wing chair flanked by Theo Siegel and Melissa Wade, opposite Cal and Doc. He signaled five fingers to the peroxided, pierced and tattooed waitress, who promptly brought over five steaming lattes.

"It's on me," Arcott said expansively.

"What do folks do for money around here?" Cal asked.

"Well," Theo piped up, "paper money's no good, obviously, though most folks are holding on to it in the hopes it someday *will* be."

"They trade services," Melissa added, "or whatever else might have concrete value."

"Such as gemstones?" Doc asked.

Arcott smiled. "We put those to other use."

Cal noted how Arcott used "we": a royal pronoun for himself when making decisions for the town; a reference including everyone else when it was something Arcott himself needed. Casting a glance about the café, Cal saw that that everyone gave Arcott a subtle deference that might be respect or fear . . . or both.

The two deputies—clearly part of Arcott's security force—stood blank-faced and watchful just inside the door.

"My, this is a treat," Arcott said, sipping his latte. "We don't get many visitors."

"Not with that bubonic horror show you've got running on the perimeter," Cal said. "And for those that can't read the writing on the wall, you've got these." He nodded at the gem-encrusted rifle perched on Doc's leg.

"We haven't had to use them inside the town . . . as yet." Arcott's eyes glittered with that sharp watchfulness that stripped you bare as a chemical peel, the corners of his lips curled in an insolent smile. "So tell me, just what do *you* do? Doctor, lawyer, Indian chief?"

"Correct on the first two," Doc said. And as for the third, Cal reflected, if they'd brought along Enid Blindman, well, he was half Lakota Sioux, if not a chief, as far as Cal knew.

"Really?" Arcott sounded impressed. "Professional men. And what brings you to this far-flung outpost of the empire?"

"How is it you have the power up and running?" Cal asked flatly.

"Ah, you'll show me yours if I show you mine." Arcott chuckled. "Very well, we have no secrets here. . . ."

Cal caught the uneasiness that bloomed in Theo's eyes. *Bullshit,* it screamed in glowing neon letters. Cal saw that Melissa Wade had noticed this, too; uncertainty flickered momentarily in her eyes, then was replaced, with an effort, by neutrality.

"A question, Mr. Griffin." Arcott leaned on the small round table, which had barely enough room for the five cups and his elbows. "Why precisely do you think the world came crashing to a halt?"

"Because all the machines stopped running."

"Obvious but, I would posit, dead wrong. It stopped because most everyone assumed the rules had changed, when in actuality all that happened was a new addendum was included."

Cal thought of the miles of crushed, scorched aircraft he had seen on his journey alongside Larry Shango, when Shango had been on his odyssey to find Jeri Bilmer and her errant information; of the hundreds, thousands who had plummeted to their deaths when the jet engines had abruptly cut out . . . and beyond that the uncounted millions who had suffered appalling injury and worse when the hideous power of the Source Wave spread out from its unknown point of origin somewhere in the west and carpeted the whole wide world.

*An addendum . . .*

"So what are you saying?" Cal demanded. "That something was added rather than taken away?"

"Yes, exactly," Arcott responded airily. "The rules that governed the Einsteinian universe are still the same, with just an addition to the cosmology that funnels energy to a fresh purpose. A new physics, some might say, but more accurately the old physics with a twist or two, a new wrinkle. Perfectly explicable, if you merely apply a clarity of observation, some logical thinking. And once you bring that scrutiny to bear"—he waved at the computers, the electric lamps, the espresso machine with its screeching din—"you can introduce a governing principle into the mix that restores balance to the situation."

"And this is what you have done?" Doc inquired. "You are, what? A graduate student, like Ms. Wade and Mr. Siegel here?"

"Until last year, when I got my doctorate, then I was promoted to associate professor. I was hoping to land tenure eventually. . . ." He smiled that Cheshire smile again, glanced around the room at the steady stream of light, the computers, the works. "But since landing the brass ring, they might just give me the town."

"And you came up with this all on your lonesome?" Cal asked.

Arcott betrayed only the slightest hesitation. "Yes, the initial theoretical underpinnings. Fortunately, it was a parallel area of research to studies we'd been doing prior to the Change, examining different strategies utilizing precious and semiprecious stones to contain elusive energies, initially in an attempt to harness fusion.

"Or putting it more simply," he added airily, warming to the topic, "we learned there were certain assemblages, specific combinations of gems, that set up a spectral interference, jangled the harmonics of the post-Change sieve effect, withholding the energy from being siphoned away to fuel the hoodoo and beasties and things that go bump in the night, and keeping it where it rightly belonged—in the matrices of the electrical and mechanical devices it had originally been designed to run."

Arcott's eyes were gleaming now, as though he himself were filled with electricity. "Once I got the basic principles down, I built the practical equipment along with Theo and Melissa here. They in turn oversaw a team of undergrads to do the scut work."

He gestured at those in the café. "We've convinced most of the student body—and practically all the town—to hang tight until we get the kinks out. Then we can teach others, restore the U.S. grid. But for the time being, we've got to keep to ourselves, for security's sake. Can't risk some invading force of yahoos thinking they can take over the whole flea circus."

It *sounded* reasonable . . . so why, Cal wondered, was it giving him the creepy crawlies?

"And what about the illusion of plague?" Doc asked. "That is, as you say, quite the new wrinkle."

"A little serendipity along the way." Arcott shrugged. "You set out to make a solvent and you discover Nutrasweet."

"I would like to study this Nutrasweet of yours a bit more closely," Doc noted.

"We'll see," Arcott said, and Cal knew his meaning was the same as when parents said it. "Now. I've shown you mine . . ."

"My sister was kidnapped," Cal replied. We're searching for her."

Siegel and Wade registered surprise. Arcott's eyes narrowed. "On your own?"

"With some friends, who are waiting back at camp for us."

"Ah. I won't ask exactly where that might be, not yet at least. But you could be so good as to tell me what *they* do."

*You're fishing,* Cal realized. *You need something . . . or someone.* Unbidden, Doc's words on the roof of the mall came floating up to him.

*You cannot know what you will need at your ultimate moment of truth . . . nor whom. So given that, it is a good idea to bring as wide a variety of dramatis personae as possible.*

"We have a former naval lieutenant," Cal said. " An Internet geek, a few laborers . . . and a physicist."

Arcott sat up at that. "What's his name?"

"Dahlquist. Rafe Dahlquist."

Theo·Siegel and Melissa Wade recognized the name and were clearly impressed. But the most dramatic change was in Arcott. There was no insolence now, no mockery.

"Take me there, I'll come alone," he said. "I need to talk to him."

# TWENTY

## Cat and Rock and Bone

For hours, the windsong of the grasses was their sole companion as, an invasion force of two, Shango and Mama Diamond soldiered on into the heart of Iowa.

Then, as dusk drew its cloak across the land, Shango pointed out a black speck in the east, moving across the sky like torn fragments of leather lifted on a storm wind. Black, and distant, and purposeful. Mama Diamond could barely make out the telltale crenellation of the distant wings.

It was a dragon, though by no means necessarily Ely Stern.

It dipped below the level of the horizon and could not be seen anymore.

A sound came rippling though the air to them, like a distant crack of thunder.

The dragon rose, was visible for just a moment, then dipped down out of sight again. A second, identical sound pierced the night, and Mama Diamond realized it *wasn't* thunder but rather something that would have been as out of place and astonishing to a Styracosaurus or Australopithecine in their day, had they the sense to know it.

It was gunfire.

When Mama Diamond and Shango reached its point of origin—

and it didn't take all that long at full gallop, having chosen to stow the bike and its payload behind—they didn't find the gun or the shooter.

But they did find one hell of a big dead dragon.

Not Stern, Mama Diamond observed with some disappointment, very clearly not Stern.

Shango crouched by the huge carcass, lamp held high as he investigated the killing mark smack dab between the creature's eyes. He studied it until he was certain, and then stood again.

"A bullet wound," he said, leaving unspoken the vast panorama of all that might imply.

Hoofprints led in one direction away, and tire prints another.

The path of treadmarks lay along a road that dipped into a valley. Peering down into it in the dying remnant of the light, Shango gasped and his face betrayed that rarest of emotions for him—fear.

Mama Diamond followed his gaze and was perplexed, seeing nothing that would draw such a response. But then she understood that what *she* perceived bore no relation to what Shango was seeing.

And Mama Diamond knew it wasn't because of what in the old days (the pre-Stern days) had been her rusty old vision, the cataract on her left eye and what she jokingly referred to as her "good" eye on the right, the sight that had remarkably become acute. No, this came up out of the part of her that was her dragon soul, that could tell the difference between false and true.

Mama Diamond spoke low and calmingly to Shango, reassured him and in due time got him moving forward into the valley, against the evidence of his eyes, his nose and all his other knife-sharp loner instincts.

Beneath the killer moon, the Rock and Bone Woman and the Cat Who Walked Alone descended into the waiting arms of the town called Atherton.

*Leather Man will have my hide,* Inigo thought anxiously as he stood at the crossroads, in what the Great Unwashed, the normals, laughingly thought of as darkness, breathing hard from the running and the fright, standing bent over with his hands on his thighs, trying to catch his breath and decide just exactly what he should do.

Take the portal on the left and head back to New York City—or fake New York City, at any rate—where Papa Sky and Christina were waiting for him, where he could report *mission accomplished* and get a gold star and maybe a hot meal or two and not risk a major ass-whipping.

Or do something *really* stupid.

But he knew, he just *knew* that where he had led Herman Goldman to was one major suckhole of a quicksand pit that old Mr. Hippie Wizard there would absolutely positively *not* be able to extricate himself from, at least not without some *major* help from an *amigo* or two or three.

And if young Master Inigo Devine, he of the blue-gray skin and pale saucer eyes (which really didn't look *that* bad once you got used to them), just slunk on back to the Bogus Apple without flagging anybody as to the whereabouts of Goldie Five Aces, well then, it really wouldn't matter where Inigo as the representative of the man in black, who was not really a man, led Cal Griffin and his little group—at least, not to Herman Goldman, who wouldn't be a member of that little group, or any little group for that matter, except maybe the constituency of the dearly departed.

And yes, Inigo knew that Goldie had squeezed him for info, and perhaps for a fleeting moment had intended to do a great deal more. But Goldman had thought better of it, because, Inigo sensed, that wasn't Goldman, not really, not the better part of him, just the small, dark fraction that was like most of Leather Man and the totality of the Big Bad Thing, and even a little black corner of Inigo himself. I mean, who *didn't* screw up now and then?

Inigo had to admit, he *liked* Goldie.

And he had just left him in a world of shit.

He swore under his breath, in that lightless corridor a quarter mile beneath the prairie grasses, under the waning moon.

What would his parents tell him to do, if they weren't both individually MIA or in the Big Hereafter, if that was indeed where they had gone?

They'd tell him to get his meandering grunter ass back to the Ghostlands and Bogus Manhattan before he was missed on his little walkabout. Because Leather Man was in the service of the Big Bad Thing, and Inigo was protected so long as he didn't cross either; he wasn't significant enough to bother with, at least while he served their *need.* . . .

But tonight, he knew, he'd been on a secret mission that very much did *not* serve the Big Bopper, *numero uno,* and right now what he was considering doing wouldn't be serving either Boss Man number one or number two (not that either could reasonably be termed *men* anymore).

Which greatly increased his chances of being noticed and squashed by one or the other, or both.

So he knew Mommy and Daddy in absentia would tell him to be *sensible,* to get on home.

But where in the Taco Bell Chihuahua had *that* ever gotten him?

Inigo turned away from the portal.

*No gold star tonight . . .*

It took him a bad long time to reach the surface, get to the lip of the silo where he had last seen Colleen Brooks writhing on the ground, temporarily blinded by the flash balls Goldie had wielded, that had allowed Inigo to slip from her grasp and propel himself into *this* universe of doo-doo.

Naturally, she wasn't there any longer. But even in the depths of night it was ludicrously easy for him to track her heat-radiating, stumbling footprints back to camp. And even if there'd been no prints, he could just as have readily followed her scent.

Mighty handy to be a little gray guy every now and then.

He found her in the bowels of the grain silo just as dawn was breaking, making him squint against the light and giving him yet another in a long line of Excedrin headaches (only, of course, there was no Excedrin to be had). Colleen was engaged in an intent powwow with Cal Griffin and that Russian doctor guy. Near them, he noticed, that husky old scientist Dahlquist was hunkered down with a newcomer, and they were holding a Coleman lantern over big unrolled sheaves of paper that looked like blueprints of some kind.

The newcomer hadn't changed his attire since Inigo had seen him before, at the train siding, but he'd have recognized him anyway.

It was Bomber Jacket.

A new day was just starting, and already it was a ballbreaker.

# TWENTY-ONE

## Apocalypse Mouse

When he'd been here long ago with his so-called biological parents (thank God that matching pair of advertisements for Flattened Affect *were* biological, Goldie used to think; it meant they had to sleep every now and then, leaving him blissfully alone for a few hours), the park had been called the happiest place on earth.

And now, well, it still was . . . if you happened to be a grunter.

Those manic little orcs were having the time of their lives, laughing their distended creepy heads off.

And the best thing, the very best thing, in the dusty old words of that toothless guy at Woodstock, was that now, thanks to the Change, it was "*a free concert, man!*"

No admission price, no waiting in line—hell, no lines at all.

*Nobody here but us chickens . . .*

And Herman Goldman, who, for some reason that seemed considerably *less* like a good idea around about now, had thought to come here.

Upon emerging topside and seeing the hyperkinetic little monsters all piled on the flying elephant ride (which, minus electricity, was even *more* going nowhere than when it had just moved in circles), Goldie backed himself up all the way to Main Street. Which was exactly like the Main Street Sinclair Lewis had described in his book of the same name, if the buildings were three-quarter scale and all the inhabitants were four feet tall with hypodermic teeth and ravenous, maggot-colored eyes.

*At least you've still got your sense of humor,* Goldie told himself.

*Yeah, and look where that's gotten you your entire Rube Goldberg life.*

So now what? Beat a hasty retreat, and live to tell the tale?

He knew the answer to that one.

Nobody here but us chickens . . . and Herman Goldman. And one other human, or near-human, somewhere in this rambling, dead faux kingdom. Not the best Inigo had ever seen, but the best he'd heard of.

The Man with the Knack.

To take the grunters where they could not go, where tunnels and caverns and mineshafts failed, where burrowing would not suffice. To bridge the gap, make straight the path, take two points and draw a straight line.

Goldie needed that knack, if he could get it. For Cal, and Tina, and the rest of them.

But mostly for Magritte, for what had been done to her, for the dead hot core that burned in him now that only blood would quench.

He had a job to do here.

*And neither rain, nor sleet, nor dark of night . . .*

Nor even—what had Inigo called them?—*little gray guys* would stay him from his appointed rounds.

Crouched in the alcove of what had been a silent-movie theater, he could hear (even with his pitifully weak human ears) the wretches scurrying about outside, could catch their fierce quick breaths, their helium-esque cries of twisted delight. They were *everywhere.*

*What kind of ticket do you need for the Meet the Wizard ride?*

But then, they'd gotten rid of ticket books years ago.

*The shortest distance between two points is a straight line. . . .*

Herman Goldman walked boldly out of the silent-movie theater (which really *was* silent now, and dead as vaudeville) and strode up to a bunch of the stooped creatures, who were feinting at each other with knifelike shards torn from the shattered plate-glass window of the Emporium across the way.

Upon seeing him, they stopped their game and turned with gleaming, malicious eyes. At which point, he spoke the words he'd waited his entire life to say.

"Take me to your leader."

At first, they'd all bared their pointy piranha teeth and, squealing like rabid Pekinese, leapt for him.

It took *mucho* fancy footwork and summoning up the granddaddy of all glowing blue fireballs to drive them back and get them to actually *listen* to Mr. Midnight Snack a moment or two.

"Cut it out, cut it out!" Goldie cried, swatting them away, his fingers trailing long threads of luminescence. "Jiminy crickets, you guys got about as much impulse control as a junket of Republicans!"

They settled down to resentful grumbling. Then they took him where he wanted to go.

Which, as it turned out, next to the pirate ride and the shrinking-inside-a-molecule ride (which was long gone even before the Source put paid to the whole notion of tourism), was his favorite of all.

The New Orleans mansion had been designed to look derelict and forsaken, so more than most things it looked essentially the same from the outside.

As for inside, from the moment he'd beheld it as a boy three decades back, the long, rectangular room with its ruined, eighteenth-century opulence had been his ideal of a banquet hall. The addition of dozens of candles flickering in the chandelier and along the walls did nothing to diminish the effect.

The dead ones still sat in their places around the table but, being automatons of ghosts rather than the real thing, they did not move any longer. At the head of the table, a massive gilt throne was positioned, and in it sat the Man with the Knack . . . which was the *real* surprise.

"Well now . . ." she said. "Look what the cat dragged in."

The dozens of grunters lining the walls all chuckled in that ugly, low way that sounded like blood pulsing from a wound.

She was twenty-five, if that, long and lean in a feline way. Her legs, which went up to here, were stretched out and perched casually on the table. With her hair like flowing black mercury and sparkling green eyes, she looked a whole hell of a lot like the Evil Queen he'd first seen in that feature-length cartoon, the one that had virtually single-handedly propelled him into puberty. I mean, after all, *she* was the real babe in that movie, not that priss of a title character who hung out with the seven vertically challenged nonunion mine workers.

But just right now, Herman Goldman was thinking there wasn't a damn thing sexy about the sociopathic personality, not when you were camping out on the other side of the mirror with it.

"My name's Herman Goldman," he ventured. "What's your name?"

"Queen Bitch."

"Right . . ." Why did the Source have to make everyone a comedian, and power mad to boot? "Nice little place you got here," he added.

She smiled at that, and stretched languorously. "For a while, I thought I'd pick Universal. But hell, this has its own castle. Sometimes I do that, sometimes I do this. Depends on my mood."

"Well, it's nice to have a choice."

She nodded, then said, "I found the crate, you know. The one everyone said was down here." Her face clouded. "Unfortunately, he'd thawed."

"Bummer."

"Mm." She regarded him contemplatively. "I like you better than most of the folks they bring round. But then, you're alive."

"Yeah, well, that kinda adds to the charm factor."

"Just don't blow it," she cautioned, her mood darkening like a storm front. Another appreciative chuckle bubbled up from the peanut gallery. This was like being on *American Idol* with Madame DeFarge in the front row.

*Okay, okay,* Goldie told himself, *don't get rattled (or anyway, more rattled), get to the point.* "I, um, hear you're pretty adept at opening up doorways."

"Wanna go to Orlando?" She glanced at the heavy oaken door at the end of the hall. It glowed *bright* around the edges, then flew open, revealing a night-drenched lakefront, the water's silver iridescence against the sand.

"Or how about Tierra del Fuego?" she taunted saucily, and glanced over her shoulder at the near door. It too burned radiance around its lip, grunters shrinking back from the light. The door banged open, showing another, similar beach, but one thousands of miles removed.

The Bitch Queen blinked her endless black lashes just once. The twin doors slammed shut, the light extinguished.

"*Sweet,*," Goldie observed. "There anywhere you *can't* go?"

"Can't go across the ocean, maybe 'cause of the water, I dunno, that's just the way it is. But North, South and Central? Most every place but one . . . and, from what I hear, I wouldn't want to go *there*."

She meant the Source, Goldie realized, and the words Inigo (who looked so much like the vicious little fiends glaring at him now, but who was so different in spirit) said on the way here exploded in his mind like artillery shells in the night.

*It would burn you up in the turnstile, It does that.*

But even so, *everywhere but one* was a good sight better than what Herman Goldman, late of Manhattan and the tunnels beneath, could pull off.

But how precisely to get Queen Bitch to *share* her delightful special skill set? She didn't exactly seem like the plays-well-with-others type. More like runs-with-scissors . . .

Or plays well with grunters while they *all* run with scissors.

Of course, as they say, *The enemy of my enemy is my friend.* Unless she *also* happens to be my enemy . . .

Orlando was looking pretty good along about now.

"So how about you, Hermie?" Her words cut into his thoughts like a scalpel. God, he hated to be called that, it always reminded him of that little weenie from *Summer of '42*. "Bet you can do a trick or two. . . ."

"What makes you think that?"

"You wouldn't be standing here still talking if you couldn't."

That was true enough. All right then. He rolled his shoulders to get the kinks out, extended his hands palms up. "Get a load of this, Your Highness. . . ."

Tendrils of light spilled out of his open palms, spelled out letters of fire in midair as he sang like an incantation, "M-I-C . . . K-E-Y . . ."

"Oh, put a lid on it," she spit out venomously. "I hate that little rat."

Oh great, mouse envy. *Then you sure picked the wrong place to land, lady.*

"What else can you do?" she asked.

He thought to tell her about some of the rest of his bag of tricks—like that nice little stunt he'd pulled propelling Eddie into the Next Life, or at least a whole new point of view—but thought better of it. This was, after all, their first date.

"That's really my encore number," he said. "It's pretty much downhill from there."

"You better have something else to tell me, Hermie," the Bitch Queen cooed.

Cold-sweat city. So he went for broke, told her the whole enchilada, about the Source, their quest, everything. Then he invited her to join their little band of merry men, and a few stout women.

The enemy of my enemy, and all that jazz.

Hey, it was worth a shot.

When he was done, she mulled it over a good long minute.

"Gee," she said at last, "that sounds like a really bad idea."

Then she did another great trick.

She made the ghosts fly out of the pipe organ and swarm all over him.

# TWENTY-TWO

## Goldman in the Power

Little gray guys," Inigo said. "A *lot* of them."

He could smell them, thick and foul and musky everywhere about him. Their traces lay on the paving stones and hitching posts, on the sign heralding GENERAL STORE and the horse-drawn fire wagons dormant in their station, on every ratty, gone-to-mold plush toy in the Emporium and amid the broken glass cases of the candy shop and the rusting stools of the ice-cream parlor.

He wondered if *he* smelled like that to the others he'd brought along with him, felt sure he didn't . . . at least, hoped he didn't.

"So where *are* they?" That was Colleen, whose eyesight had completely returned. Goldie's lightning burst may have been intense, but fortunately its effects had proved short-lived.

Not that twenty-twenty—the human version of it, at least—was much good here in the balmy autumn night. But at least there was a moon casting its silver radiance.

"More importantly, where's Goldie?" Cal Griffin added. Across his back, he carried the gem-emblazoned rifle he'd retrieved from the El Dorado, the one he could carve a dragon-shaped notch in if he so desired. One-Shot Griffin, with the dragon carcass now moldering in the high grasses to prove it. One thousand miles or more to the east, and two time zones away.

Thank heavens the portal had still proven malleable (if spongy), or Inigo could never have gotten them here.

*Welcome to Southern California. . . .*

When Inigo had burst in on them at the grain silo, Colleen had been suspicious, and Doc cautious. But Cal had instantly seized the moment. Assigning Krystee Cott and a party of three to keep tabs on Jeff Arcott as he consulted with Rafe Dahlquist over the schematics, Cal demanded Inigo lead them to where he had taken Goldie.

Inigo sniffed the air, pointed to the distance ahead, where Main Street opened onto a once-manicured, now-weedy circle of parkland that branched off to the various lands, like a roundabout. He inclined his head to the left, toward the frontier land.

"They're down there. All of them . . ." Inigo breathed deeply through his nose, speculatively, weighing the subtle, variegated constituencies in the air. "And one other . . . human, I think, and wearing . . ." He tried to place the scent, recalled it from long ago, in the time before the Change, when he and his mom and dad all lived in Ithaca, and Janet Hirschenson's mother had come along on a field trip, and he'd asked the name of her perfume. "*Shalimar.*"

"So it is a woman," Doc noted.

"Or a guy with gender issues," Colleen countered.

Cal unslung the rifle, held it at the ready. "Off to work we go. . . ."

Taking point, Cal advanced cautiously, the others falling in behind. The cheery, ruined buildings looked on as they passed, and nothing beyond the four of them moved.

"Why do I so often feel I'm in *Aliens 3-D?*" Colleen inquired, warily surveying the awnings, corners and doors.

"Because you have selected a life of activity," Doc answered.

"So that's what you call it."

"You know," Cal said softly, peering at the silhouetted spires of the castle beyond, "I always wanted to come here."

"Is it all you envisioned?" asked Doc.

"Less expensive," Cal said, and tried to make it sound light. But in his heart he knew there were forms of payment more dear than money, and that before the night was out, he might give lie to his words.

Waving them to silence, he angled off, the others following. They passed through the gate of the fort, its perimeter wall of thick timbers still straight and relatively unchanged.

A sound of water drew his attention and he looked to his right, saw the artificial lake with its small island, the water choked with algae and the big paddlewheeler at anchor abandoned and listing to starboard.

"Where now?" Cal asked Inigo in a whisper.

The grunter boy started to answer, but there was no need.

For at that moment, from the square ahead, with its curclicued railings and its Spanish moss, from within the dark mansion fronted by gravestones, a wail rose up that stopped them dead and wrapped them in a cemetery chill.

It was the grunters, in their dozens like a nest of cockroaches, cheering for blood.

And one man, screaming.

*Well, this is shaping up to be even worse than the first time I came here,* Herman Goldman thought with a curious detachment as the hideous spectres tore at him.

But then, he'd always felt most removed from himself when in the deepest guano, and on this particular occasion it was looking like he had *really* painted himself into a brick wall.

There were maybe eight or ten of the damn things (hard to keep count when he was being thrashed about so), their grimy, dusty clothes in tatters, flesh rotting off their faces and limbs, death's-head grins like the "before" pictures of scraggly, nightmare teeth in his periodontist's office. At the Bitch Queen's nod, they had vomited forth from the big pipe organ, flown shrieking at him, reaching long skeletal fingers that snatched at his padded electric-blue vest and Tommy Bahama shirt with its palm trees and China Clippers, yanked his tangle of curly black hair back hard, dug cracked sharp nails into his autumn-browned skin. They lurched him spinning up into the air as they gripped and twirled him like a maypole.

And geez, these weren't even *real* ghosts, just stupid caricature animatronics, the repli-spooks of this ride that he had once upon a time been unprescient enough regarding what was someday to be his fate to actually think was cool.

The grunters on every side were stomping their feet, banging fists into walls, just eating it up—which, considering what they intended to eat *next*, Goldie supposed, could be called the appetizer.

"My little pals dig their meals," that Bitch Queen in Goth regalia, with her weight of piercings, hoops that would set a metal detector yammering, her tattoos like the tendrils of amorous creepers reaching out to embrace her, called out over the cheers of the grunters. "But they had a request. They asked if I could turn the meat inside out, so they could get at all the juicy bits."

She chuckled then. "We aim to please. . . ."

That's when the ghost-bots really went to town, like he was a big rubber glove they were intent on removing—*reversing*. And okay, so maybe in retrospect he could say it was all part of his plan (only it would be bullshit, because really what sort of plan could you prepare for something like *this*), that he was setting up a vocal tone like a meditation to focus his energies and chakras and whatnot.

But truth to tell, he was just squealing like a girl.

Which wasn't to say he didn't do *anything*, because in the middle of this delightful little *Iron Chef vs. Norman Bates* ringside event, Herman Goldman did have the presence of mind to marshal his forces and summon every bit of talent and juju at his command. And like a Holy Roller at the peak of his gyrations or some peyote-tweaked shaman in the smokiest of sweat lodges, he could really and truly say he saw flames shooting right out of his skin.

Which, of course, happened to be precisely the case.

Herman Goldman was his very own Fourth of July pinwheel, a whirling maquette on goddam hallelujah fire, consuming but not consumed, setting alight every soulless haunt that had dared lay hands on him, their clothes and hair and skin and eyes volatilizing into glorious, blast-furnace luminosity.

The grunters gasped and fell back, shielding their eyes from the glare. Then, as they saw through squinting slits just what was happening, they began to applaud.

Because these *weren't* real ghosts, after all, just machine duplicates, and when everything was burnt away that *could* be burnt away, their metal armatures remained, still hanging from their wires in simulation of flight, still gleefully ripping away at him.

In what he supposed was his last coherent moment on this side of the veil, words came full blown to him that turned his shrieks to wild laughter born of hysteria.

*Dinner's on me, boys. . . .*

Then the head of the metal thing nearest him—which had only moments before been Marie Antoinette by way of Burke and Hare—exploded with a deafening thunderclap.

The other metal harpies instantly went dead and fell to the floor with a sound like a giant's silverware set being dropped. Released, Goldie hit the ground with a thump, landing square on his *tuchis*.

The grunters let out a shout, and Queen Bitch sat knocked back in her throne, emerald and mascaraed eyes wide with surprise (and, of course, it was her being startled—not the spooks themselves—that had rendered them inert).

The haunted house had some new arrivals.

"Guys," Goldie crooned, getting to his feet, "am I glad to see you."

"This doesn't have to get complicated," Cal Griffin said, stepping deeper into the room, the still-smoking rifle leveled at the young woman on the throne. "We're just here for him."

Colleen and Doc flanked him, crossbow and machete drawn and ready now. Out of the corner of his eye, Cal could see Inigo hanging close behind Colleen, casting fearful glances at the grunters along the walls, who were staring daggers at him. *Traitor,* their eyes said, and it was clear to Cal that Inigo would not last long among his fellows here.

By now, Her Highness was beginning to recover a bit of her élan. "Well! Dan'l Boone's got him a shootin' iron! Better skedaddle on back to the Golden Horseshoe, Dan'l. . . ." Her arms widened to take in the roomful of grunters, all glowering and baring hyena teeth. "Or go home, and come back with an Uzi."

Growling low, the grunters started toward them.

Nausea surged in Cal's stomach and he urged it down. *You have been here before, if not in this specific place, in many a place like this.* He went within himself, found that core of certainty he was coming more and more to trust, that tranquillity where ego fell away and the static was quelled.

It was a purification of self or, more accurately, a selection of certain parts of self, those that could be big enough, that could open to a process of decision beyond deliberation where instinct held sway. Cal felt his attention focus in, like a deadbolt sliding into a lock plate. He was intensely present, aware in the moment.

In one fluid motion, he raised the rifle and fired.

The Punk Queen cried out as the bullet punched a hole like a big fist in the wall to the left of the throne. The grunters retreated a pace.

"That could as easily have been a foot to the right." Cal spoke quietly, addressing the girl and her malformed legion. "Now, we disagree on a lot of things, but I think every one of us would just as soon survive the night. So chill, okay?" They seemed to consider it, or at least took no immediate action. Still holding the rifle in his left, Cal beckoned with his free hand. "C'mon, Goldie."

Goldie took a step or two toward him, then, glancing at the Punk Queen, hesitated as if a thought had seized him.

"Um, just a sec."

*Oh no, Goldie,* Cal thought queasily. *No embellishments now.*

But Goldie was Goldie, after all, as Cal well knew. Who but Goldie had seen the Storm coming? Who else cast spells out of rock oldies, laid snares for grunters in the tunnels under New York, kept Excalibur lodged in a junk pile in his sanctum sanctorum?

Only Goldie could summon lightning in his hands, walk through walls, lead them to this mad, exhilarating, insanely *dangerous* place.

And only Goldie would have the nerve, the improvisational knack for the inappropriate, the utter *chutzpah* to choose this moment to walk up to the Evil Queen and plant a long, lingering kiss on her Goth black mouth.

The girl sat bolt upright at the moment of contact as though a million volts were coursing through her, then eased back limply into the throne.

As for everyone else in the room, it wasn't often that such a disparate group all wore the identical look of incredulity.

Finally, Goldie broke the clinch. The girl looked at him dazedly, in that moment of vulnerability seeming far younger than she had. Goldie straightened, and Cal caught the expression of contemplation on his face, as if he were trying to weigh something elusive, as fleetingly insubstantial as . . . well, a kiss.

But somehow, Cal knew there was nothing the least bit romantic about any of this.

Then the Bitch Queen blinked, and started to come back to herself.

"Uh-oh," said Goldie. "Time to be moseying on."

With that, he took off toward Cal—and the door behind him—at a dead run.

The Bitch Queen yelled only one command, which, after Goldie's grand gesture, was no surprise.

They burst out of the house of the dead with every grunter and his mother on their heels.

"Man oh man, Goldman," Colleen gasped out, their feet pounding the pavement as they ran through the night—they were passing Tarzan's treehouse now—"you've pulled some weird stunts in your time, but *that* just took the Emmy."

"It's not what you think," Goldie replied, and, damn him, he seemed utterly calm.

"I don't know *what* to think."

"Well, quit it."

"Children, children," Doc interjected, and Colleen recognized that while he might indeed be her ideal of a man, he could also be a patronizing asshole. Such was love. "I would suggest we not bicker at this precise juncture."

"Oh, I think any time is generally the right time," she shot back.

Before Doc could reply, if he intended to, she saw Cal stand his ground and stonily start firing at the onrushing horde.

He dropped a good many of them before he ran out of ammo. He hadn't thought to bring more from the college town, hadn't suspected he'd be embroiled in this grunter reenactment of the Little Big Horn, with the five of them stand-ins for Custer and his men.

He slung the rifle back over his shoulder and drew his sword. Close encounter time.

Colleen leveled her crossbow and nocked a bolt into it. But just then Inigo darted past her, nose in the air, sniffing. For what? she wondered, and realized it might be for a path devoid of grunters.

"This way!" Inigo yelled, diving into the bushes behind them. What the hell, Colleen thought, and dove after him, with Cal, Doc and Goldie close behind.

She abruptly found herself up to her thighs in frigid, slimy water and saw that she had plunged right into a narrow, twisting waterway. Casting about in the moonlight, she spied a group of boats with ratty awnings clumped at a dock.

"Oh great," Colleen muttered, "the jungle cruise."

She could hear the mob of grunters tearing through the foliage, coming after them.

"Here!" Cal cried, and led them running around the bend, keeping to the middle of the shallow river, where they would be harder to track, by smell at least. The grunters were keeping up such a racket they'd be hard pressed to find Cal and company by sound.

On the move, Cal drew alongside Goldie. "Where's the exit? Get us back to Iowa."

"*No problema, mon capitaine.*" Goldie paused, looked about uncertainly. "Only I've gotten the teeniest bit turned around."

"Splendid," Colleen said. Beyond the massive, vine-strangled face replicating Angkor Wat, she could hear the grunters hotfooting it in the distance. It sounded like they were getting closer, they must have caught the scent. "Tell me, Goldman, was it worth it?"

"I'm not sure yet. I think so."

"Hey, it was *rhetorical.*"

"Those are the ones I always make it a point to answer."

"C'mon!" Cal led them onto the opposite shore, through the dense growth onto the pavement again. "We need some high ground."

Colleen glanced about, saw the silhouette of a craggy mountain, realized with a postcard shock of recognition that it was the Matterhorn—or a reasonable amusement-park facsimile thereof. But it was clearly too far away to reach, if the caterwauling of their pursuers was any indication.

"*There,*" Cal said, and she followed his gaze to stairs that led to an overhead track. Not ideal, but the best they could do . . .

They bounded off at full clip, the grunters right behind like a starving pack of hounds (which wasn't that far off, if the hounds were rabid and crazy-strong and butt ugly, to boot). As Inigo bolted up the stairway like greased lightning, Cal and Doc on his heels and Goldie behind, Colleen wheeled and fired off a bolt, catching the lead little creep in the throat. He fell like a sack of wet cement and the ones behind him tumbled over him, screeching and yelling in frenzied rage.

Colleen turned and clambered up the stairs. By now, Cal had found handrails to climb onto the roof of the aluminum train that sat silent and stilled and remarkably unworn.

It was the highest point around, and it allowed them, cursing and firing and swinging their metal cutting blades, to drive the monsters back, to hurl the demonic little brutes screaming down to smash on the hard walkway below.

Not a purpose its designers had ever envisioned, but hell, all things considered, just about now it was a damn good use for a monorail.

Suddenly, a piercing whistle rent the air and the grunters fell back, vanishing into the night.

Colleen heard the shuffling odd footsteps first, before she saw their owners.

"*Bozhyeh moy,*" Doc whispered, and crossed himself.

It was that punk bitch, that crazy queen in her haunted mansion, who'd done this, just like she'd summoned those ghosts that throttled Goldman.

The army of the undead—or more accurately, the automaton nonliving—shuffled slowly forward on metal feet. The pirates, the spooks, the smiling children of foreign lands.

And at the front, leading them on, Abraham Lincoln.

Colleen hadn't had a night to match this one since her prom.

And like that ghastly, long-ago night—in fact, *exactly* like it—she knew by the end she'd be covered in mud and blood and oil.

# TWENTY-THREE

## The Door in the Air

"I don't want to talk about it," Colleen Brooks hissed when she returned limping and bloodied along with Cal Griffin and his companions to the Iowa grain silo where Krystee Cott and the other refugees waited breathlessly for their return.

Al Watt noticed Herman Goldman carrying a battered black stovepipe hat. "What's up with that?"

"Two ears and a tail," Goldie replied, and would say no more. He tossed it onto his bedroll and moved off from the others, back out into the night, to where he could be alone with his thoughts.

Rafe Dahlquist approached Griffin, who was just pulling some jerky from his pack, handing a bit off to the grunter boy Inigo. Jeff Arcott accompanied Dahlquist. Under his arm, Arcott carried the rolled schematics he'd brought from Atherton, the plans for his dearest, most secret project.

"It's incredibly ambitious," Dahlquist confided. "I've never seen anything like it."

"What exactly is it?" Cal asked.

"A communications device," Arcott jumped in. "Let us say on rather a grand scale. I have to be rather cagey at this point, sorry about that." He cast an eye at Dahlquist. "And I would need to require your discretion, too, Doctor."

Cal glanced over at Dahlquist. "It's your call."

"I'd like to pursue this, yes. I think I can help them get it up and running."

Cal considered, spied Inigo staring at him. The boy had led them here, had said Cal would find what he sought in Atherton. . . .

And who was to say that this project might not be the door to the very thing he sought?

"You want him, you let them all come," Cal insisted of Arcott, the sweep of his arm taking in the men and women dozing, mending clothes, speaking quietly about the room. "They could use a hot shower, a warm meal, clean bed."

"Sure. Anything else?"

"I keep this," Cal said, unslinging the rifle. He thought to add, *And you give me more ammo. A lot more.*

But why fan the flames of Arcott's suspicions, tip his hand? Besides, he didn't need Arcott's approval.

He would get what he required, and go where he had to.

Through Atherton to the bloody heart of the Source Project, whether helped or hindered by anyone in this hellish, miraculous world.

Arcott nodded his agreement. Satisfied, Cal looked back toward Inigo.

But the boy was gone.

Herman Goldman stood in the night on the periphery of the derelict farm, the fierce wind off the prairie grasses making his teeth chatter, blowing clean through his many layers of clothes, chilling him to the bone. The freezing awareness of his own armature made him regard himself as a living skeleton, barely wrapped in gristle and flesh, as much a ghost as the phantoms that had attacked him in the haunted mansion out California way; more so.

Every part of him ached. Lord, he was tired. He longed to curl up in his bedroll and sleep for about twenty hours or so, the sleep of the dead, of the just or unjust, it didn't matter, so long as it was without dreams—please, for pity's sake, no dreams.

But he was here for a reason. He had to find something out, or all his adventures down this long night that seemed without end were for nothing.

Colleen had largely dropped her uppers when he'd kissed that Bitch Queen; hell, they all had, regardless of their human or inhuman status. But all of them had totally missed the point of his actions; the last thing he had in mind was romance (although now that he was safely several thousand kilometers out of her homicidal clutches, he had to admit—at least, in retrospect—that she was fairly hot).

Back in the Preserve, and later in Chicago, he had learned that on occasion he could summon up a talent, an ability to drain off, *absorb* the abilities of others. Not always, it was hit-or-miss, as was virtually everything on this loony tunes planet since the advent of the Megillah.

But when it worked . . . brother, hold on to your hat.

So when Herman Goldman lip-locked that Empress of toothy grays and not-so-amusing windup toys, he had utterly no delusions that he was Tom Cruise or Antonio Banderas.

He wasn't trying to get into her pants, he was trying to get into her *powers*.

And in that moment of intense, electric contact, he'd definitely felt as if something were being transferred. (He had also felt, absurdly, ashamedly, that he was betraying Magritte in this act, but he pushed this aside, submerged it; beyond anything, this was in *service* to her, to her memory.)

Now it was time to see how well he'd done. . . .

The harpy wind was banging a metal sign on the side of the road back and forth into its crossbeam, causing it to warble eerily like a demented musical saw. Goldie extended a hand out toward it and thought, *Stop that.*

It did absolutely nothing.

Under the pale starlight and dipping moon, he then tried similarly to animate a tractor, then a harvester, then—more modestly—the ragged remains of a scarecrow (whose purpose, he supposed, had originally been more rustically ornamental than practical).

Gutter ball.

It was a humbling experience.

All right, then, power *deux*. Portals, and the opening thereof . . .

He already possessed the ability to resummon one recently cracked by another, more skillful practitioner, or to create a transport between two sacred points, like the Adena burial mounds and Olentangy Indian Caverns.

But peering off to the black horizon where the moon was just now setting, Goldie realized he was damn short of practitioner or sacred site at this given moment.

Nothing but grass and dirt and air.

"Oh, what the hell." He made a broad round motion with his hand at the empty, cold air. "*Open*," he said.

And damned if it didn't.

The door in the air glowed purple along its periphery of mute flame, and a vista beyond showed daylight.

Herman Goldman stepped through, to see what he could see.

It turned out to be Albany, New York.

He stepped back into Iowa, then made holes to San Simeon, and Dubuque, and Alberta, Canada.

But, as the Bitch Queen had said of the warp and woof of her own special abilities, he found he couldn't summon portals to a location across the sea, or anywhere near the place to the west the dark siren call of the Source summoned him.

They would still have to find another way there.

And there might well be any number of other limitations, hiccups in his range and reliability.

Even so, he felt sure this borrowed—all right, *stolen*—gift would come in mighty handy.

The sound of horses whinnying behind him turned him around.

Cal stood with Colleen and Doc and the others from camp, all packed up and ready for bear. He saw his friends had let those who had sustained the roughest handling back at the mall ride the horses. Only one of their team members was missing, the grunter Inigo, and it felt right somehow that he was not among them; perhaps at last he had returned to the track Goldie had shunted him from earlier this evening.

"We're pulling up stakes," Cal said. "Heading back to Atherton. You game?"

He was indeed.

The town would be the same, wrapped in the chaos he alone could sense.

But better the Devil you know than the one you don't. And Herman Goldman had known the Devil, that carrion eater, that deliverer of chaos, when the scarlet gent had paid a call on him in grad school. And then again, if more subtly, when the Change had come, and when it had taken Magritte from him.

He would let the chaos that engulfed the town engulf him now. He *wanted* it, as he wanted other chaoses, other destructions that beckoned to him down the far road of the future.

With his new power humming in his veins like myriad voices along a telephone wire, Herman Goldman felt utterly sure he would get *exactly* what he wanted.

Just before the sun rose, as their party neared the slope that led down into Atherton, Doc Lysenko spied the bulk of the dead dragon that lay silhouetted amid the singed grasses.

He grew thoughtful and said to Cal, "I would very much like that brought into town, to where I might perform an autopsy."

"I'll see what I can do," Cal responded, and moved off to speak with Jeff Arcott.

In the end, it took Arcott sending out a flatbed with a full work crew to hoist the carcass and transport it to town, to the hospital morgue where Doc awaited it with gleaming knives.

And while Doc's tender ministrations ultimately proved more butchery than autopsy, no one could deny that the dragon turned out considerably more useful in death than he had ever been in life.

# TWENTY-FOUR

## The Scale and the Stones

The horses were shrieking, to begin with.

Mama Diamond spoke to them low in their own tongue, coaxing, reassuring.

"It's not real, Fine Stallion. It's not real, Brave Mare. . . ."

Just the same as you'd calm a child, waking screaming from a bad dream. Only this was a nightmare that went on and on, and you were in it right along with them.

The only difference being that Mama Diamond could see it was an illusion, nothing to be scared of—at least, as far as she was concerned.

But to a horse held in its snare, or a man . . .

Even a man made of metal as hard-forged as Larry Shango.

He sat atop Cope, and Mama Diamond atop Marsh, as they rode down the gentle slope of valley into the college town of Atherton, Iowa. Glancing over at him in the moonlight, Mama Diamond could see from the set of his jaw and the shining grimness in his eyes that it was taking all he had not to be screaming, too. Frosty breath blew from his nostrils like steam off a locomotive, as he kept his mouth clamped tight.

Mama Diamond thought of the quiet efficiency with which

Shango had wielded his hammer against the wolves around his campfire, the way he'd used fist and boot and knee to lay waste to the men who'd had the arrogance and naïveté to rise up against him in that nameless town far behind them on their road east.

*What you see ahead of you doesn't just summon up old, bad dreams, my friend.* Mama Diamond felt sure the nightmares it stirred in Shango's memory were all too real, rivers of blood he'd waded through on this broad continent or another, bound by unwavering commands that brooked no direction but forward. And she felt equally certain he had been as silent then as now.

Not a man to complain, no matter how grueling the journey, how much it shredded one's soul, tore at body and mind and heart. Mama Diamond thought back on the few words Shango had said when telling her of his ordeal in the Badlands trying to reach the Source Project.

*Not an easy trip. And fifty-three miles from it . . . I was turned away.* Not a word more, nothing of his feelings, nor what he'd suffered alone under the gaze of those granite spires.

Was he thinking of that time now, of the nameless horrors the Storm had thrown against him?

Whether he was or not, Mama Diamond knew Shango needed no soothing words, no comforting tone. He was a man on a track, headed in one direction . . . no matter how vile the smell or appalling the sight, how real or unreal the monsters.

Mama Diamond smiled then, a flinty smile, and nudged Marsh forward. She realized that just as she spoke the language of wolf and horse and cat, she spoke Shango's language, too.

The language of silence and patience and endurance.

She had learned it from her parents at Manzanar, during the time when waiting for those barbed-wire gates to swing open on that desert land, and from her brother Harry, dead sixty years and more now, who had gone on to Heart Mountain, then to the 100th Infantry Battalion and a grave outside Genoa.

Where had Shango learned this language? she wondered.

The horses were quieting now under Mama Diamond's coaxing, edging ahead reluctantly but trusting her, as surely as they had through long days of drought and Storm. They had been her steady companions for decades now, as she'd pried gem and bone from the eternal mountains, as she'd watched civilization come and go.

Focusing her mind as if switching stations on a radio, Mama Diamond found she could perceive what the horses and Shango were seeing—the rotted, scabrous bodies, ravaged, distorted, grotesque. Men, women, children, infant babes, a tableau of pestilence and death.

But looking down on this scene, it seemed to her as if everyone else were errant birds and she alone were human, and could name these gaunt welcomers for what they were.

*Scarecrows.*

Merely that and nothing more, and even less substantial. For with her dragon eyes and dragon heart, Mama Diamond could see clean through them as if they were tissue paper, or dandelion pollen on the air, or ripples in the water revealing clear hard stone beneath.

What crop were they protecting from marauding eyes, what precious bounty? And could her stolen treasure be part of it?

She could see, far below in the valley, the jeweled fairy-light of the town, and even at this distance could discern that the steady illumination was not wood nor candle nor oil light, but electricity, pure and simple.

Oh, there were mysteries to be revealed. . . .

They closed upon the phantom corpses now, the ghastly sprawled obscenities. The horses drew back, eyes rolling.

"Easy now, my Brave One. Easy, Fair Beauty . . ."

And then they were through, like clean fresh water coursing from a mountain fissure, and the bodies were gone. The horses steadied, and Shango let out a low, slow breath.

"You certainly know how to show a lady a good time, Mr. Shango," Mama Diamond said in the common tongue, no longer needing their shared vocabulary of silence.

"Yes, ma'am," Shango said, and his smile mirrored hers.

Then Mama Diamond spied the glint of the big tourmaline half buried in the dirt, and her smile vanished.

"Is it one of yours?" Larry Shango asked.

Mama Diamond squatted by the big stone and shone her lantern on it, throwing off gemfire from its surface. A good many of her semiprecious rocks were as familiar to her as the creases on her palms, the age spots on her brow. But this one had been reworked and faceted in an odd way, turned to some new purpose.

"I can't truly say," she replied.

At first, upon approaching the stone, Mama Diamond thought someone had just buried it here, and not done a very good job. But now she saw it was wired up in an elaborate, curious way to an electronic device of some sort. The whatchamacallit was about the size and shape of a Game Boy (like the one Herbie Ganz always lugged about with him before his folks had up and pulled stakes out of Burnt Stick), the guts of it worked around an odd, triangular piece of what looked like black leather but which gleamed with iridescent highlights of green and red and black.

Mama Diamond shivered; she'd seen hide like that before . . . or at least something that looked a good deal like it.

And this was not the only such object. It was wired up to dozens virtually identical to it, stretching across the slope of the valley like an electrified fence barring their way. As she held her lamp high, its beam caught answering refractions on each device, like the multihued eyes of watching wolves, but which Mama Diamond knew were gemstones.

She remembered now how the dragon Stern had first looked like a man when he'd stepped off that train—*I couldn't decide what to wear . . . so I thought I'd give you a choice*—and how she herself had cast a false consuming fire that had deceived the wolf pack and its panther king.

A good trick, to fool the eye and ear and nose . . .

And how different, really, was the illusion of a man or a flame from a landscape of dead bodies? Merely a question of scale.

It was a dragon trick, and did the dragon have to be here to do it?

Or just some pieces of him . . . ?

Mama Diamond faced Shango. "We're in the right place," she said.

Which was just when the voice behind her piped up.

"Excuse me, ma'am," the man with the gun said. "I'll be asking you to please stand away from that."

To a casual observer, the scene might have appeared a good deal more challenging than the last altercation in which Agent Larry

Shango had found himself. True, there were only three men this time rather than four, but these had guns, oddly jewel-adorned ones, and from the way they hefted them it was a good bet these weapons still worked (even if none anywhere else in the world seemingly did).

But these men made a mistake their predecessors had not: they spoke before they had Shango in hand.

Time did what it always did on these occasions for Larry Shango. It slowed infinitely down to a filament of elongated, elastic moments strung together like the gel-filled beads on a baby's chew toy. More than enough time, an absurdly generous amount, to observe and plan and act.

Shango's mind settled into an easy stance, like the low, solidly balanced crouch he assumed at karate and aikido and jujitsu sparring sessions, and all those bone-crushing events in the real world between—from the bare-knuckle brawls in narrow alleyways between mausoleums in French Quarter graveyards when he was a boy to the more recent, polished performances along the waterfronts of D.C. and Bombay, the glittering terraces of the Rue de Rivoli and reeking slums on the outskirts of Rio. Anywhere his Commander-in-Chief might choose to go, and Shango's duty compel him to follow. In the old days, at least, when that Commander was alive, not abandoned and betrayed.

The three men approached slowly, with caution, clumped together (that was a mistake), weapons leveled but not aimed. Though ranging in age from late twenties to early forties, their coloring from dark to fair, they looked as if they'd all been baked in the same oven by a smiling, doting grandma—all with identical brown, ill-fitting uniforms of small-town cops, all paunchy and rumpled, not one of them hard or watchful or keen.

In the luxurious, attenuated time sense as if he were watching a DVD on frame advance, Shango weighed his options. These guys wore no ornamentation of biker helmet or chains, no stomper boots, so they probably weren't rogues, just standard-issue cops doing their job. But this was hardly a standard-issue town, with its ghastly deterrent of fake corpses, its enigmatic machines set along the perimeter.

This postcard paradise didn't want visitors, that was clear. And here he was, and Mama Diamond, too, bound and determined to pay a call.

So what orders might these cops be under regarding trespassers? What orders would he be under, in like circumstances?

Not to kill, these guys didn't have that vibe. But not to run off, either. To contain, to imprison, to hold.

But just as certainly as Larry Shango knew how to elegantly loop a Windsor knot and fieldstrip an M-16 blindfolded, he knew that wasn't going to happen here, not nohow, not no way.

So. Show them his government-issue ID, his pass from the President, or at least the man who had once been President and whose bone and flesh and hair were now dusting away in an unmarked grave?

It might work . . . but the government as such was about as solid a concept, deserving the same respect in most parts, as paper money nowadays.

And if it failed to impress . . . well then, *adios*, element of surprise.

All this played out in Shango's mind on the whole instantaneously, like a burst of data downloaded *in toto*, preverbal, hard-wired, *known*.

As did the action he took next.

Stepping in front of Mama Diamond to shield her, Shango dropped down, grabbed the ten-pound sledge from its resting place on his back, drew it from the straps that held it there, and threw the big hammer dead midsection at the cop in front. It hit the man square in the solar plexus, driving him back with a grunt of surprise and exhaled breath into the other two, who stumbled on the uneven ground and flailed to keep from falling.

As Shango expected, the blow caused cop number one to drop his service revolver. Shango dove onto the cool wet grass, seized the gun and came up with it held steady in both hands and trained on all three.

Okay, so it was a cowboy thing to do, but along with all those *Shadow* tapes his dad had brought home that long-ago flea market day back in New Orleans, he'd also brought some *Lone Ranger*.

And if Mama Diamond didn't look a whole hell of a lot like Tonto, well, that wasn't to say the notion didn't still hold water.

The three cops were regaining their footing, breathing hard, just getting a sense of the new situation.

*Now, let's just hope none of them's a hothead. . . .*

"Gentlemen . . ." Shango began, but didn't have an opportunity to get much further into the fine art of compromise.

For just then, about the forty-eighth unanticipated, virtually *impossible* thing that day happened.

A blaring horn shattered the night and twin headlights raked over them. Shango immediately looked aside, but his eyes were dazzled and he was momentarily blinded.

The deep thrum of an engine roared up and Shango could hear big rubber tires turning off the nearby road and crunching onto the grass.

And although Shango was no connoisseur of poetry, a snatch of Coleridge rose up in his mind.

*It was a miracle of rare device. . . .*

From the corner of his eye, he saw that Mama Diamond had grabbed hold of the horses to steady them. Shango re-angled his stance to keep the gun on the three men and also on the newcomers.

The door of the big Cadillac opened and its driver stepped out. Vaguely through the headlights, Shango could see others in the car, sitting watching them.

The driver ambled up, a silhouette backlit by the brilliant light.

"Mr. Shango," the voice said, and he could hear the smile in it. "I was just thinking of you."

Then Cal Griffin stepped up and shook his hand.

# TWENTY-FIVE

## Wonderful World

The girl was asleep in the bed that looked like her bed, in the apartment that was like her apartment. For one night, no dreams visited her, and it was as close to heaven as life, waking or sleeping, could ever be now.

The old man stood over her, watching her with blind eyes, his face gentled, the dark lines etched like furrows in old bark, there in the darkness.

"Thought I might find you here," the voice behind him said in a whisper.

Papa Sky turned. He had heard the boy coming, of course, padding into the room on light, quick feet; nothing ever surprised Papa, nothing in the world of sighted men, that was.

Now, in the realm of their *minds,* that was a different story. . . .

He led the boy out into the hall, softly closed the bedroom door. "Glad to see you back in one piece," he said, without the slightest hint of irony.

"Where's—?" Inigo didn't have to finish the sentence; they both knew who he meant.

"I don't rightly know. He's a wild one, my wandering boy."

"They'll be coming soon, I think," the boy said, and there was excitement under his words, and fear.

"That's good, real good. You hungry? Carnegie Deli might still be open." Neither of them added, *If it's there at all; rather the copy of it, replicated, abducted from memory, and not gone back to mist and yearning . . .*

They exited out onto the street, which tonight at least retained its solidity, the paving stones arrayed in orderly fashion, the walls standing upright. The air was warm with a mild breeze, perfect for a late-autumn night, with none of the humidity that so often cursed the city nor the frosty promise of coming snow. This was an idealized New York, not a real one, after all—a fact that was further confirmed as Papa Sky caught the lovely roller-coaster trill of the opening strains of Pops's magnificent "Potatohead Blues" playing out of some phonograph from a distant window a street or two north. He knew this had been lifted out of his mind, it had to be; Papa Sky had actually played with Louis Armstrong once, along with Kid Orry and some of the other great old cats, fifty years back, on a paddlewheel steamboat, at Disneyland, of all places. Life was full of things so odd you had to laugh not to cry, it always had been.

Papa Sky knew where all those cats were now, under the sod, where by all rights he should be. He wondered what became of that paddlewheeler and the rest of that place.

*Well, maybe I'll just go there, or a reasonable facsimile thereof, if I ask the Powers That Be real nice, pretty please with sugar on top. . . .*

*Nah, don't even go there, Old Man, not even for funnin'. You play with fire, you get burned, even if you're eighty-three years old and blind as a stone.*

"He was like her, like Christina," the boy beside him spoke up without prompting, bringing Papa's thoughts back to the street here and now, where he was tapping out an easy rhythm with his cane as he turned from Eighty-first onto Columbus and headed south (all this being an unspoken agreement, you understand, to assign the familiar names and directions to these passing mirages, these phantasms).

"That so," Papa Sky answered.

"Quiet, and strong," Inigo said. "And patient, too."

"Fine, that's fine." Papa thought back on when he'd first met Mr. Cal Griffin and his entourage, in Chicago, in Legends, when he'd been a traveling man, even at his age, a man on a mission. "He still with that Russian doctor, and that girl with the spiky hair?"

"How you know her hair's spiky?"

"Just sounded like it would be, is all."

"Yeah, he's still with them."

"And how about that other cat, the twitchy one? Mr. Magic?"

"Goldie, yeah. He's there, too." Papa caught the tightness in the boy's voice, sensed something hurtful there, but he didn't delve further. You respect people's pain, and give it room.

"And what about Enid . . . Enid Blindman?" Papa Sky ventured, and it was his turn to feel a spear of pain in his chest, like a warm blade slipped between his ribs into the soft place beneath.

"Nah, I didn't see him." Inigo replied offhandedly. And why not? He'd never met the young bluesman, who could work his voice and four-reed chromatic harmonica and guitar of finest maple into a sweet honey sound, into miracles like angel wings.

Just like Papa Sky could blow his horn on the soft autumn nights and warm summer days, and during wintertime and springtime, too. It was a gift, one both of them had long before any Storm blasted through this old world.

It had been hard, bonechill hard, for Papa Sky to meet up with Enid in Buddy Guy's club there on the South Side, along with Griffin and the Russian and the rest, and pretend he didn't know him, act like he was just another stranger, blown in from off the street like a discarded playbill.

But then, Papa Sky supposed he really *didn't* know him, not this grown man, three decades down in his life.

No longer a baby, no, whose only music was the soft cooing he made as he lay rocked in loving arms.

The boy walking next to him stopped abruptly. "Why are you crying?" he asked in stunned amazement.

Papa Sky wiped fiercely at the wetness running down the furrows that were like old bark in maple wood. "Just something an old man does," he said. "Don't mean nothin'."

They continued on, the tapping of the cane their sole music now.

All the others were dead now. Pops and Kid Orry and Bix Beiderbecke, Wingy Manone, too. All of them, all but him. But Papa Sky knew there was a reason he was still aboveground. He had something to do.

And before it was done, he would see Enid Blindman again.

# TWENTY-SIX

## The Hinged Box

It took considerable coaxing and smoothing of feathers to convince the cops (especially the one with the spanking-new, hammer-shaped bruise to the belly) to let the big black guy and his Asian old-lady companion just sashay on into town. But then Cal Griffin put in the word with Jeff Arcott, and Arcott spoke with the cops, and that was all she wrote.

After all, Jeff Arcott was . . . well, Jeff Arcott.

In the old days, sports heroes and movie stars held sway, but now the one swinging the big stick was the guy who could get things done.

And say what you would about Arcott's people skills—or notable lack of them—Theo Siegel had to admit that, without him, Atherton would look a whole lot less like it had in the old days and a whole lot more like the far side of the moon. Which was to say, barren and picked clean and utterly devoid of appreciating real estate values.

Even though dawn had come and gone, and he hadn't gotten a lick of sleep, and his ill-used left leg was screaming like a caffeine-wired blue bastard, Theo Siegel was there waiting for them on the bench in front of the Nils Bohr Applied Physics Building when Arcott and Cal Griffin pulled up in the El Dorado, followed by a road-hardened assortment of men and women, several atop horses and others pulled in a wagon they must have secured from some antique shop or Mennonite farm community along the road in their travels.

Melissa Wade sat beside Theo on the concrete bench. She'd sought him out around seven, brought coffee and fresh bagels, kept him diverted with airy conversation. It had been thoughtful of her, and Theo was glad of it, although as always it left him with a pang of privation, of longing.

Still, she was lovely to behold in the cool morning sun, her hair with its gradients of flame like warm coals glowing, of hammered brass and pale wood, her eyes dark-sparkling as the light sought out their subtleties. Her lips were slightly parted as she looked off lost in thought. She was lush in all the right places, but also fine-boned, delicate and fragile somehow; as always, captivating.

He knew, of course, that as soon as Jeff appeared she would hurry to his side and Theo himself would fade back in her consciousness to a shade, a wisp of memory, if anything at all.

Yet in spite of this, he held an unspoken wish, locked in the stronghold of his heart, alongside all the keepsakes he cherished of her, that Melissa might someday awaken from the spell of Jeff's brilliance, might look around and see things fresh, things that were right in front of her face.

College romances could be like that, could ignite white-hot then burn out like roadside flares. He'd seen it a million times with his older brothers and sisters (scattered to the winds before the Change, who knew where they were now . . .).

Why couldn't it work out that way in this case? Why the hell not?

Because wanting something, even wanting it with all your soul, almost never made it happen. Because there were lead actors in this world and supporting players, and Theo Siegel knew precisely which category he fell into.

Even if Jeff Arcott could never love anything as straightforward as a body sharing a concrete bench on a fall morning.

A memory of an old movie bubbled to the surface of Theo's mind, of Humphrey Bogart and Edward G. Robinson in *Key Largo*, of Bogart asking Robinson, who was playing Rico the mob boss, if Rico knew what he wanted.

"More," Bogart told him. "You want more."

Jeff wanted more. More knowledge. More power.

And what would he do with them when he had them?

As the Cadillac drew to a halt before them, he and Melissa peered at the faces of the newcomers. Theo spotted the bulky man first, there in the backseat of the El Dorado, looking much as he had in the profile *Discover Magazine* had run on him last spring before the Change, if a little more care-worn and rough around the edges.

He gave Melissa a nudge. "That's him, Dahlquist."

So it was true, after all. And it explained why Jeff had allowed all these new arrivals. Hell, for that level of experimental physicist, Arcott would've let the entire roll call of the Veterans of Foreign Wars parade into town. Not to mention chew off his own left arm. Or Theo's, if it came to that.

Process had never been Arcott's thing, nor patience. Results were all that mattered, the endgame. Which was a good thing, Theo supposed, if you wanted to have piping hot water and CD players and all the swankest luxuries this extremely post postmodern world could afford.

Now things could really get moving, in earnest—whatever those things might be. For although Jeff had allowed both Theo and Melissa a glimpse into some of the details of what he was building—the parts he needed them to machine and fabricate, the marching orders he required them to delegate to the rest of the work crew—he was playing a very close hand. No matter how much Arcott tried to conceal his inner workings, however, Theo had detected his frustration at how things were proceeding, knew the new work had grown becalmed, despite all Jeff's best efforts. But Dahlquist would put an end to that.

More wonders of the New Science aborning . . .

Pandora's box, slowly cracking open.

Theo knew that his own curse—beyond that of unrequited love, and loyalty beyond all reason—was an endless, insatiable curiosity to see what precisely would happen next.

Which, thanks to Jeff Arcott, in recent times and local environs, hadn't been all that damn bad.

So why then, watching the big black car roll up like a hearse, did Theo have such a queasy feeling about the next day and the next?

He shivered, and felt the hairs on his neck rise, felt the cold dark lump under the skin there, the alien object that kept everything in check, that kept *him* in check.

Or at least, the him that he knew.

Theo envisioned all the evils of Pandora's box flitting off, flying out into the greater world, as the Storm itself had spread. Then he remembered the one thing that had been left in the box when all else had fled.

Hope.

Looking now at Cal Griffin (who had literally saved him from the jaws of death, and from its talons, too) as he emerged from behind the steering wheel of the Caddy, Theo Siegel thought he might have just enough faith left in him to believe in something more than Jeff Arcott and Melissa Wade, and the siren call that beckoned them.

Melissa had bolted up off the bench, and ran to Arcott as he climbed from the passenger side. Now Theo levered himself up, working the crutches the medic had supplied him with as an auxiliary leg.

"Welcome home, Jeff," he said. And although he couldn't really march anymore, not on that twisted, dragon-mangled leg, he waited for his marching orders.

All the while knowing, too, that soon enough he would seek out Cal Griffin and his companions and have a word with them.

Virtually the first thing Cal Griffin asked Agent Larry Shango and Mama Diamond when he got them alone was, "What brought you here?"

And the first thing that astonished him was when they answered, "Ely Stern."

The three of them sat in the Insomnia Café, along with Colleen Brooks, Herman Goldman and Dr. Viktor Lysenko, sipping lattes and espressos at a table decoupaged with images torn from a Time-Life history of the twentieth century—Hitler and Eleanor Roosevelt, Joseph McCarthy and Mahatma Gandhi. These heroes and villains of the century past, gone, all gone, and their world gone with them. . . .

"Lord, son," said Mama Diamond, surveying Cal's ashen face. "You look like someone just walked on your grave."

"Not on mine," Cal murmured, as the past unfurled like a banner bolted onto the present, shifting fiendishly in its weight and measurements.

He had thought Ely Stern most likely dead and long rotting on a Manhattan pavement, his lungs and hopefully his sadistic heart, too, skewered by the same sword that rested now against Cal's thigh.

If anyone had deserved to die, it was certainly Stern, who had left desolation and murder in his wake; who had attempted to spirit away Tina before the Source had at long last succeeded; who had done his level best to kill Colleen and Doc and Goldie—and Cal himself, into the bargain—before he had finally been sent spiraling down into the darkness between the spires of New York.

Yet why had Stern stolen Tina in the first place? Cal had long wondered about that. True, he had clearly thought she was transforming into the only other one of his kind, but that wasn't sufficient explanation.

From what Cal had learned since, it seemed obvious that whatever lived at the Source hungered for the flares' unearthly *power*, and so had gathered them in Its net.

But as for Stern, the reason seemed more personal. . . .

Upon Cal's saving her and on the journey southward to Boone's Gap, Tina had chosen to speak little of it. So Cal could only speculate from what he'd briefly overheard Stern saying to her on that distant rooftop.

There had been a tone in his voice Cal had never heard before, in all his years working for this pitiless man, before Stern's dragon self had erupted outward and revealed him for what he truly was.

His words to Tina had held tenderness . . . and longing . . . and loneliness.

Previously at the office, whenever Stern had spoken in passing of women, it had always been with derision and rage. But here was a new thing, something Cal had only had moments to wonder at before Stern had turned his killing gaze upon him, and Cal had been forced to save himself and destroy Stern.

Or at least, so he thought.

Another passing player in Cal's life, another purveyor of scars, physical and mental, safely relegated to the past, gone but most assuredly not forgotten.

But Cal knew now that Stern was *alive*, not a hideous ghost of memory but an active presence just out of sight, no longer in Manhattan but on the move, a restless wandering spirit like themselves. . . .

But no, Cal corrected, not like themselves, *nothing* like themselves. He had stolen Mama Diamond's gems, had brought them here, much the same way—Shango now informed him—that the scientists at the Source Project had coveted and accumulated such stones. . . .

With Jeff Arcott utilizing the gems that Stern delivered.

But *why?* How had this come about, this unlikely alliance, this grand design whose architecture was so elusive?

And what was in it for Stern, that consummate manipulator of self-advantage? Whose interests was he serving?

Arcott or the Source . . . or both?

Certainly himself, that was always the case. But how, to what end?

No telling, at least not yet.

Stern had removed himself to parts unknown. While Jeff Arcott was closeted behind locked doors with his armed guards and his work crew and Rafe Dahlquist, the new resident genius on the scene, all speeding toward their goal.

*While I don't even know,* Cal thought bitterly, *where my goal is.*

Until, that was, Agent Shango uttered the second astonishing statement that morning.

"I don't know how to get there . . . but I know where the Source Project is."

"It's—you could say it's an *unholy* place." Larry Shango continued, scowling. "I saw things. . . ." Shango's face clouded with the memory.

"I was turned away," he said finally. "I was turned away in a fashion I do not understand."

"You tell me where it is," Cal reassured him, "and we'll figure out how to get there."

"In the Black Hills, beyond the Badlands, outside Rapid City, South Dakota."

Cal drew in a sharp breath, glanced over to Herman Goldman, who nodded agreement, sipping his Yogi tea. Hadn't he once said it might be there, back when they'd been en route to take on Primal in Chicago, to win back Enid Blindman's contract, and his freedom? But then Goldie had quickly added that he couldn't be sure, that

Radio K-Source was an unreliable font of information. Now they had confirmation, at last.

Shango noted that Herman Goldman had changed little in the months since he had last seen him; outwardly, at least. There was something much altered beneath, he could sense though not define it, a hardness there.

He noted, too, the new thing between Colleen Brooks and Dr. Lysenko, the relationship that had grown like a fresh sapling following the winter chill. A good thing that, something for them to hold on to.

And what of Cal Griffin? He'd retained all the qualities Shango had admired on their first meeting, that so reminded him of President McKay, the calm and the wariness, the qualities of leadership that could be honed but not acquired. He was, if anything, more impressive now that he was this much farther along his road; he wore his responsibilities with less doubt.

Griffin had sent his other acolytes to their new housing and to grab some food, leaving just his core of lieutenants to compare notes around the table.

With one addition—Mama Diamond looked about her at these warriors Larry Shango had told her about back in Burnt Stick and during their long journey here—when they weren't fighting off wolves and panthers and marauders and cops, that was. It was clear from the old prairie rat's expression that she found them far less formidable than his descriptions had led her to believe. But she'd learn soon enough, he knew. Not everyone was as mild as their appearance, as she herself had amply demonstrated.

Cal Griffin leaned forward, his elbows on the table, and looked deep into Shango's eyes.

"I want to know what you saw . . . and how it turned you back."

*You cross the path of the Devil in your travels, li'l love, you keep right on walking,* Shango's great-grandmother—whom everybody called Aunt Sally whatever their relation to her—had cautioned him nearly thirty dead years back. He sat on her lap then, small and attentive and anything but intimidating, as she shelled sweet peas with long fingers like hickory branches, the wind coming off the bayou like the hot wet mouth of hell had opened up somewhere in there and was breathing out low and slow.

"And you don't tell no one who you met," she added, her twisted strong hand caressing his cheek, leaving heat trails in his skin. "'Cause he jes might hear you and come right on back. . . ."

And although Larry Shango knew in the vault of his heart that she was as right as right could be, and though he had never spoken of these things since they had happened, never seen them since but in the shrieking corridors of his dreams . . .

He told them everything.

# TWENTY-SEVEN

## Shango at the Edge

Larry Shango stood atop Sheep Mountain Table in the Badlands of South Dakota and looked west, into nothingness.

It had been a long, hard trek under a merciless summer sun that hung nailed in an endless azure sky. The cracked asphalt of Highway 44 heading west had given way to rutted, cantankerous dirt road. A sudden thunderstorm the day before had reduced the path to a slurry of mud, and although it was drying out quickly in this heat, it was still a bloody mess. He'd been forced to set aside his mountain bike and struggle the rest of the way in on foot.

Frogs heralded his way as he passed remnants of ponds, reeds waving along their perimeter in the small respite of breeze; prairie dogs yipped their echoing calls of alarm to one another like bouncing pings of radar. Amid the tall summer grasses, eroded hillocks of earth fell away, revealing gleaming bits of quartz and the fossil jawbones of departed beasts.

Shango knew he really needn't make this climb to see what lay ahead; still, some bullheaded part of him—the part he prized most, the part that had allowed him to stay on this side of the veil this long into his remarkable life—insisted he climb to highest ground to verify what his sight informed him, and his instincts confirmed. . . .

That a mile or two ahead to the west lay a shifting wall of nonreality that rose up off the land like the flat of God's hand, stretching straight up into the burning sky as far as he could see.

It hurt his eyes to look at it, somehow made him feel defiled and unclean. He knew within its borders lay Ellsworth Air Force Base, which he had visited along with the President and his retinue three years back for the dedication of a new bomber. If the B-1Bs and stealth fighters were still there, they were inert as paperweights now.

On that trip, Shango had struck up an acquaintance with Milt and Jamie Lee, documentarians whose specialty was American Indian music and culture, Milt himself being part Oglala Sioux ("Sioux" being a misnomer from the French; "Lakota" among the preferred names). They'd taken him all over the Badlands and Black Hills on a personalized tour, and he'd marveled at a terrain so different from the homes he'd known in New Orleans and D.C.

The Black Hills were so named because of the ponderosa pines that covered them, they'd told him, and in a flurry of fresh snow Milt had pulled the van over and peeled off some fresh bark; Shango had inhaled deeply of its perfume, and found it smelled like butterscotch.

The other predominant sentinels along the way were aspen trees, but Milt told him that too was a misnomer. In reality, a grove of these "trees" was actually one mass entity, its appearance as a group of individuals mere illusion.

Standing on this high tableland now amid the tall grasses, the song of the meadowlark filling the cloudless air, Shango wondered what had become of the pines and the aspen, and Milt and Jamie, too.

In the last few weeks, Shango had reconnoitered around this periphery, keeping his distance, seeing how far it reached. As near as he could tell, the protective barrier ringing the Source Project extended fifty-three miles out in all directions, allowing nothing—even a glimpse—to get through. In its voraciousness, it had swallowed up a good chunk of the Badlands and all of the Black Hills, Rapid City and Mystic and Nemo and Custer, all the way up to Deadwood and down to the Pine Ridge Reservation. Johnson Siding and Thunderhead Falls lay grasped within its nameless boundaries, Beautiful Wonderland Cave and Jewel Cave; Wind Cave, too, where some of the Lakota believed their people had originated. Not to mention (as a billboard on the outskirts trumpeted) the Flintstones' Bedrock City.

Sacred or profane, ancient or absurdly modern, all were held in thrall to whatever reigned there, brought under its scrutiny and protection.

And whatever went in did not come out.

At least, that's what the few dogged survivors in this abandoned shadowland had told him, the ones who had not fled to all parts east, west, north and south—the dominant concept being *away* from this realm of mist and fog and silence.

Most of the ones Shango had encountered as he'd drawn near had been purely mad, hallucinating and delusional. Shango had had no way of knowing whether they'd been driven to this in recent times, or had been always thus and it helped protect them now. Still, for all their crazed pronouncements, there was a kernel of information that stayed consistent from person to person, leading Shango to believe there might be truth there.

So Shango had kept a respectful distance from the swirling fog that was really nothing like fog at all.

But now he was determined to walk right up to it. Because, after all, what else was there for him to do?

Shango had been left with the Source Project as his only objective, a task he had undertaken because no other tasks remained to him.

For Cal, Colleen, Doc and Goldie, the journey cross-country had been strewn with obstacles and detours—perhaps because the Source had sensed their progress and attempted to obstruct them. If that were so, then Shango had managed to fly under the radar. He had simply walked and bicycled his way doggedly west, trading his strength for food, building stone fences or raising barns or bringing in crops, or simply scavenging his meals as he progressed through the more sparsely populated prairie lands.

He had come to the Source with no weapons but a pile-driving hammer and his own wits. He had no real idea what he expected to find nor what he could hope to do about it. He was road-crazy at that point, exhausted beyond reason, running on instinct.

Shango paused and drank from his canteen, swirling the warm water in his mouth. He supposed this was reconnaissance, what he was doing here. But like everywhere else on the perimeter, there was nothing to see.

So he turned back down the muddy, argumentative road and

made his way off the tableland, then swung southwest toward Buffalo Gap (or the unseen region that had been Buffalo Gap), deciding to see just how close he could get.

But that was the problem, as it turned out.

At the foot of Sheep Mountain stood a shaded cove of caked earth and stone as tall as two men, projecting from the dry earth like the gnomon of an enormous sundial. Shango ran his hand appreciatively over the cool rock, then abandoned it for the shadeless barrens beyond.

He had walked, by his estimate, a half mile toward the swirling fog and the Source Project beyond when he found himself standing by another similar outcropping of stone. He rested there a moment, savoring the shade. He drank once more from his canteen. The fog seemed no closer. But distance and perspective were tricky, Shango knew, in places like this.

Then he looked down at his feet. A scrawny lizard scuttled away from his high boots. But that wasn't what astounded him. What astounded him were the pressed tracks in the dusty soil.

Bootprints. Bootprints like his own.

They *were* his own.

A wave of vertigo washed over him. Somehow he had come full circle, back to the same stony overlook where he had stood scrutinizing the barrier of the Source.

But he had walked consistently *toward* it. . . .

"*Damn*," Shango said aloud. Heat prostration, he thought. Dehydration. He must have turned himself exactly ass-backward.

He rested a good twenty minutes and drank water freely. Then he set out toward the wall of mists again. In places, the soil was loose enough that he was able to follow his own footprints. He was doggedly careful to keep the barrier ahead of him, avoiding gullies that would take him out of line-of-sight, not letting his eyes leave the shifting wall of evanescence that seemed alive and malevolent, for more than a few seconds. And then he came up a slight rocky rise to a pillar of rock—

Full circle.

This was useless, Shango was finally forced to admit. There was a kind of coiled space surrounding the Source Project, a sort of fence. A fence he couldn't climb, because it was impalpable, immaterial.

*What goes in doesn't come out,* the denizens of the Badlands, the crazies, had told him.

What they hadn't added was how it *got* in.

He rested his spine against dust-spattered rock and contemplated his next move. Clearly, the Source Project was unapproachable. At least by daylight.

Just east of here and one day back, at the juncture of the White River and Medicine Root Creek, Shango had encountered a balmy white man of indeterminate age, resplendent in eagle and wild turkey feathers and rusted beverage cans, who called himself the King of Empty Spaces and Nickel Redemptions. Although the man studiously avoided looking at the shifting wall stretching up into the sun-wrinkled sky, he clearly knew much about the barrier of vapors and the power it projected.

*It's different at night,* the King had said, shuddering at some unspoken memory.

*It's different at night.*

We'll see, thought Shango.

Shango watched the transformation from the shelter of the pillared rock.

As the sun set, the wall of noncorporeality seemed to take life and potency from the gathering dark. Shango had brought with him a pair of costly binoculars, for which he had paid nothing at a deserted camera-and-optical shop in a town called Reliance. By the last of the day's light he was able to see long streaks of multicolored light glowing and slowly twisting within the mist-structure like contrails illuminated by a sun that had dipped below the horizon.

On other nights at other stopping places, Shango thought he had discerned this phenomenon. This vantage point was the closest he'd gotten to the barricade; despite the hall-of-mirrors trickery played on him, it confirmed his suspicions.

The rainbow of comet tails divided and multiplied, gaining in number until they covered the fogscape like an incandescent quilt some titan might wrap himself in.

Shango could not divine the purpose of this display, but he

assumed it was a means of drawing or accumulating energy. The Source, he thought . . . source of what? Of power. Of preeminence.

What affected the world, Shango suspected, had not simply originated here. It was sustained here, controlled here, manipulated, given its unique nature, its *personality*.

Shango stood a moment watching the sun slide lower, wondering what his next step should be.

Stealth would gain him nothing. Shango shouldered his hammer and his canteen and walked to the roadway of Bureau of Indian Affairs Route 2 heading west, where in the dimming light the gravel still showed erratically through a skein of drifted dirt.

He set himself firmly on the path, striding deliberately toward the frosty wall of light, like a supplicant or a pilgrim, and this time he was not turned back.

He pierced the skin of the fog, felt it moving damp and electric on his skin, like a convocation of lightning bugs, and curiously smelled hot chocolate and gunpowder and evergreen. He wondered if those smells were truly there, or if something within the fog were somehow conjuring them from the well of his memory.

The last natural light of day fell away, and if there were stars overhead they were lost to the feverish glow of the fog.

Shango moved cautiously forward as the light trails coiled and danced about him, painting their colors on his shiny dark skin and battered clothes and the hammer he bore.

Some yards ahead of him, the haze seemed to be coalescing, gathering itself together into a form. At least, that was the impression it gave; it could be that Shango's wearied mind was playing tricks on him, that someone was walking toward him through the fog and becoming visible, rather than actually *assembling* itself from the constituent atoms, drawing into solidity from the particles of mist.

But he didn't think so.

And as he drew closer to the apparition, he was sure.

What stood in his path was a man—at least, partially. But the texture of its hair and skin, the cable-knit sweater, plaid flannel shirt and faded jeans it wore, were all wrong, constantly shifting and rearranging themselves with subtle, unceasing movement, like an ocean seen from a height or a colony of termites. Rather than being illuminated from the light trails, Shango could see that the creature glowed from within, casting its own muted nimbus onto the vapors about it.

And something even more disconcerting—at times, the phantom looked whole and complete, then in an instant the sweater, shirt and jeans would appear altered, stained and, in some places, torn. The man's face was ghastly pale, bone peeking here and there through parchment flesh. Part of that face looked as if it had been sandblasted away. Its eyes were cloudy and distant.

A suggestion perhaps—and Shango shuddered at the thought—that this being had been horribly injured at some time in the past.

It was like one of those pictures of Jesus where he opened his eyes from a certain angle, closed them from another; both realities true at the same time, and both an illusion.

"You're not allowed here," the ghost-thing said. It gazed coolly into Shango's tired eyes.

Shango collected himself, cradled his hammer in his hand.

"What place is this?" he asked.

"You know what place," the being of mists and vapors replied flatly.

*True enough,* Shango thought. *But how did you know that?*

"Who are you?" he said, and wondered why he hadn't asked *What are you?* But then, Shango knew *that* answer, some of it, at least, if not in his mind then in the instinctual, resonating part of his gut that clenched tight before this appalling guardian.

"My name . . ." it said, as if the question were a difficult and troubling one, "is Fred."

*Great, a monster named Fred.* "Fred what?" Shango asked.

Again, the question seemed to perplex the creature, to propel it into rumination as though diving into murky waters. At last, it answered, in a hollow tone redolent of longing and loss, "Wishart . . ."

"*Wishart,*" Shango exhaled. It was one of the names he had seen on the list of Source Project scientists, the list he had salvaged from agent Jeri Bilmer's purse in the crumpled wreckage of United 1046 out of Houston, its debris trail scattered and forgotten in the woodlands of Albermarle County.

The list that had cost Jeri Bilmer her life.

And a name, too, Cal Griffin had told Shango there in the woods of Albermarle, that Cal's sister Tina had murmured in fevered dreams back in Manhattan; when, heat-melting like a waxen thing, she was transforming into a being of radiance and inhumanity.

"You know me?" this nightmare that had been Dr. Fred Wishart asked.

"I know of you. You're from West Virginia, from a town called Boone's Gap." A town that Griffin and his friends had been journeying to when Shango had encountered them in the woods, although they had mistakenly thought the *town* was named Wishart—until Shango had taken it upon himself to break his oath to President McKay and tell them it was a man.

He wondered now if that intelligence—and the little else he had known of the Source Project at the time, the little he'd been able to share with them—had been sufficient to save their lives.

And if somehow—despite the unlikelihood, the clear impossibility of it—Fred Wishart could have been there as well as here.

The spectre paused distractedly, as if trying to process this information. But Shango could glean no clue whether this horror could fathom what Boone's Gap might be, or West Virginia.

"I'm a federal agent," Larry Shango said, feeling the absurdity of trying to impress this entity with the weight of his authority. At any rate, the statement may or may not have been a lie, as it spoke to what Shango had once been and since discarded, or tried to discard, like a garment set aside but the ghost tattoo of whose fabric and pattern still adhered to the skin.

Wishart stared unblinking at him, his skin twitching creepily now and then, his face betraying no comprehension, as though *federal agent* were as meaningless a string of nonsense sounds as *Boone's Gap* or *West Virginia* had been.

"It doesn't matter," it said finally. "Go back now . . . while you can."

Shango disliked the sound of the creature's voice—like wind blowing through an empty house, making vowels of gutter troughs and consonants of loose shingles. It made him *want* to go back, to run far and fast and keep on running. But he had come this far—

"I would be happy to leave," Shango said. "But there's something here I want." Shango knew it to be true, but could not have given voice to what precisely that might be.

"There's nothing here for you."

"You're wrong."

The Wishart-thing appeared to be growing brighter, the fog rapidly darkening, the night coming on in earnest. Shango saw that the mist about Wishart was spiraling in around him, like he was a drain emptying it of its energy and essence.

"Take me in there," Shango pressed.

"I can't. . . ." Wishart stared more intently at him, and there was something blinding and frenzied behind its eyes, like a nuclear core running out of control, that made Shango squint and glance away.

Seemingly in answer, the air around Shango grew thicker and hotter. Shango leveled his hammer, as much shield as threat. The head of the ten-pound sledge left vaporous phosphorescence flowing after it in its wake.

Wishart took a step back, his eroded eyes widening, ravaged skin and clothes emitting their coal-stove light.

*I do have some power,* Shango realized. He wasn't entirely helpless.

The wretched haunt tilted its head oddly, as if hearing a distant call, then straightened. "This isn't a good place to be when the sun's gone . . . for a man."

"Aren't you a man?" Of course it wasn't, but Shango wanted to see if there was any remnant of the man within this cobweb-thing, any echo of it.

Hesitation, uncertainty, silence.

"You don't understand," Wishart said at last.

"Then explain it to me."

"We're bound by what we set loose. . . ." It fixed its gaze on him again, making it clear Shango was included. "All of us."

"What binds you?" Shango might as well have asked, *What did you set loose?* It was all the same thing.

"I can't answer that question."

Frustration and impatience flared in Shango, and he was surprised at its intensity. He had the sudden memory of his mother long ago with her church ladies in their white gloves and fancy frilled hats at the séances they would infrequently attend, despite their loud and long-professed piety, behind closed-shuttered, paint-peeling doors in the French Quarter. The dearly-departed and resummoned spirits invariably provided irritatingly oblique replies to the most direct questions, as if God would only allow them to quote responses from some Magic Eight Ball in the hereafter.

*Why can't ghosties and ghoulies and things that go bump in the night ever give a fucking straight answer?*

*And why can't you, Dr. Fred Wishart, or whatever the hell you are now?*

Shango lifted the hammer to a present-arms position, his right hand up the shaft near the weighty steel head. "You need to stand aside."

Wishart said nothing, his dead eyes on Shango like banked suns, not giving way. The air was hot and simmered with red light.

Shango hefted the hammer, prepared to swing it—

Wishart held out one pale, bloodless hand—

"And *what*?" Colleen Brooks demanded. The morning had slid effortlessly into afternoon as the five of them had sat listening to Shango around the gouged old table in the Insomnia Café with its ratty furniture and soft rock music, its litter of glasses.

"I don't remember," Shango replied.

"You don't *remember?*"

"Well—it might sound ridiculous."

"Are there any fucking skeptics left on earth?" Colleen retorted. Cal Griffin put a calming hand on her arm.

"Just tell us what happened," he said.

"I closed my eyes and went to sleep," Shango said. "It was kind of involuntary."

"And when you woke up?" That was Doc Lysenko, who maintained a watchful composure although he was on his fifth espresso.

"I was lying in the dirt in an empty rail yard in some hard-luck town near the Mexican border."

"You don't know how you got there?" Cal asked.

"No, sir, I do not."

Mama Diamond watched the dust motes floating in the light shining through the big front windows. It was a hell of a yarn, better maybe than the one about the old stone-and-bone lady and the dragon who paid a call, the dragon that took her treasure and left a secret thing between her and the animals, a secret gift of tongues.

Where was Stern now, whom these new companions of hers had

known, and Dr. Fred Wishart, and Cal Griffin's vanished sister, Tina? All sitting around some table like this one, somewhere else in God's creation?

It was ridiculous, of course, but no more implausible, really, than the unlikely assemblage of the six of them sitting here. Mama Diamond marveled at the complex tapestry of loss and event that had knit them together.

Where might those threads, those lengths of time and chance that had so entwined them, had brought and bound them together here, draw them next . . .

And with whom might it further entangle them?

Cal Griffin leaned in toward Shango, his chin resting in his hands, his elbows propped on the table. In his spare efficiency of frame he seemed about one-third the heft of Shango, with none of the other's broad muscularity. But Mama Diamond noted that they both shared the same unspoken ease of command, the same instinct of decisiveness. Both of them had long been used to relying on their own judgment.

Two Cats Who Walked Alone . . . but were doing so no longer.

"You ready for a rematch?" Cal Griffin asked Shango.

For the first time that entire day, Shango smiled.

# TWENTY-EIGHT

## The Map of the Flesh

The sign on the building said Married Student Housing.

*I'm neither,* Colleen Brooks thought sardonically, *and not likely to be anytime soon.* But even so, she was grateful for the soft bed and running water.

And Doc there with her.

After their time with Larry Shango in the Insomnia Café, the afternoon found them in the quarters Jeff Arcott had assigned them, beyond the physics building and the student store, past the sculpture garden with its Rodins and Henry Moores and Degas ballerinas, to the utilitarian block of apartments where Melissa Wade led them and then—with a delicacy Colleen appreciated—quickly departed.

The two of them dropped their dusty packs just inside the front door and divested themselves of the crossbows, machetes, cutting blades and other miracles of lethality each favored (although Colleen always kept her big Eviscerator Three close by, while Doc retained the straight razor in his boot).

Colleen got the water in the shower running, waiting for it to heat. Doc was in the bedroom now; through the open bathroom door she could see him hiss with pain as he worked to remove his scuffed and sun-faded leather jacket.

She glided over to him, helped him off with it, hung it in the closet, where there were wooden hangers.

"I groan like an eighty-year-old man," he commented.

"No, just like a forty-five-year-old with mileage."

"I'd say, rather, the truck that dragged me has the mileage. I fear my odometer broke long ago."

She smiled. She was down to his blue denim shirt now and worked undoing the buttons. But the blood from the numerous cuts he'd sustained in the lovely grunter vacation spot that evening had dried and adhered to the inside of the shirt.

She ushered him into the bathroom, foggy with steam from the showerhead. Wetting a wash towel she found hanging on the door, she bathed the wounds as she gently peeled away the fabric. His torso was olive dark, long and lean with muscle, and as ever she admired it for its efficiency and its strength.

But she pitied it, too, for its many scars, and saw the night's work would add to them.

"Geez, Viktor," she said, "you're starting to look like a map of Bosnia." (Not that she herself was without significant marks from any number of beings human or otherwise.)

"I have never been one for scrapbooks, so I carry my keepsakes here." He pointed to a long gash running alongside the base of his lowest rib, by the abdomen. "Here is where you saved my life in Greenwich Village," and another, higher, "here where you saved me in West Virginia, here in Illinois." (He pronounced it in his thick accent "Ill-in-noy-is," which oddly charmed her, though she couldn't say why.)

"All these almost deaths," he added, melancholy eyes smiling, "all these fates deferred. You swoop in like Lady Liberty—"

"Or Mother Russia?"

"Or an avenging angel, sword held high, and cheat finality at every turn. You challenge my pessimism, *Boi Baba.*"

*And you challenge my despair,* she thought, but did not say. All the losers she had been with, all the Rorys and Eddies and Jacks—not to mention the ones she'd blown off from the get-go, the pond scum even lower on the food chain, if possible, than the bottom-feeders she'd selected. All the guys more likely to be in a police lineup than at an awards dinner, whose only distinguishing feature was their cynicism, the only bar they set the one that held their beers and chasers.

Looking back over the long line of these specimens—like an evolutionary chart that never got much beyond *Australopithecus*—Colleen reflected that the only thing she could count on with them was that she couldn't count on them . . . and that, whether they stayed or went, she knew she wouldn't have much taken from her because she never gave them the keys to her heart.

Not so with her sad, competent, loving father, whose face she knew as well as her own, even after all these years. In dying he had left her, and torn away a piece of her that was precious and core.

That was when she had first learned that love was a wound, and without ever putting it in so many words, even to herself—*especially* to herself—had determined to lock her heart away from further harm.

And yet, she marveled, here she was all over again. With a man so admirable, so much finer than herself . . . and so dangerous to the self-protection she so prized.

Love was a wound, and an enduring, foolish risk . . . but then, hell, so was everything now.

She kissed the scars on Viktor's chest, and on his rib cage and his arms, and drew him with her into the shower, then to the bed, where for a time it was sweetness and immediacy and flow, and neither of them thought of the future or of the past.

As day eased into night, she released herself into his keeping, and slept.

Later, when they were both awake, he held her in the darkness, skin touching skin.

"What was it like," she asked softly, "there in the reactor?"

He was silent a time, thinking of Chernobyl, and then he said, "I never was in the reactor. I only saw those who were. They paid out their lives, knowing they were dead men already, keeping the hoses trained on the core, buying others time. I cannot conceive of such courage."

*And yet you have it, Viktor,* she reflected, *I've seen it so many times. How can you not know that?* But then, she supposed, it was always most difficult to see one's true self.

"Why do you ask this?" he said, and she could make out his eyes in the dark, studying her.

"Once, when we were talking about the Source, you said, 'Into the reactor.' I think we'll be there soon. . . ."

He held her tighter, and nodded. "Yes, I think so, too."

"Funny, you know, I can't wait . . . even though it's gonna—"

He put a finger to her lips. "Shh . . ." No need to say it would assuredly kill them; they both knew.

Later still, she said, "I always figured I was kinda like a toaster. It shorts out, it's done, it goes in the trash. It doesn't move on to some higher plane."

"Your resemblance to a toaster is somewhat remote."

"Don't be obtuse." She fingered the cross on the chain around her neck, the gift Viktor had given her long months back, after he had saved her in the frigid waters en route to Chicago. It was the only thing she wore now, along with the dog tags, and the dragon scale he had returned to her. "Do you believe in an afterlife, Viktor?"

He pondered it. "I would like to, yes. But who can say? I'll know when I get there . . . or I'll never know." He kissed her on the head. "Or perhaps I'll merely be a toaster beside you on the shelf."

That begged the question, but she didn't press him further. Anyway, it wasn't really the question she'd wanted to ask. . . .

The one that spoke in her heart, that thrust like sheared metal off a car wreck, like the screams of a mother and daughter dying in the frigid waters of a swollen stream outside Kiev.

*If there were an afterlife, who would you choose to be with?*

Feeling his lean, scarred arms around her, lying back against his wounded self, Colleen Brooks felt haunted by a woman she had never known.

# TWENTY-NINE

## DRAGON SKIN

"I want you to take a look at this," Doc Lysenko said.

They stood beside him in the morgue, Cal and Colleen and Goldie, in the hour before dawn, on their second night in Atherton. (Mama Diamond and Larry Shango were still getting some shut-eye up in their separate rooms in what had formerly been the Ramada.)

When they made their delivery here, the work crew had been forced to improvise, shoving twelve tables together and rigging a block and tackle to hoist the big carcass up onto their surface.

But then, nobody had said this would be easy.

Observing him now, dressed in hospital blues, covered from head to toe in blood, Colleen Brooks reflected that her lover looked in all his equanimity like some maniac physician in a splatter movie—Dr. Bloodhappy, or Surgeon Kill-Scalpel, or something equally sanguinary.

In reality, though, he'd merely been following a line of inquiry . . . which, among other things, just happened to involve taking a chainsaw to a dead dragon.

Fortunately, Dr. Waxman and the rest of staff at the college Med Center, the nurses and interns and student volunteers, had been all too happy to provide Doc with the equipment and elbow room necessary to perform this most singular operation—or autopsy, to be more accurate—although the brute strength required to open up the body and heft the organs seemed more befitting butchers at work on a steer, or even some Hemingwayesque safari taking souvenirs off a fallen bull elephant, than your standard sawbones examining a cadaver.

When Doc had first set about cracking open the rib cage and extracting and weighing the internal organs, the room had been filled to the rafters, SRO with medical staff and the panoply of grads and undergrads who had heard what was going on in the subbasement. It was the first such autopsy ever performed at this facility; possibly performed anywhere in the world, because dragons were rare as hen's teeth and one gave them a wide berth when crossing their shadow. Besides, no one—not a man nor woman in attendance there as the bone and fluids, scales and gristle flew under the screaming metal blades wielded by the surprisingly serene Russian—had ever seen one of the big flying reptiles dead, or met anyone who had killed one. Incredibly, examples of both were in their town tonight, two miraculous visitations at once.

Now, many hours later, the component parts had been disassembled and notated, placed in their separate receptacles of glass and metal and plastic. Young and old, accomplished and callow, hardened and untried, the observers had found themselves hushed and wide-eyed . . . and finally, one by one, had drifted away to pursuits less gaudy and brutal.

Until Doc, alone and sure now, summoned his friends.

He gestured at the enormous fretwork of the skeleton atop the joined tables. "Truly a remarkable structure, an edifice as elegant and durable as a Gothic cathedral."

"Yeah," Colleen said, "but a cathedral rarely tries to bite your head off and swallow you whole."

"Only some of the clergy within do," Goldie commented, but no one rose to the barb.

"So what have you got for us?" Cal asked Doc.

"Some preliminary data, Calvin, and some educated guesses. Upon close inspection, I verified several long-standing suspicions. See this structure, and this one here? They are human in their lineage, undeniably so. Oh, amended and built upon and added to; in some cases to an astonishing degree. But any knowledgeable scrutiny reveals that this is, in fact, a man—changed, most assuredly, capable of much a normal human being could not do. But still a man."

Doc leaned back against the wall and rubbed weary eyes. "The organs bear this out, too. And I feel certain the DNA resequencing I'm having performed will again verify these findings, down to the molecular level. . . . It confirms what we ourselves have seen firsthand, and although one must be cautious when drawing conclusions from only one sample, I would express a conviction that were we to cross-section another dragon, or any of the grunters"—and here Doc's voice dropped down and grew more gentle, eyeing Cal—"or the flares, they would all be clearly derived from human beings; would, in the truest sense, still *be* human."

None of them spoke for a long moment, then Colleen said, "Okay, so that's reasonably creepy. . . . Where does it get us?"

"Do you recall the devices set into the ground at the edge of town? The ones we encountered when we returned and found Mr. Shango and his lady companion? They told me of their belief that these were the instruments that projected the appalling false landscape of corpses and plague."

Colleen shuddered, remembering the ghastly landscape that had nearly driven them away from this place before they had learned the wonders it held (which, of course, had been the whole idea); and she thought of her amulet, the dragon scale she wore, that had allowed her to pierce the illusion and behold the truth.

"Dr. Waxman was kind enough to substantiate that this was indeed their purpose, and that there was a spare apparatus being stored at a facility nearby. A new friend of mine, an intern named Lewis, was good enough to fetch it back here. And I removed *this* from it." He opened a drawer and withdrew a dark object, held it out in his open palm.

Colleen recognized it instantly, knew it as well as she knew the feel of what rested on its chain against the soft place at the base of her throat.

It was a dragon scale.

"Dr. Waxman tells me that each of the devices has one of these scales embedded in it," Doc continued, "along with the gemstones that focus its power." He glanced at Colleen, and there was tenderness there. "I have examined it under the electron microscope, and it appears a match with the one you wear around your neck. Again, DNA analysis would confirm this."

Cal's face was grave. "If I understand you correctly, Doc, you're saying that the scale that saved us back in Chicago, and the ones in the devices here . . . are from the same dragon."

"Yes, that's a strong likelihood." He nodded at the dragon bones on the tables. "And a different individual from this gentleman here."

Colleen had only known one dragon up close and personal (where they'd actually had a word or two, between the bastard's attempts to incinerate her), and that was Ely Stern. She herself had seen Cal put a sword clean through him, seen the monstrous lizard plummet a thousand feet to the New York pavement, to an almost certain and grisly end.

But Mama Diamond had told them only yesterday that Stern had not stayed put. He'd survived and hit the road. . . .

"It's Stern," Cal said coolly, and Colleen somehow knew in her bones it was so. "Shango and Mama Diamond followed him here. He stole her gems and brought them to Atherton." Cal took the leather scale from Doc, weighed it in his hand. "It's a reasonable bet he left these behind, too."

"Yes," Doc agreed. "But then, that would mean—"

Cal finished it. "That he tried to kill us in New York, then saved our lives in Chicago."

They fell silent, meditating on the imponderable flow of events. Like so many things down these crazy long days, it was impossible . . . but that didn't mean it wasn't so.

And how did Papa Sky fit into all this? Colleen wondered. The mysterious jazzman who had given her the scale in the smoky thick atmosphere of the Legends club in Chicago. Where might that old blind man be, if he wasn't dead by now?

Still hanging with dragons, or one dragon in particular . . . ?

"But why would Stern *do* that?" Colleen asked. "I mean, I can't see him particularly giving two rats' asses about saving our bacon. So was it to bring down Primal, so the Source could get at all those flares he was protecting?"

"I don't know," Cal said simply. "It's possible he was serving the Source there, and here, too."

"Lovely," Colleen said. And yet, something didn't sit right. Stern was a rotter through and through, it didn't take a degree in advanced physics to figure *that* out, but she hadn't gotten that vibe off Papa Sky, not at all. And for all her flaws, Colleen prided herself that she usually read people pretty right (despite her choices in men).

So why would Papa Sky be helping Stern?

Questions, with no answers . . .

What else was new?

Cal handed the scale back to Doc. "Tell me everything you've learned about this."

That was the lawyer part of him, the pragmatist, Colleen thought admiringly. File away what you can't deal with now, and get on with business.

"It would appear to have several unique properties," Doc noted, "whether on the living dragon or not. First, as we witnessed when Colleen utilized it against Clayton Devine in Primal's palace, it has the capability of repelling both the flares and the powers they wield.

"Secondly, given the way Colleen's charm allowed her to pierce the illusory tableau outside of town, I would venture that the dragon scales have the power both to project an illusion . . . and let one see through it."

"Any notions on how we might apply this knowledge?" Cal asked.

"I thought to design this." From the same drawer, Doc pulled out a strip of yellowish, translucent material, about the thickness and texture of parchment.

"I will not tell you which part of our friend here I obtained this from." Doc held it up before his face; Colleen could make out his eyes blurry behind it. "I tested it myself on the loathsome panorama. It dissolved like a tissue of lies in a cleansing flood."

Cal pondered it solemnly. "So you think we might be able to avail ourselves of that ability, and the other properties, too—"

"Yes, exactly," Doc responded. He strolled over to a big vat immediately adjacent to the skeleton. "Although it will require us to set aside any qualms we might have."

Walking after him, Colleen saw that its label read EPIDERMAL TISSUE. *Oh brother . . .*

"Let me see if I've got this right," Colleen said, facing Doc. "You've just said this monster on the slab is actually a human being . . . then you're proposing we cut him up and use his skin."

"Not precisely how I might word it, but that is the gist of it, yes."

"Okay, I just wanted to be sure," she said, and tried to make it sound light. Because she knew there was no room in the future that laid itself out before them for anyone to be squeamish, or allow false scruples to deny them a tool that might give them the edge, tilt the balance enough for them to do some good (she wouldn't allow herself the luxury to add, even in her thoughts, *And maybe just save our lives*).

But in the turmoil of her thoughts, in the craggy inner landscape of her mind, she wondered which of them—Ely Stern in his fierce, unfathomable actions, or the dead thing on the slab, or she and her friends standing around discussing its cannibalization—were truly the monsters.

Doc replaced both the scale and the parchment strip in the drawer, slid it shut. "An effective material," he said, "and they've put it to remarkable use here. Which gives me pause."

"How so?" Cal asked.

Doc sighed. "Perhaps when Ely Stern delivered his inventory of gems, he informed Jeff Arcott of his ability to repel energy, to cast illusion. But to design an instrument to project an illusion such as we witnessed . . . ?"

Cal understood. "Stern's no scientist."

"No," Doc concurred, "and it's not plausible to believe the physicists here in Atherton were embarked on such a line of research prior to the Change. It's a true melding of the old science and the new."

"Arcott spoke of a new physics," Cal said.

"A convenient turn of phrase, Calvin, but truly there has not been sufficient time for such a thorough melding of theory and application to have arisen—not within the scope of human research and development, at least."

"What are you saying?"

"I'm saying that Jeff Arcott is . . . how do you say it? Talking through his buttocks."

Colleen snorted (which was something she *really* hated to do). "Do you possibly mean talking out of his ass?"

"Out of his ass, yes."

"You mean lying," Cal added.

"Indeed."

"So who's the man behind the curtain?" Colleen asked. "The guys at the Source Project? I mean, assuming they *are* guys, and not . . ." She mimed something with tentacles.

Doc shrugged. "What would they have to gain?"

"Depends on what Arcott's working on now," Cal said. "That supersecret project of his." He gestured at the overhead bank of lights, the refrigeration equipment and, by extension, all the restored machinery in the town. "The reason for all this preamble."

"I suppose we might ask him," Doc offered.

"Yeah," Colleen said. "And his security goons might dance the *Nutcracker.*"

"Mm." Doc agreed. "Of course, we can presume he has allowed Dr. Dahlquist into his confidence, if only for expediency's sake, to get the project completed."

"Maybe so," Cal said. "But we're not going to know anything till we find some way past Arcott's guards."

Which seemed like a perfectly good occasion for Goldie—who had not said a word for a good deal of this—to reveal just what nifty little knack his lip-lock with the Bitch Queen in the magic kingdom had given him.

# THIRTY

## The Hole in the Wall

Rafe Dahlquist was having the dream about Neville Chamberlain and Anna Paquin again, when a sound startled him awake.

He opened his eyes just in time to see the door in the air appear and Herman Goldman step through.

"Don't try this at home," Goldie said quietly, so as not to alert the two guards just outside. Then he led Dahlquist back through the portal to where his friends waited.

"Arcott calls it a Spirit Radio, but it's a damn sight more than that," Rafe Dahlquist told Cal Griffin and the others, as they sat in the kitchen of the cramped lodgings in Married Student Housing, where Melissa Wade had assigned Colleen Brooks and Doc Lysenko.

"What exactly does it do?" Cal asked.

"Not much, at least not yet. We've only got it up to about one-ten-thousandth strength. Believe me, that baby takes a mother lode of power, not to mention calibration so exact it could give you hives."

"What does Arcott *say* it will do?" Cal pressed.

Dahlquist sighed, took a gulp of the Instant Sanka Doc had

cooked up in the microwave. "Okay, here's the official line. . . . With broadcasting and telephones down, there's no way to readily have discussions with anyone beyond your immediate enclave. The world will stay fractured and every city, town and suburb isolated and plunged back to the Middle Ages until we can change that. Hence the Spirit Radio, which will allow two-way communications again. But because it requires such a tremendous outlay of power, they had to get the grid operational first."

"But the design is . . . complicated?" Doc inquired.

"Yup," Dahlquist agreed. "Sorta like the Manhattan Project was complicated.

"I'm not saying this is a nuclear bomb or anything like that," he added quickly. "It's just hellishly ornate. It definitely *does* have features of a very powerful receiver."

"If it's a radio," Colleen asked, "doesn't it need a similar device on the other end?"

Dahlquist nodded. "Arcott says he's been writing to a sister community, sharing plans and materials. With our help, they should be ready to launch when we are. . . . Then it should just fan out from there."

"Where is this community?" Cal asked.

"Supposedly a few hundred miles to the west."

There was a sudden chill in the air. Cal glanced about, caught the same thought mirrored on the faces of Colleen and Doc and Goldie, felt the familiar heaviness in his gut.

There was far more to the west, he knew, than the Source Project. And yet . . .

Dahlquist caught the vibe, too, addressed Cal. "You want me to pull the plug on this, boss, say the word. I gotta tell ya, the deeper I sink my elbows in, the worse feeling I get."

"Why's that, Rafe?"

"Hell, this thing ain't no friggin' radio. I mean, Jesus, it's just made to *seem* like one."

"What do you think it is?"

"An access point, an entryway, a transferal device . . . for Christ's sake, a *door.*" He shot Goldie a sharp glance. "Not like that fancy little trick you did in my quarters, nothing sweet and benign like *that.*"

He swallowed down the rest of his coffee and shuddered. "There's something on the other side, and you turn this hungry beast on, I mean, really rev up the juice, I think it's gonna bust on through. This precious gizmo is designed to withstand terrific stresses and energies, for long-term duration—so whatever comes, why, it'll keep right on coming. Just an educated guess, but I gotta tell ya, I'm pretty damn educated."

Cal considered a moment, then said, "You have any idea what's on the other end?"

"No," Dahlquist replied. "But the other day we ran a test, y'know, just minimum strength to get things going. I heard these . . . *voices* . . . coming through, sounded like thousands of 'em, all overlapping. Couldn't make out anything, 'cept one word. . . ."

The word was "Wishart."

It was a rare thing for Jeff Arcott to propose a toast. But then, it had been a damn satisfying day, no two ways about it. With Rafe Dahlquist stirred into the mix, they were advancing miles at a stretch now, not fucking inches.

Which, of course, Theo Siegel reflected, didn't say a thing about what they might be advancing *toward*. . . .

The hour was late now, and bone-weary from the day's labors, he was dining with Jeff Arcott and Melissa Wade in what had once been a faculty conference room on the third floor of the Nils Bohr Applied Physics Building, in the college town of Atherton, at a table that seemed too big for just the three of them.

The walls were decorated with framed NASA photographs: the earth from geosynchronous orbit; the *Mars Pathfinder* on the ancient floodplain of Ares Vallis; the International Space Station. Icons of a lost age. Was the ISS still in orbit, Theo wondered, or had it come plummeting down through the atmosphere, to impact, perhaps, on a newly medievalized Europe or Japan, startling the serfs and the samurai?

Melissa had done the cooking, had cadged together the ingredients for chicken pasta with tequila cream sauce and a side salad of field greens, candied walnuts and gorgonzola. It was incredible, like everything she set her mind to, remarkable; she must have been striking bargains all over town, even after logging in her own full day on Jeff's grand mechanism, his Infernal Device.

Theo savored every bite, filled with gratitude . . . all the while knowing that Melissa had offered up this delectable sacrifice to Jeff, with Theo himself merely a collateral beneficiary, a side effect.

As with so many of their meals together, Theo recognized that, for himself at least, sour grapes was invariably on the menu.

He willed himself to let it go, as much as he could. In this life, the road went a whole lot smoother if you resigned yourself to what was rather than what you'd like it to be, or supposed it should be.

Particularly since the Change had locked its jaws on the planet. A whole hell of a lot came down that you had precious little say in: where you'd live; what you'd do. . . .

Even whether you'd be human or not.

That's when it really counted who your friends were.

Theo looked about at Melissa and Jeff, and reflected that it wasn't such a bad bargain after all, compared to what might have been, what he might have become.

He shuddered, remembering the convulsive curvature of his spine that been mere terrifying preamble, just as Melissa no doubt recalled her fevers, her lightening body.

If Theo reached behind his neck, he could feel the small lump where Arcott had sutured a garnet into a pocket of his skin. Melissa, he knew, possessed a similar lump.

Of all those resident in town when calamity had struck, only they two had been granted reprieve, Jeff's godly dispensation. Of the rest, the luckless ones, the glowing changelings siphoned away by the Storm, the disfigured wretches condemned to hide in shadow and belowground, Jeff hadn't lifted a finger to avert their fate.

*He rescued us because we were his friends. And so we remain his friends.*

Or perhaps it was merely because he'd had continuing need of them. . . .

Jeff himself had required no such intervention. He had remained resolutely unchanged, utterly human—at least, as human as he'd been to begin with; incandescent, elusive, cryptic.

How had he known to perform this service upon them? The same way he had known to reelectrify the town, to mount this blazing fresh project that now consumed all three of them. Like everything with Jeff, it stemmed from his brilliance . . . and from the secrets borne to him on the night winds.

Melissa had been talking about the visitors. "I don't know," she said, sighing. "They seem like good people, but this Griffin guy definitely has an agenda, and he's being cagey about his ultimate goals."

Jeff Arcott swirled his glass of wine thoughtfully.

"They make a good argument, though," Theo said. "I talked to the woman, Colleen. Her attitude is, we have this new tech, why don't we share it?"

"And what did you tell her?" Jeff inquired.

"That it's all luck and trial-and-error, and we don't even pretend to understand it ourselves."

"That's good," Arcott said. "It's even true, more or less."

"It felt like a lie."

"What would you have us tell them?"

"Everything. Why not?"

"*Everything* is a pretty tall order."

Theo could feel his expression growing icy. Then Melissa stepped in.

"We're not unsympathetic, Theo," she said, with that voice like music, like wind chimes, and he felt himself warming again, even knowing that, while she claimed she and Arcott sympathized, she was really the only one who did.

"It would be wonderful to be able to share everything," Melissa added. "But things are still precarious here. If you signed on to a hunting party sometime, you'd see how hard it is to keep all this going."

Melissa herself had put in some scavenging duty, Theo recalled. The Atherton "hunting parties" hunted gemstones, not animals. In the early days they had raided the town itself, ransacking abandoned homes for jewelry—a macabre exercise, Theo thought, like plucking gold from a corpse's teeth. Over the course of more recent months, the search had been expanded to nearby towns. And word was out on the trading routes that some wandering "gypsies" would pay handsomely in dry goods and matches for otherwise useless decorative stones. This was both good and bad: it increased the supply but also drove up the price.

And no amount of gemstones was enough to feed the voracious appetite of Jeff Arcott, whose experiments sucked up every stone not allotted to transportation or basic support.

But then, Jeff's supply was far beyond what the hunting parties supplied; he had another source, one he chose not to discuss. Theo had seen him, however, on his late-night forays to the outskirts of town; had watched from hiding as the furtive shadows delivered the vast supplies needed to construct the new device of enigmatic design and purpose.

Theo knew these lurkers were not the benign, timid ones he sometimes drove supplies to out beyond the periphery of town, the grunters that had been eagerly awaiting him when that dragon had swooped down out of the setting sun and nearly filleted him; would have, too, if Cal Griffin hadn't scooped up that fallen rifle and put paid to it.

No, these were creatures of a supremely nastier stripe. And while Theo sympathized, no, make that empathized—hell, tell the truth, *identified*—with the malformed, sad-sack bastards shivering out in what had once been soy and corn fields beyond town, he didn't want to even *consider* any similarities between himself and those muttering dark little monsters that did the grunt work (literally) for Arcott under cover of night.

Even though the sight of them moving rapidly on stealthy feet set off some unspoken call within him that screeched like a smoke alarm.

"If it was widely known what we do," Arcott was continuing, snaring Theo's attention once more, "we wouldn't be able to do it. We'd be fighting over resources."

It was a good excuse, Theo thought, for maintaining a monopoly. It was probably even true.

"Whereas," Arcott went on, "given a little time, a little understanding, we can maybe learn to synthesize the effect in a way that's both affordable and exportable."

Oh, noble dream. This would have been less convincing had it come from anyone other that Jeff. Arcott had been blessed with credibility. He was tall, raven-haired, with dazzling blue eyes, damn near angelic, if a dark angel. He looked utterly guileless in his jeans and ratty bomber jacket.

Theo pushed aside his glass of wine. It was making him surly.

And after that, if he kept drinking, it would make him loquacious, which was the last thing he wanted to be right now. Because Theo Siegel had a secret, one newly minted.

On his way here through the crisp night air, walking behind the dark bulk of Married Student Housing, he had heard the murmuring of a voice that should not be there, should very much be under lock and key elsewhere.

Not that Theo should have been able to hear that voice through so many layers of lath and plaster, and at such a distance. But there were times, fleeting moments, when his hearing was preternaturally sharp, his eyesight and sense of smell uncannily keen. And other times when he felt unusual aches and pains in his muscles and ligaments and bones, brief discomfitures that thankfully passed and left only dread.

He owed Jeff a lot, Theo knew. And Jeff was his friend—or, at least, had taken actions that a friend might take.

But nevertheless, he chose not to tell Jeff Arcott that the man playing hooky, the errant voice he'd overheard, was Rafe Dahlquist, or that Cal Griffin was there with him.

In spite of his history with Jeff, or perhaps more accurately *because* of it, Theo realized he was coming to trust Griffin a good deal more than Jeff.

And down what twisting, divergent path, he wondered, might *that* ultimately lead?

Time would tell, as it always did. Every story had an ending, whether good or bad. For now, he would keep mum, and let the newcomers have their secrets.

Still, Theo felt just giddy enough to offer up one further tidbit from his earlier conversation. "The woman Colleen mentioned something called the Source Project." He paused. "Almost like she wanted to see if I recognized the name. Whether I would flinch or frown or something."

*The way you just did,* he thought, watching Arcott.

"What did you tell her?" Arcott asked.

"That I'd never heard of it."

"Good," Jeff Arcott said, but his expression remained thoughtful.

And he kept a careful, sidelong watch on Theo the rest of that night.

# THIRTY-ONE

## Sun and Heart and Stone

In the apartment Melissa Wade had assigned him in Married Student Housing, across the hall from where Colleen and Doc lay sleeping, Cal Griffin was restless.

He had slept fitfully for a few hours atop the old mattress, vagrant springs pressing insistently into his back, dimly aware of the stubborn odors of this room that had seen much use: the array of cold pizzas, textbooks running to mildew, sweatclothes piled in heaps; all of it cleaned out now but too late to exorcise their ghosts. Twice, he thought he heard bells ringing in the distance, or imagined it.

He woke again, at some hour after midnight but still well before dawn, and couldn't find his way back to sleep.

Awake in the dark, he heard no bells but was alert to a thousand other subtle sounds. The tick and crackle of the old building as it gave up the last of its stored heat to the dark.

From outside, he heard the brittle conversation of autumn trees; he heard an animal, maybe a raccoon, trundling through the unmown grass. His hearing had become very acute.

Hours before, he had sent Goldie to escort Rafe Dahlquist through the door in the air, back to his room. Neither the guards standing unaware at their posts outside his quarters nor Jeff Arcott nor any of his lieutenants must have the slightest inkling that Dahlquist had taken a little sojourn tonight, and told all.

Nor that Doc had shared his day's researches and findings with Dahlquist, and that together with Cal and Colleen and even Goldie, they had come up with an alternate plan.

One that, if it worked, would put the Spirit Radio to a very different purpose than its designers intended.

But for now, Dahlquist was merely to keep right on working, to draw not the least suspicion down upon himself.

Meanwhile, he would pull a double shift, moonlighting on a series of experiments and tests to see if what Cal had in mind had the faintest prayer of working.

Because if it didn't, then their only option was to bring this whole place crashing down around their ears, and that was a far from pleasant prospect. . . .

Which explained more or less why Cal was having trouble sleeping.

He climbed out of bed in his T-shirt and boxers, pulled on his 501s and buttoned them, grabbed a jacket from where he had dropped it at the foot of his bed, and eased on his shoes without undoing the laces. He buckled on his sword and walked out of the apartment.

There was a little more light in the hallway despite it being after curfew, with battery-powered LED emergency lights posted on the walls, each tiny white box equipped with a set of garnets arrayed in the shape of a horizontal 8, the infinity symbol.

He found the stairwell and climbed up to the flat roof of the aging apartment building. The moonlight was bright enough to make the town seem cased in white ice. It was almost cold enough tonight for genuine ice—well, chilly, anyhow. The breeze was from the north, and it carried the faint sound of calls that weren't quite wolves and weren't quite men. Cal didn't care for that noise. It was too human, too heartbroken.

Cal practiced his moves on the roof of the school building, where he wouldn't be seen, shuffling his scuffed Nikes over gravel and tar. The night sky was clear and deep, and soon the wind fell off and the air hung motionless. Despite the cold, with the effort of movement he soon felt the sweat on his arms and back.

This sword had taught him a great deal. Even back when he had discovered it atop a heap of trash culled by Herman Goldman from the profligate curbs of Manhattan (and before that, when he'd first seen it in that disturbing, prescient dream), he had recognized its style and quality. As metalwork, its design held simplicity and sturdiness. No need for gaudy ornamentation, it effortlessly wore its purpose and primacy; it took an edge and kept it exceeding well. Its leather scabbard was dyed rust-red and worked with depressions for fingers that exactly matched his own. There was also a subtle design embossed around the finger grooves that could be barely discerned, it was so worn now, of a sun and a heart and a stone.

In the long journey here, both sword and man had been tested and seen hard use; and while it could not be said they had emerged unscathed, they had not been broken, merely further tempered.

The sword itself had been his best teacher. It moved smoothly in certain ways, resisted him in others. It wanted his wrist turned thus, wanted his shoulders squared, his body balanced. It counseled him to use its mass and momentum, not fight them.

He worked for twenty minutes in the autumn night, emptying his head and letting the sword take him. Thrust and parry, crouch and whirl. Had anyone been watching, they would have marveled at the speed and efficiency with which blade and wielder moved as one.

But to Cal there were only the myriad flaws and shortcomings within himself, the many missed opportunities, and the long road ahead toward the proficiency that so eluded him . . . at the same time sensing that that *other* road, the one to his dark objective, to Tina and the Source, would be shorter by far.

Time was no ally, Cal knew; it was a merciless, relentless adversary.

At length his arm tired. He let the swordpoint drop. Finished.

But the sword still felt alive with . . . something. Readiness? Impatience? Perhaps both, and a good deal more. It held mysteries and secrets, of both its destination and origin, a puzzle box that might open if it chose to reveal itself.

"Thought my pal with the hammer was greased lightning . . . but you put him to shame."

He whirled at the sound of the voice.

It was the old woman, Shango's odd traveling companion, the flinty, sun-weathered one who called herself Mama Diamond, near the doorway that opened onto the stairs. She stood with her back to the steel frame of the ventilator outlet, a faint smile on her lips.

Cal realized his right hand had arced the sword instinctively around to aim at her heart. Vaguely ashamed, he let it drop. "You appear out of thin air?"

"Remember when questions like that used to be rhetorical? No, I just walk light. Heard you cutting capers up here, saw you from the street. Decided I'd pay a call."

Cal didn't ask how her aged eyes had spied him in the dark, her creased old ears had caught the sound. Let her have her secrets, for now.

The blade lost its willfulness and felt heavy again. He returned it to its scabbard. Tonight he would oil it to preserve the metal against corrosion.

"Cold time to be out walking," he observed.

"Sleep and me, we're only sometimes on speaking terms," Mama Diamond replied, a cold wind gusting up to ruffle her short hair. Cal wondered idly how many people this reedy, self-reliant woman might be on speaking terms with, as well. She had the feel of someone folded in on herself; if not antisocial exactly, then not needful of society.

"It's different at night," Mama Diamond said. "The town, I mean."

Cal followed her gaze to the big autumn moon, grand as a sailing ship up there in the ebony ocean, its pale face as cool and eternal as the face of God. A silhouette fluttered across it, and was gone. A bat, Cal thought. Or maybe the cold shadow of a dragon.

An eerie sound wafted through the air to them, so distant and forlorn it almost wasn't a sound but merely a remembrance. Still, it made Cal's hackles rise.

"It's not Stern," Mama Diamond said with assurance. "I know his call."

"So do I," said Cal. *Or at least, I thought I did.* Today's revelations had shaken his conviction.

Stern had stolen Mama Diamond's gems, had brought them here, apparently under orders from whatever dwelled at the Source, whatever now held Cal's sister captive, if indeed she were still alive.

(But she *was*, Cal's heart insisted, she *must* be. . . .)

Stern had traveled from New York to Chicago to Mama Diamond's shop, and then here to Atherton.

Ahead of them, always ahead.

Stern had drawn Mama Diamond and Shango here. And, Cal thought, wondering about the grunter boy Inigo, perhaps himself and his companions, too.

Whose lives Stern had chosen to save . . .

Cal was suddenly conscious of the heft of his sword in its scabbard, of the singing ache in his arms and shoulders and legs, of the pathetic *limitations* of his humanity.

The dark road ahead stretched off to an unknown future . . . under a shadow from above.

*Am I leading anyone, or merely being led?*

Cal saw that Mama Diamond was scrutinizing him, far more closely than she had studied the moon. "You look like a man with a question."

"It's not one you can answer," Cal replied.

Mama Diamond walked to the edge of the roof, held her face immobile in the frigid wind.

"I had a man once, Danny," she said, not looking at Cal. "We kept company, for a time. Then he was gone. I truly cannot say why he did a single thing he did, beginning to end. . . . I don't think he could, either."

She turned to Cal, and her eyes were hard and clear. "Most of what happens just happens, and most everyone's plans go bust, one way or another.

"And maybe, just maybe," Mama Diamond said, her cracked voice so quiet it was like the wind rubbing against itself, "every now and then, a bad heart can do good. . . ."

Another cry came on the wind, a different one, close to the ground and high-pitched.

"Coyote," Mama Diamond said. "He's just found some pizza in a Dumpster."

"You say that like you know."

She gave him a Mona Lisa smile, and rubbed her arms against the cold, like sticks trying to start a fire.

"I ran into that pal of yours," Mama Diamond said, seemingly changing the subject. "The one with the shirts that are a conversation all by themselves."

That would be Goldie, of course.

"He told me what's on the other end of what they're building . . . and what you're gonna try doing with it."

Cal felt a momentary flash of irritation, then realized that if Goldie had let Mama Diamond into their confidence, it must be for a reason. His wild airs to the contrary, in certain ways Herman Goldman's actions were the most deliberate and considered of all of them.

"What do you think?" Cal asked.

"That you're crazy . . . but it's a good crazy. Don't mean it won't fry you on the griddle, though."

"True."

"But I'll tell you this much—you get your foot in the door, you'd best take me with you."

Looking at this frail old woman, Cal thought to protest, but the words died in his throat. There was something below the surface in her that belied appearances. Underneath, he sensed, she was hard stone, *diamond* hard. . . .

And Cal knew in that moment that it was not Shango's iron will that had brought them here, but hers.

*What monstrosities would walk the streets were men's faces as unfinished as their minds,* Stern had once said, quoting the philosopher Hoffer.

But that wasn't always true. Sometimes the face beneath the mask was finer and stronger than the mask itself.

"Why do you want to come?" he asked Mama Diamond.

"Maybe just because I'd like to see what all this has been for." She smiled, making the lines in her face crinkle up like a paper fan. "And maybe I'd like to meet that little sister of yours."

Cal nodded. "I'll do my best, when the time comes."

"Of that, I have no doubt." Mama Diamond yawned hugely, and stretched. "Time this old night owl went to roost."

"Good night, ma'am."

Mama Diamond walked slowly and cautiously to the door that led to the stairs. Then abruptly, she turned back.

"Do you think there's forgiveness in this world, Mr. Griffin, or just atonement?"

The question startled him, but he found the answer readily there. "I think every day's a new one . . . and we do what we can."

She ran back and kissed him on the cheek, surprising them both.

"You go get some sleep now, son," Mama Diamond said. "And you have yourself some sweet dreams."

Then she was gone, down the stairs.

Cal peered over the lip of the building, but curfew had come and the streets were dark. He heard Mama Diamond's steps echo away into the night, and knew she meant for him to hear it, a lullaby and good night.

His eyes lifted again to the moon, bright as God's serene, eternal gaze.

Proficiency was not everything, Cal realized, nor even readiness. Sometimes, he had seen, compassion and consensus and mutual need won the day.

And sometimes not . . .

In the distance, in the night beyond, Cal thought he heard, or only imagined, the sound of wings.

# THIRTY-TWO

## Rendezvous in Lost Places

"Okay, in the old days, the guy with the M-80 leads. It looks like a machine gun and makes a firecracker-type sound that is loud, bright and stuns the senses, basically disorients everyone inside." Krystee Cott, the former naval munitions expert, had the floor and was educating Cal and the others as to just what "doing things by the book" might mean. "This is a breaching charge and is also used to blast open a window or door, with a train of guys outside waiting to enter."

There were close to thirty of them gathered in what had been the rec room in Married Student Housing—Cal, Colleen, Doc and Goldie, plus Shango and Mama Diamond, and the fugitive slaves that had accompanied them to Atherton, those judged not too infirm to lend a hand. Guards were posted on the perimeter to make sure no one overheard them.

"The M-80 isn't meant to kill anyone, just blow open the door and stun the enemy," Larry Shango chimed in. "Basic Navy SEAL advancement on a building. The shooters go in, Command and Control coordinates the guys invading."

"Yeah, I get it," Colleen Brooks said. After all, her dad was Air Force, this was for the most part second nature to her. "But we've scouted the town. No heavy firepower at all, just a few reconditioned rifles and handguns."

"We work with what we've got," Cal said. "The good news is because whatever's at the Source is so hot to get the Spirit Radio constructed, they've been forced to reveal a fair amount of how the new science works—which is *why* the guns are working." He addressed Krystee Cott and Shango. "Think you can rig up some munitions using stuff from the college chem lab?"

"Yeah, sure," Krystee answered. "Might be a little twitchy, though."

"Aren't we all?" said Goldie. That got a nervous laugh.

"Let's talk about manpower," Cal said.

'There are two forces," Shango explained. "The blocking force isolates the building, delta force goes inside."

"So we have one group keeping the portal open while the other goes in," Cal said. "Now, we're not going to know what's on the other side till we get there, so we want to get in, see what's up"—Cal didn't say, *Hopefully get Tina,* he didn't need to—"and get back out again quick, shut everything down. The second assault can be more prepared, utilizing what we learn first time out."

Cal spoke with assurance, knowing what was required of him. He wasn't fooling anyone, that wasn't the point. They were all volunteers here, knew full well what a rickety structure this was, how prone to disaster.

Still, in creating the *illusion* of confidence, Cal understood it increased their chances, gave them renewed hope . . . including, he was surprised to realize, himself.

*Print the legend. . . .*

Which was, he supposed, how legends got started in the first place.

Cal then asked Rafe Dahlquist to describe the modifications secretly being made to the device, which might contain the whirlwind, if only for a time. Then Doc explained the outré accoutrements *he* was stitching together.

Which didn't exactly make anyone want to order lunch.

"Any questions?" Cal asked. "No?"

There would be soon enough. He called the meeting to a close, and everyone dispersed to their various assignments.

Emerging out into the brisk coming-winter day, Cal took the steps to the sidewalk two at a time, kicking the golden-red leaves aside, sending them flying.

We just covered the *what,* Cal thought worriedly, but not the *who.*

What intellects vast and cool and unsympathetic would be waiting on the other side of that door?

He and Shango had both met one of them, Fred Wishart, who was no longer a man, but who still had some buried part of him that felt human emotions, that could be reached if one knew the key.

Cal had utilized that knowledge back in Boone's Gap, when he had played upon Fred's love of his twin brother, Bob, to get him to relent, if only momentarily, in his ferocious attack on Tina and Cal himself.

In the autopsy room here in Atherton, Doc had said that the dragons and grunters and flares were all in some fundamental way still *human.* And Wishart had been, too; at least, enough to be reminded of the loss he had sustained, to summon up a longing that could be transmuted to empathy, to compassion.

What else waited at the Source Project?

Something incredibly powerful, a force of will that had yanked Wishart back to its core, and drawn flares mercilessly from wherever they lacked a sufficiently armored protector.

What lurked at the Source was unimaginably strong, and growing stronger every day. Cal knew he had pitifully little with which to oppose it . . . except perhaps knowledge of what that power might have secreted unknowing within itself.

In the aftermath of their battle at Boone's Gap, Fred Wishart's brother Bob told Cal that the consciousness at the Source made a mistake in seizing Fred back, that now Fred was a virus, perhaps one that Cal might trigger, awakening his humanity once more.

Fear and brutality reigned at the Source; Cal had seen the result of it spread over the land like ink spilling across a map.

But if Fred Wishart was a virus, it was because there was more to his nature than brutality and fear, despite the havoc he had wreaked upon Boone's Gap; gentler impulses that his human soul might bring into play.

And he might not be alone.

So perhaps the question Cal needed to ask was not *what* lurked at the Source, but rather *who.* . . .

In his pocket, Cal could feel the crumpled paper he'd carried with him since copying it from the list Shango had shown him in the woods of Albermarle County.

On the fifth floor of the Atherton University Research Library, nestled among dusty tomes, Cal found the volume he was searching for. He withdrew it from its place on the shelf, and settled at a desk beside a window to read.

To some, *Who's Who in Applied and Molecular Physics,* eighth revised edition, might have seemed the next best sleep aid to a Steven Seagal film festival. But to Cal, it was utterly enthralling.

Including, as it did, virtually every scientist at the Source Project.

Herman Goldman walked in the sunlight, wishing he could empty all the querulous and contrary thoughts from his skull. He was tired of it. Tired of the constant chatter, the nagging self-recrimination and self-justification, all the cacophony of words running in his head like water from a broken faucet. He wanted the frigid sun of waning autumn, like a white circle painted on the dome of the world, to dry it up.

He walked through town, and the cool wind felt good on his face, fresh and clean and a little sharp. Towering white clouds like mountain peaks skimmed the horizon.

The day was bright if austere, and the storefronts and dingy brick warehouses by the river gleamed in the sun, grand in their tawdriness, faded and ethereal, trapped in the silvered afternoon like bugs in a gossamer web.

Like when you were young, Goldie thought, and still going to school, before the madness, but it was a Wednesday and you'd skipped out and all the row houses were unnaturally quiet, as if the neighborhood had declared a holiday from children and all the adults had elected to celebrate with a nap.

He wanted that isolation and that quiet, away from all the people and their noise; to center and quiet himself, too. It was in that silence and solitude that he could best summon back the sight of her, and the sound, and the smell.

That he could be with Magritte.

He let his footsteps follow the river. There was a kind of boardwalk along the riverbank beside some scrubby parkland, some municipal manager's halfhearted attempt at beautification currently overgrown with devil grass and assorted thistles. Power lines crossed the river here.

Goldie walked past them, and past the deserted subdivisions now surrendered to weedy fields, past the zoned but undeveloped properties with their sidewalkless streets, past civilization, to a place where the Powdercache River flattened into a silver braid that stitched prairie to prairie. There was duckweed here, and a few faint trails flattened into the tall grass.

He crouched by the river, plunged his hands into the chilling current, brought forth the cupped and bracing water, and drank. It quenched and burned icily going down, forcibly reminding him of the many things in his foolish life that had sated and brought thirst, soothed and pained him, all at the same time.

He caught his reflection in the bright surface, and was surprised at the hardness in his eyes, the lines around his mouth that others might have deemed fretfulness but he thought more telling of rage.

Would Magritte have loved this face, as she had the gentler one he'd worn upon their first meeting? Would she love it still were they to meet again?

He didn't believe in such an absurdly sentimental notion as heaven, of course, but he longed for it; Magritte was the first person he had lost with whom he ached to be reunited, the first love he hadn't severed himself from and fled.

In the rippling, elusive surface, he thought he could discern her face, a ghost of liquid and light. He wondered if she would approve of the path he had set himself on, the acts he planned in the days ahead.

Were they for her, for her memory, as he told himself by way of justification . . . or only for himself?

He stifled the answer he already knew, and chased the words away.

It was beautiful here, the long sunlight raking the high yellow grass, the occasional sound of insects, a V of geese subdividing the meridian. He rose and continued walking, the brittle reeds crackling under his feet. This must all be marshland, Goldie thought, when the river runs high.

The sun, which had seemed fixed and motionless in the sky, was suddenly lower; soon he would be in the dark. Dangerous things were abroad in the land; one shouldn't be out alone. But along this particular stretch of river, he knew he was the most dangerous creature of all.

He caught a sound of footsteps behind him, and knew who it was before he turned. In their hajj across the continental United States, they had all of them become accomplished trackers.

Cal Griffin approached him in the gathering dark, and Goldie saw in his face a mirror of his own, weighted with the future. Cal held out a sheet of paper.

"There's some places I'd like you to go," he said.

# THIRTY-THREE

## Another Nice Mess

Waiting had always been the worst part for her, even when she was little and it was the endless anticipation of scanning the horizon for Santa Claus or summer to appear on the glide path coming in on approach.

Which wasn't a patch on waiting for some Union of Concerned Scientists, Hearty Man TV-dinner sweet old pencil-pusher—namely, Dr. Rafe Dahlquist—to give you the green light to step over the threshold into hell.

As the days slid one into the other and winter came on in earnest, Colleen Brooks had to admit that it was her own damnable impatience and not everyone and everything getting on her last nerve that made her want to haul off and kick a puppy.

So contrary action was in order. . . .

"What's the deal here?" Cal inquired as Colleen led him slogging blindfolded along the slushy sidewalk of the main drag toward the Art Deco structure that was still in reasonably good shape, despite being subjected to more than sixty corrosive Iowa winters in its long and distinguished tenure here in town. Doc obligingly brought up the rear, as did Goldman, who had been mostly absent in recent days—and infuriatingly mum on the subject, to boot.

Colleen had made it a point to seek out the surprisingly young Bohemian who still kept the place running and charm the socks off the guy (not that hard a trick, really, when she set her mind to it; hell, she could walk and talk with the best of the bipeds). So he'd led her downstairs to his Fortress of Solitude, the big basement that doubled as a storage vault, and let her peruse what turned out to be his fairly impressive holdings.

Now, some days later, Colleen drew Cal out of the winter chill into the steam-heat warmth of the lobby, then to the larger hall beyond. Contrary to the exterior façade, its interior style was not Deco but rather a neo-baroque eruption of gilt chandeliers, cherub sconces and rococo stairways—a Depression-era proletariat vision of grandeur.

She sat Cal down front and center, and whipped off the blindfold.

The acoustics of the theater were pretty damn good, so the ovation that erupted was close to deafening.

They stood arrayed along the rows of seats and up the twin aisles, grinning broadly at him, Krystee Cott and Mike Kimmel and the rest, the orphaned wayfarers Cal had led through the valley of the shadow and other perilous realms to the respite and relative safe harbor of Atherton (all in attendance save Rafe Dahlquist, naturally, who was under lock and key with the full chorus line of guards, not to mention the unholy troika of Arcott, Siegel and Wade, building the Son of the Megillah).

"Surprise," Colleen said.

"It's not my birthday," Cal said.

"Shut up," she said. She waved her arm up at the little high window in back, and the house lights dimmed.

For the first time in a long time, they watched a movie.

Kenny Escobar, the manager-cum-projectionist, had a number of fairly recent releases (recent prior to the Change, of course) available for screening. But Colleen had gotten to know Cal pretty well by now.

So she chose Laurel and Hardy in *Sons of the Desert.*

Cal laughed until the tears rolled down his cheeks.

(Goldman, meanwhile, sat watching totally stone-faced. "Don't think I'm not enjoying this," he explained to her in a whisper. "It's just that when I was a kid my Uncle Vaclav had a complete collection of Stan and Ollie flicks that he'd screen in his weird old mansion and make me sit watching without cracking a smile, 'cause he was of the conviction they weren't comedians but rather great *tragedians*—a theory which I suppose has its merits." "Christ, Goldman," Colleen responded, "does *everyone* in your family have a screw loose?")

Then she showed Cal *North by Northwest.*

It was only as she sat watching there in the dark, alongside those with whom she had inextricably bound herself, the three so-very-different men who had entrusted her with their lives, that she realized how much like these films their journey had become. They were all of them as helpless as dandelion fluff in a hurricane, totally at the mercy of whatever weird shit the Fates threw at them.

Give in to the moment, it invited, surrender to the currents of storm and flow with them, be uplifted.

Which, paradoxically, didn't mean that she shouldn't fight like hell at the same time—just not be so preoccupied with the struggle that she failed to recognize what resources might avail her.

In the darkness around them, Colleen could discern the other baby birds Cal had taken under his wing, and the townies and college kids who had filtered in to watch the show, who were now sharing the experience along with them.

*We aren't alone in this,* Colleen thought. *We never were.*

Ely Stern may have brought them here, all the legions of the damned might be awaiting them at the end of the road, and she might not be able to do a damn thing about it, none of them might.

But that wasn't for her to say.

Remarkably, with that awareness she felt suddenly unburdened, so light it was akin to weightlessness, and it occurred to her that this flush of exhilaration might well be labeled hope.

She sat anonymous and totally present, her eyes filled with the timeless, fleeting images on the screen—Eva Marie Saint dangling from Mount Rushmore, Cary Grant extending his hand out to her, grasping her wrist and pulling her effortlessly up into what was now transformed into the interior of a sleeping compartment, as they kissed and the train that bore them vanished howling into the blackness of a railway tunnel and the unknown future beyond.

Amid the torrent of applause, the music of communal experience, the houselights rose again. Colleen perceived the bulky, rumpled figure awaiting them in the aisle, Goldman standing behind him, having spirited him here.

"We're T minus thirty-three minutes," Rafe Dahlquist said.

The light was like nothing in this world, and Jeff Arcott couldn't take his eyes off it.

The resonance chamber was banked down like logs gone to ash in a fireplace, barely glowing now. But it was hypnotic in its lazy, ceaseless motion, the flashing bits of evanescence winking in and out of existence in the vacuum of the huge cylinder, leaving vaporous rainbow trails like fingers dangled casually in a stream. As he watched it entranced, it seemed almost to be talking to him.

And scant minutes from now, Jeff Arcott knew, it literally would be.

No longer murmuring in myriad whispers like the legions of the departed, it would soon be invested with power on a scale that would heighten and focus those voices to crystal clarity . . . and quite a good deal more.

It elated him, and scared him, too.

The letter of introduction Ely Stern had brought with him all those months back—along with the first delivery of prime gemstones—had been written in a delicate, almost feminine hand. But the power it promised, the secrets of the universe it offered to reveal in the fullness of time, had been anything but demure.

The driving force, the intellect behind all of this, was brilliant, sublime, commanding—a mind undeniably beyond anything human history had previously produced.

*It has come to my attention*, the letter began, *that you have been embarked on a line of research that might yield considerable benefit, were it combined with several areas of inquiry and experimentation in which we ourselves have recently excelled.*

The letter was signed *Marcus Sanrio.*

And it invited Jeff Arcott to collaborate.

In the letters and breathtakingly original designs that followed, Sanrio had taken Arcott's initial work and built on it in a way that was mesmerizing, counterintuitive and unexpected—but, in hindsight, undeniably *correct* in its assumptions and execution.

Arcott had given himself over to its siren song, and followed where it led.

This much he knew, or at least had been able to read between the lines: for reasons unknown and unstated, Marcus Sanrio, the greatest thinker of the twenty-first century (and who always in correspondence oddly referred to himself in the royal *we*), had been previously unable to join Arcott here in person. But via the Spirit Radio and the instantaneous matter transmission it permitted, Sanrio would soon be with him.

Then the pace of the work would accelerate to a phenomenal degree. And this post-Change world would no longer signal the arrival of a new Dark Age of suffering and ignorance; no, with Sanrio and himself at the forefront, the wild energies let loose on the earth would be tamed and brought into orderly service to mankind. It would be the dawn of a new Industrial Revolution, one that made the pace of the first look leisurely by comparison.

Thus far, Arcott had merely been able to apply a few of Sanrio's principles in order to recapture some of the technology that had been lost, a pallid replication of the old ways of the world. Soon, however, very soon, they would be able to eclipse those accomplishments, create a new understanding and application of that understanding that would allow remarkable new strides.

A rebirth, a renaissance, an enlightenment; a total redefinition of virtually everything, starting most importantly with men's minds.

It was the way of things, Jeff Arcott recognized.

With his laws of motion in the *Principia Mathematica*, Isaac Newton had defined a coherent, observable cosmos around him, the natural world for all to see. But he little dreamed of the transcendent gospel that Einstein would unveil several centuries hence, the crazy-but-true universe where matter and energy were equivalent, gravity bent light, and velocity defined the pace of time; moreover, that the universe was a hyperbolic paraboloid and, wherever you went, if you traveled long enough you invariably arrived back where you started.

The epiphanies Marcus Sanrio's line of inquiry promised were every bit as profound and disconcerting as Einstein's; more so.

Sanrio, with his self-reverential double pronoun and unwillingness to travel via any method but the Spirit Radio, might be a major eccentric and fucking pain in the ass, but hell, Einstein never wore socks or got a haircut, and it only added to his charm.

What mattered was what you *thought*, and what you *did*.

Together, he and Sanrio had brought this town back to life again, and now they would open the door to a radiant new future.

Sanrio and Arcott. Nothing wrong with being the number two man, nothing at all . . .

Arcott thought of Nils Bohr, whom the building he was standing within was named for. He had not been the prime innovator but rather a follower of Einstein, a willing hand that put the breakthrough concepts to practical use; still, Bohr had walked away with his own Nobel Prize.

Arcott tore his gaze away from the lights that writhed like cobras under the spell of a fakir's music, and glanced over at Theo Siegel, who was just tightening the connection on the final bus bar. Theo thought *he* was the number two man. All well and good; no reason to disabuse him of that notion until everything came off as planned. Melissa Wade hovered nearby, monitoring the minute fluctuations of current, the pressure variances of the vacuum with its frisson of argon, at a billionth of an atmosphere a mere ghost thrown in for seasoning.

As Marcus Sanrio had written on many an occasion, there was room for everyone.

Arcott glanced at his gem-encrusted digital watch. Twenty minutes earlier, at Rafe Dahlquist's request for a break and a bite of lunch, he'd dispatched him under guard to the lab's kitchen several doors down. But neither had returned, and time was marching on.

"Flag a guard out in the hall to fetch Dahlquist," he told Theo. "It's high noon."

Theo nodded and sprinted to the heavy steel door, muscled it open and stepped through.

It was only moments before he returned, walking backward, hands raised timorously over his head.

The guards, unarmed now, followed him, and behind them came Cal Griffin and a good many others, hefting sparkling, gem-augmented ought-thirties and nine-millimeters they could have liberated from nowhere but the armory.

Arcott was incredulous; the armory was guarded by his most loyal men, its computer lock triple-encoded. To get in there, a man would have to be able to walk through walls.

(Which, he found out soon enough, was precisely what Herman Goldman—who himself was nowhere to be seen—had done.)

Cal Griffin strode up, and Arcott saw now that Rafe Dahlquist had entered behind him.

"Little change of plan, Jeff," Griffin said.

Then Dahlquist unlocked a storage cabinet and got out the damping equipment.

# THIRTY-FOUR

## Big Blue

"You're gonna fucking ruin everything."

Theo Siegel had to admit it was the first time he'd ever seen Jeff Arcott lose his cool, and it wasn't a pretty sight.

But then, being held at gunpoint and watching someone take over your big nasty toy was likely to spoil anyone's day.

Jeff had ranted awhile and then, seeing Cal Griffin wasn't inclined to listen to Jeff's version of reason, had settled down to a hateful silence. Griffin's guards covering him, Jeff stood leaning against a wall, smoking a cigarette and glaring at the assembled throng—all except Theo, whose glance he contemptuously avoided.

Theo felt jettisoned; his stomach hurt and his insides were ashes. But then, he figured he probably rated such treatment.

At first, Theo had tried to act surprised by the invasion, but he'd always had a lousy poker face and, after a few moments, had set about actively aiding Griffin's troops.

Not that they'd needed much help. Under Rafe Dahlquist's direction, Colleen Brooks and two other of Cal Griffin's followers—who introduced themselves as Al Watt and Mike Kimmel—had efficiently set about getting the dampers wired up and spaced around the hundred-meter-long resonance chamber. Theo noted that Griffin's other lieutenants, Doc Lysenko and Herman Goldman, were nowhere to be seen; on duties elsewhere, no doubt. But Griffin clearly had made his plans well, and brought the personnel he needed.

Theo found he couldn't keep still; he kept pacing, making note of this piece of equipment, that calibration and setting . . . all by way of avoiding the one person he knew he would have to face.

Finally, he turned her way, found himself snared by her beautiful, betrayed eyes.

Melissa Wade sat perched atop a packing crate. "I thought you were our friend," she said, and her voice was cobwebs and razor wire.

Theo nodded—what was there to say?

But the way he saw it (and he could have been wrong, goddammit, could still be wrong), it had boiled down to a choice between helping Jeff turn the key on what well and truly could have had monstrous repercussions, or do his bit to throw a monkey wrench into the works, and just maybe save the whole damn world.

A world that included Melissa. Or more to the point—at least, as far as he was concerned—a world that pretty much *was* Melissa.

So when it came down to the short straw, Theo knew he'd have to choose saving Melissa's life over keeping her regard for him.

Which didn't mean it was one whit less of a gut-shattering soul ache, that he wouldn't regret having done it to the end of his days.

Theo slowly moved close, so it would be just the two of them. Voice shaking, eyes blurring wetly, he whispered, "I am your friend."

Through the rippling distortion, Theo saw Melissa still staring at him, but her expression had clouded over with uncertainty. She opened her mouth as if to speak, then thought better of it and turned away.

He moved off to where Cal Griffin stood marveling at the Infernal Device. It was the first time Griffin had seen it in the flesh, and Theo could well understand his awe at the sight of it.

"She's a beauty," Theo observed. "How about I give you the ten-cent tour?" It would feel good to lapse into data speak, to put aside feeling if only for a moment, if only in pretense.

He led Cal closer to the big cylindrical vacuum chamber, its enameled-iron skin gleaming bright blue, thick orange bands of metal spaced along it at regular intervals.

"Big Blue here started life as a plasma generator, a fusion energy research project. You know, studying alvan waves, lower hybrid waves, drift waves, etc. . . ." Theo caught himself, flushed with embarrassment. "Oops, just veered into major geek territory, sorry, pardner.

"Anyway," he continued more simply, "prior to the Change, there were four brands of matter—solid, liquid, gas and plasma. Only plasma didn't exist naturally on earth, it was far too hot, millions of degrees, core-of-the-sun hot—I'm talking the rigorous scientific definition of plasma here, not that fluffy stuff you get in those globes at Radio Shack alongside the lava lamps. So Jeff and four other PhDs—gone to their various native stomping grounds now—set about building this baby to generate it, working with grad students such as myself and"—here his voice faltered, and he had to work to steady it—"and Ms. Wade, plus various other grunts and techies.

"Made everything right here ourselves," Theo added with obvious pride. "Lathing, milling, welding; epoxy, acetone and elbow grease. Took three and a half years, with funding from the Navy, National Science Foundation, Department of Energy. . . ."

(Which explained at least partially, Cal supposed, by which circuitous route those at the Source Project had learned of the research in the first place, and had known to contact Arcott.)

"Those electromagnets generate a field up to eighty thousand times greater than Earth's magnetic field." Theo gestured at the orange bands, then at the row of big copper clamps bolted onto the electromagnets and secured to the walls. "Bus bars feed in the current—thirty megawatts, enough for a small town—supplied by big turbines in the power room. Water pumps cool the bus bars, heat exchanges recirculated from the building's water supply."

He ran loving fingers along the big cylinder as he strolled the length of it, Cal following. "Initially, pulse lasers were employed to excite the argon atoms, create instabilities to measure. We used different materials for the lasing medium, cultured crystals, ruby, neodynium, YAG—you know, ytrium-aluminum-garnet and the like. . . ." Theo paused, and his expression grew thoughtful. "Plasma is alive, in a way. It has waves in it, it has memory. It's not passive, it's active. External magnets alone can't contain it; it uses its charge to neutralize the field and escape. It's squirmy, always finds a way out."

Indefinable and ungovernable, Theo knew, like the human heart itself, every bit as elusive and determined. He was quiet a moment, then came back from whatever distant land he'd been visiting, and gave Cal a shy smile. "Not so different from what we're trying to lasso now . . ."

He continued walking, but his tone remained hushed, reflective. "Then Storm-day happened, and it all changed. Jeff got his inspiration . . . from whatever source," he added pointedly, "and we got *this.*"

They had reached the far end of the device. Attached at complex but regular intervals around the periphery of the blunt end of the cylinder were gold-plated studs and a staggering array of gemstones, a coral encrustation of garnets, opals, tourmalines, rubies, sapphires and emeralds, a glittering mosaic. Anaconda-thick wires insulated with yellow Teflon crossed from stud to stud in a spiderweb pattern, looping in nouveau curlicues around a massive oval of blue crystal.

Theo saw that Griffin was holding his breath, then caught himself and let it out slowly. The massive blue crystal was not a doorway, not yet. Not until the juice was turned on.

Then the trick would be keeping whatever waited on the other side where it belonged.

"My stars and whiskers," a voice close behind them said, and Theo knew it for Mama Diamond's, realized she had been following them, had heard every word.

He turned and saw that she was peering past them, up at the wall of gems. "I know every one of them," she said incredulously. "Those stones are mine."

As a child in San Bernardino and then at the camp in Manzanar, Mama Diamond had sat often in church, sneaking in despite her parents' Buddhism, listening raptly to the liturgy, letting the Latin wash over her in its power and mystery, the unknown words like an incantation, an unfurling of God's secret plans, back when she'd believed there might be a God.

That young Theo Siegel's description of his machine had been much like that; Mama Diamond hadn't understood a word, but recognized the force behind them, the moving shadows of great and terrible things. . . .

Which had led her, unknowing, to the very place she had sought. Her treasure, her gems.

She approached the glittering wall of stones until it filled all her sight, reverent as a pilgrim arriving from a long sojourn lost and wandering. She knew each of them like the rough air in her ragged lungs, like the blood in her veins; their flow, their color, their flame.

Seeing them here, unprepared as she was, was like seeing them for the first time, like she had never really seen them before.

She had to confess, it was a rare gift.

Ely Stern hadn't stolen her treasure, not really. He had merely relocated it, and her as well, changed and put to a different, perhaps better use.

*People leave you, and possessions, too. . . .*

Mama Diamond was back with her possessions, and had come to know a good many people along the way. People whom she realized, with a warmth like a Pendleton blanket enfolding her, she had come to value even more than the cold, inert objects she had gathered and held close to herself down the dust of years.

But not so inert after all, she corrected herself. She ran her fingertips above the gleaming gems in their new matrix, careful not to touch them. With her heightened senses, she could feel the power throbbing in them, waiting to be unleashed, teeming with every bit of mystery and certainty the good Lord held in His keeping.

Soon enough, she would step through that ring, and the stones that had been hers would gather her up as she had gathered them, would hold her to them and do with her what they would.

Cal Griffin walked over to where Rafe Dahlquist labored on the final adjustments with his crew. "How we coming?"

"Just about ready to crank the body up to the roof, see if lightning hits it." Dahlquist was speaking facetiously, but it might as well have been literal, considering what they were about to try.

"Let me just make sure I've got this straight," Colleen Brooks said, striding up to them (she found it was becoming her theme song, of late). "We push the big red button, that thing hopefully opens up onto South Dakota, the Source Project, right?"

"Uh-huh," Dahlquist said, not looking at her, his eyes on the elaborate series of connections he was running from the damping devices to the large blue crystal. "And if this does what it's supposed to, we keep the field contained, so there's no surprises."

"There are always surprises," Colleen said.

At which moment, Herman Goldman appeared literally out of nowhere and tapped her on the shoulder.

"Judas Priest, Goldman," Colleen yelped, spinning on him, "don't *do* that."

"Why not? It's one of the best perks." He tipped his straw cowboy hat with the five aces, which struck Colleen not as a courtesy but rather as the impertinence it was clearly intended to be.

"Where the hell'd you spring from anyway?" she asked.

"*Where* is not the pertinent question," Goldie replied, stifling a grin. "But rather, with *whom*."

He stepped aside, to reveal the hyper little grunter known as Howard Russo . . . and the serene ebony presence of Enid Blindman.

# THIRTY-FIVE

## The Rainbow Door

"Last stop on the way," Goldie said to Cal. "Man, you sure kept me hopping."

Despite her ire at Goldman, Colleen found herself smiling broadly.

"Hey, Mr. Bluesman." She clapped Enid on the shoulder. "How's life down on the Preserve?"

"Plenty quiet, compared to where I hear we gonna be goin'."

Colleen had last seen the remarkable young blues player at Magritte's funeral pyre in Chicago, just after the ordeal of their battle with Primal; in fact, Enid had been the whole reason for that battle.

Colleen and her companions had first met Enid along the banks of a peaceful river valley as they'd traveled out of West Virginia, had discovered that the siren call of his music could both draw people to him and protect them from the Source (while the flare Magritte in turn protected *him*)—until such time as Enid could lead them to a portal that opened onto the Neverland of Mary McCrae's Preserve.

Cal had hoped to employ Enid's talent to shield his group as they journeyed to the heart of the Source; had hoped it might give them a chance to save Tina and perhaps change the world back to the way it had been.

But they soon learned there was a terrible cost to Enid's gift. Due to the terms of a demonically transformed contract Primal held the rights to, whenever Enid utilized his music to good purpose, it also twisted and distorted *other* souls, rendered them into tortured beings of smoke and flame, and sharded the landscape into bizarre crystalline shapes.

So with the assistance of Enid's former manager-turned-grunter Howard Russo, they had plunged into Primal's black fortress, had ultimately destroyed that insane dark being (whom they only later learned was once Clayton Devine, security chief of the Source Project). They had brought Primal's tower crashing down, liberating the countless flares Devine held captive there and removing Enid's curse in the process . . . but at the cost of Magritte's life.

Enid had taken it upon himself to conduct the surviving flares to the Preserve, to safeguard those who were not beyond aid, to honor what Magritte had sacrificed her life for.

But now he was back, his engine fine-tuned and humming.

Enid looked considerably healthier than the last time Colleen had seen him. His skin was darkly vibrant, no longer the sickly gray that marked how his Pied Piper gift had drained him prior to their extricating his contract from Primal. She noted, too, that he'd brought along his guitar and harmonica—the weapons he used, along with that remarkable velvet-gravel voice of his, to shield those near and dear to him from the loving attentions of the Source Consciousness.

*Which damn well better include our little scouting party very shortly, or it's gonna be a mighty short trip. . . .*

Howard Russo bulled up to her, and she saw he was outfitted in a screamingly loud yellow checked suit and matching fedora that had been tailored to fit his dwarfish frame. He grinned from beneath mirrored Ray-Bans. "Not bad, huh? I'd say I got my look pretty well nailed."

"You put Goldman to shame, Howie." Colleen didn't add, *And if someone ran you down, it wouldn't be by accident.*

"Here's the rest of the boodle." Goldie handed Cal a battered leather portfolio, tied with a string. "Better be worth it, my head's spinning from all the time zones."

Cal opened the portfolio and studied its contents. It didn't look like much of anything, as far as Colleen could see. Some scribbled notes in Goldman's chicken scratch, a handful of dog-eared snapshots.

"What's all that?" she asked Cal.

"Maybe nothing," he murmured, sliding the papers back into the portfolio and stashing it inside his jacket.

Rafe Dahlquist looked up from his position by a bank of computer screens, where he was monitoring the power. "We're optimal. Just give me the high sign when you're ready."

Cal nodded. A low hum of electricity, of turbines whirring along with increasing power, vibrated through the room and through all of them, like the steady pulse of a giant.

Cal glanced at his watch, then at the big steel front door. Colleen could detect his impatience, the pregame tension in him, which they all felt one way or another. But she knew that he wouldn't set things rolling until he had this one last piece in place.

He didn't have long to wait, as a moment later the door swung open and Doc entered, rolling in a dolly with a big cardboard box strapped to it. He set it upright and released the strap, easing the box to the floor. Crouching, he opened the flaps.

Everyone gathered around, acutely curious, because even though Doc had prepped them on exactly what he was doing, hearing about it was one thing and seeing quite another.

"You will have to excuse the workmanship," Doc said by way of apology. "My needlework is usually confined to stitching up incisions."

He withdrew the bulky pieces, and a number of the onlookers gasped. Their surface was blackly iridescent, roughly pebbled and ridged, bespeaking power, even put to this new purpose.

Colleen found the padded shapes oddly familiar, and in a rush it came to her. "Don't tell me, you raided the athletic department."

Doc nodded. "I utilized shoulder pads and other protective pieces for the framework. As for the rest . . ."

He didn't need to finish; they all knew.

The thick leather garments were from the skin of a dragon—the dragon that Cal had killed, Arcott had brought here at their request, and Doc had autopsied—fashioned now into body armor and visored helmets.

"Sadly enough, there was only sufficient, um"—Doc searched for a delicately appropriate euphemism—"raw material to provide three full ensembles." He glanced inquiringly at Cal, who drew near the box.

Cal lifted out a helmet, tunic and pants. "Mr. Shango?"

Shango approached and took them, eased his big frame into them.

"Goldie?" Cal said, proffering the next set.

"Thanks, but I'm uncomfortable enough in my *own* skin."

Cal nodded acceptance, then glanced inquiringly at Enid Blindman, who sat cross-legged on the floor nearby, tuning up his jumbo maple guitar, limbering up his harmonica.

"'Preciate the offer," Enid piped up, and Colleen was struck again by how even his speaking voice was musical. "But I need to keep loose, so's I can spin my *own* kinda shell."

"Right," Cal agreed. Colleen knew as well as Cal that Enid's ability to weave a musical cloak about them, to shield them from being detected by whatever dwelt at the Source, might be their most vital armor of all.

Cal turned to Colleen, raising the garments.

"Uh-uh, no way," she said, backing. "Only two more sets, I know which of my favorite bookends are gonna be in them."

Cal moved to speak, but Doc cut him off, took Colleen aside.

"Don't give me that kindly Russian doctor act, Viktor. I mean it."

Ignoring this, he said, "We both know that you are by far the better fighter, Colleen, and in any skirmish you will be on the front lines, no matter what any might command to the contrary." He stepped close, peering at her with those gray eyes that had seen so much anguish and retained such compassion. "It would ease my mind greatly."

*Dammit, trust him not to fight fair. . . .* She felt her resolve melt like an Eskimo Pie shot into the sun.

Scowling with extremely bad grace, she stalked back to Cal. "Gimme that," she said, snatching up the grotesque rig.

She slid her arms into the loose-fitting tunic—which smelled thickly of musk and other loathsome things that made her want to lose last year's lunch—and pulled it on. Christ, she felt lost in this thing; it made her feel like a little girl wearing Daddy's clothes. She pushed the thought away, subdued her rising gorge. Seeing that the sides had leather laces (she didn't even want to think about what part *they* came from), she tightened the garment until it fit better and allowed a proper range of motion.

She saw that Doc was holding the remaining suit of armor toward Cal. "No arguments, Calvin. We both know what is required here."

"Gandhi only wore a loincloth," Cal said.

"Yes, and look what happened to him."

Cal sighed and took the armor.

"*Spacibo,*" Doc said.

Cal gave Dahlquist the thumbs-up.

As soon as Rafe Dahlquist keyed in the initiating sequence, the gemstones encrusting the Spirit Radio took on a numinous glow, a largeness and purity of light like the clarified essences of color produced by a prism. And like a wall dissolving to reveal an unknown territory beyond, the blue crystal faded from sight, replaced by a glowing fog . . . a fog that stayed bound within the parameters of Mama Diamond's gems.

It no longer looked anything like a blue crystal, Mama Diamond mused as she stared into the hypnotic, swirling mists writhing voluptuously within the flashing circle of gems. If she had to describe it (and she was grateful she would never be called upon to do so), she supposed the closest she could come would be to say it looked like every light on the Vegas Strip as seen through her milky bad eye (her *formerly* bad eye, she corrected herself; since the tête-à-tête with Stern at her shop, she was seeing just fine through it, thank you very much), if someone at the same time were slowly flipping her ass-over-teakettle so everything in her field of vision did a languorous three-sixty.

"The field's holding steady, we've got it contained," Rafe Dahlquist reported to Cal. "But I wouldn't trust it longer than twenty minutes, not at this point."

"Okay, so the meter's running." In his rough-hewn black armor and helmet, Cal Griffin looked incongruously like some slightly undersized biker from hell or mountain man who skinned and tanned his own duds—certainly not like the modest young man who'd been surreptitiously practicing his sword moves on top of the dorm building so no one might see him being so lethally beautiful in his movements.

Cal nodded toward Colleen Brooks and Doc Lysenko, Herman Goldman, Shango, Howard Russo and Enid Blindman. Howie had a ruby-glittered, Tech Nine automatic stuck in his belt, while the others sported gem-encrusted rifles slung over their backs, plus their usual weapon of choice—machetes, sledgehammers, crossbows and the like. In addition, Enid was outfitted with his big guitar and the Hohner Meisterklasse harmonica he favored. Larry Shango carried the heavy-duty bag Mama Diamond had seen him load up with the homemade explosives he and Krystee Cott had been cooking up in the chemistry lab.

But of course, there was no telling whether old-style explosives would work on the other side, Mama Diamond knew; that they did so here was certainly no guarantee.

And if there was one thing Ely Stern's unheralded arrival in Burnt Stick had taught her—and nothing along the way had dissuaded her since—it was that the best course of action was to expect the unexpected, and rely on nothing.

The seven of them approached the roiling portal, its van Gogh palette of lights playing over them, making them look as though they were adorned in living war paint.

"Now, you remember, Enid," Howard Russo said, dogging the bluesman as he sauntered toward the rainbow font, "anything grabs you by the short and curlies, you cut and run. No heroics. You don't want to live on in your music—you want to live on in your *body*."

"'Spect you to do the same it comes to that, Howie," Enid responded.

"You can take that to the bank," Russo muttered.

Colleen Brooks made a preemptive move to step through the portal, but Cal restrained her.

"You threw me a party, this one's mine. I test the water, then you can dive in."

"*Cal—*"

"No, Colleen."

She ran an exasperated hand through her short, spiky hair. "How do we know it's a transporter device, and you're not walking right into the disintegration chamber? I mean, I think I can confidently say we all saw that *Star Trek* episode."

"*Uno momento,*" Goldie said. He moved closer to the misty wall of light, turned an ear toward it. "I can hear voices on the other side. Plus I'm getting a murky picture . . . nothing clear, just a feeling of elbow room. There's considerable real estate over there."

"Well, that certainly reassures me," Colleen grumbled. But she relented, stepping aside to let Cal take point.

Concentrating, Mama Diamond felt she too could hear the sounds on the other side, dimly. The noise was an impasto of voices too thick to be comprehensible, but each layered syllable was somehow distinct, embodied, solid. Mama Diamond imagined that if she closed her eyes she would see a legion of ghosts crowding around her. Which was why she kept her eyes firmly open.

Cal turned to Dahlquist. "If something starts to go south, if it heads toward meltdown, kill it, shut it down. Don't worry about us." Mama Diamond read the uncertainty in Dahlquist's eyes, but he nodded his agreement.

Cal addressed Krystee Cott, whom he had delegated to command those left standing guard. "Keep everything cool, no one in or out." He shot a glance at Jeff Arcott, glowering but silent against the wall. Arcott deliberately ignored him.

As for Theo Siegel and Melissa Wade, Mama Diamond saw each was staring into the portal as though hearing a music being sung only to them—and perhaps, she realized, that was the case.

Cal turned back toward the portal, was about to step through. *It's now or never,* Mama Diamond thought urgently. Three quick strides brought her up to him.

"Forget something, Mr. Griffin?" she asked pointedly. She might also have said *someone*, given the promise he'd made her on the roof of the dormitory building. Up close now, she could see that blue sprites of static electricity danced in his hair.

"I'm sorry, ma'am," Cal said, not unkindly. "But we're going to have to take a rain check on that."

"Well, that's all right, dear," she replied demurely. "I suppose you'd know best about that."

Mama Diamond caught Larry Shango's eye. Did she detect amusement there, or just imagine it? More like he had been there before, and knew her better than that now.

She stepped back. Cal Griffin gave her a shy smile—*ah, there was that boy on the roof again*—and walked into nothingness.

In an instant, Colleen Brooks, Herman Goldman and Doc Lysenko followed him, then Larry Shango and Enid Blindman and Howard Russo were gone into the mist.

The hum of the massive generators rose up, and Mama Diamond became aware of a sharp metallic smell in the air. It brought to mind the electric Fender guitar Arnie Sproule used to play from time to time; his old tube amp smelled like that when he turned it on after lengthy disuse. Only this was about a thousand times more intense.

Mama Diamond's heart was pounding like the hammer on her rusty old alarm clock, like John Henry's sledge right toward the end before he dropped; she could hear it in her ears, feel it in the veins in her temples.

It was talking to her, had been talking to her since she had first seen Mr. Shango standing over her on that train platform in Burnt Stick, since she'd encountered Griffin and his friends as she had crouched beside that fear projector in the night-kissed outskirts of Atherton.

Staring into the shifting curtain of light, ringed by her own glowing treasure, Mama Diamond knew with surety those young ones would need her, desperately and soon.

*Better to ask pardon than permission,* Mama Diamond thought, and leapt through the portal of the Spirit Radio.

# THIRTY-SIX

## City on the Edge

*Sometimes,* Larry Shango thought as he moved cautiously through the glowing fogbank, rifle at the ready, *what's new is old again.*

At least, that's how it felt to him now, déjà vu all over, exactly the way it was when he'd been all by his lonesome, Sheep Mountain Table faded to invisibility behind him and Fred Wishart, that humorless spectre, about to appear and dispatch him to the land of Emiliano Zapata and cactus soda pop.

Only this time, Shango had Cal Griffin and his retinue of Colleen Brooks, Doc Lysenko, Herman Goldman, Enid Blindman and Howard Russo along for the ride—which didn't mean they had any more of a clue as to where they'd landed or were headed in this glowing, impenetrable soup.

Shango glanced at his watch, which he could just barely make out in the shifting, multicolored light. Eighteen minutes to go . . .

"Welcome to South Dakota," Goldie murmured.

"I'm open to suggestions," Cal said.

Colleen let out a cry. Shango wheeled to see that Mama Diamond had appeared out of nowhere and collided into her from behind.

Shango smiled to himself; at least, this was one thing that was no surprise.

"Come on in, the water's fine," said Goldie, utterly unperturbed.

Cal sighed but said nothing, indicating his acceptance. He continued forward—then halted abruptly, raising a warning hand.

Shango squinted into the mist ahead of him.

A figure was appearing.

It drew closer, gained clarity and solidity.

But unlike Fred Wishart, this was no phantom assembled from the atoms, from the mist itself. . . .

Simply a boy, or something a good deal more than a boy, who strode up to them, intent on keeping an appointment.

"Let me show you the Bridge," Inigo said.

Theo Siegel found himself sweating profusely, even though the room was outright frosty, the air circulators keeping the atmosphere at an even low temperature. He wanted everything to go smoothly, for Cal Griffin and his friends to emerge unscathed, for no mishaps to befall them on the other side.

*The dangerous side . . .*

Which might well have been this side, too, had not Griffin interceded and replaced Jeff Arcott's hand on the wheel with his own.

Theo cast an anxious glance Jeff's way. Jeff glared back at him, finally willing to acknowledge his existence, at least. Theo realized this felt neither better nor worse than Jeff's initial response of ignoring him entirely.

Theo chose not to look at Melissa, however, not wanting to risk a second encounter with those accusing eyes, that wounded voice.

How he wished he could somehow demonstrate to her what dreadful thing he feared would have happened had Jeff's plan come to fruition.

In later times, Theo would recall that errant thought and add ruefully, *Be careful what you wish for—you might just get it.*

"Ten minutes and counting," Krystee Cott said to Rafe Dahlquist.

Suddenly, there was the sound of rending metal, and the bolted steel lab door tore clear of its hinges.

Flame erupted into the room.

Amid the screams and pandemonium, Theo heard Krystee Cott shouting orders, saw gunfire erupt toward the doorway. Mike Kimmel grabbed the extinguisher, unleashed it futilely at the growing blaze. The others in the room were dashing this way and that, trying to get clear. As far as Theo could see, no one was seriously hurt—perhaps a deliberate choice on the part of their attacker—

*But the damping equipment, my God . . .*

It was aflame, melting to slag.

Through the smoke, Theo became aware of a vast, bony form striding into the room, sweeping people and machinery aside, tearing wiring loose in great, taloned handfuls.

He had seen this one before, in the night, at the train siding.

Jeff Arcott had called him by name.

With claw and fang and fire, the man in black, the dragon thing, destroyed all that held the Infernal Device in check.

Unhindered now, tendrils of insane purple light shot out of the Spirit Radio's riotous maw, uncoiling into the room like living things, spreading outward to infect and corrupt all they touched.

Arcott's laboratory was alive with energy. Huge sparks, like phantasmal blue lightning, arced between the portal and the laboratory walls. The portal itself was as bright as a sheet of sun—a mirror of flame.

The source of this energy was clearly no longer the massive diesel generators in the physics building's basement. This energy came from elsewhere, and Theo realized there was *nothing* he could do about it.

"Out! Everybody get out!" That was Krystee Cott, shouting to the others over the din, helping them find their way as they flailed and crashed about, blinded by the blaze, gagging on the smoke.

Through the roar and fumes and glare, Theo could just make out a handful of others clearing the room; from their dim outlines, he thought he discerned Rafe Dahlquist and Al Watt and Mike Kimmel, moving under Krystee's urgent direction. He saw others, too, furtive smoke shadows, frantic silhouettes of vapor, but could not identify them. The bulk of the destroyer, the dragon thing in the shifting, thick plumes of smoke, seemed unconcerned about them now.

Theo cast wildly about for Melissa, heedless of his own welfare. His eyes located Jeff Arcott against the far wall, falling back and screaming horribly just as one of the tentacles of pure power seized him and whipped him about, hurling him into walls that threw off great plumes of sparks with each impact, as the tendril expanded to cover Jeff entirely, consuming him whole.

Sickened, Theo turned away and dove deeper into the room, crying out Melissa's name.

He found her on the sidelines, wavering in the smoke like a heat phantom, a dreamy mirage. She was staring with a quizzical, unfocused gaze, mouth half open, at the wildly pinwheeling gateway.

"Melissa! *Melissa!*" She made no sign of hearing him, registered nothing at all.

Desperate, Theo grabbed her up and slung her over his shoulder, noting only momentarily the effortless strength that seemed to fill him—and the curious fact that there was no pain issuing from his injured leg, that he needed crutches not at all.

He plunged with her toward the exit as the demon power surged up out of the portal, gaining ever more purchase here. A bolt of shimmering plasma passed perilously close to Theo's head, singeing his hair and causing Melissa to twitch against him as if she were gripped in a nightmare.

Stumbling, choking, he carried Melissa out of the laboratory. The corridors of the Physical Sciences Building were likewise blazingly bright, as if someone had cranked up the voltage to the ceiling lights. He felt dreadfully strange, *ached* in every part of his body. Looking over at Melissa, he could see that she still seemed dazed, her gaze dull and removed. In the pitiless glare, her body seemed more fragile than ever. Her rib cage fluttered with her breathing like an ancient bellows, and her body was as light in his arms as a butterfly or a moth.

He reeled out of the building with her, lost his footing rushing headlong down the stairs and nearly fell, narrowly gaining his balance on the greensward of Philosopher's Walk.

He heard a shattering of glass and looked back just in time to see the skylight of the physics lab explode upward into the night, followed by a monstrous dark shape.

Ely Stern, having accomplished what he had set in motion so many months ago, the elaborate series of events he had planned and directed and now at last achieved, unfurled himself and took wing.

He vanished into the starlit sky.

# III

# STRONGHOLD

*You have to know what your center is, so you can stand everything.*

—Ann Cedarface

# THIRTY-SEVEN

## STRAWBERRY FIELDS

Normally, it's considered sound advice, when intent on not drawing unwanted scrutiny, to be as quiet as possible.

But then, these were hardly normal times.

So when Cal Griffin advised Enid Blindman that it would probably be advisable for him to start playing anytime now, everyone concurred that was mighty fine idea.

Enid began strumming softly and singing low to himself as the nine of them moved cautiously forward through the mist, its cool dampness like the gentle kiss of a cadaver on their skin, the grunter boy Inigo leading the way.

Upon encountering him in the fog, Colleen had been inclined to skewer the little blue-gray rodent, seeing as how his advice on leading them toward sanctuary hadn't exactly been five-star up until now. But Cal stayed her hand; they wouldn't have gotten this far without the boy, and even though Inigo undeniably played a very close hand, he had taken no action so far that Cal sensed as treachery.

"Besides," Goldie added with his characteristic glibness, "it's not easy being blue."

"Ain't *that* the truth," chimed in Howie.

Colleen made no reply, although she ordinarily would have. A sidewise glance at Goldman, shimmering insubstantial as a mirage beside her, revealed a face set in a humorless mask. His mouth might be on automatic with feigned levity, but his mind was elsewhere, and intent on a grimmer purpose.

Not surprising, really, considering their present environs. For they all knew in this frigging haze they might as well be marching down the throat of whatever monstrosity called the Source Project home; might, in fact, be forging blissfully unaware straight on through to the acid-pool of its cavernous belly at this very moment.

But, fatalist that she was on most occasions, Colleen didn't really think so—not yet, at least.

As she inched through the fog, the midnight-blue chords and harmonies of Enid's song lulled her, brought calm and reassurance. It hadn't always been thus. When she and Goldman first encountered him roaming among the tall cedars in that river valley along the Ohio/West Virginia border, Colleen thought Enid a malevolent Pied Piper and had predictably gone on the attack—a typical berserker stunt that succeeded only in landing her upside down in a tree, skewered by a branch (she still had that jagged, lightning-bolt scar down her right side, which Doc—adorable diplomat that he was—said merely added to her charms).

But if she'd learned anything from their travels with Enid from there to Chicago and beyond, it was that his music had power not only to soothe the savage breast but also to block out whatever lurked at the Source from seeing him and his friends, from reaching out its long, invisible tentacles and plucking them away.

At least, that was the story back then, when they'd been one hell of a lot farther away from it. Still, the best they could hope for now was to play the odds and hope they caught some breaks along the way.

"Fourteen minutes and counting," Larry Shango reported.

"When will we come to the Bridge?" Cal asked Inigo.

"We've been walking along it," Inigo said, and drew to a halt. Before him the misty streaks of neon vapor were swirling concentrically as if spiraling down a drain. Colleen could just now make out the sky beyond, which held a rosy glow of late afternoon or dawn; hard to tell which in the overcast sky. The landscape began to clear, to resolve itself into a body of cool blue water, flanked by rolling green hills. Narrow flat rowboats were tethered together at the shore, a gentle wind nudging them against each other.

Colleen knew this lake well. As the fog dispersed even more, she could see the flower-bedecked rise ahead of her known as Strawberry Fields, and to its left the wedding-cake structure of Tavern on the Green. A glance ahead to her right showed her the vast Romanesque stonework of the American Museum of Natural History, and beside it the Hayden Planetarium.

"Oh my God," Colleen whispered.

She, Cal, Goldie and Doc all knew this place for a certainty, although only Inigo had truly been here before.

It was Central Park.

"I thought you said we were in South Dakota," Cal said to Goldie.

Goldman was squinting intently at the vista ahead. "We are . . ." he replied hesitantly.

Doc stepped to the forefront, peering at the solidity of the structures before them. "Colleen, Calvin, Mr. Shango—your visors, please."

Colleen lowered the visor on her helmet, and peered through the tan membrane covering her eyes. "I'm still seeing Big Apple," she said.

"Me too," Cal concurred. They glanced at Shango, who nodded his agreement.

Doc mulled this over. "Offhand, I would say that the likelihood is what we are seeing is not an illusion but rather solid matter, a replica of some sort."

"Great, we're in a diorama," Colleen muttered. She wondered where all the flares might be hiding, knowing that the Source had abducted thousands, if not millions of them. At least in Chicago, the Ruby City, the glow of them had lit up the skies. It had been a beacon, making the myriad of those that powered Primal distinctly easy to find.

Cal turned to Inigo. "Why is this here?"

Inigo peered up at Cal and said meaningfully, "Because it's her home."

Colleen saw Cal's eyes register surprise, then fill with a comprehension far deeper than the words the boy had uttered.

And despite all his months of preparation, despite his determination to keep a cool head, to be the leader they all needed him to be, Cal took off running full-out across the manicured grassland, darted over the bicycle path and out onto the street and the city beyond.

East to the broad thoroughfare of Columbus, and north to the weathered but well-maintained brownstones of Eighty-first.

To home . . . and Tina.

"After me!" Cal cried, knowing they would follow.

He could hear Colleen pounding after him, and the others behind her; it was no more than he expected, what he counted on. But Cal didn't have time to look back nor slow his pace. There were only thirteen minutes or so left, and he knew he could no more return to the portal without discovering if Tina were here than he could tear out his own heart.

He dove past the variegated street denizens of Manhattan, who remarked on him not at all, past the gleaming parked cars and trucks. It registered on him that this was a simulacrum of New York City before the Change, but one muted, damped down, with none of the clamor nor haste, as contemplative and unchanging as an aquarium.

Then he was on the familiar street, bounding up the short flight of stairs to the heavy oak door he knew so well, the one whose original had been there in the time of Fiorello LaGuardia and Al Smith and before. He threw it open, bounded up the stairs.

But at the same time, he was no fool; he knew where he was, or rather where he wasn't. He drew forth his sword—he felt sure *that* at least would still work; let those behind him wield their rifles—and vaulted up the stairs two and three at a time.

He hit the landing, turned hard right and found himself facing the apartment door that was identical to his own, a perfect replica. He could hear the others thundering up the stairs behind him, felt the reassurance of their presence, their constancy. He tried the knob, felt it turn. The door was unlocked. He plunged inside.

The curtains in the living room were drawn tight, casting the room in dimness, and for a moment Cal couldn't see detail in the gloom. He looked about wildly, spied illumination coming from the hall. He bolted for it, his feet making cushioned, echoing thumps in the worn carpet as he ran. He saw his own room, dark and untenanted but incredibly exact in what detail he could discern, then he spun toward Tina's room. Its door was slightly ajar, and light was pouring forth from within.

*God, let her be there,* he pleaded to the unseen, uncaring deity that had taken their mother's life and gifted them with an abhorrent, fugitive father, had cast him and his sister onto the foreign shores of Manhattan and then split them apart. *I don't care what she is, what inhuman, damaged thing. Just let her be alive, let me care for her and get her home. . . .*

He opened the door and stepped inside.

The girl sat in her chair by the bed, in the rocker (or cunning replica of it) that had been bought on the day of Cal's birth, that his father had torn the runners off of in a fit of rage before Tina was born. A reading lamp sat on a shelf above her head, glowing like a halo, shining its radiance down on her glistening hair.

She held a book open in her lap, was glancing down reading it. Cal knew it from its scuffed leather binding; it was *Great Expectations.* He had read it aloud to her, in their life together, the life that had been theirs so long ago.

"Tina . . ." Cal said, and his voice cracked, had no volume to it.

She looked up, and two thoughts struck him at once, with the force of blows. Her hair was not silken and white, her eyes not an alien blue; both were dark, and she appeared utterly human.

And in those human, dark eyes as she regarded him calmly, quizzically, there was not the slightest hint of recognition.

*She doesn't know me.*

He was staggered. He had not expected any of this, and he felt a flood of fresh grief, of raw anguish that cut him as if with the sword he carried in his hand.

"Tina, it's Cal," he prompted.

"I go by Christina now," she responded abstractedly, but underneath there was no hint of familiarity.

*Of course,* Cal realized, a more adult name. He could see she looked older than when he'd last seen her; she was thirteen now. And they had been separated by what each had experienced since their parting, yet another gulf between them.

The others were behind him now.

"We have eight minutes," Shango murmured.

Enough time, barely, to get back, if they left now.

"Take her," Cal said.

But before they could move to do so, Goldie suddenly moaned, grasping his head with both hands, and fell to his knees.

Cal peered at him in alarm. With an effort of supreme will, Goldie forced his face up toward him. His eyes were slits, pain filling them wetly with tears. "The way back," he gasped, whispering. "It's *closed*. . . ."

The floor abruptly shuddered with a pulse, a tremor that shook along its length like a bear awakening from slumber and stretching to rise. Outside, the air rumbled with a deep, sonorous roar.

"It knows you're here," Inigo said, and there was dread in his voice.

The far wall of Tina's room melted and reached for them.

"Shango!" Cal cried. "The explosives!"

Shango dug in his bag and pulled out one of the homemade metal canisters he and Krystee Cott had constructed back in Atherton. He pulled the pin and hurled it at the shifting, amorphous shapes stretching out toward them.

*Now we'll see how good a cook you are,* Cal thought, as he shielded Tina and drew her back away with the others.

There was a breathless moment of expectation, then a satisfying explosion of fire and smoke, blasting what had been the wall clean apart.

"Yeah!" Colleen shouted in triumph . . . then fell silent along with the rest of them as the smoke cleared and what was revealed filled them with horror.

Littering the scorched area of the blast, lying piled atop each other by the gaping hole in the wall, were what looked like frail, delicate children, bloody and mutilated, torn to pieces, their glow damping down to nothingness.

Flares, dead flares.

And though Inigo had not told them—had not until that moment even known—Cal and the rest of them grasped exactly what this hideous spectacle meant.

"It's flares," Cal whispered, thunderstruck. "All of it . . ."

With the exception of Tina, who somehow had been made human again, everything they had seen in this cruel parody of New York

City, every building, every street, every tree and cloud and lamp fixture, was composed of flares. *That* was the substance that made up the matter of this place, that powered it and gave it solidity. The thousands, the *millions* of innocents abducted by the Source and turned to this brutal purpose.

Cal realized they couldn't—*mustn't* strike out at it.

*They would be killing the very hostages they had come to save.*

And in their moment of terrible uncertainty, of hesitancy, the room rose up against them, like ocean waves crashing up out of the floorboards, and separated them, one from another. Mama Diamond and Goldie, Shango and Colleen, Doc and Howie and Enid all cried out in surprise and alarm, frantic exclamations that were quickly stifled and fell to silence.

The room resumed its formal shape, with no sign of the mangled flares; they'd been absorbed into the greater, secret whole. Cal found himself alone with Inigo and Tina.

The others were gone.

"We have to get out of here!" Inigo tugged insistently at Cal's sleeve, at the scaled dark dragon hide encasing him. "Now!"

Stumbling blindly, bereft, Cal dragged his sister out of the building and, led by the wild, abandoned boy, made his escape into the void.

# THIRTY-EIGHT

## Soi Cowboy

As any profound philosopher and serious scholar of the natural laws of the universe has discovered at one time or another, there are occasions on which the most appropriate and jejune observation regarding one's immediate situation is *Fuck this!*

Which was certainly the epiphany presented to Colleen Brooks in the moments immediately following the little funhouse shenanigans the doppelgänger of Cal Griffin's Upper West Side apartment pulled on her, when the floorboards bucked like Roy Roger's horse on locoweed and she was hurled forcibly backward and suddenly found herself in surroundings utterly unlike New York or any place on the North American continent.

This wasn't to say she didn't recognize her surroundings, however. She knew *exactly* where she was—or rather, where they wanted her to think she was. The air was musky and thick with humidity, as hard to breathe as if she were trying to inhale syrup. Her skin was instantly sticky with sweat, her clothes beneath the dragon armor plastered to her skin, and yet she felt as cold within as if her insides were tombstone marble.

While it had been daytime only moments before, here it was night (as it was always night in her remembrances) and the garish, ugly street was clogged and raucous with subcompact Toyotas and Nissans belching exhaust; with huge and gaudily decorated trucks over from India blasting their horns as they inched precariously forward; with the brightly colored, three-wheeled taxis known to the locals and *farangs* alike as *tuk-tuks* zipping between the swaying, ill-balanced vehicles. The black asphalt of the street was shiny with recently departed rain, and in its reflections the boisterous cacophony of neon signs was rendered double in its seedy enticement, blinking and flashing with images of overendowed, underdressed woman and smiling, dangerous men; Marlboro Men, to be exact, the American male being the *ne plus ultra* of invitation, of reckless power and release.

The smell on the air was the same, exactly the same as she remembered it, the fetid stink of sewage, and rotted fruit, and spices in hot cooking oil, of a city of five million left to decay and sink on its foundations slowly back into the marsh and swampland from which it had been dredged and excavated by men long dead, their dreams of glory dead with them.

The street was called Soi Cowboy, and it was the pulsing heart of Bangkok's red-light district.

Colleen Brooks knew this street well, although the last time she saw it waking was when she was ten, when her Air Force father had been briefly stationed here to perform triage on a squadron of aging, hard-used B-52s left over from the Nam, to render his usual, uncompromising miracles on these gorgeous, terrible death machines. Her mother had flown over from her family's home in Lacrosse, Texas, to join him, and had brought Colleen along, notwithstanding how she felt about bringing her child into "that kind of environment." She knew damn well that if Colleen got left behind, there would be hell to pay—long weeks of surly silences, uncooperative sulks, and guilt-inducing looks of raw reproach that could reduce a mother almost to tears.

Colleen, victorious, was just happy to be going somewhere other than Lacrosse, Texas. There wasn't much to like about Lacrosse in Colleen's estimation, and flying willy-nilly to Bangkok seemed the height of adventure to a ten-year-old. It was something she would later speak of to schoolmates as if it were merely a weekend trek to the Gulf. *(Yeah, we just got back from Thailand. It was okay, I guess. I didn't see a single horse the whole time.)*

Best of all, central to all, they were a family again, at least for a while—reunited with her father.

On this particular night—or the original of it, at least—Daddy had been called upon to locate a young GI who'd escaped into the dark splendors of the city for diversion and return him to his quarters before he was considered AWOL. In the darkness of a foreign hotel room, frigid with over-amped air-conditioning, Colleen had silently eased into T-shirt and jeans and crept out a window to follow and find her father.

After three weary, tear-streaked hours, she located him in a dreary club that was actually fairly innocuous considering the environs, where he was knocking back a few Singha beers with the wayward and depressed young tech sergeant and feeding quarters to Hank Williams on the juke. The boy had just heard from his fiancée back home that she'd determined a mutual friend to be a better marriage candidate (at least more likely to be alive in a year or two) and had cut him loose via a long and rambling Dear John letter.

Colleen remembered the look of grave sympathy on her dad's face as he watched the younger man spill his pain onto the drink-stained bar.

"Chief," he told her later, when they were safely back in their hotel room, "all I could think was, 'There but for the grace of God . . .' I wasn't sure I wanted you and your mom to come to Bangkok. But sitting there listening to that poor kid, I was damn glad you were here."

"Language," her mother had said, giving her dad a look that was at once loving and reproachful.

Knowing full well it was not that time, that she was not ten, that she was still in South Dakota no matter *how* it looked, Colleen still felt that same long-ago fear that scythed her breath into short gasps and made the blood pound in her ears and pulse behind her eyes. She hurried breathlessly along the tawdry street, the seedy tourists and dissolute expats and servicemen on leave not shooting her so much as a glance.

She wondered what awaited her beyond the black-enameled door of that dive at the end of the street—some ghastly re-creation of her father consoling the wayward airman like a waxwork tableau in Madame Tussaud's, that would move and speak despite their utter lack of souls . . . or something unfathomably worse?

And dammit, in spite of everything she knew, in spite of the fact that she was utterly sure that whatever was behind this fucking charade had no object in mind other than to distract and delude and almost certainly ultimately *kill* her, she still found herself longing to see her father again—even if it *was* just some copy of him, some image raided from the vault of her memory. To see his cockeyed smile that made the corners of his eyes crinkle up, see the sandpaper stubble no razor seemed entirely able to subdue. To look into those brown, forgiving eyes, to feel his callused hand with its grease-stained nails ruffling her wild mop of hair and hear his voice.

"How goes it, Chief?"

Just once, once more. To call him back from the grave . . .

*How goes it, Chief?* Not fucking well.

*Language, Colleen. Language.*

But before she could reach that door, unlock its secrets, she found herself snared by another storefront on the vile, raucous street, lured by the lilting music wafting from under its door and around the edges, by the smell of incense curling out on the sultry air.

She felt drawn against her will, beguiled the same as she had been fifteen years back and more. She hadn't thought of this in a long time, this perplexing dark vision, as alluring and ruined as a poisoned wedding cake.

There was a big window set in the door, and she remembered that her first time round she'd had to stand on tiptoes to see through; this time, she could look right in.

The room was the same, wide but not deep, with glaring, unadorned bulbs casting the room in a harsh, unforgiving light. Staggered wooden tiers stretched the width of the room, like baseball bleachers or a section of Roman amphitheater peering down at gladiatorial blood sports.

There was a birdcage hanging on a hook from the ceiling beside the wooden tiers. Within it perched a shiny black bird with a bright orange bill, chattering along in Thai, and Colleen found herself thinking the same absurd thought she had at ten—

*Boy, that's one smart bird, speaking a foreign language.*

Perched sitting on the tiers were rows of fragile young women and pale, delicate boys, some in shorts and tight T-shirts or bathing suits, some in frilly nightwear. Each held a piece of white cardboard before them with a number written on it.

As a child, seeing these pale, underfed women and boys, with their blank, apathetic faces, she had been confounded by what they might be doing there, although even then the frank air of carnality and commerce made something churn in the pit of her stomach.

But now, she knew them for what they were, understood that beyond the inner side door would be a long hall with tiny, unadorned rooms like monks' cells, a narrow, worn bed in each.

*Pick a number, just like a deli,* she thought with distaste.

It was the same, exactly the same as she remembered it. But then she saw the one thing different, the dissonance that made the sweat on her skin go clammy, made her heart skip a beat.

There was an old woman, an old Asian woman, sitting dead center on the middle tier among all the others, the bored ones waiting to be picked, if only for the variety, the change in the tedium.

*She* hadn't been here before, not the first time around, Colleen was sure of it—*and the woman was looking dead at her.*

Although she was about the age of Mama Diamond, of her race and coloring, with eyes that held a similar alertness, this woman had none of the other's kindness nor regard. She was all hard edges and coldness. She rose from her place on the tier, took several small, precise steps to floor level and approached.

Colleen felt the hairs on her neck rise, felt the jolt of adrenaline hit her heart, her pulse quicken. She felt the strong urge to run, but instead drew her machete. When it came to fight or flight, she generally found herself of the fight variety.

*Let's see how dumb a decision that is this time.*

The Asian woman drew near within the room, reached the door and, rather than opening it, was suddenly just *on* the other side, out in the sticky night air.

"You shouldn't be here, little girl," the woman said with a lightness that made it all the more ominous.

"Who are you?" Colleen replied, and fought to keep her voice even. "I don't know you."

Up close, she could see that the texture of the old woman's lined parchment skin was odd, composed of a subtle, transient energy that flickered like galaxies of stars blinking on and off, endlessly extinguished and reborn.

"Funny . . ." the old woman said absently, glancing about at the street rather than at Colleen. "I—we—I"—she seemed to be having trouble with pronouns—"was actually here, you know, at about this period. I fled the Cultural Revolution . . . dreadful times, the savagery, the destruction. . . . My own father was beheaded by the white-boned demon."

There was a sense of all this being said distantly—mere ghosts of memory, shreds of feeling and expression—an old tape playing, not the least connected to how this women (or whatever she truly was) existed now.

Then the old woman focused on Colleen and, for the briefest moment, Colleen thought she could discern sympathy in those eyes, the fleeting scrutiny of someone both kindly and human.

"Fear is what drives this world, my dear," the apparition whispered, "fear and the remorseless need for *security*. . . ."

Her eyes slid away and all emotion drained, replaced by that dreamy, distant quality.

"I came to this sewer," the woman-thing said. "I did what I had to, I *survived*." She said this last with the faintest echo of defensiveness, guiltily, as if Colleen might well have grounds to accuse her.

"Who are you?" Colleen repeated.

"Agnes Wu," the old woman responded. But once more, she seemed to be speaking by rote, as though the answer held no meaning, the syllables in an unknown language, mere nonsense sounds.

Colleen recognized the name. It was on the list of Source scientists Cal carried with him, copied off the one Larry Shango had shown them, that Shango had found hidden alongside the corpse of Jeri Bilmer.

*So now I've met two of the bigwigs who fucked up the world,* Colleen thought, Wu here and Fred Wishart back in Boone's Gap—and neither of them human anymore. Wishart must be around here somewhere, too, and how many of those other clowns?

Beyond that, and far more important to her, Doc and Cal and dammit even fucking irritating Herman Goldman, too, not to mention Enid and Howie, Shango and Mama Diamond, somewhere nearby, she *knew* it. But how to find them in this maze of conjured memory, this shell game of misdirection and illusion?

"You're in a bit of a predicament, my dear," Agnes Wu said with the cool aplomb of a Bengal tiger stalking a gazelle. "Can't go forward, and can't go back."

"So where's that leave me?" Colleen asked, her hand tightening on the machete.

"Where does that leave anyone?" Agnes Wu asked philosophically.

The clamorous Thai music from within shifted to a throbbing disco beat, and the words blared out through the glass. "Stayin' alive, stayin' alive . . ."

Agnes Wu's placid features twisted into a mask of rage that for a moment was *another* face, an old man's face Colleen did not recognize, pale and thin, with sightless eyes blank as eggshell.

"I *hate* that song!" the Agnes Wu thing spat, and reached out to Colleen with a hand that was a hand no longer but instead a churning mass of multihued energy, a vortex of will and nothingness that Colleen could feel pulling her toward it, inhaling her like a drowning man breaching the surface of the sea.

And in the midst of this, in some distant-observer part of her mind, Colleen got a visceral flash, an instant-message comprehension, that while the memories presented might be Agnes Wu—at least drawn from her consciousness—the homicidal rage erupting from behind the façade seemed dissonantly *someone else*. That pallid blind man perhaps, in all or part; if not a puppet master, a dominant awareness . . .

With a cry, Colleen grasped her machete in both hands and brought it down hard across Agnes Wu, hacking her from shoulder to hip in a move that would have sundered her in two had she been composed of meat and bone and blood, or any material that could be so affected.

But it was like trying to cut lightning, like severing smoke. It had no effect at all, except possibly pissing off the thing that was Agnes Wu—or was composed partially of her—even more than she was previously.

The abomination gave a hideous, deafening roar that shook the ground and sky and all its stars. Its force hurled Colleen windmilling back, struggling to maintain her balance—which is what saved her ass, in the long run. For as she flailed wildly to stay on her feet as she was driven backward, her arm glanced against a wall, which *shrieked* and flinched away.

*Now*, that's *interesting*, Colleen reflected.

Agnes Wu was striding toward her and she didn't really look human anymore, unless humans were made of the molten hearts of suns, made of reactor cores in full meltdown. Colleen could feel her skin sunburning as she faced her, her eyes crisping like she was peering into the fires of hell. She turned quickly away and plunged her arm again into the wall. Her bare hand hit blunt stone, was turned aside, but where her arm glanced the wall, the brick surface rippled and screamed and irised away.

*It's the armor,* Colleen realized, the armor of dragon skin that Doc, Lord bless him, had made for her and Cal and Shango. Just like the scale that had burnt Clayton Devine, that crazed, homicidal half-flare, back in Chicago when Colleen had pressed it into his flesh, the armor was doing the exact same thing here.

Because—as that bloody, horrific explosion had so clearly demonstrated just minutes before—*the walls and doors and everything else here were made of flares.*

With the possible—no, make that *probable*—exception of Dr. Agnes Wu, who was bearing down on her right about now with all the loving tenderness of a rabid Mack truck.

Not wanting to test the proposition at this juncture, not in the least, not one little bit, thank you very much, Colleen finally chose the *flight* side of the equation and threw herself bodily at the wall. As the armor encasing her legs and torso connected with the hard brick, the wall let out a wail of pain and opened up. She passed clean through like a knife through butter, like a B-52 through a cloudy sky, and was gone. It sealed up behind her, a fast-healing wound.

Colleen found herself on the other side, not Bangkok or New York but rather an undifferentiated area, murky and dim. The floor under her feet was substantial, however, and as she moved forward she noted that the matter in the air—not fog, precisely, denser and more still—avoided touching her, shrank away as she pressed through. Keeping an eye on the path behind her, just in case Agnes Wu or whatever it was took a notion to come after her (which thankfully, she did not), Colleen slowly advanced.

She discovered that by waving her arms in a broad arc, she could clear a bit of space around her, actually get a look at where she was. She saw now that she was in a vast corridor hewn from solid stone, blasted out of the rock itself. Not like a cavern, nor a mine, either, it was puzzling. She noted there were porcelain panels set in the walls, with writing on them. But in the dim illumination from the fog, she couldn't make out the words.

She reached out and touched the rock wall, found to her relief it stayed solid and silent. It was *real,* or as real as anything could presume to be nowadays, which was about as far as you could throw it.

But no, she corrected herself, what she felt for Viktor was more real than that. He had made her wear this freaking armor against all her protestations, her contrariness. He had saved her.

She longed to see his gray, forgiving eyes, his knowing, sad smile, feel the tentative sureness of that touch that unmanned her, that made her small again and opened her heart like a surgeon's scalpel that would only heal and not harm.

And unlike the fraudulent tissue structure overlaying some twisted armature that would have been the likeness of her father had she reached the end of Soi Cowboy, she knew that when she found Viktor (and she *would* find him, and the others, too, get them the hell out of here, if it could be humanly done), he would be *alive* and present and no mocking ghost.

Her arms waving like some crazed Leopold Stokowski on speed, Colleen Brooks made her way down the vast corridor of stone, the murky thick air around her—that had once been fragile young women and pale, delicate boys—clearing a path before her.

# THIRTY-NINE

## The Dacha by the Sea

"Wake up, Viktor," the sweet, soft voice said, and he felt a caress on his cheek. "You've been dreaming."

It was only as he opened his eyes that Doc Lysenko realized she had been speaking Russian.

She filled his field of vision, she was that close, peering down at him lovingly, with him all the world to her.

That tangle of auburn hair was unmistakable, the long, long lashes, those incredible, unforgettable eyes, darkest green with flecks of gold in them, like sunlight casting through dense leaf cover onto a forest floor.

It was Yelena.

"This is not real," Doc said in alarm, sitting up, throwing back the covers. He, too, was speaking Russian.

"Sh, sh, my love," Yelena said, kissing his cheeks and brow, touching him with light fingers like a whisper. Oh God, it was familiar, so precisely right. He realized with a shock how much he had forgotten, and now remembered.

"Nurya . . . ?" he whispered in a croak, the pain like an icicle from a Moscow winter thrust into his heart.

"In the other room, of course, asleep. It's early." She drew him out of the bed, enfolded him in the thick sable robe she had bought him in Odessa on their third anniversary. He saw that she was wearing the pale shift he so loved. She pulled her hair back into a ponytail—which only made her features all the more elegant and refined—and secured it with a band.

"Come," she said, taking his hand. "Let's step outside, to the beach."

"No . . ." he protested weakly, and felt his own consciousness dimly, or rather as if everything that had come before was growing dim, retreating from him despite all his efforts to hold on to it.

He pulled away from her languorous grasp, stepped out of the bedroom into the common room, with its fireplace of the twelve massive stones quarried from near the Sea of Azov. He knew this place well, felt overwhelmed by the sensation of returning home, of nostalgia like a consuming wave.

*This is what it is like to die*, he thought, to be lost in an embrace.

Ignoring her whispered entreaties, he strode to the opposite bedroom and eased open the door. In the darkness within, a small figure lay bunched under the covers. Hesitantly, his breath held like a treasure within him, he approached the bedside and peered at the tiny form. Her face was pressed into the down pillows, and she wore a frown line between her brows as though concentrating on life's deepest dilemma. But she still looked every bit an angel.

Yelena was behind him now, her gentling hands on his shoulders. "She's fine, she's perfectly well," she assured him, her breath soft as memory in his ear. "Don't you dare wake her."

He turned to his wife, and she shimmered through the wetness of his eyes. "Goodness, Viktor, you act as if we'd been gone an eternity. Come, let's see the dawn."

He let her lead him then, to dress him in his summer clothes of linen, his soft hide sandals. The two of them emerged out onto the fine white sand, he and the woman who was his bride. The sun was warm even though it was the break of day, the wind mild and salt fragrant. They were alone on the beach, all the other gingerbread cottages closed up tight, the world at peace. He looked out at the sea that stretched forever, the gentle waves lapping like God welcoming a road-worn pilgrim, a prodigal son.

They were at the dacha on the shores of the Black Sea, their summer idyll when Yelena had persuaded him reluctantly to go on vacation, to set aside his crushing workload at the hospital in Kiev, to fob it off on other, equally competent (although not quite so gifted) doctors.

It was an impossible luxury for most physicians, he knew, but then Yelena's father was high up in the Party, and it was the family retreat, had been since the days of Stalin and Molotov, before the Great Patriotic War and the frozen dead of Stalingrad.

A seabird called from on high, and he looked into the rosy, lightening sky to see the gull hovering overhead, could make out the perfection of its outstretched wings, the ordered rows of its feathers. It floated bobbing on the currents of air, then folded its wings and plunged like a spike driving down, crashing into the water, sending a spray flying upward as it speared a fish and gobbled it down.

*I have seen that movement before,* Doc thought, but it had been no bird and its prey no fish, but something of considerably more weight and moment.

He tried to call up the image of those dark forms and found them elusive, could not summon them in his mind's eye. It filled him with dread closing on panic. But even as the feeling speared up within him, he felt it damped down and muffled, as if from some will outside his own.

Vague forms and structures moved within his mind, the towers of foreign buildings, faces he felt should be familiar but were alien and born of far lands.

Not now, but belonging to another time, one that was paradoxically both future and past, in a time beyond the horror that was to come. It was all receding from him, misting away. He felt a sense of desperate unreality, and suddenly did not know whether it was the present moment or the insistent call of memory that was unreal.

Yelena was studying him, the ocean breeze playing with her hair, and her smile was sympathetic and sad. "You look so weary, my love. It's good you'll be able to rest here."

And, dear God, he felt that, too. So good to be here, to release the grief, the demand of duty, of obligation to others. To relax into ease and comfort and belonging, like floating on the warm, forgiving sea.

No, something inside proclaimed to him. *You get your fucking ass out of there right now, Doc Lysenko.*

It was a voice that spoke in his heart, an American voice, a woman's voice.

*Boi Baba . . .*

"I cannot remain here," he murmured to the exquisite, serene woman beside him. He began stumbling away, along the lip of the ocean, his sandals pressing into the damp sand as the foam retreated back from him into the waves.

Yelena moved quickly to overtake him, stood blocking his way. Her eyes were no less loving, but more firm as she held him in her gaze.

"You had a dream, Viktor," she said, not unkindly, "and in your dream we died, Nurya and I, and you were a refugee washed up onto a distant shore, and the world died, too. . . ."

"*No,*" he breathed, and could not have said whether he was denying that it was a dream or that it was so.

"Is that the world you want, Viktor? A world of corpses? Or *this,* to be with the living?"

But it hadn't been just a world of the dead. There had been *someone,* someone who had brought him back to life, when he himself had been the walking dead.

*Why could he not remember her name?*

Yelena drew close to him, and he let her kiss him on the lips. He felt her living breath, felt the perfume of her, the promise with no hint of the grave.

"It is no accident that we are here," she said, and the emphasis she put on the word "accident" made him shiver and called up a distant echo of tires shrieking as they lost their grip on a rain-sheened road, the roar of a stream that was too swift, too deep, and too hungry, of two bodies he once had forced himself to identify.

Her caress banished the phantoms. "We're safe here," she said. "No harm can come to us."

"And why is that?" he said, a tremor of cold running through him despite the warmth on his skin.

"Maybe there is one who provides you sanctuary, whose name we cannot speak . . . but who wishes you well."

*Wish . . . ?*

Wishart.

The name blossomed in his mind but meant nothing to him, although he felt it should.

But named or not, that was how power worked, how it always worked. Without that protection, that favor, all you loved could be washed away as casually, as disdainfully as skid marks off a road.

*Sanctuary . . .*

He could stay here, wrap the sea about him like a winding sheet, entomb himself in safety within this eternal moment, embrace and become like these two he loved.

But then, that was hardly a new sensation, a fresh novelty. No, if anything, it was the state that long years had made familiar to him, a decision he had chosen before the earth on two graves had grown smooth and cold.

Before a young man and woman had sought him out to help a little girl, before they and a wild-eyed mystic had called him back from his torpor, back to an existence of uncertainty and hope and pain.

*Wouldn't you rather be with the living?*

Yelena stroked his cheek and smiled again. "I'll make you breakfast. We'll rouse Nurya. Wouldn't you like that?"

He made to speak, to voice a question, but suddenly there was a tearing sound, and he turned from her to look outward.

There was a woman there, clothed in scaly black leather garments, a black helmet crowning her. She held a machete, and a multiplicity of other weapons draped across her back and hung from belts and bandoliers. Behind her, a ragged tear in the sky was sealing up. He supposed she had done that with the machete.

She was standing on the ocean.

And in that moment, Viktor felt a door close in him, and it was a good closing, not a forgetting but definitely an ending. He let out his breath, a release, and felt himself relax into ease and comfort and belonging, like floating on the warm, forgiving sea.

"Time for me to go," he said to Yelena, and it surprised him only a little how easy it was to make his decision.

He found that he himself could not walk on water, so he splashed out to the ludicrously armored woman in the warm surf. He grabbed her hand, and she hauled him up to her level.

Before she led him out of there, he felt a giddy urge to turn back to Yelena (who still stood there watching him, and had not yet changed into a Gorgon or the goddess Kali or any other improbable thing that was indisputably *not* Yelena) and shout back, *This is my American girlfriend!*

But he only had so much tolerance for the absurd.

# FORTY

## Goldman in the Glory

"Save your hate for the Source," Magritte had told Herman Goldman way back when, in Howard Russo's dusky apartment on the outskirts of Chicago.

Her subsequent, pointless death had given him formidable reason to build that hate into an edifice more towering than the fortress deranged Primal had erected against the Source; to nurture and preserve it as a focal element that could unleash his power in all its terrible wrath.

Now at long last, he was finally where he could do something about it.

Scant moments before, the place had looked precisely like New York. But it *wasn't* New York; hell, he could've told that with his eyes closed, could have told it Ray Charles blind, because the music of the Source, that jangly, Village-of-the-Damned, ninth-level-of-Hell swarm of voices, that white-hot electric wire that had been jabbed into his brain and reeling him in ever since before the Change, was shrieking like God Himself was Ethel Merman being tortured.

Radio Goldman was *definitely* on the air.

He had been saving up his pennies, putting any number of items into his portmanteau of juju, for just for this occasion.

Now he just had to zone in on the insane, beating heart of it, really put the *home* in homicide.

When Tina and Cal's mock apartment did its little rumba number and sent him flying Adidas over Stetson, spinning him round and round like a Protein Berry smoothie in a Jamba Juice blender, the lights had gone out for the briefest instant, only to come up again like a curtain rising on this fresh and utterly diverting little vacation spot.

Still South Dakota, he told himself, even if it looked anything but . . .

Nevertheless, he did not recognize the new digs. Unlike the Manhattan apartment, which he knew must've been derived from either Cal's or Tina's memory, this scenery was nothing cobbled from *his* database.

Postcard lovely, though, with its beachfront of faded grand hotels like a chorus line of dowagers, the bulky forties American cars plying their way down the streets, the olive-and-cocoa-skinned men and women bustling along the sidewalks, the lilt of Spanish floating from every window.

Somewhere in the Tropics? Undoubtedly . . . but not any time around now. This was a scene from fifty years ago, and more.

"Quaint . . . but I call it home," a voice behind him said languidly.

Goldie turned, and commanded himself not to drop his jaw.

The face was familiar, and the horns, too, not to mention the tail.

*Better the Devil you know . . .*

He looked exactly as he had when first he'd appeared in Goldie's classroom dog years back, when he'd levitated the classroom and engaged Herman Goldman in a week's worth of frothy debate and badinage.

With one staggering difference—*that* particular fallen gentleman had been a projection of Goldie's mind, he knew that, had even somewhat known it at the time, no more a distinct individual than a ventriloquist's dummy or an American President.

But *this* Red Boy, well now, he might *look* the same, but what was under the hood was another story altogether.

For while the face was familiar, filched from the well-fertilized fields of Herman Goldman's frontal lobes, the Foul Fiend smiling back at him was a complete and utter stranger.

Not the real Devil, certainly, any more than he'd be the real Santa

Claus or Easter Bunny (though they might be arriving on the scene anytime now, no telling). And the fact that he was smoking what Goldie's finely tuned nostrils identified as a Pall Mall and gazing at him with blind, milky-white eyes (although he seemed perfectly able to see him) only gave further proof, if that were needed.

"Who's in charge here?" Goldie asked.

"Batista," the other replied, gazing out at the passing parade. His voice held the faintest trace of accent, cultured and lilting, caught more in the rhythms than the pronunciation.

"Very funny," Goldie said. "You wanna tell me whose past we're looking at here?"

Somewhere a band was striking up "Manteca," a jazzy little Afro-Cuban number Goldman had first heard on a musty Dizzy Gillespie LP his dad had stowed long ago in their attic. The other inclined his head, as if to catch it better.

"Quantum physics teaches us that the space between particles is more real than the particles themselves," the apparition said dreamily. "That everything material is an illusion, beauty included, *especially* beauty."

He drew the smoke deep into his lungs and held it there, gestured out at the buildings with his cigarette. "An elegant façade, nothing more . . . one that can be blasted apart by a hurricane or an errant thought."

He brought his cold coffin eyes to look on Goldman once more. "I was a busboy here, in the Hotel Nacional . . . being spat on, cleaning the vomit of the *turistas Americano,* when their bored wives—as high strung and finely bred as racehorses—were not giving me their loving attentions . . . while their husbands practiced free trade in the casinos."

"Y'know, I just can't see the Prince of Darkness moonlighting as a busboy," Goldie observed. "Howzabout we take off the mask?"

"I will if you will, Mr. Goldman."

Now, *that* sent a Popsicle straight up the old backbone. Not that it should be that much of a surprise, though, if this clown could peruse folks' gray matter like strolling the aisles at Wal-Mart. . . .

*Only how much has he been shoplifting?*

Goldie tried for an offhanded manner. "Mine doesn't come off, try as I might."

The other shrugged as if discarding an overcoat draped over his shoulders, and with no seeming transition he was suddenly human, or appeared so; a pale, lean man with sickly white hair and long, nicotine-stained fingers holding the same cigarette, appraising the world with the same blind eyes.

"How'd you get from here to South Dakota?" Goldie asked, figuring he might as well advance a few more feet along the tightrope, try to glean as much as he could.

"An itinerant lecturer passing through on sabbatical recognized this untouchable, this invisible one with the phenomenal gift for numbers, for abstract thought. Was it any more unlikely than Einstein working as a patent clerk? No, although I was somewhat more striking than dear Albert, more *compliant*. . . . And so I was spirited away to Cornell and the Ivory Tower."

Goldie found his mouth was dry. He licked his lips, tried to keep his voice level. "You know *my* name . . ." he prompted.

The corner of the other's mouth lifted in the barest trace of a smile. "In life, I was known as Marcus Sanrio . . .."

Bingo, a moniker right off the list of Source Project mucky-mucks, *director* of the whole nine yards, in fact.

It may not have been Hawaii, Goldie realized, but he felt a vibrating certainty within himself (like that endless chord on *Sergeant Pepper's*) that odds-on he was talking to the Big Kahuna himself. No floating green head with a man behind the curtain, but the man himself.

"So I'll ask again," Goldie repeated, striving to sound casual, to sound anything but what he truly was. "Who's in charge here?"

Sanrio looked off into the distance and considered; not the answer, Goldie realized, but whether to answer at all. He parted his lips, and let the ghost vapor of the cigarette curl lazily from his mouth, the smoke gray-white like his empty dead eyes.

"It's a collective, of a sort," he said languorously, at last. "But as for the governing aesthetic . . . you could say that it's mine."

Bingo again.

So the only question now, Herman Goldman knew, was how best to kill him.

# FORTY-ONE

## The Time of Blood and Storm

*It's like tearing through different flats on a theater stage,* Cal Griffin thought, ripping away layer after layer of illusion.

Along with Inigo and Tina (who still stared blankly at him, seeming not to recognize him at all), Cal had managed to utilize his armor to burst through the barriers and reunite them with Colleen and Doc, then reach Mama Diamond, Howard Russo and Enid Blindman. As he suspected, they weren't far apart at all, just separated by walls of different settings, like themed rooms at some fantasy hotel.

So now here they were, Cal and Colleen in the lead, bursting through tiers of unreality in search of Larry Shango and Goldie.

"Cripes, what's the deal here?" moaned Howie. "I mean, why not just kill us and get it over with? I do *not* need to be seeing that 1976 production of *The Fantasticks* again."

"Old Devil likes his games, Howie," said Enid. "But don't you be dissin' it. We still breathin' here."

"It seems to be rooting around in our minds," offered Mama Diamond. "Searching out the threat to it there."

*True enough,* thought Cal. But given what Doc and Colleen had told him of their forays in mock Russia and Thailand (Mama Diamond pointedly choosing *not* to share what picture postcard had been summoned from *her* memory; Cal's quick glimpse of it revealing only that it looked like some kind of prisoner camp), the answer seemed more complex, the motivation and purpose of what set the scene and manipulated the players more diverse. Perhaps the Consciousness at the Source was *not* simply homogenous malaise in a bottle; maybe there were majority and minority opinions at work here, discrepancies and deviations. . . .

"You got an opinion on this?" Cal asked Inigo.

Inigo looked furtive, hunched his shoulders. "I don't ask questions."

"Yup," Howie agreed, "that's always served me pretty well, kid—leastways, till *now*. . . ." He shot Inigo a grin.

Cal caught the look of gratitude on the boy's face, of recognition; the two grunters were outcasts both, even among their own kind.

Abruptly, they punched through to Goldie. He was standing beneath the swaying palms on a bustling, old-fashioned resort street, talking to a lanky old man blanched as an albino.

Cal heard Inigo suck in his breath. "Aw, *man* . . ." He sounded profoundly dismayed.

"It's the second blind man," Tina murmured, gazing at the old man. She turned her face to Enid and whispered enigmatically, "You're the third." Cal wondered who the first might be, and had an inkling he just might know.

"Who is that?" Cal asked Inigo.

"Sanrio," Inigo said.

Cal shot Doc and Colleen a glance; they all knew that name from the list.

"Is he real?" Doc asked.

"That's kinda complicated," Inigo replied. "But yeah, mostly. Listen, we gotta get outta here before he spots us."

But it was already too late. Cal saw that Sanrio had raised his head and spied them. Sanrio canted his head upward, as if in silent supplication, both a prayer and a summons.

A tumult rose up from ahead of them, insane shrieks of rage and belligerence, growing in volume.

Cal motioned for Colleen to flank him. "Get behind us," he told the others; his and Colleen's armor would help shield them from whatever the flare matter formed itself into.

"Goldie, get over here!" Cal cried out. Goldman seemed frozen in place beside the pale figure.

Abruptly, the buildings and sky and people *shivered*, and hunched, muscled figures burst through, screeching hideously and rushing toward Cal and the others.

Grunters, hundreds and hundreds of them.

"Hoo boy, some time for a family reunion," moaned Howard Russo.

"They're real," said Inigo.

"Yeah, I figured that," Cal said, drawing his sword while the others unslung their rifles and Howie pulled the Tech Nine from his belt. Cal glanced over to Goldie, just in time to see him rush up to Sanrio and embrace him.

Cal heard him scream as the world exploded in light.

Too late, far too late, Herman Goldman realized that something was terribly wrong, that he had miscalculated and this pillar of fire he was embracing, this mocking dark entity, was not Marcus Sanrio at all, at least not his physical self, but merely a projection, like the voice at the end of a telephone line, and Goldie could no more kill him than smacking a receiver against a wall would give the caller a concussion.

But hell, that didn't mean taking a bath with the phone couldn't electrocute *you*.

He had intended to draw all the power out of Sanrio, had in his hubris assumed he could do it as readily as he had sucked the ability out of that E-ticket Bitch Queen, and then hurl Marcus Sanrio into the distant reaches of nothingness, where he could be one with the space between particles until hell froze over and there were no innocent fragile ones for him to fuck with anymore.

But instead, grasping this radiant nonbeing, it felt to Goldie pretty much like someone had thrown lighter fluid on the hibachi of his mind and dropped a match.

The last conscious thought he had was, *Oh Magritte, forgive me. . . .*

But if there was an answer, he didn't hear it.

"*No!*" Cal shouted, and ran forward as Goldman fell. The others were right behind him. His eyes still strobing from the flash, Cal saw that the army of grunters had halted in their charge, too, blinded and momentarily dazed.

Goldie lay crumpled on the ground, his straw cowboy hat fallen away. His eyes were rolled back, unseeing. Currents of energy were coursing and snapping all over his clothing and skin, making the hair on his head snake about as in a blow dryer; in fact, his hair was the only part of him that seemed even remotely alive.

There was no sign of Sanrio, or whatever part of Sanrio had been there.

Doc bent beside the still form, reaching out a hand to touch his neck.

"Be careful, Viktor," Colleen urged.

His fingers grazed Goldie's carotid artery, and Cal could hear the arc of electricity as it bit at Doc. Doc winced, but kept to his task.

"No pulse," he said, ashen.

"Get back," Cal said and pulled Doc clear, for he saw now that the energy was surging up to envelop Goldie entirely. In an instant, there was nothing to be seen of him but the manic light playing all over his body. Then all of a sudden, he crumpled in on himself and turned to winking bits of dust, which the air seized and whirled away.

He was gone.

"Oh, dear God," Colleen breathed, and Cal could hear her voice crack.

Then, with a cry that tore at their ears, the grunters were upon them. Cal drew Christina behind him, and turned to face the foul creatures, sheathing his sword and unslinging his rifle. He saw that Howard Russo was likewise shielding Inigo.

Colleen and Doc began firing, then Howie, too. Cal joined in their fusillade, choosing his targets, firing again and again, as the tang of gunpowder stung his nostrils and gray smoke swirled about them. White anger rose up in him, for what had been done to his sister, to Goldie, to all of them, and he felt a savage, guilty pleasure as the bullets found their mark, tore meat and gristle and flesh away from the brutes. Shrieks of agony rent the air, and blood was everywhere. The grunters that weren't hit slowed in their advance but did not stop.

Enid was firing, too, and made a curious sight, rifle leveled and guitar slung over his back. Cal noticed that Enid's gun had a fixed bayonet; he knew that blade well. Enid had wielded it back in Chicago, and told Cal of its heritage—Enid's great-grandfather, the Lakota warrior Soldier Heart, had taken it off a cavalryman at the Little Big Horn.

Cal glanced at Inigo and saw that the boy was baring his teeth and growling at their attackers, his muscles taut steel waiting to spring. Cal put a hand on the boy's shoulder, restraining him.

"Not yet," he said. Inigo mastered himself, and nodded.

As for Mama Diamond, Cal could see that she held no weapon but was instead speaking in a low voice to several grunters who faced her. He couldn't make out the words, but saw to his amazement that the grunters she was addressing were backing away from her in terror. Now wasn't *that* interesting. . . .

They kept firing until their ammo was gone, and *still* the little monsters kept coming, until it was close work now. Cal swung his sword in wide, practiced arcs as the others wielded machete and crossbow and razor, and whatever else came to hand. The grunters, for their part, brought their hideous strength to bear, reaching out with long arms to claw, darting their heads in with gaping, snapping mouths full of scalpel teeth.

Cal realized that he and his companions were outnumbered ten to one, that the grunters were driving them relentlessly back, until their backs were literally to the wall. Cal kept Christina (who was staring out in mute horror) behind him. It occurred to him that the grunters were making no effort to reach her, as if somehow she were exempt, or of a nature they preferred not to come in contact with.

Cal unleashed Inigo at the last and the boy threw himself into the fray with fang and claw, fighting with surprising ferocity. But he was clearly outmatched.

Three of the grunters leapt at Cal, brought him down hard. His sword went skidding away along the ground. They tore off his helmet, shredded the rough leather leggings and tunic over his clothes and ripped them away.

"Get the hell *off* me, you little creeps!" Colleen cried from nearby.

Out of his peripheral vision, Cal could see they were doing the same to her, deliberately stripping her of the dragon armor.

As *if they were ordered to.*

Cal rolled and managed to throw the fiends off himself, scrambled for his sword and brought it home into the neck of one as it again leapt at him. He then dove for Colleen, kicking and slicing at her attackers, sending them scurrying away.

But then more were on them, burying them, hauling them down again. All Cal could see now were grunters in closer detail than any sane person would ever want to, their foul breath filling his lungs and nostrils. From the cries of Doc and Enid and Howie, and even Mama Diamond now, he assumed the same was true of them.

Suddenly, Cal heard a new commotion from some distance away, low squeals and shouts of pain, bones cracking. The grunters grappling with him paused to look up, and Cal did, too.

Larry Shango, grunters hanging off his arms and from around his neck, his armor torn clean away, was wading into the mass of grunters, hammer flailing. He pulled several clear off Doc and Mama Diamond, hurled them into a mass of their fellows.

Then he threw the homemade grenade at them.

It exploded magnificently, made mincemeat of them.

And okay, so maybe it was a double standard and, unlike their moment of horror with the flares, they felt little squeamishness about blasting these puny bastards to smithereens. But then, these guys were just plain *nasty.*

Shango, his face sweaty and glorious, turned to face the grunters still wrestling with Cal and Colleen, with Howie and Inigo and Enid.

"You want the same?" he cried, a god of serene fury. "That can be arranged."

As one, the grunters released their prey and took off running, straight at the buildings. They connected with the stone façades, went right on through and were gone.

Shango helped Mama Diamond to her feet. "You all right, ma'am?"

"Yes, thank you," she replied. Shango looked about at the others, who were on their feet now, bloody and breathing hard but intact.

Taking count, he said, "Where's Goldman?"

Cal felt grief flood over him anew, was about to speak when suddenly there was a voice in his head, human and inhuman at once, incredibly powerful and malign.

MEMORIES HOLD POWER. . . .

He gasped with the intensity of it, saw from the pain on the faces of his companions that they'd heard it, too.

He had known such a voice before; it had been Fred Wishart's mind speaking to him in that devastated house back in Boone's Gap, before Tina was spirited away.

This held some of Wishart in it, Cal could detect that, and others, too. But the main will, the dominant force of it, was someone far different.

*The second blind man . . .*

I WAS TWELVE WHEN THE ONE IN '44 BLEW THROUGH HAVANA, it added, and even its thoughts held that distinctive Spanish lilt. LIKE A LIVING, MALEVOLENT THING COME TO RULE THE WORLD. . . .

*He's talking about a storm, a hurricane,* Cal realized with a growing sense of dread. He looked at the others, at Colleen and Shango, and his own unshielded self. *We have no armor.*

Then the mind that was Marcus Sanrio—and myriads and complexities far beyond—said, BUT WHY TELL YOU WHEN I CAN SHOW YOU?

Cal heard a roar like the soul of the world splitting in two. He turned toward the beach. The sky was black with storm clouds, and the sea was rising up to meet it.

It reached out and seized them.

*It's not touching me,* Christina thought with a strange, calm horror. *It's not touching me at all.*

But the storm was killing the others.

The rain and wind tore off the face of the ocean like a murderous Fury, blasting up onto the shore, tearing away the palm trees, hurling cars aside, ripping away awnings and knocking buildings to their knees, scattering the bodies of the dead grunters, and the living humans and Inigo, too. It reminded her of films she'd seen as a child, of the blast wave of nuclear explosions.

Then the wavefront came, rising up off the water a hundred feet and more, crashing down onto the land, flooding the street with foaming, turbulent mayhem. The level of the water was high above her, yet she felt none of its force, could breathe just fine.

*I shouldn't be able to do this,* she thought. *It's not human.*

And then the thought came to her, suddenly, shockingly—

*But then, I'm not human.*

Through the churning, deadly water, she could see the others slammed and tumbled like rocks carried along in the rapids to smash against boulders and shatter, their mouths opened in silent screams, the air bubbling out of them. They were drowning, all of them—Inigo, and the powerful black man and old Asian woman, the guitar player and the little gray man, and the younger woman and the Russian man, too.

And Cal.

Oh God, it all came back to her in a flash, like a curtain torn away, dawnlight cutting through the night. The one she had been waiting for all this time, the one she could not call to mind, no matter how hard she tried. Not the dragon man in black, nor Sanrio or Pollard, Sakamoto or Wu, nor any of the other shadows that peered over her shoulder . . .

But her brother.

*I'm not gonna leave you,* Cal had told her long ago in their apartment that was the *real* one, not the one that was just exactly the same.

And he *hadn't,* he was here, finally, at last he had *found* her. . . .

Only to die before her eyes.

By the will of the Thing that was driven by Sanrio, whose attention was away from her now, she understood, distracted by his whim of maelstrom, so that finally her mind could clear. . . .

Cal was gasping and flailing, spinning in the murderous flood, helpless in its power, the power of those ones—

Just like herself.

She looked down at her hands, her *human* hands, and knew this outward form that had so assuaged and comforted her was a fiction she could no longer afford. She reached down into herself, searching, and found the dissonance, the alien music she had deafened herself to for time without mind. She embraced it, called it forth and opened herself to it.

The radiance blossomed within her.

She could see her fingers elongating and losing their color, the nails vanishing, and felt a lightness in herself that might have been mistaken for a body floating in water but which she knew was weightlessness of another kind. It filled her with despair and joy.

The corona about her flared to life, flowing with power and brilliance and certainty. She reached out with her mind, and the nimbus about her extended to encompass the others and draw them back to her. Looking out with her azure eyes, her face bloodless and wreathed in hair of palest silk, she merely had to will the water to keep back, and it was so.

The human ones, and the boy Inigo and the gray man who were neither human nor like her, slumped in on themselves, all water fled from them, gasping in great lungfuls of air, reclaiming their lives.

She held her brother in her arms, like a mother with a child, and kissed his fair, soft hair.

"I'm not gonna leave you," she said, and for the first time in a long time she knew truly where she was.

She was home.

# FORTY-TWO

## The Rubble Field

The zone of Christina's aura that enveloped them was so bright, with its shifting pastels, its mesmerizing, kaleidoscopic play of patterns, that for a good long time they couldn't see what, if anything, lay beyond it.

Cal still held her, or rather they held each other. With infinite tenderness he said to her, "We need to see outside, Tin—Christina." Cal had told them all of her requested change of name, and he was working hard to get used to it.

Christina nodded, and inclined her head. The aura's radiance shifted from opacity to a hazy transparency. Now they could see that beyond it stretched an open, bare area, which faded off to dim insubstantiality.

It seemed that Sanrio had withdrawn, at least for now, and taken with him any attempt to create the illusion of a coherent environment.

"Hey, it's an improvement," Colleen said. "At least, nothing's trying to kill us." Her expression suddenly darkened, and Cal knew that she, like all of them, was thinking of Goldie.

"We have to find a way out of here," Cal observed. "Before he has time to remarshal his forces."

"I agree, Calvin," said Doc. "But I don't recall seeing any exit signs recently."

"How about you, Pathfinder?" Colleen asked Inigo. "You got any helpful hints about now?"

"His name's Inigo," Christina said, sharpness in her voice.

"Right, right," Colleen replied, abashed. "Sorry."

"There's this tunnel . . ." Inigo suggested tentatively. "But it's not a great bet."

"Show us," said Cal.

Inigo led them down a sharp incline that led deeper and deeper, until they could all feel the suffocating weight of the earth, the countless tons of stone above them.

"I know this may sound funny, all things considered," Howie rasped, "but I've always been *majorly* claustrophobic. . . ."

"I've heard better," said Colleen. She knew from the cramped, bent-over way the passage was forcing her to walk that her back would be killing her come nighttime.

*If they survived till then* . . .

Mama Diamond was running her fingers along the rock face as she went, tracing the glistening seams that caught Tina's glow and reflected it back; the gleaming bits of red and blue and gold whose nature Colleen could only guess at, although she felt sure Mama Diamond was intimately acquainted with them all.

Mama Diamond caught Colleen watching her. "You're looking at the kitchen where all those gemstones were baked, deep in the heart of the earth. . . . Kitchen goes on and on, everywhere in the world."

Listening in, Enid nodded. "Guess everythin' connects up one way or another . . . and it ain't always bad."

"Not even usually, in my experience," Mama Diamond added.

"I'd welcome hearing more of that experience," Shango spoke up. "Sometime when we get a breather."

Mama Diamond smiled. "You can consider that a promise, Mr. Shango."

The passage grew more and more narrow, until even Inigo was forced to duck his head.

"We're gonna have to crawl from here," he said, apologetically. "And be *real* quiet . . ."

They crawled through the darkness, Inigo in the lead, Cal, Colleen and Doc following, with Christina floating behind, Shango, Howie, Enid and Mama Diamond bringing up the rear. Christina's nimbus cast a glow ahead of them into the void.

*It's like being born,* Colleen thought, inching through the tight passage, her bare hands scraping on the rough, cold stone. But then, that had been largely true of this whole experience, from when she had first met Cal by the bank of recalcitrant elevators she was repairing in the lobby of the Stark Building, back before the Change, when even then he had risen to her defense against some asshole mouthing off to her.

And what had she—ever the lady of grace and etiquette—said to this knight in shining armor, who was merely trying to aid her?

*Hey, hotshot, I need a personal savior, I'll ask for one, okay?*

Perfect.

But then, he'd gone and done it anyway.

So she'd gotten to see the U.S., made real friends for the first time in her friggin' unfunny joke of a life, been more or less courted by two remarkably decent men and ultimately chosen one of them.

And not three-quarters of an hour ago, she'd gotten to see that man's late lamented wife and daughter—or a reasonable facsimile thereof—and wonder of wonders, the miracle she hadn't even dared to ask in her secret heart had happened. . . .

He'd chosen *her.*

In all this melee, she and Viktor hadn't even had a chance to talk about it yet.

She felt clammy wet, and her chest ached whenever she thought of Goldman, goddamn his brave, impetuous hide.

*Why'd he have to go and pull a crazy stunt like that?*

She'd never even told him that underneath the vast sea of irritability he continually seemed to rouse in her, she really *liked* him.

*Too late now, Tough Lady . . .*

She remembered a line from a book she'd read, or maybe she'd heard it as a question on *Jeopardy*—

*It was the best of times, it was the worst of times. . . .*

Now wasn't *that* the truth?

Ahead of them, Inigo raised a warning hand. They all stopped. Cal motioned for Christina to hang back along the passageway. She retreated, her glow about them diminishing as she withdrew.

Colleen could see Cal and Inigo had reached a wider section of the passage that seemed to terminate in an overlook. She shimmied forward, the others—save Christina—joining them.

Colleen peered at the open area below and, from the feel of the air breezing up at them, she could sense that it was immense. At first, she couldn't make anything out, but in a few moments her eyes adjusted to the gloom. She and the others lay on their bellies staring at a huge tunnel, steel tracks set out along the length of it.

Sitting on the tracks, black as a starless, abandoned sky—but somehow also throwing off a dim glow that allowed her to see along the tunnel—was a long train with featureless cars and an ominous, vast locomotive, huffing steam like a dragon waiting.

And on either side of it, scurrying about and crawling over each other, shouting and shoving and hissing in all their foul glory, were thousands and thousands of grunters, like a Shriners convention of gargoyles.

*It's not a great bet,* Inigo had said.

*You got that right, Blue Boy.*

Making not the slightest noise (Enid holding tight to the bells worked into his dreadlocks, to make sure even *they* would not betray their presence), the eight of them hurriedly edged back the way they came.

"Now what?" Shango asked once they'd gotten clear of the passage.

"Maybe it's time we got clear on exactly where we are," Cal offered. "I mean, past all the illusions and false starts. Something more specific than that we're in South Dakota." He turned to look questioningly at Inigo.

"We're . . . kinda inside a mountain," Inigo responded hesitantly.

"Great," said Colleen.

"Beyond that tunnel," Cal asked, "what are the ways out?"

"Um, well, a lot of them are knocked out," the boy answered, "since the, y'know, thing or Storm or whatever. The only way I ever got out was that tunnel. But I've heard there's another place, only I couldn't tell you where exactly. . . . It's called the Hall of Records."

"What's it look like?" said Cal.

Inigo shrugged. "It's sorta long and squarish . . . and it's got these things in the walls with words on them, like you make plates out of."

Colleen was dumbstruck. "I've seen it."

"Honey," Mama Diamond said, smiling, "you surely do get around."

*We have been buried alive,* Doc Lysenko thought as they hurried along the stone passageway, *and now at last we are clawing our way to the surface.*

In the far distance, he could see a bright rectangle of light and knew it for what it was—the doorway out to the open air.

In the glow cast from Christina's nimbus, he glanced over at Colleen and gave her the faintest smile. She returned it, uneasily.

*Almost there . . .*

Abruptly, the walls and ceiling and floor beneath their feet trembled and rocked, and he could hear a rumbling, an enraged roar that grew quickly and filled every corner of his mind.

*NO!*

It was Sanrio, he had detected them. Doc could see his own look of fear and alarm mirrored on the faces of the others.

Cal picked up his pace, broke into a full-out run, motioning for the others to follow him. But as they sped toward the light at the end of the tunnel, Doc could see an illumination rising up from behind them, reflected on the backs and shoulders of the others.

He looked back and saw a roiling, riotous mass of shifting color filling the chamber and rushing at them, felt its obscene heat speeding toward them.

*Fire,* fire made up of flares.

"Tina! Enid!" Cal shouted, not slowing.

Christina concentrated, and her aura intensified, spread out to enclose them. Enid grabbed up his guitar from around his back and began playing for all he was worth, incredible, gorgeous riffs of power.

The hungering wall of flame rebounded as if striking a barrier, then came on again, slower but not stopped. It was clear to Doc that, fast as they might run, they could not possibly reach the doorway before the fire engulfed them.

*The reactor would have them. . . .*

Silently, he said a prayer as he felt the ferocious heat pursuing him, his ears full of the echoing percussion of their footfalls, the triumphant roar of the flame, the wild beauty of Enid's guitar.

And then, something *else* . . .

Faint, at first, barely perceived, but then louder, more assured, weaving around Enid's magnificent, fierce chords.

An accompaniment.

Low and throaty, and every bit as intricate and skilled. The two formed elaborate harmonies and counterpoint, danced and built upon each other, driving the flame back.

He could feel its hellish warmth retreating. He dared to glance behind him, saw the churning wall of rainbow fire folding *back*.

And impossibly, emerging out of it and walking toward them, a *man* . . .

Playing a saxophone.

They had reached the portal now and plunged through, into daylight and fresh air. Doc saw that they stood on a broad landing set high in the rock face, a twisted stairway descending from it.

They were all out on the landing now, the sax man included, a cool wind blowing their hair. From within the corridor, the flame still swirled and pursued them.

The sax man stopped his playing. "Close that door, sweet girl," he said to Christina.

She glanced up at a boulder above the doorway, and with her mind brought it down. It landed with a resounding impact, squarely sealing the door.

The old bluesman smiled then, turned white, cataract eyes toward Enid Blindman. "Am I glad to see you, son." His voice shook, and held such a depth of emotion that Doc realized there was something profound and unspoken, a mystery there.

As if remembering himself, Papa Sky addressed the others, adding, "Mighty glad to see the rest of you, too."

Which was a figure of speech, of course, because of all of them, he alone could not see where they were.

On reflection, Doc couldn't say whether that was a blessing or a curse.

But regardless, the old man could certainly *hear* it.

Above them, at the summit, a geyser of incalculable *power* shot up from the heart of the mountain through an opening that had undoubtedly been blasted out of the rock itself months ago, at the exact moment of the dark miracle called the Change, the Storm, the Megillah. . . .

That miracle was clearly continuing. The dazzling geyser of energy pierced up into the sky, into twisting, undulating black clouds that rippled out to the horizon in all directions. A reverse whirlpool, a centrifuge throwing off power to the four corners of the world.

And it was clear, too, that the first eruption of this force must have been horrendous, for the rock face all about them had melted and reformed, into appalling, grotesque new shapes.

Even so, they could all still recognize the summit nearest them for what it had once been, and at last they knew exactly where they were.

"My God," murmured Larry Shango, and it occurred to Doc that he had never heard the man so shaken.

Once, the massive portraits had been distinct and recognizable, shaped lovingly with jackhammers and dynamite, each grandly resplendent in their various accoutrements of powdered wig, beard, pince-nez. . . .

But since then, the four gigantic stone heads had melted, oozed together, lost all definition as individuals, and resolidified into one loathsome visage that was a tumble of gaping mouths and horror-filled eyes.

"Mount Mushmore, Goldie would have said," Colleen remarked, and there was loss and pain in her voice.

Helping the old blind man along, they made their way down the stairs and onto the rubble field, descending to the sacred Black Hills beyond.

# FORTY-THREE

## The Unquiet Dead

"Them's some powerful riffs you got there, Old Man."

The first words Enid Blindman uttered once the group of them had cleared the shadow of the ruined, disfigured monument were addressed to Papa Sky. The next were to no one in particular.

"This is one scary-ass place."

True enough on both counts, Mama Diamond reflected. But the statement of more burning urgency was clearly the latter.

Because *everything* was bound and determined to kill them.

As they struggled their way along the melted and re-formed face of the mountain and down the rubble field (the stones of which still bore the jackhammer gouges made when Rushmore was first carved, sixty years ago and more), great ragged boulders tore clear and pounded after them. Blasted, burned vestiges of ponderosa pine came alive and snatched at them with blackened branches like spear-points.

Her companions fought back the onslaught, shattering rock and shearing wood with light, and sound, and blades of keenest metal.

But the party was just getting started.

*It's not nice to mess with Mother Nature. . . .*

Only this wasn't Mother Nature. No, she and Mama Diamond

had enjoyed quite a cordial relationship over the last seven decades, as Mama sought out a good deal of the fine lady's bounty, prying it lovingly from earth and stone and riverbed.

No, if Mama Diamond was to understand the information Cal Griffin and Agent Shango had shared with her, this was Dr. Marcus Sanrio at work—Sanrio and whatever else held sway there inside that mountain.

Mama Diamond had thought until now that dragons and their little gray workforce were about the worst this world had to offer.

*Old Woman, you had no idea. . . .*

They'd reached a roughly level area now, a broad expanse of cracked concrete with a big oozy bowl shape at the center. Mama Diamond saw that it had once been an amphitheater, before—as with the mountain itself—it had melted like an ice-cream cone and then resolidified.

Beyond the flat expanse lay a collapsed structure that Mama supposed had been an information center, a museum and a gift shop, but that now was so much fused wreckage of stonework, girders and glass. And out past that, rows of scorched granite stumps that (she knew from photos Katy and Samantha had sent from their vacation back in '98) had once been tall, ordered pillars like something out of that movie she'd seen on public TV, what was it called?

*Triumph of the Will . . .*

There'd been a triumph of the will here, all right, but it wasn't the U.S. government or Nazis, or anything particularly human anymore.

The shards of glass and tortured sharp metal and smaller hunks of rubble quivered and launched themselves careening at them. Christina screwed up her face in concentration, extending her forcefield to encircle Mama Diamond and the rest. Enid and Papa Sky played duets for all they were worth, while everyone huddled inside the blazing halo.

"We are still within the Source Project's sphere of influence," commented Doc.

"I'd say you're not gonna lose any bonus points on that one, Viktor," said Colleen.

"What the hell is the Source Project doing inside Mount Rushmore?" Howie piped up.

"Originally Rushmore was conceived as a far grander project," said

Cal. "The Presidents were supposed to be full figures, not just faces, and there was going to be a huge museum and repository carved out of the inside of the mountain."

"How in the name of fried green tomatoes do you know all that?" asked Colleen.

Cal shrugged. "Tina did a social studies paper once. Anyway, supposedly all they ever actually blasted out was the Hall of Records."

"That tunnel with the porcelain plaques," said Doc.

"Yes," Cal answered. "But in actuality they must've carved out the rest of the mountain secretly . . . and put in the Source Project."

"Let's hear it for American ingenuity," said Colleen.

"How far to the periphery?" Cal asked Shango.

"I'd reckon fifty miles, as the crow flies."

"I hate to break this to you, Larry, but we're not crows." Colleen had to shout now over the din of the rocks and glass and metal crashing against the barrier. "More like paper targets, or soon to be chalk outlines."

"Really, Colleen," Doc chided, "I wish you would try to be more positive." His eyes smiled, and Mama Diamond saw some of the tension ease out of Colleen's shoulders as she accepted the taunt.

"Makes no nevermind if we reach the borderland," Papa Sky added in his smoky cigarette rasp, lifting his lips from the bamboo reed set in the mouthpiece of his gleaming alto sax. "You try to pass through it into the world outside, why, it'll just burn you clean away."

Mama Diamond saw that the boy Inigo was nodding somberly in agreement.

"And how exactly did *you* get here?" Cal asked Papa Sky, but Papa only smiled inscrutably and would speak no further regarding his travels here, nor any possible companions, human or otherwise.

Cal sighed, and let it go. "We can't stay here, that's for sure." He let out a slow, considered breath. "Mary McCrae's Preserve was in the Olentangy Indian Caverns of Ohio. A sacred site, that helped lend it its power. Now, the Source Project might hold sway here, but it's smack dab in middle of the Black Hills—"

Mama Diamond nodded; she knew the lore well. "The granddaddy of all sacred sites."

"That's right," Cal said. "So odds are it should have a power all its own, too."

"In theory," Doc said. But theory was all they had now.

They fell silent then, the only sound the fusillade of debris continuing to batter their defenses.

Finally, Papa Sky spoke, his ancient, musky voice barely audible. "There's a place I know. . . . Least, I heard tell of it. Rumor is some folks tried to get there once, long time back, old men, women, children . . . It's called the Stronghold."

"Tell me it's fifty feet from here," Colleen said.

"More like fifty miles," he replied. Colleen groaned.

"Where?" Cal asked Papa Sky.

"A tableland just past the Black Hills . . . in the Badlands."

"Well?" Cal asked the others.

Mama Diamond felt she really shouldn't have a vote. After all, despite the conviction she had felt that the others would *need* her along, thus far she'd been little more than baggage. She saw the others nodding their assent (reluctantly, of course; it would be fifty miles of long, hard road, a royal sonofabitch, and no two ways about it) and added her own.

Cal took this in and rose, Mama Diamond and the others following suit. Slowly, fighting the whole wide world every inch of the way, they journeyed past the melted pillars and out through the parking lot, to the twisting roadway leading down to the Badlands.

Enid Blindman and Papa Sky continued playing all the while. As they made their tortuous way, Mama Diamond touched Papa on the arm. "Those folks who tried to get there, a long time back, what happened to them?"

Papa Sky stopped playing, and his face was gray under its cherrywood sheen.

"They were on the run," he said, looking out at her with troubled, unseeing eyes. "A whole lot of them got rubbed out. At a place called Wounded Knee . . ."

Farther down the slope of the mountains, they found the terrain less ravaged than at its apogee, or rather ravaged by the natural sweep of earth and time; the flow and retreat of ocean, the exhalation of molten rock, the layers of stone that had rippled and overturned like blankets on a restless sleeper.

All under a storm-wracked sky that held little sympathy, and a great deal of threat.

The ponderosa pines were thicker here, and green-needled once more, the aspens speckled white and brown, not charred as by a dragon's breath. The air presented a fitful, elusive intensity of humid heat radiating off the mountainside behind them; a whisper of the Source. But for the most part, the wind wore its winter coat, and chilled them despite their heavy clothes. Icy rain pelted at them, alternating with flurries of snow. Their legs felt leaden; Colleen longed for Big-T, her redoubtable steed whom they'd left stabled back in Atherton, and for Cal's Sooner and Doc's Koshka. She thought then of Goldie's horse Jayhawk—whom he had renamed Later, in a predictable fit of Goldie-ness—and it brought her a fresh pang of grief and regret.

As the afternoon waned, the assaults on them from all directions (rail fences flying at them, barbed wire coiling and springing like pythons) grew less determined and more sporadic, until they ceased altogether. Cal directed Christina to conserve her energies; in answer, her aura withdrew from about them until it encompassed only the pale, hovering girl herself. Papa Sky and Enid continued to play, but more softly, Doc leading the sightless old man with a gentle touch on his arm.

Walking alongside Cal, Colleen could sense his wariness. The cessation of attacks hadn't lessened his anxiety; rather, it had served only to increase it. Colleen shared his concern. She had learned on her father's knee that you pull back your ground forces to make room for the artillery bombardment.

As their boots crunched on the newly fallen snow, she wondered what new hell they would soon face.

She didn't have long to wait for the answer.

Descending, rounding a bend in the cracked highway amidst towering granite needles that (as Mama Diamond coolly informed them, as if they were nothing more than a nomadic tour group and she their seasoned guide) had been thrust out of the earth two and half billion years ago, they hit a level patch, a shelf on the slanting hillside.

Cal drew to an abrupt halt, motioning the others to stillness.

They were not alone.

Cal drew his sword from its scabbard, and Colleen unslung her crossbow and nocked a bolt into it soundlessly. She saw the others readying themselves, too, although she felt certain they knew as well as she did that they had about as much chance as a canary at a cat convention.

There were hundreds of them, arrayed along the hillside in the tall grass, amid the thick pines, snorting blasts of steamy breath from big nostrils, the snow like powdered sugar on their massive shoulders and heads. Some still grazed on the wheatgrass and bluestem, tearing up great hunks of sod, with blunt sounds like great machines gouging out the earth.

Blood dripped from their diminutive mouths, and ran from their fathomless black eyes like crimson tears beneath vast horns like polished granite, black speckled in gray. Great gashes in their hides showed glistening meat with marbled fat and bone beneath; violence had been done to them, wantonly and on a grand scale.

They were dead, of course, but had been called forth from the womb of the earth to face them now with blank malevolence.

The buffalo covered the land, and hungered for their blood.

# FORTY-FOUR

## The Ring and the Sea

*I'm a science geek, not an English major,* Theo Siegel thought as he fled bearing Melissa Wade from the shattered ruin of the Nils Bohr Applied Physics Building, on the campus at Atherton. He knew he would never adequately be able to describe the shining, avaricious mass that oozed from the wrecked building and began its inexorable advance on the town. Its aurora glow of purple and blue and green was something like the night-washed waves pounding the shore along the Sea of Cortez, where his late father (a geek, too, from a long line of geeks) had taken him and his girl cousins back when he was a kid. But it was also like some sickly mold on a basement-damp orange, like something repulsive coming off a gone-to-liquid corpse.

However you described it, though, you sure as hell wouldn't want to *touch* it, or have it touch you.

As he staggered away, trying to put as much distance as possible between them and that freakin' portal (which he knew as surely as the waist size on his jockey shorts was continuing to pour fiendish energy like water from a gut-burst dam), he saw townies and college gits alike disgorge from buildings on all sides, gape at the shining crud coming off the physics quad, then take to their heels getting the hell away; clear out of town, if they knew what was good for them. Word was spreading, and *fast*, which was a damn good thing. 'Cause what didn't get *out* got *ate*. Theo felt that one right on down to his Converse All-Stars.

The sky above him was dark, apart from fitful light reflected from a passing cloud; the moon was down. But the weird, expanding glow illuminated the streets and buildings, too. They didn't need Jeff's streetlights—dead as Mussolini now—to see which way the wind blew.

Melissa seemed to gain substance as he carried her farther from the portal and perhaps, therefore, from the Source. But substance wasn't health. Although she felt heavier, less ethereal, she was clearly sick. He could see a pallid sheen like fevered moonlight on her face, her eyes swept closed. Unconscious, she spasmed in her sleep, and one particularly violent convulsion threatened to shake her out of his arms altogether.

Even in the pulsing, cold dimness he could observe that her hair was starting to blanch, her face grow thin, the cheeks more pronounced.

He knew what was happening to her; it didn't take a rocket scientist (or even a physics grad) to figure *that* out.

Somehow, that eruption of bad news, of pure evil crud vomiting out from the Source, had rendered the stone in Melissa's neck null and void; it was no longer stopping her transformation.

She was *changing*, transmuting into what Jeff Arcott had been able to defer only for a time, the gates of the portal swinging wide now serving to unleash it.

Melissa burned hot in his grasp. His arms were heavy with fatigue, they ached dreadfully. But then, so did his legs and neck and back; his entire musculature, in fact, and skeleton, too. It felt to him paradoxically as if he were both lengthening and compressing, and the dread that filled him made him want to tear open his chest with bloody fingers and let loose a scream beyond anything his voice could proclaim.

*I'm changing, too.*

He knew it for a certainty, in the shivers that cascaded along his flesh, the agony that drove like a railway spike through his skull.

But this time, there would be no reprieve. Because there in the physics lab, Theo had seen Jeff Arcott consumed by the result of what he himself had built.

Jeff, who had not previously transformed into anything, who had stayed completely human . . .

Jeff had fixed them once upon a time, he and Melissa, had *cured* them. That had been shortly after the Change, when Atherton was still dark and increasingly empty as the population drifted away in search of some better place or succumbed to personal transformation, became drifters and refugees, and grunters and flares and the occasional hulking dragon, and other nameless things.

It had been a breathless, perfect evening in late summer, Theo recalled. Jeff had just gotten his first great brainstorm, had begun feverishly working on the set of wonders that would restore the town. They had been picnicking, the three of them, when Melissa took a chill and grew wan. Theo recognized the signs; he had seen it happen to others.

She was turning into a flare.

It was he who had thrown a blanket over her, hustled her with Jeff to Medical Sciences and put her on a gurney. They'd wheeled her to a room where, by candlelight and without benefit of anesthetic, Jeff had opened a flap of skin at the back of her neck above her spine and inserted a ring of sterilized garnets and amethysts, then sewn the skin together again with a surgical needle and lengths of coarse black suture.

For Melissa, all this had passed as in a fever dream. But when she woke, the fever had broken, the pain was gone, and the curious lightness she felt had yielded to the familiar sumptuous draw of gravity.

Jeff would never explain how he had known what to do, how the gems had conserved her humanity (or Theo's, when soon after it had seemed inevitable that he would become one more grunter).

It was only much later that Theo tracked Jeff along the shadows to the railroad siding outside of town, discovered the black train and its towering master, its crew of deformed curs who were what he himself would have become . . . and learned from just where Jeff got his *inspiration.*

At the time, however, Jeff had claimed he'd simply known. Just as he had known how to revive Atherton from its extinction, give it back some semblance of normalcy.

The normalcy that had been mockery, mere illusion, now shredded and cast away.

Theo found his breaths were coming in short gasps; he couldn't get enough air into his lungs. He reached the periphery of the Sculpture Garden, stumbled onto its grassy rise and set Melissa on an iron bench.

*Only for a minute,* he told himself, to regroup, get a second wind. *We can't let that shit catch up to us.*

He ran a hand over what had been his injured leg, felt wonderingly that it was completely healed. True, it might *ache* like a Tin Woodman left to rust a million years, but say what you like, this metamorphosis crap sure beat major medical.

Curled in on herself there on the bench, Melissa looked like a child in an iron casket. Theo shuddered, and chased the thought from his mind.

He gazed back toward the physics building. The radiance was brighter now, surging in all directions, picking up speed as it gained assurance. *Time for us to be making tracks,* Theo realized, no matter how crappy he felt.

But when he turned back, Melissa was gone.

# FORTY-FIVE

## VOMIT, THEN MOP

*Well now, that's a relief,* Mama Diamond thought, even as she felt a chill run straight from the crown of her head to her little toe. She knew, too, that no one else in her party was thinking anything even *remotely* like it.

But then, the rest of them hadn't been feeling particularly like a fifth (or in this case, tenth) wheel, and wondering if their insistence on accompanying this little expeditionary force into the mouth of hell hadn't been merely the first cranky expression of a nascent second childhood raising its senile voice.

Which was merely a roundabout way of saying that Mama Diamond had been doubting her finely honed instincts right along about now.

But hotfooting it in the snowfall paralleling Highway 40 out of Rushmore, skirting the deserted, fallen structures of Keystone and its blasted, twisted billboards touting the Flying T Chuckwagon Supper and Show, Old MacDonald's Petting Farm, the Reptile Gardens and the National Presidential Wax Museum (not to mention the Holy Terror Mine—and if *that* description didn't fit the whole damn area nowadays, Mama Diamond didn't know what did), Mr. Cal Griffin and his stalwart band of adventurers had come upon a whole herd of rusticating herbivores that might have been candidates for a petting zoo themselves if not for a little thing or two.

Namely, that they were dead, skinned and in a *real* bad mood . . .

The bitter cold wind was lifting low off the ground now, and it carried to Mama Diamond the sticky iron blood smell of the beasts, a stink that seemed to weight the air, make it hard to breathe in. There was another smell, too, the musty odor of their thick winter coats; the parts of their carcasses that still had coats on them, that was, that hadn't been cut away by the long-departed buffalo men who were bones and dust as ancient as these animals themselves.

As if they all abruptly heard some call on the air beyond the range of human hearing (and who was to say they didn't), the brutes raised their heads as one and appraised the interlopers with clear challenge, and imminent threat. The lead bull was grunting his displeasure with throaty deep exclamations, blowing puffs of pungent air from his nostrils. He tensed his huge shoulders and raised his tuft of tail, readying to charge.

Out of the corner of her eye—never taking her gaze off the lead buffalo—Mama Diamond could see Griffin gesturing the rest of his band closer together, keeping himself at the forefront, all of them hefting their varied assortment of absurd weaponry.

Weaponry that would no more dispatch this enormous collection of tainted meat on the hoof than a rolled newspaper. Which was, Mama Diamond felt, just what Dr. Marcus Sanrio and his ghastly inhuman buddies back in their mountain fastness had counted on.

But these hideous rejects from a meat market studding the landscape ahead as far as the eye could see weren't the only things that had been called here—Mama Diamond herself had, too, though by a different, unknown agency and for a far different purpose. She had been touched by a dragon, and it had left its mark, awakened the dragon part within her. She understood now that her journey from Burnt Stick to Atherton to this lonely, cold highway outside Keystone, South Dakota—and for that matter, the entirety of her roving, long life, from San Bernardino to Manzanar and the fossil beds beyond—had been aimed to arrive her at this precise moment; the trajectory of her life like a toy arrow fired at a guard shack.

She realized, too, that her parlays with the horses and wolves and panther had been no more, really, than practice sessions.

At last, at long last, Mama Diamond knew *just* what she was here for.

"Out of my way, boys and girls," she said to Griffin and the others as she strode to the head of the group, confidence filling her like wind in a clipper ship's sails.

They were the last words she said in the tongue of man.

The lead buffalo tilted its head to look at her with its dead black eyes, sniffed at her with its broad, flat nose, incarnadined with shiny, black blood. Behind it, the others of the herd regarded her, waiting, lethal.

"Ho there, Grass Eater!" Mama Diamond called to the leader, in the dragon tongue she knew it would comprehend, her voice booming out so all would hear. "You Dead Thing, you Killer of Flies!"

(From her peripheral vision, Mama Diamond spied Colleen starting to pipe up, saw Cal grab her arm, commanding her to silence. Sharp boy, that one, quick on the uptake. He'd know how to play this out, without Mama having to draw him pictures—a damn good thing, seeing as how Mama Diamond felt sure she wasn't going to have spare time to haul out pencil and paper. . . .)

"You're insolent for such a small thing," Old King Buffalo replied to Mama Diamond, then added, "It will be a pleasure to rip you apart."

"Listen to Old Cow brag! Did you boast that way when man and horse ran you down, when they laid you low? They should have cut out your tongue, too, Braggart Cow!"

King Buffalo was shifting his weight from side to side, still readying himself but with the slightest hint of hesitation, made unsure by Mama Diamond's belligerence, her lack of caution.

"Old Cow doubting himself? Lie down, Old Cow, you and your sheep herd with you! Back to earth and worms with you! And bother no more your betters!"

That last jibe hit home; Old King Buffalo lowered his head; his breath was coming in short, enraged grunts.

*Let it be now*, Mama Diamond thought, reaching down into herself, summoning every bit of resolve and conviction from the deep dragon part of her. And the human part, too, the part that had scratched treasures out of the earth and dispensed their gleaming delights to Native boys and passing travelers alike.

That had left her family behind without a glance.

That had been loved by a boy named Danny once, and lost him to the wider world that had so scared her.

Well, she was in that wide world, now.

With a roar that echoed to the sky, Old King Buffalo charged, and the rest of his herd with him, thundering the earth, the cracked road and ground trembling, their hooves throwing up great clots of snow and grass and dirt.

"*BURN!*" Mama Diamond screamed and felt herself ignite like the world bursting alight. She extended her arms and willed herself outward in an expression of blaze and consumption.

And *this* time, her utter surety in the unwavering fact of it made her *see* it:

Gouts of blue and red and white-hot flame spewed from her and struck King Buffalo, knocking him backward into the others as he screamed and burned. The others were on fire now, too, and the trees and grasses, too. The buffalo plunged aside, bellowing in their terror, dead as they were, some plunging off the cliffside, flipping down and away, screaming, while others stampeded blindly away, shearing off tree trunks and stones in their blind panic.

Mama Diamond risked a glance at her companions, and from their puzzlement it was clear they saw none of the flames, had no understanding *why* the beasts had rioted and parted. But none of that mattered. Mama Diamond could feel her power ebbing, starting to falter. . . .

"*Run!*" she cried to the others, and could not say whether she said it in the dragon tongue or not.

But Cal Griffin didn't need more. He took off at a run, the others following, bolting down the roadway in the opening she'd made for them as the corpse buffalo shrieked and rolled in the dirt and fled.

Mama Diamond stumbled after them, but her legs were watery under her, she had no *oomph* left, as she continued to fire the stream of flame at the brutes, this way and that, keeping the path open as long as she could.

And maybe the flames were just an illusion, Mama Diamond knew, no more real than a lonely girl's wish on a summer's night, but how real were these dead things? (Real enough to kill, she knew that.) The scorched ones were staying scorched, the shredded remnants of their fur and skin and the muscle beneath smoking and filling the winter air with the smell of charred meat.

With a *phht!* Mama Diamond's flames abruptly cut out, and her body was intact and cold and frightfully mortal once more as she shivered there.

Coming aware that there was no further threat, the buffalo slowed in their headlong, chaotic rush, turned back toward her again, those that hadn't plummeted clean off the mountain.

Slowly, cautiously, they drew near, circling her, their crisped hooves crunching the grasses and snow and asphalt. Over their heads, Mama Diamond could discern Griffin and the others clear of them, safe now, just slowing and glancing back, seeing to their dismay that she was not right behind them, that she was cut off and trapped.

Nothing in the world they could do, nothing at all, Mama Diamond reflected, and that was all right. Or at least, it would have to be.

Utterly spent, she sank to her knees in the fresh snow, no longer able to stand, to do anything. A ludicrous phrase came to mind, something from her childhood, from a lesson on writing, of all things. *Vomit, then mop.* Well, she'd vomited out all that flame, but she didn't have a lick of energy to mop now, not no way, not nohow.

She saw Old King Buffalo had righted himself and gained his feet, every bit of him black now, burnt clear down to the skeleton. He approached her, was scant feet away.

"You got a bone to pick, Old Cow?" Mama Diamond croaked, and she laughed, although it wasn't really funny.

Old King Buffalo shrieked like all the damned souls echoing up from the mouth of hell and charged, the rest of them coming on, too.

Mama Diamond closed her eyes, the hammering of their footfalls all the sound in the world, knowing it would not be long now.

Then she felt a hurricane beating of wind surge from above her, and heard angry, rasping words that cut through the din.

"Leave her—she's *mine.*"

Mama Diamond opened her eyes and looked up, but all she could see was a vortex of whirling black cloud whipping down out of the storm roof, something winged and dark within, hauling the tempest down with itself as it dropped.

Enormous, taloned fingers wrapped about her midsection and yanked her high into the storm.

In the moment before consciousness left her and she knew no more than the stones in the earth, Mama Diamond put a name to the voice.

It was Ely Stern.

# FORTY-SIX

## The Morlock and the Moore

Since the time he was ten, Theo Siegel's favorite book had been *The Time Machine*, and its most harrowing chapter the sequence where the Time Traveler lost his beloved Weena to the burning woods and the Morlocks.

(Not that Theo ever suspected he himself would someday *be* a Morlock . . .)

Now he ran wildly about for a time, calling frantically for Melissa, peering in the shelter of trees and any dark vacancy she may have crept into in search of solitude and clemency. He stayed mostly to the rolling expanse of the Sculpture Garden, knowing full well that in her weakened, transmutative state she could not get far.

He found no one. Finally becoming mindful of his own danger, he looked out to see that the onrushing tide of foul, purple-blue-green moldlight was almost upon him. From his vantage point on a grassy rise, he saw to his alarm that the crashing waves of luminance had encircled his position, that he was trapped, with no way out. Living and conscious—no, he corrected himself, with some nameless consciousness *driving* it—it swept up splashing, stretching toward him, his small realm of greenery shrinking rapidly as it encroached.

Casting desperately about, he peered back and saw the grouping of glowing, diseased structures on North Campus, the physics and other natural science buildings, all engulfed, devoured, transformed.

All save one; although its base was roiling and shimmering with the Source corruption, its domed crown was unsullied, intact. Almost as though the Mind behind the invasion was deliberately keeping it separate, as—what?

A *holding place, a nest* . . .

Theo knew where Melissa was.

Hundreds of yards off, impossibly away, across the undulating sea of devil light.

Just then, the gleaming blue tendrils surged up and grabbed him. He cried out, it stung *hot* like burning cold ice, shooting all the way up his arm into his cheekbones and the sockets of his eyes. He pulled free and scampered away from it, scurried up into the canopy of the lone, untouched tree standing sentinel at the peak of the rise.

*Aw man, this is just not my day,* Theo thought, and barked out a frenzied laugh as it occurred to him how much he looked like a newspaper cartoon at that moment.

He quieted abruptly as he heard the sound of metal creaking and distorting. From on high in the damp gleaming, he could see the sculptures, Rodin's *Walking Man* and Degas's *Little Dancer Aged Fourteen* and that funky thing with arms like a windmill, all suffused, inundated with hell-light, coming to life and crunching toward him, with a racket like a demolition derby.

They smashed into the tree, battered it, leaving smears of patinaed bronze on its bark, brought it thundering down. Theo flailed through the air, landing square in the midst of the energy pool. He felt it course over him, submerge him.

The pain was like a swarm of wasps adhering to him. But even so, it wasn't as bad as he thought it would be. For one thing, it wasn't devouring or absorbing him, somehow wasn't able to get *inside* him (although he could dimly sense voices in his head trying to—well, the best description would be *mind-fuck* him, mess with his thoughts, get an upper hand on his will; but it wasn't happening, it felt more like a customer in a restaurant shouting for some attention while being roundly ignored).

*It can hurt me, but it can't kill me,* he thought, and it gave him an odd, giddy confidence. And he knew something else, too, although he couldn't have said how—that the part of him it could hurt was the part that was still human, that had not completely changed.

The realization was momentary, fleeting—just before the huge bulk of metal surged up and encased him.

He recognized the piece, could put a name to it, thanks to the modern-art-appreciation class he'd taken to fulfill his breadth requirements, so he would have what the administration deemed a fully rounded education.

*This is fucking ridiculous,* he thought as the Henry Moore squeezed the life out of him.

With a rush of adrenaline, he felt the inhuman strength pervade him again, pushed with all his might against the crushing, indifferent bronze. He felt it begin to give way.

Shimmying and grunting, he pulled himself clear of the mass of metal, fell and gained his footing and ran through the living light as it whipped at him and stabbed deep with glowing barbs like Portuguese man-of-wars. The pain was screeching at him, filling his universe. Strobing black flashes filled his vision. He knew any moment he'd pass out, and then it would be *adios, amigo.*

Theo tripped and sat down hard, gasping as the light overwhelmed him. The world fading out and retreating on him, he felt the last reserves of his strength dissipate, eddy out into the larger, glowing sea.

Suddenly, he felt a strong hand grab him by the scruff of the neck and yank him roughly to his feet.

"Jesus, boy, whatcha doin'? Waitin' for a streetcar?"

The other figure got a firmer grip on him, around the waist with one long, wiry arm, and then leapt almost straight up, grabbing hold of a ledge on an untouched building with his free hand (Theo knew it to be the Aaron Copland Music Building). He dragged Theo along the precipice, then pulled him into an open window.

The room was pretty dark, but Theo found it was getting easier and easier for him to see in almost no light. There were a number of folks there, and he recognized them all—Krystee Cott, Rafe Dahlquist, Al Watt, almost everyone who had been in the plasma lab; relief flooded him at the thought they'd all gotten away.

*Except Jeff . . .*

"Christ, son. You look like shit."

He turned and saw that the speaker was the one who had hauled him up here and saved his bacon. Brian Forbes, the grunter who had joined Cal Griffin's band of strays in the blood-drenched snows outside the Gateway Mall, gaped at Theo with enormous eyes the color of albino cave fish.

"Yeah, well, you aren't exactly an American Beauty yourself," Theo retorted. Then, abashed, he added, "Thanks."

Forbes shrugged, and nodded.

Theo recalled how the other had moved through the stinging light, seemingly unharmed.

"That energy crap," Theo ventured, inclining his head toward the open window and the campus beyond, "Did it hurt you to move through it?"

"A little, not much," Forbes replied. "Gets kinda noisy in your head, but hey, I've hadda screen out crazy bad noise my whole life. I'm from Detroit!"

*So I'm right about it,* Theo thought. The less human he became, the weaker grip it would have on him.

Krystee Cott stepped up to Theo. He saw she had three rifles strapped across her back, along with ammo belts. "We've got the horses saddled and waiting on Coulter Street. We're getting out of here, away from town, while we still can. Then we'll regroup and formulate a response."

*What kind of response? We got our asses kicked.* Thanks to that dragon, the one who had arrived on metal rails and departed on the storm.

Theo gazed out the window, at the dome that rose above the sea of infection, that gleamed pure in the moonlight.

"I can't come with you," he said to the others.

He climbed back out the window, and was lost to the night.

# FORTY-SEVEN

## The Parameters of Absolution

Stumbling down the mountainside, bitter with the cost of their survival, the winter wind stinging their eyes to slits and icing their lashes, they might all have appeared blind ones to a passing observer, although only one of them truly was.

*Do you think there's forgiveness in this world, Mr. Griffin, or just atonement?* Mama Diamond had asked Cal on the moonlit roof of the dormitory back in Atherton.

From the safe distance Mama Diamond's act of courage had bought them in their confrontation with the butchered, reanimated buffalo, Cal had seen the merciless black shape wrapped in storm cloud swoop out of the darkling sky to seize her up and carry her off into the gale.

Whatever that dark messenger had been, there was no telling where Mama Diamond might be now. Still alive? Cal could only hope. Lost, certainly, to the Storm. Would she forgive him, wherever she was? Could he ever atone for bringing her here?

Or any of those that had followed him: Magritte, Mike Olifiers . . . Goldie.

Enid Blindman had been a Pied Piper to lead others to sanctuary, Cal reflected. But what had *he* led them to? He looked over at his sister, the glowing halo of her floating, changed self casting illumination on the night-dark path ahead.

He knew there was no point in flagellating himself. He had done what he'd had to, as had the rest of them. The world turned every moment, it hurtled through space; stillness was no more than an illusion, a cunning self-deception. Every action, even inaction—*especially* inaction—was a choice. And the assumption that one held responsibility for all the wild vagaries of the universe was simply arrogance.

*I am the captain of my ship, not of the sea. . . .*

Cal had listened to the voice within him, and taken the wise counsel of others. It was *right* to be here, a testament to their tenacity and courage and will—which didn't lessen the ache of loss in his chest.

Still, he had Christina with him; he had kept that promise, at least. And in doing so, he'd forced changes on himself perhaps even greater than those imposed on his sister, albeit more subtle, less telling to the eye.

He came to an awareness that his sister was scrutinizing him with her strange, opalescent eyes. He smiled at her, and she gave him the ghost of a smile back.

They had traveled through bleak, uncharted territories, the two of them, both together and alone, and had neither safety nor security now. But then, safety and security were illusions, too; everyone died, that was the way of things.

Gravel and the dust of ages crunching beneath his boots, Cal reflected that if the journey of his life were marked by two ports of call, one of them fear, the other love, he knew at which destination he had arrived.

His sister was beside him, and that was enough.

As they struggled along the looping, switchbacked path of Route 40, thick grasses twined and stretched to grasp at their legs; prairie rattlers and bull snakes uncoiled out of their winter sleeping places to leap snapping at them; slumbering hordes of grasshoppers and mosquitoes and katydids swarmed up to envelop them. The night and land were alive, suffused with a muted, blue St. Elmo's fire that pulsed and writhed over all that rose to meet them at the bidding of the Thing unseen.

Christina drove them back with her luminosity, Enid and Papa Sky with the heat of their music. And what they couldn't deflect, Cal and Colleen, Doc and Inigo and Howie and Shango stomped and hacked to bits with boot and sword, machete and knife.

Inch by inch, yard by yard, mile by mile . . .

How much farther now? Hard to tell in this blackness. Thirty miles? Twenty-five? An infinity.

They were coming down out of the Black Hills onto the Badlands now. The snow, with its odd taste of defilement when it brushed their lips, was abating, giving way to a cruel, unrelenting wind that had teeth in it, that chilled them clean through despite the many layers of clothing they wore. Their teeth chattered, and their limbs shook as they pressed on in grim silence. Tina alone seemed untouched by the cold, serene and enigmatic in her weightlessness.

The attacks appeared to be lessening, becoming more sporadic, less intent. Perhaps whatever lived at the Source drew in upon itself as night came on; perhaps even *It* needed to sleep sometimes.

Cal hoped so.

Alongside the roadway, rows of white metal signs banged a percussive rhythm against their wooden poles in the fierce wind. Cal could see the triangular signs all bore the same scolding admonition—THINK.

Following his glance, Inigo came up beside him. "That's to show where someone died here. You know, in an accident."

*We may die here, too,* Cal reflected. *But it won't be any accident.*

To the boy, he said, "Are you from around these parts? Before the Change?"

Inigo nodded. "Came here when I was ten. My dad worked at Ellsworth for a time, the Air Force base outside Rapid. Then he got a job in the mountain. . . ." The boy's face darkened in the gloom, remembering. "We didn't see him much after that, my mom and me."

"What happened to them, your folks?" Cal asked. He realized he was speaking low, so none of the others could hear, although he couldn't have said why.

Inigo shrugged. "Dad ran off before things came down. . . . Ma went to find him."

"They just left you?"

"Mom had this lady friend she put me with. . . . When the Storm came, I didn't see that lady anymore." He shivered, and added cryptically, "I didn't want to."

"Is that when you changed?"

"Around then, yeah. I kinda kept my head down, found stuff to eat. . . . You can do okay, if you don't make waves."

*Yeah, but somewhere along the way you radically altered your operating philosophy, kid.* It occurred to Cal this was the longest conversation he'd had with the grunter boy, and the most Inigo had chosen to reveal.

"So how'd you get inside the mountain?" Cal asked.

Before Inigo could respond, his pale big eyes went wider still, as he saw something ahead in the darkness that made him stop dead.

Cal halted and peered into the blackness. Behind him, the others stopped, too.

Ahead of them, the night sky was lit with flashes that burst staccato across the heavens, like strings of immense firecrackers going off, or gigantic Christmas lights exploding.

The lightning was coming for them.

And beneath it, swarming across the vista of ragged terrain, the strobing stormlight giving their matted, wet fur fleeting illumination, packs of gray buffalo wolves, spat dead, reincarnated, up out of the earth. They were still many miles away, but the thunder carried their maddened howls echoing up the mountain face to them.

Christina brought her lambent protection around Cal and the others once more.

*It's going to get worse before it gets better,* Cal thought grimly, drawing his sword.

*If it ever gets better . . .*

They plunged forward to meet the storm.

Morning found the group of them weary, singed and bloodied, but still alive.

"It comes in fits and starts," Cal observed. "Like the Source is pacing itself."

"Ours not to reason why," Doc added, applying a salve and bandage to a scorched patch on Colleen's arm. "Merely to take respite where we can."

They broke out the food from their packs, the few delicacies they'd brought from the Insomnia Café back in Atherton, and rested on tumbled boulders amid melting snow and mud, short grasses and anemic cacti. Cal saw that Inigo had pulled the hood of his jacket over his head, donned sunglasses against the light. Howie, too, had pulled his fedora low and affixed his Ray-Bans.

"I reckon we got maybe another fifteen miles or so," Papa Sky commented between bites of Swiss on rye, his creased face turned southeast into the wind. Cal wondered anew how the old blind man could sense so much more than they.

"Funny thing, you knowin' all about these parts, and me knowin' diddly," Enid said, rubbing his chin, the bells in his dreads jingling softly. "I was born here, y'know? Pine Ridge. My mama was Lakota."

"I thought it was your father who was Lakota, not your mother," Colleen noted. "I mean, that's what Goldman said."

"Yeah, well, ol' Goldie didn't always listen too good," Enid replied. "Depending on the occasion."

*True enough*, Cal thought.

"I left here when I was a baby," Enid continued, standing to stretch. "My mama married a real estate guy, and we moved to Decatur. Cancer got 'em both, way before the Storm."

"Just as well you didn't grow up in these parts, son," Papa Sky said. "Folks round here sometimes got a bone in their craw 'bout black folks. Comes from the buffalo soldiers and all, in the Indian Wars."

"Well geez, that's hardly a week ago Wednesday," Colleen observed. "Maybe it's time to get over it."

"First thing you learn about this land," Papa Sky said evenly, "is history ain't history. It's pretty much the same thing as right now. Everything's all mixed up together."

"What about your real father?" Doc asked Enid.

Enid's face grew stony. "Mama never talked about him. She figured what's gone is gone."

Like Inigo's father, Cal thought, and his own, and Tina's. Orphans, the lot of them; foundlings and scatterlings, abandoned to wind and storm.

Papa Sky said nothing, looking off at the horizon with empty dead eyes.

They moved on.

As morning eased toward afternoon, the fractious cloud cover broke, and a high, brilliant sun cast a clean, hard light over the land. Traveling along the path of what had once been Highway 40 skirting Custer, they passed Red Shirt along the 41 and transferred onto the narrow, rutted path of Route 2 stretching toward the Pine Ridge Reservation.

The Black Hills gobbling down the last of the daylight, Cal and his companions crested a plateau from which they could spy seventy miles in all directions under a fiery sunset, the soaring formations of the Mauvaises Terres striated with bands of red and brown and yellow, an ancient land of erosion and fossil bones in the crumbled, weathered earth. From far off came the cries of western meadowlarks and cowbirds, rugged survivors of this scourged, enduring land.

And like a brilliant, long nail pounded into the cross of the earth, the beacon of power bursting into the heavens, pinwheeling endlessly from the Source.

He had gotten Christina back, Cal thought ruefully, but beyond that they hadn't changed anything.

With night descending and the last remnants of their strength waning, they staggered across the flat expanse of tableland—which Papa Sky informed them was about halfway between Buffalo Gap and Porcupine, and was called Cuny Table by the locals. Finally, Papa Sky brought them to a halt before a rickety, paint-peeled wooden stand, with the whitewashed words ICE-COLD POP AND MORE.

There was nothing and no one else in sight, as far as the eye could see in the wash of moonlight.

"This is the Stronghold," Papa Sky informed them.

"*This* is the Stronghold?" Colleen asked incredulously. "Gee, and I coulda had a V8." Cal was glad Colleen at least had the diplomacy not to add, *This is what happens when you let a blind guy lead you.*

"Sir, are you sure—?" Cal began.

Then the land ahead of them rippled and shook and turned over.

The ground opened up, revealing a cavernous space beneath. Cal could discern torches burning within, and a multiplicity of passages branching off, and countless people gathered together.

"*Hua kola!*" Papa Sky called out.

A lone figure backlit by torches stepped up the slope toward them, boots crunching on gravel and snow, emerging into the light cast by Christina's glow.

Cal drew in a sharp breath. The figure was a woman clad in leather and furs against the cold, wearing more sheathed knives than he had ever seen on any human being. Her eyes were green and wary, her hair long and black and platted down the back.

Beside him, Inigo gasped as he saw the woman, and took off at run toward her.

"No!" Cal cried, but the boy paid him no heed.

Seeing him come on, the woman dropped into a defensive stance and pulled a long, deadly blade from its scabbard.

Drawing near, the grunter boy cried out, "It's me! It's *Inigo*!"

The woman's mouth opened in soundless surprise, her eyes astonished. She threw the knife aside into the snow as he leapt for her, and she enclosed him rocking in her arms. They sobbed, the two of them, for all the time lost, for this meeting.

Inigo's words were muffled in her embrace, but Cal caught them as they drifted on the night wind to him.

"Mom . . . Mom . . ."

In time, she rose, and with her boy's hand in hers, walked up to Cal. She extended her free hand, and Cal took it.

"I'm Cal Griffin," he said.

Her eyes reacted with surprise; something raw and primal flared there, and was quickly suppressed.

"May Catches the Enemy," the Lakota woman replied by way of introduction, and led them into the waiting earth.

# FORTY-EIGHT

## MUSIC AND STEEL

*It's like descending into a grave,* Cal thought, and knew it was not the first time he'd had such a thought in the journal of his adventures. In truth, more than anything, his life had become a collection of experiences and exploits he never dreamed he would have, and more often than not would have preferred forgoing.

His body anchored with weariness, muscles singing with the ache and bruise of the long trek and its travails, he staggered into the heart of the earth. Christina drifted shining beside him, Colleen and Doc half supporting each other, Howie limping along while Shango and Enid helped guide Papa Sky down the sloping terrain. Inigo and his mother, still holding hands, followed close upon.

The gateway of soil sealed up behind them, entombing them in the massive space beneath. Cal tensed as it closed, then detecting a like anxiety in his companions, forced himself to relax.

The air underground was fresh and moved with a cool breeze from several pathways. The pungent, pleasant smell of burning sweetgrass and sage wafted on the air. May Catches the Enemy led them to low tables with soft cushions, where buffalo stew and flatbread and strong, hot coffee were served up. Cal ate greedily, for the first time aware of how hungry he'd been, and felt considerably better.

Inigo's mother came and crouched nearby, studying him keenly, as if trying to weigh who he might be by the way he chewed his food, how he sipped his coffee.

In time, she said, "We were told you were coming, but not who you'd be."

"Yes?" Cal replied. "By whom?"

She hesitated, and her eyes darted to Papa Sky, who sat across the table, nodding his head in time to a beat only he could hear.

As if he'd caught her glance, the old blind man said, "By my special friend . . ."

A shudder ran through Cal. He thought of the first time he'd heard Papa Sky use that phrase, back in Buddy Guy's club when he'd given them the dragon scale that had come from his mysterious, unseen traveling companion.

"That the same friend who sent you to us in Chicago?" Cal asked.

A smile spread across Papa Sky's face, like honey on good dark bread. "That's mighty sharp of you, Mr. Cal. . . . But then, my friend always said you were bright."

Colleen started to speak, but May cut her off with a raised hand. "The white people joke about Indian time . . . but we like to wait till everyone's here who's s'posed to be. We still got one or two coming. There'll be time for talk. But right now, y'all need some rest. You come a long, hard way."

Colleen looked questioningly at Cal.

Yawning, he rose. "Show us to our suites."

The others were led to various alcoves where warming fires blazed, given sleeping bags and blankets from Wal-Mart and Prairie Edge and wherever else folks had been able to scrounge supplies before they'd been locked in here, trapped in their tiny enclave of safety from the encroaching, malign power at the Source.

May Catches the Enemy found Cal and Christina a cozy place in a shadowy corner away from everyone, where Cal was surprised to find fluffed pillows and a goose-down comforter and thick buffalo robe waiting. The woman withdrew, and Cal settled into the robe, wrapping its lush dark fur around him as he lay on the dry, hard earth. Christina floated onto the comforter and grew still, closing her eyes, her aura fading to faintest eminence as she eased into rest.

Her eyes fluttered open and focused on a distant spot, to the darkness where Doc and Colleen lay unseen. "Things are different," she said drowsily.

"Uh-huh," Cal said.

"She's with him now, huh?"

"They're good together," he said. "It's a good thing."

"You're different, too. . . ." Her eyes came to rest on him. "Good different. You're strong, Cal."

"I can't move boulders with my brain."

She gave him the faintest smile, then her face clouded. "Goldie . . ." she said, and didn't finish it.

He nodded, feeling the loss, knowing there was nothing to make it right.

"Maybe we're alive in who remembers us, at least a little," his sister said. "Maybe we're alive in what we set free. . . ."

"Maybe," he agreed.

They were silent then, alone with the crackling fires, the weight of air.

At last, Christina spoke again. "Back in the mountain, when I was . . . you know." He sensed she couldn't bring herself to say *human*. "It's all fuzzing away now, like a dream when you wake up, I can't keep hold of it. But the one you mentioned to Papa . . . he was there."

Cal felt chilled, within the warm embrace of the robe. Neither needed to say his name; they both knew. Cal was wide-awake now, his senses keen. In the distance, down the rock passages, he could hear the whistling of the wind, and a sound like something calling.

Christina huddled deeper into the comforter, her pale fine hair fanned atop it. As sleep enfolded her, she murmured, "Inigo calls him Leather Man."

As night drew on, Cal found sleep eluding him. Restless, he moved off from his sister as she slumbered, not wanting to wake her. Wrapping the buffalo robe about him, he walked to the mouth of a passage, peered down it. Air swirled up out of it like a titan exhaling, and he heard a rhythmic, deep pulse. But it was dark as a coal miner's esophagus. He felt like seeking out Inigo, with his night-sharp grunter eyes, and asking him to search out its secrets.

He was weary of mysteries. . . .

Suddenly, he was gripped hard from behind, felt cold steel at his throat, the edge of a long blade.

"I been a long time waiting for this," the voice behind him said softly in his ear. It held music in it, and steel.

He knew the voice.

He'd placed his sword by the pillows and comforter; still, he had his short knife in its scabbard under his ribs. He could reach it easily, might be able to do something with it. Or he could call out to his sister. Rousing fiery awake, she could shatter this one's bones where she stood, blast her to dust on the air.

He did nothing.

"You've got something to say." He worked to keep his voice level, and as quiet as hers. "Or we wouldn't still be talking."

She released him then, and came around to face him.

"My married name was Devine," May Catches the Enemy said.

As the night waned and morning came on, Cal came to know that long months ago, nine hundred miles away in Chicago, he had killed this woman's husband, and Inigo's father.

They drank coffee, just the two of them, beside a low fire, out of earshot of the others. The flames leapt and sparked, made light play in her raven hair, her emerald eyes.

"He never wanted it, what happened to him," May said, not looking at Cal. "He left to keep us safe. Maybe that's what he was doing with them flares, too. . . . Then it all went to hell."

"Have you told your son?"

"Not yet . . . I'll tell him when the time's right. We got a lot of catching up to do. When I got back, I couldn't get to him. With everything I could pull off, the farthest I could get was here."

Cal thought back to the deserted mall in Iowa, to his first encounter with her son, when he'd heard the boy's name and recalled the line from *The Princess Bride*.

*My name is Inigo Montoya. You killed my father. Prepare to die. . . .*

Incredible, Cal reflected, the turns of fate, the dance of loss and grief and inexorable parting, of sins committed, and allies made. . . .

"That thing with the knife," May said, "I just needed to get it off my chest." Her eyes found him, held him pinioned there. "You did what you had to," she added, an absolution.

Nevertheless, Cal blamed himself, even knowing he could have chosen no other course, that Clayton Devine, in his guise as both Primal and Primal's toady, would surely have killed them all had they not gained the upper hand.

Guilt and necessity, that was the rule of the day. So what separated the pure from the defiled, the evil from the good? Compassion? Could that possibly be enough?

Or did the old definitions, the dividing lines, no longer hold sway? Had they changed like everything else in this twisted world?

"You have a busy head," May Catches the Enemy said, intruding on his thoughts. She touched his hand, and he was surprised to find that her touch discomforted him more than the blade at his throat had.

Catching this reaction, she smiled. It was the first time he'd seen her smile, and it transformed her, rendered her girlish and appealing. He saw she had a dimple in one cheek, the fire lending her skin a warm glow.

"It's a good thing you're here," she said, growing serious again. "Mostly, those who made it here are old folks, some kids. We only got one or two holy men, and that won't be enough. . . ."

"For what?" Cal asked.

May Catches the Enemy gave him another smile, but with mystery in it, and the promise of coming things.

"Better get some sleep while you can," she said, rising.

"I haven't slept much since the Change," he replied.

She gazed down at him. "The world hasn't changed," she said, "just revealed more clearly what it always was, so everyone can see it plain."

She fell silent, meditative. Then she murmured, soft as a feather touch, "Folks got so busy, everything so noisy and fast, they forgot who they were. Things had to get quiet again, so they could find the being in human being, get connected to the universe again, to the world, to their power. . . ."

It was amazing, Cal thought, that here, surrounded by the forces of darkness, cut off from anything that might bring reinforcements or aid, she could so effortlessly, so simply summon up hope. Her certainty, her self, was like a golden spike driven straight through her to the center of the earth.

Cal felt something inside him come alive and warm. And for the second time since he had entered the Ghostlands, he felt he was home.

With a start, he realized he was staring at her. She lowered her eyes. "I didn't mean to make a speech," she said.

"It's okay," he answered, then added, "I like your world."

She brought her eyes up to him once more, and he floated in her gaze. "The big circle of everything," she concluded. "The four quarters, four winds, four directions, four races . . . all balanced in unity."

*Unity?* At this last, Cal found his mind rebelling. *What about the Evil inside that mountain?*

As though answering his thought, May said, "No such thing as the Devil, only a sickness at the heart of things, an imbalance."

She bent to him, kissed him lightly on the head. "Pray to see what's real, Mr. Griffin . . . and you will."

Cal wasn't aware of having fallen asleep, but he was awakened by the rumble of the earth opening up and daylight pouring in.

A man stood facing him from the gaping mouth of the land, a man all in black, his gleaming black hair pulled into a ponytail and held in place with a white gold clasp.

"You may have wondered why I've asked you here," the man said with a voice like acid-scraped rock.

Cal's eyes darted to where he'd lain his sword in its scabbard. Christina was no longer there. He dove for it, rolled and came up fast.

The man was sauntering up to him, his face and body melting in the morning sun like candle wax, shifting and re-forming into black iridescence, into truth, into reptilian splendor.

He laughed as Cal drew his sword.

"You don't want to kill the man who saved your sister," the dragon said.

Cal lowered his sword.

"I didn't think so."

A figure appeared from behind the dragon, walking on spindly old legs, her tan, lined face like the land itself, with its patience and wear.

"We've got a good deal of catching up to do," Mama Diamond said, putting a hand on Cal's arm.

Together with Stern, she took him to where the others waited.

# FORTY-NINE

## THE KING OF INFINITE SPACE

N*ow, this is really interesting,* Herman Goldman thought.

In the terrible moment when he'd tried to leech the life force out of the blazing projection of Marcus Sanrio and found it to be a *horribly* misguided style choice (much akin to all those Blind Dates of Dr. Moreau he'd gone on in his college days, when his aberrant behaviors could be fobbed off as merely the excesses of youth), Goldie had assumed that he'd pretty much bought the farm.

*And what the hell was he gonna do with a farm?* . . .

But no, seriously, he thought he'd cashed his chips, sounded the trumpet, kicked every bucket from here to Poughkeepsie.

In short, that he was dead meat. In fact, in that one, endless, eternal second, he'd fast-forwarded through every damn Kübler-Ross stage of dying—denial, anger, bargaining, depression, acceptance—and all seven dwarves and thirty-one flavors, to boot.

But most of all, he saw his entire life. Not flashing before him like some preposterous VCR playback on crystal methamphetamine, but rather the *shape* of it—a multidimensional object rendering every action, intention, memory into a complete and seamless whole.

And being *his* life, its form was naturally . . . *unusual.* Gaudy and eccentric; sort of like the entire universe laid out as a bird of paradise, all bright colors and odd angles.

It was all there, in hyperrealistic Technicolor. Every time he'd fallen on his face, ranted when he should have whispered, sang when he should have stayed mute—and that last, impetuous *jeté* with Sanrio, when he'd failed big-time.

But he could also discern that there was honor there, and forthrightness and valor; the attempt, at least, to render on the canvas of his existence something worth doing.

All in all, it was a life he could live with.

Which, surprisingly, was exactly what he found he was doing.

The abstract construction of his life winked out, and Herman Goldman, Esquire, *didn't.*

He was still alive, still conscious, still experiencing things.

It was just that things happened to be, well . . . kinda *funky.*

For one thing, he didn't exactly seem to have a body. No hands, feet, mouth, nose—in fact, none of the parts you'd need to have a complete Herman Goldman collection.

Just a rather nebulous consciousness, an ongoing, stable (as stable as he ever got, that was) awareness of self. He felt like a helium balloon floating through the clouds, untethered, unconnected to anything.

Yet for some reason, he felt okay. He also felt damn certain this was *not* some wacky expression of the Afterlife. After all, he'd read pretty damn thoroughly on the subject, and this *wasn't* it.

So just where the hell was he? . . .

"Welcome to my world," said a voice in his mind.

Then it introduced itself as Fred Wishart.

Herman Goldman had met Fred Wishart before, in the desolate and devastated house in Boone's Gap, West Virginia, when Wishart had almost nixed the whole town in an attempt to keep his twin brother, Bob, alive and incidentally keep himself out of the clutches of the ravenous Gestalt Entity at the Source that was equally bent on reeling him back in.

But back then, Wishart had possessed a physical manifestation, a sort of überbody made up of starlight, glowing nuclear embers that flared and extinguished themselves and were continually replenished out of the life energy of everything around him.

It was a description that jibed with the way Shango described Wishart when he'd encountered him on his first delightful little jaunt into the Badlands.

But it was nothing like what presented itself as Wishart now.

For one thing, this manifestation had no body whatsoever, no more than Herman Goldman himself had. Instead, it was merely a cloudy presence, a distinctness apart from the generalized hazy nothingness about them, just as Goldie himself seemed merely an *apartness* rather than a physical presence.

Which he supposed made them, in the inimitable words of Stan Laurel, *two peas in a pot. . . .*

"Um, how's it hangin'?" Goldie asked.

"You're in great danger," the Wishart cloud replied.

*Oh, marvelous.*

"Yeah, well, that's not exactly a surprise," Goldie replied. It had essentially been his general state, waking and sleeping, for a good long time now, and he certainly didn't need Mr. Cumulus here to point it out to him.

"I tried to protect the Russian one, the doctor," the Wishart consciousness continued absently, as if to himself, "I drew a place from his mind, a place of serenity, to shield him . . . but he wouldn't stay put."

"Yeah, well, that's Doc, always antsy." Goldie realized that neither of them was exactly *talking*—a good thing, considering their notable lack of tongue, teeth and larynx (not to mention anything that could even remotely *hang* . . .). "Say listen, you think you could point me toward an exit?"

*And while you're at it, maybe a body?*

"There's no leaving," Wishart responded dolefully. "And no hiding place, once *He* awakes . . ."

"He? He who?" Goldman asked, although he felt reasonably sure he already knew. Despite his total lack of a body, he shuddered nonetheless.

*Sanrio . . .*

"Yes . . ." Wishart replied, and Goldie realized the other could read his thoughts. Or, he amended, his *private* thoughts, the ones he intended for himself.

It filled him with dread, a sense of violation. Wishart, or what was left of him, seemed to mean no harm. But Wishart wasn't the only teddy bear on this here picnic, and the casualness with which he invaded Goldman's mental garden of verse gave a hint of darker things.

*Fuck it, I'm outta here,* Goldie thought and, spurred by his fear, felt his consciousness plunge forward—

Which happened to be right *through* Fred Wishart.

Goldie felt a sudden rush of memories and sensations, a headlong tumult of images and sounds and smells and feelings. Little League and Stanford and the movie house in Beckley, and that fishing trip with Bobby when they were both teens, the two of them with Wilma Hanson along, all three of them laughing their asses off, even though she was older, of his mother, Arleta, and his doctor father, who died young . . .

The memories that were the totality of Dr. Fred Wishart.

*Oh God* . . . Goldie thought, and he'd have tossed his cookies right then and there, if he'd had cookies to toss or a stomach to toss them from.

"Where *am* I?" Goldie asked.

"You know that, don't you?" Fred Wishart said.

Yeah. Yeah, he did. . . .

Beyond Wishart, he could sense murmurings, harmonies and cacophonies of other minds. He extended his consciousness outward, tentatively brushed the other dominant psyches held in thrall there. Sakamoto and Agnes Wu, St. Ives and Pollard, and the other names he knew full well from Larry Shango's list.

And out beyond them, like an asteroid belt or Oort Cloud of mentalities, lesser minds, banked down, orbiting, tethered fast.

Thousands and thousands of them . . .

The flares.

He could sense them distantly without even trying, sense their variant stories, their divergent histories, each an individual who'd once been human, once had a family.

Trapped here.

*No leaving, and no hiding place* . . .

He could invade them, pick the lock on the strongbox of memory, pilfer their thoughts and keepsakes, just as Wishart had done with him, and he with Wishart.

But beyond them, within them, he sensed another thing, resonant and myriad. . . .

"The flares hold all the minds they have touched," Wishart said, discerning his thought. "Even those who have gone before."

*Oh sweet Lord,* Herman Goldman thought, the impossible, wild hope born suddenly within him. He extended his mind like a great hand stretching out, passing through the multitudinous awareness like a mighty wind striking many trees as it roared through a forest.

And at last, at last, at last . . . he found her.

*Magritte.*

Not alive and whole, not all of her, but the *essence,* the core, preserved, held pristine.

He inhaled her, embraced and enfolded her, took her into himself and made her inseparable, as he had once recognized the one he'd labeled the Devil as himself, as he had once welcomed madness.

The part of him grown bitter and mean since her senseless, pitiless death—that had jettisoned mercy and nearly tortured a poor innocent grunter boy in the missile silo back in Iowa, and had tried so desperately to kill Marcus Sanrio, that *Thing* who was no longer a man—dissolved like thirst in quenching waters.

For the first time in his life, and despite the fact that he had no body, Herman Goldman knew that he was whole, and healed, and sane.

Then everything outside him fell away, and all was Fred Wishart's futile, terrified warning.

*"He rises!"*

And a mind at center, all the other wills revolving about it and lending it certitude and power, brought its scrutiny to bear on Herman Goldman.

YOU KNOW A GOOD DEAL I CAN USE, it thought at him, utterly remorseless and cold.

Marcus Sanrio went into Herman Goldman's mind and emptied it, turned it inside out and shook it like a pocket on a pair of jeans.

The pain was appalling, and went on and on. Goldie screamed and knew there was nothing he could hold back, no secret he could keep, no sanctuary set aside.

It was crazy badness, and it was only going to get worse.

But Goldie had known craziness before, and he could ride this wave, even as it shattered him and blew him apart.

With the last bit of will he could muster, he envisioned a board beneath his feet, a board he could ride.

The board was Magritte.

# FIFTY

## The Dragon's Tale

S*oon you'll be past the pain . . . where no one can touch you,* Ely Stern had said.

It had been night then, too, but not bone-cold like this, no, sticky-hot and humid, where the summer air plastered your clothes to your skin and all you wanted to do was shear a hydrant clear off its base so the cooling geyser would give you some momentary relief.

Not that he'd been wearing clothes by then . . . unless you counted the pebbled, iridescent black leather that was a second skin to him; his appalling, magnificent dragon's hide.

He had flown up to perch atop the night-wreathed tower overlooking the dying city that had been New York. Flown up with the delicate mutating girl whom he had fancied his guest, although other, less generous souls might have dubbed her his captive. She was shaking, wracked with delirium, blue devil fire eddying about her, altering her cell by cell, remaking her into something new and strange and fine.

Incredible that, at that point, she'd been the only one he'd seen touched by the hand of destiny like himself; he'd even fancied the two of them might be the only such in the world. Now he knew there were thousands, millions like them; the post-human beings.

Not that the knowledge made him feel any less alone.

In his fear and impulsiveness and solitude, he had seized her away from her home and the brother who raised her, the one who had once been his employee, and brought her to this barren rooftop to complete her metamorphosis, not merely into this new, inhuman form, but into his companion, his confidante.

What madness.

He had worried she might be frightened, but if she was she'd masked it and—in spite of her fever, of the pain coursing through bone and muscle and flesh—had substituted defiance.

"'What monstrosities would walk the streets were men's faces as unfinished as their minds,'" he'd exulted, quoting the philosopher Hoffer, and adding that, to him, they wouldn't be monstrosities but rather *masterpieces*, rendered beautiful by their undeniable truth.

Then he'd offered her the world.

"I don't want your world," she'd replied, and ran staggering to fling herself off the building.

What fire, what glorious certainty and contempt.

She hadn't known then—*couldn't* have known—that in time, like him, she'd be able to fly. And at that moment, still more human than not, she couldn't have; she'd have plummeted a thousand feet and died.

She would have, too, if not for the timely arrival of her brother, with his bravado and ridiculous sword, intent on saving her from the monster.

From him.

So he and Cal Griffin had gone on their wild ride flying through the black skyscraper canyons of New York, the aerobatic *danse de mort* that had culminated in his big-shouldered reptilian self getting skewered like a shish kebob at a sidewalk falafel stand.

A night of surprises all round, as he, not the girl, had fallen eighty stories to the unyielding pavement below, to hear his bones smash like a bag of glass and have nothingness enfold him like leather wings.

Then, like a tentative touch on his shoulder, rousing him to agonized half-consciousness, the sound of echoing light footsteps, a tapping cane.

And the querulous words "How we doin' there? . . ." in a voice that crackled like autumn leaves.

"I've had . . . better days," Stern had croaked through the pain, which elicited a laugh that had no meanness in it, that shared a wealth of understanding and suffering.

"Well, you just take it slow," Papa Sky had answered, putting a gentle hand on his bloody, broken hide. "We gonna see what we can do about that."

The old blind man had been a fool. To take him in, to nurse him back to health. What could it possibly bring him, except the likelihood of an abruptly shortened life and painful death?

Not that Stern would have wanted that; it was just the way things tended to sort themselves out. It was a violent world, and to survive one had to take violence on.

But that wasn't how things had worked out.

Immobilized, lying in Papa Sky's ludicrously cramped flat, in his absurdly small bed, Stern had found himself with nothing to do with his time but talk.

And Papa Sky had been more than willing to listen.

Not that Papa seemed to have any agenda, nor even any judgment—or at least, judgment he expressed.

And absurdly, impossibly, after a dozen *pointless* years of therapy, in which the only discernible change to his life Stern had perceived had been the financing of a yacht and any number of Caddies for the sedentary quack who'd sat silently listening to him those interminable hours, with none of the empathy nor wisdom this old black music man brought to bear . . .

Ely Stern found himself changing.

Not that he didn't still have that same burning rage that drove him to smash and destroy, to lash out blindly . . .

But now there was a new thing within him, like Papa Sky's gentling hand on his bloody, fractured self, urging him to pause, to *reconsider*, to look at the world with fresh eyes.

Incredibly, Papa Sky, that old blind man, had given him new sight.

He could choose to be the destroyer, could act upon his blazing dark impulses, and be utterly alone.

Or he could try another path, one far more dangerous to him, exhilarating and fraught with peril.

But did the world, at this absurdly late stage of the game, allow the possibility of such change?

Silly question.

The world of late had been nothing *but* change.

Which left him with the question of who he was, and what precisely he was going to do with the rest of his life.

As Papa Sky served him hot chicken soup and serenaded him with soaring saxophone medleys of Gershwin and Irving Berlin and Cole Porter, Ely Stern had looked into himself for an answer, for meaning, and to his amazement discovered . . .

Christina.

To find her, to protect her, that and nothing more, was all his soul desired.

Remarkable.

It was self-interest driving him, of course, as it always had been, but now bent to a different purpose.

He knew by then where she would be drawn, inevitably, and knew the only course that would lead him to her.

He opened his mind to the voices, to the One Voice, to the Source. The wind would carry him there, and the barrier he had seen in his dreams, the barrier that would burn lesser creatures, would not burn him.

He rose before he was properly mended, groaned with the effort . . . and found Papa Sky facing him on the doorstep.

"I figger you gonna need me around to keep you honest," the old man said.

Stern laughed. Like his own monstrous self, it was the undeniable truth.

And as the two of them traveled their scorching road, Ely Stern found to his amazement that Papa Sky held within him not only wisdom but power, too, that he could more than stand on his own two feet, as well as ride on the back of a dragon.

They made their way to South Dakota, and knocked on the Devil's door.

"You really expect us to believe that?" Cal Griffin asked Stern, as he sat around the big circle with the others—Colleen, Doc, Mama Diamond, Papa Sky, Shango, Enid and Howard Russo, Inigo and his mother. Christina floated nearby like a bubble containing all the world's rainbows, while the other inhabitants of the sanctuary, the Indian families and the shamans, the holy ones and medicine men, busied themselves in the deeper recesses of the cavern.

"No, Mr. Bond, I expect you to *die*," Stern replied, in his best Ernst Blofeld *Goldfinger* impersonation. He crouched low in the vast cavern, wings tucked in against his body, arched cathedral-like above his demon head, a black thing in the blackness. He glowered at Cal, showing switchblade teeth. "You really expect me to give two shits what you believe?"

"Now, now, we not gonna get anywhere like that," Papa Sky soothed. "We all on the same side here."

"I must admit, I find that a challenging concept to accept," Doc Lysenko remarked.

"Yeah, lizard boy," Colleen added, "if you're such a reformed character, how come you've been the Source Project's delivery boy? What's with all the smash-and-grab in those gem shops?"

Stern fumed, but Papa Sky said simply, "Tell the folks, Ely."

Stern sighed, glanced at Christina, who hovered glowing nearby, her face a mask that betrayed little of her feelings. "It wasn't going to let her *go*, that was certain from the git-go, and It had half a mind to atomize Papa and my humble self right fucking there and then, it's *touchy* that way. . . ."

Stern looked off, and his eyes narrowed, remembering. "But then I realized—it was a potential *client*. So the pertinent question wasn't what *I* needed but what *It* would need. I had to put myself in *Its* shoes, even if It didn't have shoes anymore, or feet to put them on."

His eyes slid back to Cal and the others. "This was all surmise, you understand. I wasn't really seeing *It*, just a manifestation, that fucking glowing scarecrow that changed from one to another to another. . . ."

"And what precisely did you discern was Its need?" Doc asked.

Stern shrugged. "Even though It was growing in power, It still had limitations, vulnerabilities. It had plans, ways to safeguard Itself and gain primacy, but It needed someone to put matters into motion, and those gray mental midgets It ruled"—here he glanced at Inigo and Howie—"no offense, didn't have, let us say, the *initiative* to run things on the ground."

He looked at Christina, and his expression softened. "So I cut a deal with It. Reconstitute her as human, or at least *looking* human, before she was burnt up like coal in an oven, fodder like the rest of the flares, set her up in digs like she had back home.

"Round about then, I came upon *this* one," he flicked a clawed finger at Inigo, "stuck like a fly in jelly. He couldn't get out, but It didn't seem inclined to pick him off, either. He was under the radar, It wasn't paying attention to him. So I figured I'd give him a job. . . ."

Colleen shook her head. "And you did all this 'cause you're wearing the white hat now?"

Stern's eyes blazed. "You may not have noticed, but this isn't a comic strip. *Christ*, I am so *glad* I didn't have to travel with the lot of you."

"Now, now, Ely," Papa Sky crooned. "We all gettin' hot under the collar here. You remember your blood pressure."

Stern nodded, and Cal could see him struggling to force calm.

"You're telling us," said Cal, "that you stole all those gems, helped set up the Spirit Radio, just to keep Christina safe?"

"Not just that . . ."

"What then?"

May Catches the Enemy spoke up. "That Thing in the mountain, it's crazy scared, wants to swallow up the four corners, swallow up everything, so it can be safe."

"How do you know that?" Shango asked.

May Catches the Enemy shrugged, the firelight catching highlights in her black hair. "You feel it. It's in the air, the water, in everything."

"So eventually, there'd be no more dragons," Stern added, "no more people or grunters or flares—just *It*, a totality of everything."

He glared at Colleen. "So if you don't want to believe I did this all to help *her*"—he nodded toward Tina—"you just tell yourself I did it for self-preservation."

A tense silence descended over them.

"So It designed the Spirit Radio . . ." Doc prompted.

"Stuck here in the Black Hills, It knows It's a target," Stern observed. "But if It can open up conduits to other locales, exist simultaneously in a number of places—"

"No one thing can kill it," Shango finished.

"Give the man a set of dishes," Stern said. "The one in Iowa's the first of many. There's a bunch more in the planning stages all across the U.S. That's why we have to move now."

"Why didn't you just kill It?" Colleen asked Stern. "I mean, Judas Escariot, you're the one who can breathe fire."

"It never let me close enough," Stern replied, with a hint of ire. "I dealt solely with Its projections, all those images that look human. I saw It once, you know—what It *really* is, just for a second." Stern shuddered then. "Just a blur, I couldn't say exactly. Then It slammed the lid. But It could have killed me anytime it wanted. It doesn't suffer fools gladly, or anyone, for that matter."

"Wouldn't it have been simpler," Shango asked, "just to bring Christina back to Griffin, and tell us the whole deal?"

"Did people get *stupider* while I was away? I told you, It wouldn't let her *go*."

*And maybe*, Cal thought, *you liked having her to yourself.* Sharing her only sporadically with Inigo and Papa Sky; a contained world of four.

"So you brought us here," said Cal, nodding toward Inigo and Papa Sky. "Using them."

Inigo began, "I'm sorry I couldn't tell you—"

Stern cut him off, addressing Cal. "Had to play a close hand, bunky. The Big Bad Thing can get into your mind, read it like the morning paper—particularly little peanut *human* minds like yours. Couldn't risk It getting the drop before you got here."

Doc looked concerned. "But It *must* have. . . . After all, It closed the portal behind us."

"Mm? Nah, that was me. I kicked the shit out of your damping equipment, let the whole thing run wild."

There was an explosion of outraged protests. Stern shouted them down. "I didn't *kill* anyone, all right? And that was a major bitch to manage, believe me."

Silence settled again, like snow in winter light.

Finally, Papa Sky said, "Let 'em know the rest of it, Ely."

Stern blew a contemptuous breath from his reptilian nostrils, but surprisingly Cal could detect something like regret in his gravel voice. "There's what you might call a *downside*. . . . We've kind of *jump-started* things. It's spreading out there in Iowa, the Bad Thing's power, Its control. Slowly at first, but once It gets a head of steam up, It'll gobble up everyone and everything."

Cal was horrified, saw his emotion mirrored on the faces of the others. He thought of the ones he had left in Atherton, the ones who had made their journey here possible—Rafe Dahlquist, Krystee Cott, Mike Kimmel and the rest. To have them subsumed into the Source, crumbled to nothing and destroyed . . .

Like Goldie.

Despair surged up in him again, the impulse toward hopelessness and defeat. Then his eye caught Mama Diamond's, and she gave him a wink. He had thought her lost, too, and she had returned. Not every surprise was a bad one, and the Source Entity wasn't the only one holding a hand of cards that could still be played.

"How long will it take?" he asked Stern.

The dragon shrugged. "Let's just say if we're gonna do something, it'd be advisable not to take an extended lunch."

Cal rounded on him with a sudden fury. "*What the hell made you do that?*"

"Two reasons," Stern answered, the regret giving way to cold pragmatism, the lawyer in him. "First, it's like Hitler with the Russian front. Establishing a second beachhead, gaining dominance, weakens It, takes Its attention and resources. That's why It couldn't stop you getting to the Stronghold here. It gives us a window of opportunity."

"And second?" prompted Shango.

"There's this Lakota thing called *Napesni*. . . ." Stern looked to May Catches the Enemy.

"The No-Flights," she explained. "Warriors who staked themselves to the ground in battle so they'd have to triumph or die."

Stern nodded. "I figured, no back door, you're gonna take it to the max."

"Lovely," said Colleen.

"Why us?" Cal asked. "Why me?"

"I'm not a people person," Stern replied. "You are, cupcake."

May Catches the Enemy canted her head in apparent agreement. "Folks generally fall to pieces or rise to their best depending on who's around to lead them." She turned to Cal. "Way I hear it, you done pretty good on your way here from New York."

"Besides . . ." Stern hesitated. "I had this dream."

He spoke lower now in his sandpaper rasp, and Cal could see the memory shook him. "It's dark all around, and you're at the heart of it, holding that damn sword, and everyone's begging you to *do* something. . . ."

Cal found he'd broken into a sweat. "And do I?" His voice was barely audible.

"I don't know," Stern answered frankly, looking at him with a gentleness, a *humanity*, Cal had never seen before. "But you're the only one who can."

Mama Diamond could see that the others were having a hard time taking this all in, just as she herself had, soon after Ely Stern had plucked her from amidst the buffalo of the living dead and saved her bacon.

Even so, she had learned this was a world that demanded you looked at it for what it *was* rather than what you thought or wanted it to be.

Whatever he might seem, in the end Stern had been no thief, merely a conservator and strategist, setting a pace that led them all here, and kept them effective and whole.

It was whatever dwelt at the Source that was the real thief, that wanted to steal away not only all they possessed, but their precious selves as well—while the journey Ely Stern had set in motion had served only to bring Mama Diamond to her own true self.

As for what awaited them at the Source, if they succeeded in reaching and confronting It, might It be as different from what Mama Diamond imagined as Stern had turned out to be?

She didn't know.

On the way here, as Stern had borne her through clouds blown along the frigid eastern winds, the dragon had told her that the strongest person was the one who could look *anything* in the eye and not blink.

Now, sitting here in the belly of the earth that had enthralled and beguiled her for so long, Mama Diamond prayed for the strength to see (with the unclouded eyes so recently brought to humming clarity by the dragon's gift) what lay at the Source for what It truly was.

"Let's recap, shall we?" Colleen said. "We're trapped in the Badlands with dwindling food, almost no weapons, buried under the ground with a dragon and a bunch of Indians. Yeah, we're on rails here."

May Catches the Enemy bristled. "Lady, you could use some spirituality."

Colleen bulled up to May, getting right in her face. "First, I'm no lady, and *second*—"

Cal stepped between them before it could escalate into a knife fight. "Drop it," he said to Colleen.

Cooling, she backed off. Cal took May aside, away from the others, and spoke softly. "You got a problem with any of us, you bring it to me, okay?"

"Yeah, sorry. . . . Guess I'm not Little Miss Centered all the time."

Despite the urgency, despite the weight of grief like a stone in him, Cal smiled. "It's just what you told me. No divisions between people anymore, we don't have time for it. We want to live, we get over ourselves."

She smiled back. "You're a good listener . . . and a fast learner." She cocked her head quizzically. "How are you at dancing?"

"Dancing?" he asked, puzzled.

She led him along with the others to a big steamer trunk and unlocked it. Cal saw that it was filled with fringed garments made of leather that were painted white with various markings. She held one up to him.

He knew it for the forbidden thing it had been, had seen one like it in a museum once. Long ago, it had been the last, sad expression of a ravaged, defiant people, and the sorcery it had claimed had been only an empty promise, like a dry wind on parched lands.

But whether May Catches the Enemy thought this was a new world or not, Cal knew the rules of the game had changed greatly . . . and this garment once made of dreams might hold a very different substance indeed.

It was a Ghost Dance Shirt.

# FIFTY-ONE

## The Jeweled Ring

Crouching like a gargoyle on the high ledge of the Aaron Copland building under the silent moon, Theo Siegel looked down upon the rolling expanse of malignant light.

*I've got to get through that,* he thought, *and I can't do it like this. I've got to speed things up.*

And there was only one way he knew that might do that.

His fingernails were growing sharper, becoming almost like claws. With one hand, he reached back to his neck, felt the hard bump under the skin where Jeff had implanted the jeweled ring that had kept him human, that might still be doing what it could to hold on to the remnant of his humanity. . . .

He gritted his teeth, and with one fierce motion, slashed open the skin.

He threw the ring, glinting in the moonlight, far out across the sky.

Then, changing, he set off for the cupola. For Melissa.

All Melissa Wade knew was that she hurt. She hurt, and she burned. And she felt light, as light as a dandelion clock (she'd learned that term from her departed English professor dad, with his love of words and mechanisms; funny that such a delicate thing would have a name that conjured up wheels and gears), almost as light as the air itself.

As in a dream, she'd come here from the Sculpture Garden, to the place she invariably went when she was troubled. Her aerie, she called it. The little observatory on campus.

Sitting on the floor in a litter of sidereal charts and astronomy journals, she heard an echoing, metallic knock, and at first glanced foggily at the door. But then she realized the sound had come from above, and looked up.

A figure was peering down at her from around the open lip of the dome beside the telescope, silhouetted against the night sky.

"Melissa?" it rasped, in a guttural voice that sounded somehow familiar. The figure climbed in, began scurrying down the roof of the dome, upside down, like an immense spider.

She felt a distant horror, but could not command herself to move.

But as the creature approached and gazed down at her with immense, gentle eyes, despite the terrible alteration she recognized him.

"Hello, Theo," she said.

Theo had seen people turn into flares before. Melissa was going through the process at a terribly rapid rate. Already, her skin seemed nearly transparent. She held her hands palm-flat to the floor, as if she were afraid of losing contact with the planet. Her golden eyes were luminous in the shadow of the telescope.

"Melissa," he said.

Her attention flickered but held.

She said, "What happened?"

"The Spirit Radio. It won't turn off, and it's letting something through."

"Is that why we're . . . changing?"

As if on cue, Theo felt a spasm clench the muscles of his legs as the bones slowly morphed. Tendons coiled, skin flexed and loosened. The persistent itch grew worse. At least the ragged wound at the back of his neck, the self-inflicted gash he'd made, was healing fast. Along with the night vision and superhuman strength, it was one of the perks of his growing nonhuman status.

"We need Jeff to fix us again," Melissa whispered.

"Melissa . . . he's gone."

"No . . ."

"Melissa, I saw it. It got him." Whatever *It* was . . .

"He'll come," she murmured, half delirious. "He always does."

True enough on past occasions, for good or ill, and mostly ill. But Theo felt reasonably certain all bets were off now.

At the back of the cupola was a small maintenance room with a window overlooking Philosopher's Walk and the campus quad.

"Is the window open?" Melissa asked with trepidation.

"No," Theo said.

With an incredible effort of will, she rose to her feet in a series of halting motions that were painful to watch, and hobbled over to the window.

He understood why Melissa was cautious of the window. She was afraid she would forget about gravity and loft away like a child's balloon. He pictured her adrift among the stars. One more distant light in the sky.

At the window, she stood with her hands against the sill and her eyes resolutely fixed on the campus. "Hold me down," she said. "I'm dizzy. Anchor me."

Tentatively, Theo stood behind her and wrapped his arms around her waist, as he had longed to do on so many days past.

The heat of her was shocking. He pressed himself against her.

She watched through the window for Jeff.

His own pain increased, along with a foggy sleepiness that became irresistible. After a time he slid down to the floor, his arms still loosely wrapped around Melissa's feverish ankles, and closed his eyes.

When he woke, she was gone.

In his panic, Theo looked to the window. But the window was still sealed. He saw his own reflection in the glass. Saw the whiteness of his eyes, the gray maggot skin, the glinting sharp teeth. The image was mesmerizing, and appalling.

His mind felt blunted, and he wondered with a thrill of fear how much longer he might be able to think.

Even now, words were coming more slowly to his mind, like hieroglyphs carved in sandstone being eroded by the wind. Words fading to a fine, flat geometric plain.

Outside on Philosopher's Walk, he saw that the glowing sea of infection had settled, muted down to cover each surface like a coating of Christmas flocking on a tree. He spied a figure shambling away from the physics wing, and knew from the shape of him and the familiar way he moved, favoring his right leg, that it was Jeff.

And hurrying to catch him, half running, half floating over the eerie, arc-lit blue of the grass, was Melissa.

As she reached him, he turned to her.

Seeing him fully now at last, she began to scream.

# FIFTY-TWO

## Our Strange Man

"Dig it," Colleen Brooks said balefully, scowling at the Ghost Dance Shirt she held up before her. "I *don't* dance."

Months earlier, May Catches the Enemy had known that if any of them were going to get anywhere at all, she would need some warriors, a few musicians and a natural-born leader.

Now, looking out at Cal Griffin and her other new comrades as they stood on the grassy plateau of Cuny Table, the sky a searing cold blue above them, not a cloud in sight to the end of the world, she knew she had gotten her wish.

The snow had melted off mostly, and the land was a dusty green where foliage grew and cracked brown earth where it didn't. Minutes before, she had signaled Walter Eagle Elk, a frail elder with a sun-lined face like the Badlands themselves, to open the earth to let them emerge out onto the land.

Which was risky, she explained to them, as it could draw the attention of the Sick Thing at the Source . . . but vital, nonetheless.

She'd handed each of them—with the exception of Ely Stern and Christina Griffin, who watched from the sidelines—a Ghost Dance Shirt, which she herself now wore, and requested they don them.

And they all had done so, even Howard Russo and Inigo, looking like kids trying to wear Daddy's clothes.

All except Colleen Brooks. A real pain in the ass, that gal, and a ballbuster to boot.

But when the chips were down, May reflected, that might not be such a bad thing.

Doc Lysenko sidled up to Colleen, gave her a playful nudge. "Come, Colleen, you don't want to be a wet blanket, now do you?" The fringe on the arms of the white leather shirt he wore rippled in the breeze.

"Viktor, what the hell are we doing here? I want to kick some Source Project butt—not boogy on down."

May Catches the Enemy came up to her, gestured at the breathtaking vista about them. "Crazy Horse said, 'My lands are where my people are buried. . . .'"

"Yeah? And where's that get us?"

May saw that Cal Griffin was studying her intently, a contemplative expression on his face. "Maybe nowhere," he murmured. But she could tell from his tone that he intuited what she had in mind.

"We pray for all living things," May Catches the Enemy said to them all, by way of preamble. "We pray through all the spirits of the world, through the two-legged people and the four-legged people, through the animal people and the bird people and the fish people, and especially the tree people. We pray through them to the Great God Creator. The spirit world is the real world."

She fixed her gaze on Cal Griffin, and said in a quieter tone, "And when we speak to the dead, we say, 'We shall see you again. . . .'"

May nodded at Walter Eagle Elk, and to his grandson Ethan, whom he'd been training (the playfriend who, as a child, May had tauntingly called Ethan Ties Shoelaces Together). They began to beat their drums and chant in a mournful, hollow tone that rolled out over the tableland, drawing lilting responses from the cowbirds and meadowlarks, and the wrens who had not fled the brute winter.

And maybe this had once been a dance only for men, May realized, her pulse quickening with hope and excitement, and maybe only men had once been the warriors. . . .

But this was no time for such distinctions.

May Catches the Enemy, who was sometimes called Lady Blade

and who had once been May Devine, drew her knives and, circling, began to dance.

One by one, the others followed suit—including, at the last, a grumbling Colleen Brooks.

Griffin's sister Christina was moving now, too, flowing in the air with deft motions that left streaks of entwined color and light in her wake. May Catches the Enemy found herself staring openmouthed at the fairy girl, knowing that her soul was that of a dancer.

Watching May and doing what she did, moving to the beat, Cal came up alongside Enid Blindman and Papa Sky. "Play with all you've got," he called to them. *"Play to wake the dead."*

They set to it with a will. Their music swirled and spiraled around the drumbeat and voices, gained assurance and majesty, filled up the sky and the land.

And from the Black Hills, from the rotted, cancerous Thing at its core, an answer came.

Angry black clouds spread out like a carpet unrolling, suffocating the sky, and from within them flared blinding flashes like worlds exploding.

The lightning rained down.

Howling, Stern took to the sky, breathing flame up at the heavens, deflecting the raging death strokes. Christina, too, extended her radiance, twisting the sizzling current away from the dancers to scorch prairie grass and barren trees scant yards away.

The lightning bolts increased their fury, pounding down like blazing fists, ravaging the land. Tortured, unthinking animals, summoned by the Mind that could not be denied, streamed out from the hills, shrieking maniacally, launching themselves with fang and claw, to be immolated on this killing ground.

"Keep dancing!" May called out to the others, and Cal took up the cry.

Slowly, barely perceptibly, the lightning began to die off, the clouds took on colors of red and blue and gold within the blackness, moving like the breath of a living thing.

The thunder came.

It boomed out like the universe clearing its throat and issued, not from the sick core of the Hills, but from somewhere deeper, and older still.

"The Thunder People!" May Catches the Enemy shouted over the roar. "The Thunder People summon their children!"

It reverberated through them and went on and on, rattled their bones and teeth, shook the ground beneath their feet, tumbled rocks and raised great plumes of dust into the muted and shrouded air.

"Son of a bitch!" Colleen Brooks exclaimed.

The land about them was rippling, turning over, like a rumpled sheet being reversed on a mattress. The ancient soil cracked, vented, bent away. . . .

And where it folded, something rose up from below.

Shadow forms, many hundreds of them spreading over the land, wraiths of smoke and ember and will.

As one, they turned toward the dancers and advanced on them.

Larry Shango slowed in his gyrations, edged up to Cal. Their eyes were locked on the coming forms.

"Is this a good thing," Larry Shango asked in a low voice, "or a bad one?"

Cal Griffin considered the figures, drifting toward them like fog. He could see now that some were shaped like men, and some like horses.

"A good thing," he said at last.

The others had stopped dancing now, the music fading off and the thunder banking down to a low rumble.

The shadow ones stopped before them.

"*Hua kola* . . ." the warrior in front said, and his voice was shadowy, too. He was no more than smoke and vapor, but Cal could see he stood well-muscled and tall, and the shadings of color within the smoke revealed curly brown hair and pale gray eyes. He wore a single eagle feather and behind his ear, a stone. Painted on his chest were a lightning bolt and two shapes that, in time, Cal would learn were hailstones.

Ely Stern had come to ground beside Cal, and Christina floated down silently, in awe. The others, too, gathered around him to face this newcomer and his brothers, who had been called forth by the thunder and not the Storm.

May Catches the Enemy stepped up to them and smiled. "I'd like you to meet my ancestor," she said, and introduced them to the one some had called Curly, and others Our Strange Man.

The one most had known as Crazy Horse.

# FIFTY-THREE

## Jewel and Wind

To say that May Catches the Enemy had made a believer of her was to overstate the case.

But as Colleen Brooks stood among the legion of ghost warriors and their shadow horses, she definitely had to admit her skepticism had been put somewhat on hold.

As the daybreak star rose and the Moon of the Popping Trees set, May Catches the Enemy led the lot of them, phantoms and all, back into the big hole in the earth, and sealed it up tight behind them.

"So how's all this getting us to Source Grand Central?" Howard Russo asked her.

May gestured toward one of the branching passageways. "These tunnels are uncharted extensions of Jewel and Wind Caverns, twelve hundred miles and more," she explained. "Some of the Lakota believe human beings first came up out of Wind Cave. . . . We're goin' back down."

*Lovelier and lovelier* . . . thought Colleen.

Stern stepped daintily to the passage mouth on ponderous feet, flexing his wings, limbering them. His nostrils stretched wide, drawing in the scent of what lay beyond in the darkness.

"What do you smell?" Cal asked, joining him.

"Death," Stern replied, then cast him a narrow glance. "How's your irony quotient?"

"Shoot."

"Borglum, the guy who built Rushmore, back in the twenties was in the KKK." Stern's lip twisted in a mirthless grin, revealing piranha teeth. "At the top was an Imperial Wizard, running an Invisible Empire. Under him were Grand Dragons, and the grunts were called goblins. . . ."

"Hilarious," Cal said.

Stern nodded, and his hooded eyes regarded the passage again, and the unseen things within.

"Any goblins left down there?" Cal asked.

"Wait and see," the dragon said.

Christina wafted up to them like a toy boat on a mild stream, regarded the tunnel with cool aplomb. Inigo followed close on, never taking his eyes off her.

"Might be best if you stayed here," Cal advised her.

"No way. I'm going, Cal."

"That's a deal breaker," Stern snapped in a tone that was . . . well, stern.

*It's like she has two fathers now,* Cal thought, and felt a pang of jealousy, resented how Stern had insinuated himself into her life; knowing, too, that she would not be here if not for that fact.

Stern was glaring at Christina as she hovered high off the ground at his eye level. She gazed right back, not giving an inch.

"You lose, how much chance you think we'll have that It won't come for us?" she said evenly.

Stern blinked, knocked back. Cal smiled inwardly; how many times had he encountered that same remorseless drive, the raw determination that had fueled her back when the only fortress she assailed was that of ballet, bent on conquering it and bringing it to heel.

With a sigh, Stern shook his head, yielding. She held within her such delicacy, such fragility, he felt as if he could snap her like a match.

But he knew it was not so. He thought of her on the precipice atop the tower in New York; she'd shown that same resolve.

*I don't want your world. . . .*

Well, now they were all sharing the same world, the lot of them—one with a monster lying in wait for them.

A monster that, for once, wasn't him.

They would all die, of course, no matter how many fucking ghost Indians had their back.

Nevertheless, his heart felt ridiculously light in him, and he cursed himself for a fool.

He'd given up job security, and one hell of a pension plan. I mean, talk about eternal life—even if it *did* ultimately entail getting devoured by a grotesquerie bent on not just *ruling* the world, but *being* every last fucking bit of it. . . .

It was laughable, and so that's precisely what Ely Stern did.

Like a great gout of flame, the laughter erupted from him, went booming down the passageway, preceding them into the entrails of hell.

When his mirth finally subsided, he turned to Cal Griffin, who had once been his underling and now was a great deal more than his better (not that he'd ever dream of *saying* that).

"Let's get this show on the road," Stern said.

The ghostly warriors unslung their weapons, carbines and bows and arrows made of vapor, and climbed aboard their shadow steeds. Indian fashion, the war ponies had no bridles nor saddles, no stirrups. Their tails were tied in a knot.

May Catches the Enemy followed suit, clambering aboard a dappled gray made of mist, which supported her just as though it were entirely substantial.

Colleen saw that nearby, Mama Diamond was speaking softly to one of the spectral mares, in a tongue only she and they could understand. Then she mounted it, with an effortlessness that was uncanny in a woman of her years, not to mention one that had endured such rough handling of late.

Colleen approached a pony that still remained riderless and recalled the words her father had said to her, of how he chose a dog.

*I look in its eyes, and if I see a soul there, I take him home.*

Cautiously, she drew near the creature's head, looked it square in the eye . . . and found reassurance there.

She climbed aboard.

It sat her well. She pressed her knees gently into its sides and wove her fingers into its insubstantial mane.

Seeing Doc hesitate, Colleen called out, "C'mon, Viktor, it's just like riding a bicycle." She was careful not to add, *One called back from the dead.*

Enid mounted a sorrel mare, hauling Papa Sky onto its rump behind him. Enid had his harmonica secured on its holder around his neck, Papa his sax on its strap.

The others climbed aboard their horses, Inigo and Howard Russo; even Walter Eagle Elk and his grandson Ethan, too.

Cal was the last to mount, and before he did Colleen saw him stash the battered leather portfolio inside his Ghost Shirt; the portfolio Goldman had brought him upon returning from his mission to fetch Enid Blindman, that she knew held an enigmatic collection of photographs and notes.

"What do you say to make it go?" Cal asked May.

"*Hoka hey*," she said.

"*Hoka hey!*" he cried, and the legion of them thundered off down the passageway, the horses' hooves flying into the darkness.

*It's kinda instant replay, but not exactly*, Inigo thought as he flew along the endless rock tunnel, down and down, back toward the place he'd lived in but never called home.

The last time he'd tried a stunt like this, he'd been clinging to the top of the hellbound train, plunging through the darkness to burst up out of the earth and deliver its gleaming treasure to Jeff Arcott and the waiting town of Atherton. Right now, he was holding on for dear life to the wispy mane of a nag that'd probably been bleaching bones on the prairie before Teddy Roosevelt was out of short pants.

This was better, if only marginally; the wind whipped at him, howling like a lost soul—or an army of them, more precisely. But the real army was the one riding alongside him—the ghost warriors and the human ones; Howard Russo, who was a creature like himself; the dragon Stern; and Christina, ever fair and flowing. If necessary, Inigo knew she was a beacon he would follow to his own burning death, or beyond.

He was not alone in this. Her brother Cal had done the same thing. It's what had led him to trust Inigo in the first place, despite the misgivings of his closest advisers; what had led him here, where'd he finally rescued his sister, only to return to the dread place of her imprisonment, in a wild attempt try to finish things up right.

Inigo realized that he liked Cal, he liked him a lot. And from the little he'd seen of the two of them together, so did his mom. Yet there was something else there, too, something troubled, that seemed to have a history in it. He didn't think the two of them had met before, didn't think they *could* have. Still, he made a mental note to ask his mom about it later . . . if there *was* a later, that was.

He realized his heart was pounding like a drum machine on meltdown, that he was scared right down to the soles of his leathery big feet. He forced himself to take a deep breath, tried to slow his pulse to a level below tachycardia.

Just then, the spirit horse banked around a sharp bend in the passage. Inigo yelped and clutched tightly to the beast's compact, muscled body so as not to be thrown clear. There was a roar from up ahead, and a burst of hot air surged past him, tingling his face like sunburn.

It was Stern, flying fast at the forefront, exhaling great explosions of flame every minute or so to clear the road. It lit up the cave spectacularly, making Inigo wince with the glare, providing flashbulb brilliance to accompany the more muted light provided by Christina's aura and the cool glow of the spectral warriors and their steeds.

Inigo wondered how long Stern could keep this up; did his flame come from some internal gas tank, or was it replenished from some other font?

*We'll see soon enough. . . .*

Apart from Stern's warming blasts, the tunnel was cold but not freezing, and the air was fresh. Behind him, Inigo could hear Enid Blindman and Papa Sky atop their mount, playing full out over the wind. The music hardly echoed at all, which surprised Inigo.

But then Mama Diamond explained that was due to the boxwork, the odd crystal formations in the ceiling, so-called because they looked like square post office boxes all in rows.

They didn't look like that to Inigo, though; they seemed like thousands of bats, just waiting to wake up and swarm down at them. He shuddered and fought to banish the thought.

"And see that there?" Mama Diamond shouted to him as they thundered on. "That white bumpy stuff's called cave popcorn, calcium carbonate deposited through limestone pores. And that curtainy stuff hanging down off those high ledges is called drapery, though it always reminded me of Wells's Martians, fat jellyfish with all those tentacles. Nailhead spar, and dogtooth . . . It's just crystal, though, laced with different minerals like iron and manganese."

Inigo suspected she was telling him all this because she sensed his apprehension, saw him as just a kid, and was trying to distract him from what lay ahead. It was quaint, courtly even, and it touched him—rather than pissing him off with its condescension, which it normally might have done.

Hell, they all had to look out for each other any way they could, even with the small stuff.

"I reckon we must be five hundred feet down, if we're an inch," Mama Diamond continued. "And will you *look* at what's up ahead. . . ."

Inigo cast his gaze forward, feeling a hint of trepidation for an instant. But then he saw it, stretching out wide before them. . . .

A *lake*, huge and black and serene, showing not even a ripple, save where an occasional droplet of water fell from the vault above. Stern winged above it into the darkness beyond, a perfect dragon reflection skimming below him in the water's mirror sheen. The wraith horses sped after, their hooves barely kissing the surface, throwing up light, bracing sprays.

Then they were past it. Inigo looked about him at the walls and ceiling, seeing deep into them with his night-blessed eyes, really studying them for the first time as they flashed by. They *were* incredibly beautiful, rose and blue and gold sparkling in the quartz, an astonishing array of shapes, spires and projections all honeycombed, with rivulets of water dripping down from fissures in the rock.

And because he was looking right there, and had the vision to discern it, he saw them first.

Oozing out of the boxwork, squeezing through, clambering down on the craggy rock face, flowing slick as oil.

*Grunters*, baring their snaggly, fanged teeth, glaring down with hungry, crazed faces, coming on fast. The massed, thick smell of them hit him like a blow, that stink of rotted meat and other unclean things; he wondered if it came from what they ate or just from *them*.

Inigo let out a shout, waving wildly upward. The others saw now, too, and unsheathed their blades, nocked arrows into bows. Stern swung about in a great arc, beating his black wings and climbing, inhaling deep to unleash the inferno.

The grunters let out wild, triumphant shrieks and released their holds, dropping down to land among them. Seeing this, Stern clipped off his exhalation; he couldn't let loose the torrent without claiming them all.

Cal was shouting orders, and Inigo heard the cries of Shango and Colleen Brooks, too. And something else, weird and creepy, that raised the hackles on his neck, a piercing ululation like nothing a human throat could make. There were words in it, but not English, and Inigo couldn't make them out.

Then he saw and understood—it was Crazy Horse, and the other warriors, taking up their war chant, plunging into the mass of writhing, attacking fiends, driving them back with rearing hooves and arrows and spear.

Abruptly, a body struck Inigo from above, one his own size, wild and hard, hurling him off his horse. He hit the stone floor, the breath knocked out of him, the screaming mad thing atop him ripping and biting. Inigo punched at it, kicked hard, bit into its neck. But more of them leapt on him, holding him down, tearing out flesh and meat.

Then Cal Griffin was there, driving two away with thrusts of his sword. The third turned on him, knocking the sword aside with a wild blow.

Cal didn't dive for the sword, didn't hesitate. Instead, he bulled into the beast, driving it back, lifting it clear off its feet—and plunging it down onto a crystal stalagmite, impaling it in a fury of cracked bones and screams and gushing hot blood.

The killing began.

# FIFTY-FOUR

## Answered Prayers

Jeff Arcott felt limitless power surging within him, and it was unspeakable.

His eyelashes and his cracked, dry lips flashed and snapped with blue-green fire. His hair writhed like severed high-tension lines, and his eyes were glorious suns held nailed within burning sockets. His flesh pulsed with midnight blue and lavender and Sucrets-green pure neon flame. He was hideously, vibrantly *alive*, abrim, overfull with momentous energy as he reeled across the common in the hell-light that coated everything like a sick sheen of radioactive vomit.

Like a moth held prisoner in a killing jar, Arcott felt his consciousness immobilized within his body, unable to command the slightest movement.

Sanrio was moving him, he knew. Sanrio had done all of this; it was what he had planned all along. Arcott had been no equal partner, merely a flunky, a dupe, in service to a distant, uncaring god.

He prayed only to die.

But his god was not one given to answering prayers.

Through blast-furnace eyes, Arcott made out, silhouetted against the glowing, infected surfaces of pavement and adjoining structures, a tenuous figure rushing toward him from off in the distance, floating rather than running, her unshod feet barely grazing the pathway.

*Melissa . . .*

Plunging headlong toward him, driven by need and love, the twin currencies that motivated her still, despite the inevitable change Arcott could see had finally overtaken her.

She would reach him in a moment, would embrace him and, he knew, be consumed like an autumn leaf in a bonfire.

*Melissa, no . . .* He tried to shriek, but could utter no sound.

He was Sanrio's bitch now. But he'd always been, hadn't he?

In the asylum of his mind, Jeff Arcott began to laugh hysterically.

He saw Melissa slow before she reached him, saw her get a good look at him at last and begin to scream.

What must he look like?

*Run, Melissa.*

But Sanrio was making him stagger toward her, arms outstretched like some fucking Frankenstein's monster. He felt Sanrio's hunger to absorb her power, her light, just as he was eating up everything else in sight, absorbing it and growing strong.

Melissa was down on her knees, shrieking, shaking her head as he drew near. Funny, he thought, she should be able to fly. . . .

Maybe she didn't know that yet. She wouldn't ever now.

He reached out to her. . . .

Suddenly, something *hard* struck him in the midsection, drove him hurling back.

There was another agonizing blow to his ribs that threw blazing sparks off his radiant self. He lost his balance and fell.

Looking up, he saw a hunched form standing over him, wielding a length of metal pipe like a baseball bat. Even though the other was mightily changed, Arcott recognized Theo Siegel.

Theo's mouth opened to bare impossibly sharp teeth, and he cried in a voice that was equal parts sob and roar, "Forgive me!"

As he swung the pipe toward Jeff's head, Arcott thought, *Good for you, Theo.*

OPEN YOUR MOUTH AND SCREAM, the Sanrio-mind commanded him, BURN THE LITTLE WRETCH AWAY.

*No,* Arcott protested silently, and fought against the command with every scrap of will he could muster; not enough, he knew, to hold long, only for a moment. . . .

A latticework of all-consuming nonfire shot out of Arcott's frame despite his efforts to oppose it, and the disintegrating flood would assuredly have swept Theo into the ranks of the post-living had he not been suddenly yanked sideways by—

*Melissa.* Saving him, at the last moment.

A marionette, damned, Jeff Arcott wheeled to face Theo again, to devastate him.

But impossibly quickly, Theo regained his balance and sprang full at Jeff, bringing the pipe down on Arcott's skull. There was a hideous wet *crack.* Theo shouted with the impact, an anguished cry.

Arcott staggered back, knowing that the demon energy overflowing him would repair the damage, would not allow him surcease.

But then another thought intruded from the Sanrio-mind, a desperate, frightened thought not directed at him.

I/WE ARE ATTACKED, INVADED. . . .

NEED POWER.

And all of the dread energy, all the hellacious, diseased light flowed out of Arcott and the streets and the buildings, out of the trees and the grasses, back through the Spirit Portal to South Dakota to fortress the Big Bad Thing, to defend the Sanrio-mind.

All of this happened in the briefest instant, too swift to register.

Arcott sank back, his body crackling and crisped as a blackened leaf, relieved, knowing he would have died anyway, but this hastened it.

He could move his body again, a little, and tried to speak. He motioned Theo closer.

But if Theo Siegel heard him, Jeff Arcott never knew.

# FIFTY-FIVE

## The Iron Road

*I've fought them dead before,* Cal Griffin thought, cursing.

But at least last time, they *stayed* dead awhile.

He was swinging his blade wide, sweat coursing down him despite the chill of the cave.

In Boone's Gap, outside the barricaded Wishart home, the gluey, fragmented corpses of the decomposing grunters had risen to battle them, only staying down when their feet and hands were severed clean through.

Not so now. Cal could see in stolen, quick glances, where Shango was flailing his hammer, Colleen wielding her crossbow and Doc his machete, that the moment the loathsome curs were run through or bludgeoned, or otherwise had their clocks thoroughly cleaned, the light would go out in their eyes but this would stop them only momentarily.

Then, as if an unseen puppet master had taken over (which, Cal recognized, was *exactly* what was occurring), each grunter would shudder like a dog waking from a bad dream and resume the attack with even greater frenzy.

Fleetingly, he caught sight of May Catches the Enemy amid a group of the fiends. She was a wonder of motion, seemingly effortless, throwing, spinning, leaping, stabbing. Drawing knives from a multiplicity of sheathes and hiding places in the folds of her clothing, she slowed her attackers, pushing them back, living, dead and dying alike. Cal saw that Inigo kept close to her now, that she was shielding him even as he attempted to tear at the monsters himself.

At the same time, Enid and Howard Russo were flanking Papa Sky, keeping the attackers at bay as best they could. Christina, too, was driving a group of them back with the force of her light, and Stern was smashing, crushing and squashing as many as he could reach as he stalked forward.

Crazy Horse and his phantom warriors, still mounted on their war ponies, were faring even better, the power of their spectral weapons causing the dead things to stiffen as if electrified and then dust away to nothing.

"Aw shit, *Rory* . . ."

Cal looked over to see that Colleen was gaping at a little gray brute she'd just shot with a crossbow bolt to the head. He stood staring blank dead eyes at her, the shaft protruding from a point just above his eyes, black blood leaking down. He was in tatters, mere remnants of clothes, but even in the weak light Cal could make out the brown bomber jacket, filthy, faded jeans and "I ♥ NY" T-shirt that hung on his shrunken frame.

It was Colleen's old boyfriend, who had lurked in the dark confines of the Manhattan apartment he and Colleen had shared, then disappeared down a manhole into the sewers below . . . only to emerge here.

Rory gave a liquid gurgle and lurched toward her, arms splayed, mouth in a hideous, vacant grin, spittle and blood and bile bubbling out.

Without thinking, Cal leapt for him, tackled him, took him down to the unyielding stone floor. The dead grunter let out a deafening high screech of pure agony, flared like a moth immolating itself on a hot bulb, and *vanished.*

Cal stood shakily, he and Colleen staring at each other in puzzlement. Then Cal understood—

"The shirts! The Ghost Shirts!" he shouted to Doc and Colleen, Mama Diamond and Shango and the others, grabbing up another dead, flailing grunter and hugging it close to his chest. Like Rory, it screamed and evaporated.

The others got the hint, wading through the howling, writhing mass, grabbing them, drawing them close. One by one, the creatures sparked like strings of firecrackers, wailing, and were gone.

*But there were still a hell of a lot of them. . . .*

Just then, Cal spied a shadowy figure on the periphery, emerging out of the depths of a branching passageway coming off the main, stepping toward them. The sea of grunters parted to let him pass.

"*Stop your fighting, friends,*" the figure called out to Cal and the rest, and even though there was something under the words, an indefinable quality that was not quite, well, *human,* Cal recognized the voice even before Christina's glow revealed his face.

It was Goldie.

Cal shot a questioning look Christina's way. Slowly, she shook her head. Cal looked to Stern, who caught his meaning.

The figure was ambling toward them with a crooked half smile on his lips, a twinkle in his eye. Stern drew a deep breath, like a huge bellows being extended fully open, then spit out a projectile maelstrom of flame. It caught the figure dead on, knocked him back and transformed him to a pillar of incandescence. Pure nova, he flared up in Catherine wheels of blue-white energy, spiraling out and extinguishing, leaving no evidence he had been there at all.

"You sonofabitch!" Colleen cried and dove for Stern. But Cal stepped between them, facing her.

"It wasn't him," he said levelly. "Just a projection, an illusion, like the rest." Colleen quieted, nodding. Cal turned again to face the grunters.

But by now, those that were still living had taken to their heels, scrambled up the slippery rock walls, and disappeared back into their hidey-holes and the other dark places that succored them.

The rest, the cadavers, the undying dead, dropped as if their batteries had been pulled, lay still and wet and broken on the cold hard ground.

*It's not done with us,* Cal realized, this Thing that was Sanrio and the others, this Thing that took Goldie. But then, they had barely started what they were going to do to *It.*

"Take me to where you saw It in the flesh," Cal said to Stern. "Take me to where we can hurt It."

"That way," Stern said, pointing a bloody, taloned hand toward the passageway from which the facsimile of Goldie had appeared.

The phantom warriors had ridden up alongside them now. Cal saw Colleen and Doc and the others who'd dismounted for the close fighting remount their steeds. He was gratified that all of them were still there; although bruised and bloodstained, none had fallen in battle.

He moved toward the ethereal pony that had borne him here.

But before he could reach it, a tremor shuddered up out the mouth of the passage, and an angry roar issued from within.

Cal was closest to it. His nose caught a sharp tang of creosote and wooden ties, the echoes of foundries long since abandoned, Pennsylvania coal and Pittsburgh steel.

Like a great black serpent, like a Worm God of nightcrawlers and machinery, the helltrain shot out of the tunnel. Driven not by steam or diesel but by an altogether darker power. The engine was driving toward him now, glittering ebony-black, its antique iron cowcatcher arrayed in a demonic grin. Its unholy scream drowned out the shouts of his companions.

He could feel the envelope of air it was pushing ahead of itself, could smell its sour greasy-iron stench, its momentum and enormous mass.

"*Stand your ground!*" Cal wasn't sure whether Stern had cried it, or he'd heard it in his mind, or both.

At any rate, it was all happening so fast there wasn't time to do much else. Cal grasped the hilt of his sword with both hands, braced his toes against the filthy rubble mound on which he stood.

Steel against steel. In the world as it once had been, this would have been futile; more than that, suicide and madness. The sword blade would have cracked or broken, and the train would have sustained little more than a nick, if that, and driven Cal under its wheels, crushed and chewed him up, just as the Thing at the Source was chewing up the world.

But times had changed, and this sword had never met anything it couldn't cut.

The blade bit into the train as if into living, screaming flesh. Cal felt the jolt up the length of both arms; whole rivers of energy flared up him. His heartbeat stuttered in its rhythm. With a sound like glaciers calving, the train opened in a wound.

And exploded around him.

He felt steel part under the impact of his blade, felt it continue its lethal momentum.

Then something sharp struck his face, and something else struck his body, and he dropped away from the impact and rolled aside as the train, severed from the Source, detonated into a hundred thousand parts. . . .

Not parts of *metal,* as Cal had expected, but fluttering and buzzing parts, a cloud of them too thick to see through: black beetles, houseflies, bluebottle flies, crows screaming at the unseen moon, ravens. . . .

The train had been a prison composed of its own captives.

It lost all resemblance to a train, the way water scattered from a broken cup loses all order and definition. The various crawling and flying things of which it was made beat the rushing air with their wings, soaring up and out and away from the thing they had been constrained to be.

Some, inevitably, were crushed against the rails or flew headlong into the rock walls and ceiling. Cal smelled broken chitin and the blood of birds. But most of the captives simply scattered.

Distantly, Cal heard Mama Diamond call out to them, a command in a language he could not comprehend. With a great *whoosh* the flying mass of them whirled off into the dark unknown like chaff before a storm, and were gone.

Cal stood up slowly, beating a swarm of carpet beetles off his hair and skin and clothes. He was bruised where the body of a crow had struck him and scratched where another bird's talons had raked across his face, but he was basically all right. He had managed to keep his grip on his sword, one hand curled around the hilt.

He turned back to the others, breathing hard, fighting to keep his legs from giving out under him. They were staring at him in awe, all but Stern and the wraith warriors, whose expressions were unfathomable.

"Let's finish this," Cal said.

Stern led them deeper into the mountain.

# FIFTY-SIX

## The Luminous Dark

Jeff Arcott was dead, to begin with.

But Theo Siegel didn't have time to ruminate on that, or agonize over it, or ponder the fact that no one would ever call him Theodore again.

Or even wonder if the life choices he'd made that had led to the inevitable moment of bashing in Jeff's head with a steel pipe had been better, say, than going to vocational school or joining a cycle gang or simply running away to become a snake handler when he was ten.

Because although Jeff—or rather, the tragic, mangled, power-riddled vessel that had been Jeff—was no longer a threat to Melissa or Theo or anyone, the dark sensibility at the heart of the Source very much *was*.

At this given moment, It was summoning back every bit of the sickly, glowing energy It had disgorged out of the Spirit Radio onto the pavements and streetlamps and upright brick structures of Atherton, drawing it surging and splashing back the way it had come, like a tidal wave receding into the sea. . . .

And drawing Melissa Wade with it.

Jeff Arcott had tried to whisper something in his last living moments, as Theo had crouched horrified over him.

But before Theo could discern what that might be, he'd heard Melissa's wailing cry on the wind and spun to see her blown whirling away like a paper doll on the wind, engulfed in lambent dark energy.

She was twenty, forty, seventy yards from him now, blasting toward the ruined shell of the Nils Bohr Applied Physics Building and the portal within.

"*Melissa!*" he cried, and vaulted after her on thick powerful legs, through the churning emerald-topaz radiance that could buffet him and prick him like a thousand needle-hot wasp stings, but couldn't possibly *stop* him.

Legs pounding, leaping over great swaths of concrete, Theo drove forward, cutting down the distance. He sensed dimly about him that, as it retreated, the luminance left behind only arid stone and dead foliage, leeching out every last ounce of life force, stealing it away for other, urgent use.

But not Melissa; it had taken everything else, had ravaged and perverted Atherton, corrupted and destroyed Jeff—

*But it wouldn't have her.*

He could see the twisted skeleton of the physics building ahead of them now. What shone out from the interior of the building was not light but a kind of luminous darkness, a viscous black of such intensity that it made Theo want to shut his eyes.

Instead, he let out a savage cry and gave a last Olympian leap high into the air, reaching out with great wiry arms. . . .

He struck Melissa midair, seized her by her frail midsection, held hard to her; close now, he caught the scent of her sweat and her Changing, pure and bitter, like some exotic herb.

But the compacted weight of him was not sufficient to bring the two of them down; they were still driving through the air, the momentum of his leap speeding them even more rapidly toward the inhaling maw.

Ahead of them, scant feet from the physics building, he caught sight of a splintered power pole, frantically stretched a long gray arm toward its gem-encrusted crossbeam. His fingers wrapped tightly around it, and the force of the wave carrying him pulled him horizontal as it tried to tear him away from the pole. But he held fast to it, and to Melissa, until his fingers on the faceted stones and rough wood were bloody, until his bones wanted to crack.

He howled his rage and his pain against the Storm.

He was still howling when the roof of the Nils Bohr Applied Physics Building came apart in an explosion of beams and tiles and rebar, plywood and brick and drywall. Pieces of it fell about the two of them like hail—some pieces big enough to crush them, though they were spared. Oddly, there wasn't much sound. Only the soft initial *thrump,* and the pattering sound of debris raining down on Philosopher's Walk.

The building was gone, and with it the light-darkness that had shone coldly out of it, and all evidence that the Spirit Radio had ever been conceived, built or activated.

Except for the two of them, clinging trembling to each other atop a power pole, Atherton was silent and dead and dark.

# FIFTY-SEVEN

## THE SIX GRANDFATHERS

The holy ghost legion drove on, into the heart of the mountain that had been named after Charles Rushmore, a lawyer from far New York, and had been called the Six Grandfathers for time out of mind before that. The great reptile beast that had been a lawyer king flew on beside them, and also the flame-girl that had been a ballerina, now speeding like a hummingbird. The boy Inigo and his blade mother, too, and the other mortal beings who had journeyed long and hard, holding their souls in their hands.

They drove like a wedge, parting all that stood before them . . . for a time.

Then the Thing at the Source gathered Its forces, and brought them down.

"*Where? Where is It?!*" Cal was shouting at the top of his lungs over the clamor, the screams of the spectral horses, the cries and blows of his companions, the death screams of whatever ungodly nightmares were being thrown at them.

They were in the great hall now, Cal was sure of that, but there was no way to *see* that, because the Big Bad Thing was reaching into their minds, summoning forth all their bleakest memories and best-beloveds, the cornucopia and totality of their lives, to shape into solid form from the unborn clay, the writhing power at its command—to hurl these bloodless facsimiles at them to rip out their hearts, to kill them stone-cold dead.

The Ghost Dance Shirts Cal and his companions wore were growing less persuasive—perhaps there was a limit, a fading terminus to their power—and so they needed the added impetus of steel and grit and brawn.

"Torment me not, you fraudulent things!" Doc was yelling, his English growing absurdly formal with the stress, as he flashed his machetes and cut to ribbons the pustulent, glowing radioactive forms in ragged uniforms and other trappings, the dead of Chernobyl whom Cal knew Doc had tried to save long ago, and failed. There were others, too, Cal saw, a willowy woman and small girl, who flung themselves at Doc.

Doc could not bear to cut at them, but shoved them hard away; and Stern roasted them to whispers.

Colleen, too, was up to her elbows in a rogues' gallery of men and women summoned from all the hours of her life, who launched themselves hissing at her. Women in business attire and tatty thrift-shop dresses, men in overalls and T-shirts and work clothes—and most notable of all, a handsome, weathered simulacrum of a man in an Air Force uniform that Cal saw she had the hardest time of all slicing and taking down, but did so with grim determination, her eyes brimming with tears.

It was the same for all of them, for Shango and Mama Diamond and Papa Sky, for Howard Russo and Enid, May Catches the Enemy and Inigo, Christina, too. A relentless, unceasing force cobbled up into the specifics of elderly Asians, young Nisei men in Army uniforms, camp guards, old black church ladies in their Sunday best, roadies and hophead musicians with dreamy grins and lethal hands, tribal elders and sun-wizened earth mothers, hot young gas station mechanics . . .

And *children*, children like a maddened, stampeding herd, predator-crazed into blind, rushing panic, tousle-haired and rumpled, freckled and dewy-eyed, friends and schoolmates and neighborhood kids dust-deviled into solidity, driving at them to knock them down and trample them to death.

As all about them, buildings rose and shifted and fell, the counterfeit sky wheeled and stormed and cleared and stormed again, mountains thundered up and avalanched to dust, desert plain gave way to skyscraper canyon and black, turbulent shore, shearing off and re-forming from the evanescent landscapes in their minds.

But not once, *never once*, showing the true form of what lay only yards beyond . . .

"*Where is It?!*" Cal screamed again at Stern, as he drove his sword clear through the shape that was wholly his dead mother made flesh again, forcing himself to feel nothing, or as close to it as he could come.

Stern tried to speak, but there were dozens of forms like humans flinging themselves atop him, bringing him down with their sheer weight, swarming. Some Cal recognized as replicas of Stern's former clients and underlings, while others—beautiful, contemptuous women; elderly, corpulent men—he didn't know.

Stern flipped his hulking body and rolled on the ground, trying to extinguish them like flame. But then even more were on him.

Still, he managed, with a wild gesture, to fling an arm out toward a space some feet behind Cal.

Cal cracked the hilt of his blade into the face of the fourteen-year-old girl who'd been his first love, sending her flailing back away from him, and turned to face what lurked behind him.

The air quivered about him; Cal had the strong sensation that whatever lay hidden there sensed his intention. The illusory stores and tenements and shacks about him gave way as the *real* stone walls on either side of him trembled, fractured and extended out in hard gray fingers, crushing together to form an insensate wall blocking him from whatever was sheltered and watching from within.

Then the stone shuddered and reached out for *him.*

Cal grasped his sword hard in both hands and braced himself. The blade had hewn steel, had cut the hell-bound train in two.

*But what about stone?*

Well, hell, he'd pulled it from Goldie's towering trash heap in the tunnels under Manhattan, hadn't he? Just like some postmodern Excalibur . . .

But Jesus Christ, that didn't *make* it Excalibur!

It didn't matter, none of that mattered, only that he see what was on the other side of that wall, see what was true.

*Pray to see what's real,* May Catches the Enemy had told him, *and you will.*

In the instant before the rock could seize him and crush the life out of him, Cal turned to Our Strange Man and his followers, the sacred dead ones in the midst of the fray.

"Brothers!" he cried out. *"Help me!"*

They and their war ponies curled in on themselves, turned to vapor and surged over Cal like a cleansing stream, flowed past him along his arms into the holy blade, which gleamed and throbbed and sang with the power of the sky and the water and the land.

Cal brought the sword down hard as the cold stone reached him, and there was a cry like every wild, crazed beast in the unseen places of the world, and the stone wall shattered to pieces and fell away.

Cal saw what lay behind it, and gasped.

# FIFTY-EIGHT

## The Man Behind the Curtain

P*eople*, they had once been people, maybe a dozen of them, men and women, some old, some not, it was hard to tell. Melted together, flowing like wax into an obscenity that was all horrified, screaming mouths and nightmare eyes resembling nothing so much as the ruined, melted stone heads on Rushmore itself.

But worse, indescribably worse.

Vestigial limbs like unformed, aborted fetuses, patches of brittle black-brown, golden-white hair erupting higgledy-piggledy from blotchy, pitted skin with infection runneling down from uncounted, unsealing wounds.

And most nightmarish, most unthinkable of all . . . it was still alive.

The scientists of the Source Project, Marcus Sanrio and Fred Wishart and Agnes Wu, Sakamoto and Monteiro and the others, transfigured into this monstrosity when everything went wailing out of control and the energy they had endeavored to seize like Zeus with some lightning bolt had instead seized them.

They had ripped a hole clean through to someplace unimaginably *else*, and that breach remained gapingly open—was, in fact, still flooding out its savage, ungovernable power from the point at which it had first come thrusting, erupting into this virgin world.

Cal Griffin glared and squinted at the dreadful gash in existence just behind the quivering mass that regarded him with rolling, hateful, terrified eyes; the useless, foul body that housed the gestalt mind Stern and Inigo had called the Big Bad Thing.

The light behind it was blinding black, all color and nothingness, a light that was not a light, *not-beingness* that was nothing of this universe, that was indescribably *other*, but that had been called forth into existence here, that had been torn out of elsewhere and was fed, replenished from the unthinkable, unknowable font.

The Source.

Cal couldn't help staring at it, couldn't *bear* seeing it. It was so alien, yet had become as all-encompassing, as much of this world, as the air about him, the fundamental pulse that had changed Stern and Inigo and Christina, Goldie, too—and the helpless multitudes like them.

In that quick-flash moment of perceiving it, Cal sensed that he had been right, that the power itself held no consciousness, no agenda; it was like pure, primal electricity, like the nuclear forces themselves.

But the baleful, nauseating creation regarding him from in front of the Source was another thing entirely.

"*Kill it!*" Cal heard Colleen scream from behind him, and he raised his sword once more, whether to strike out at it, or—

He felt it reach out with its adrenalized, myriad mind, felt it summon every last bit of power from its hostage flares, from the primacy of the Badlands, from all it had been able to leech out of Iowa, *focusing, willing it* to burn all these trespassers *down*.

He felt that power surge like hot fire needles along every nerve, felt its cancer invade every cell. He shrieked and fell to his knees, heard his companions screaming, too.

He could feel them in his mind, Sakamoto and Wu and Brinkowicz, Corning, Feldstein, St. Ives, Pollard, Monteiro—every one of them, all the scientists on Shango's list—could sense them in that tortured, sullied lump of flesh. And at the core, subsuming and commanding them, dominant and undeniable, leading them as he had always led them, Marcus Sanrio.

DIE, Sanrio thought at them, DIE NOW.

Cal felt as though a hand were squeezing him, but also inverting him from within, felt the wave of unbeingness washing over him, inviting him to release, to surrender, to die. . . .

But just then, he felt the grip release just a bit, felt the tide flow back by inches, and he sensed, distantly, a force in opposition. Weaker, but throwing all of itself against the greater mind, holding it back, if only momentarily, from dealing the final stroke.

Cal reached out with his thought to seek it, to identify it—and found a name.

Wishart.

And, surprisingly, remarkably, one other . . .

*Goldie.*

Not dead, no, merely held, absorbed, enclosed.

Cal felt his heart rush. Where he sat crumpled there on his knees, he still held the sword.

He released it now.

"Cal . . . *no* . . ." Pleading, moaning, a whisper behind him. Colleen, her life a flickering candlelight held in a breath.

But Cal needed his hands free now, needed no sword. Fighting the agony, fighting to stay conscious a few seconds more, he withdrew from within his shirt the battered leather portfolio Goldie had brought him from the travels Cal had dispatched him on, when Goldie had returned with Enid Blindman and Howard Russo. That had not been Goldie's only port of call, far from it.

The Sanrio mind bore down, tore at Cal like a freezing river, stealing away his life force piece by piece.

*Hold on, Goldie, hang on, Wishart. . . . Just give me a moment more. . . .*

With fingers grown numb, Cal worked to untie the string, to throw open the portfolio, to lay claim to the irreplaceable treasures Goldie had brought from the four corners of the land. His hands trembled; its contents spilled out onto the floor.

"Light!" Cal screamed. "*Give me light!*" He sensed Tina behind him, battered and assailed. She willed it, and light flooded out, washed over him as he dove down and scooped up the varied flat paper shapes, held them out before him like talismans.

The fleshy abomination was watching him now, gaping eyes brown black green blue, curiosity in them, the same curiosity that had driven them to slice open the world, *insatiable* curiosity that withheld the death blow.

Cal held out one of the creased, shiny rectangles, colors and shapes parading across it.

"Agnes Wu! Your son, your daughter!" Cal cried. "They're safe, in Ithaca! They're waiting for you!"

Another photograph.

"Bernard Sakamoto! Your wife is in a shelter in Baltimore! She's there with your granddaughter!"

Another.

"Stanley Monteiro! Candace, she's in the hospital in Hannibal! Her back was broken in a fall, but she's healing! She needs you there!"

And so on, through Brinkowicz and Corning, Feldstein, St. Ives, Pollard and the rest. All the names Cal had researched in *Who's Who in Applied and Molecular Physics*, discovering their hometowns, their families.

All the ones who had been kept apart from them due to the security lockout at the Source Project, prior to the Change. All those who might have a claim on them, on their hearts and minds, their allegiances beyond Sanrio.

Who, alone of them, had no one he loved, or who loved him.

They had not *chosen* to become this monstrosity, to absorb a world out of fear and madness; that accident had been visited upon them, that drive imposed on them.

Perhaps only Sanrio, their merciless, killing leader, had ever wanted that, had hungered for it since his days of degradation in Havana, his powerlessness. . . .

Cal had learned at last, after all the long days and hard miles, the tortured road from Manhattan to Boone's Gap, Chicago to here, to differentiate between the action and the actor, to jettison notions of evil and perceive only the *fear*. . . .

*Pray to see what's real, Mr. Griffin . . . and you will.*

Cal felt the gestalt mind tremble and hesitate, felt the wills of the others pull back, tenuously rebel.

"You're human!" Cal pleaded. "*Be human again!*"

But then, like a relentless tide flooding back, Cal sensed Sanrio gaining mastery once more, reeling them in again.

*They're not strong enough,* Cal thought despairingly, *they need a leader. . . .*

*Take me!* he thought at It, with the same fierce will that had driven him across this devastated, phenomenal land; that had gathered together Goldie and Doc and Colleen to follow him, and Enid Blindman and Lady Blade and the escaped slaves off the farm at Unionville; that had defeated Primal, and Fred Wishart, and Stern, in their time; the will that might also be called love.

*Take me!*

He opened himself to It.

He felt his body fall away and dissolve like dying, felt himself swept up and plunged into a heaving, boiling mass that was pure thought and memory and being, that held no time and all time at once, that was pure *now* with no past or future in it, a moment held frozen and eternal.

And that moment was terrifying. . . .

*Blurred streaks like blood smeared on a mirror. Men, women, booted, hooded, gloved in white, running, shouting. Machines spinning, pinwheeling sparks, a thrumming rising to a whine and then a wail. This is not right, this is not how it's supposed to be. A rectangular door lined with lights. A gateway. And something emerging, slashing into existence, all colors and none, a whirlpool blaze of pure, savage power. The men, the men and the women all tumbling over each other, pitching headlong to get away, but the whirlpool surges up, seizes them and spins them back into itself. Faces shrieking as they melt together, a chaos of eyes and mouths, not dead, alive, not many but one, frozen in that horrified moment, screaming, screaming—*

As Cal suspected, the gestalt mind was frozen, locked into that molten instant of horror and fear. No wonder it had taken the actions it had to safeguard itself, to wipe every contrary will like chalk off a blackboard. The lesser minds had given themselves over to Sanrio, to guide them, to keep them safe. Crazy and paranoid, and no wonder. Madness maddened, and turning the world mad, too.

*But now there was a new sheriff in town. . . .*

Cal found himself floating in the blackness. But he could sense the other minds there, could hear them like voices in the night.

*Come to me,* Cal thought. *Come to me and I'll be your sanctuary.*

He felt Goldie first, sensed him surge up and lock on. Then Fred Wishart, who had tried, he knew, to keep them safe when they had first invaded this realm, and who had turned Shango away when he had trespassed, too, before Sanrio could discover him.

And Agnes Wu, who had protected Inigo when his own mother could not, when he had been forsaken and transformed.

Cal felt Marcus Sanrio then, felt him attack with a consciousness like a knife, felt his own mind scream as Sanrio tried to cut him to pieces, to gather the others to shred him like wolves tearing apart a deer.

But Cal was on the inside now, and Sanrio couldn't hold them.

Hesitant at first, but with growing determination and velocity, Bernard Sakamoto and Stan Monteiro, Agnes Wu and the others reached out to Cal, holding on, giving over their will to him. He felt their dread and their longing, felt them gain stability as he soothed and reassured them. He felt himself grow with power, felt it fill him like hot air in a balloon, felt himself expand and extend his dominion.

Sanrio fought it, then fell back and fled.

Cal reached out with his mind, pursuing. . . .

And sensed, beyond him, the flares in all their multitudes, heard them like a plaintive, echoing chorus.

Then, as Sanrio diminished further still, Cal caught on the distant edge of perception, barely detectible, like a whisper in another room, a whisper wrapped in cotton . . .

Something else.

*Minds* . . .

Not from *this* side, Cal could *feel* it. . . . *Other*, unimaginably *other* . . .

And behind them, a boy, somewhere in *this* world, a boy with a mind like no other, a boy who had been a boy for a long, long time . . .

Then, like a door slamming determinedly shut, the awareness was gone.

Cal was in the blackness, surrounded by the countless minds held captive here, pleading that he help, pleading that he *act*. . . .

And Cal realized that, at last, his long-ago dream had arrived.

But it was different in its details, there was clamor and chaos, but not the sounds of battle, of metal on metal, of metal tearing flesh. And no sword for him to claim . . .

These had only been the *symbols* of things, the metaphors, of confrontation, of *power*. . . .

Cal could sense Sanrio coming back, drawing on the power of the void itself, on the power of the Source.

He was returning to reclaim what was his.

Cal felt the power of the others within himself. Like Sanrio, he could draw upon the raw power of the Source, too.

The flare minds called to him.

He stood at the black heart of the tumult as they cried their anguish, their despair, *demanded, pleaded*—

*That he act.*

But act *how*?

He reached out with his new, expanded awareness, felt the tenebrous borders of the rent, the tear in the universe. . . .

And he knew with utter conviction that he could seal it, plug the hole, cut off the torrent of the Source.

But it would take drawing upon all the force at his command. It would take bringing the mountain down in on itself, cascading tons of rock crashing down on their heads, crushing them.

In the lighthouse beacon of his mind, Cal could make out the frail, delicate form with hair fine as white spiderweb and eyes a scorching blue. . . .

*Christina.*

And the others beyond her, among the multitude of souls . . .

Colleen. Doc. Goldie. May Catches the Enemy. Inigo. Papa Sky. Mama Diamond. Enid Blindman. Howard Russo. Larry Shango.

Cal knew he could do this, stop the energy that had flooded the world, and destroy Marcus Sanrio, too. . . .

*But it would kill them all.*

And would it change the world back, back the way it had been?

Who could say?

With the will that had brought him here, the will that could also be called love, Cal made his choice.

He brought his vast attention to Sanrio and blasted him back, sent him hurtling, tumbling away, before Sanrio could regroup, draining him as he went, bleaching his bleached, cadaverous soul, inhaling the fiercesome wildfires as they burst out of Sanrio like nuclear mandalas of psychotic glory made flesh and lightning strike, and then blowing them back at the albinic stick figure, vomiting forth the torrent of withering black-star corruption to scour raw this child's scrawl of phosper dots and malignity, until only the barest remnant of the being remained, a tenuous loose affiliation of particles that had once been a man, had once been known and known itself as Dr. Marcus Sanrio.

Cal tried then to draw the entity back in, to hold him still and mute and captive.

But with the last bit of power that was his, Marcus Sanrio fought to evade these filaments, to slip from Cal's grasp. There was a moment of fierce struggle and then, in a searing implosion of mind and will, Sanrio winked out, spiralized and compacted to nothingness, vanished from distance and time, and was gone from all awareness.

Extinguished, destroyed? Cal *thought* so, but then . . .

He couldn't be sure.

But this much he knew—either way, Sanrio had been dead a long time, soul dead. . . .

*Let go of the dead, and attend to the living.*

He turned his attention to the others that orbited about him . . . and repeated what he had said before.

*You're human. Be human again.*

He summoned up all the power that was within him, within the scientists and the lost ones and the flare children, the power he could draw from the flood coursing out of the rent in the universe, felt it suffuse him and erupt and flow outward in a great, warming deluge. . . .

*You're human. Be human again.*

And it was so.

The first thing Cal realized as he sat up groggily on the scorched tile floor was that he had a body again.

The second was that he had no more power than an ordinary man.

May Catches the Enemy was there, helping him shakily to his feet.

"Not bad, Griffin," she said, smiling broadly. "Not bad at all . . ."

Cal looked about him, and saw that the room was a shattered wreck of what had once been a laboratory, the walls chiseled out of bare rock. It was what it had always been, at least since the Change, at least in reality.

"Christina . . . ?" Cal croaked out worriedly, and his sister floated up to him. Still a flare, not human, but thankfully, not harmed. In her glow, Cal could make out Inigo and Howard Russo huddled concernedly about him, still grunters, as well. Colleen stood close on, Enid and Shango silent and watchful alongside, Papa Sky and Mama Diamond there, too.

"Man, you sure know how to throw a party," said a voice behind him.

Cal turned and—even though he knew the man was generally leery of human contact—hugged Goldie until he nearly turned blue.

The shadow warriors and their horses were gone, May explained, fled back to the Spirit Realm. But then she led Cal to where Doc Lysenko stood ministering to Fred Wishart and Agnes Wu and the other Source Project scientists, human again, who sat blinking and moving like sleepers gone far from the world, awakening at last from unquiet dreams.

Of Marcus Sanrio, there was no sign.

"What about the flares?" Cal asked.

May led him through the Hall of Records to the staircase beneath the watchful, ruined heads of Mount Rushmore.

In the autopsy room at Atherton, beside the ravaged body of one that was not Ely Stern, Doc had told Cal that the dragons, and the grunters and the flares, were not inhuman, but rather *alternate* humans. . . .

*Pray to see what's real,* Mr. *Griffin. . . .*

Humans, all of them, in all their forms, in the world as it truly was.

From his vantage point high atop the Black Hills, which had been called He Sapa since time out of mind, peering over the Badlands as they lay timeless under a rising sun and a cloud-wracked sky, Cal had to admit that the glow of the multitude, flying home to all four corners of the land, was spectacular indeed.

# FIFTY-NINE

## Old Man Waiting

In these recent days of miracles and wonders, Garrett Lambert had seen some freaky things, truth to tell and no fish story, my man.

But it went without saying that the cobwebby dude sitting on the bench by the dead old train depot was right up there with the contenders.

"What'chu doin' there, old-timer?" Garrett ambled up to him in the noonday sun only mad dogs and Englishmen would dare sashay out in. In his era, Garrett had been a pretty mad dog hisself, and once upon a time had been enough of a blueblood to pass for a Brit on a five-buck dare, if need be.

"Waiting for a train," the old dude exhaled, his voice as silken and insubstantial as cobweb, too. His skin was pale, faded parchment locked away in a tomb, and his hair and clothes were leeched of all color, too, diseased somehow.

Garrett squinted hard at him; what with the glasses he'd misplaced in Laredo, and the four Dos Equis he'd quaffed as his morning Breakfast of Champions, he was having a hard time getting a lock on this particular member-in-good-standing of AARP. He seemed to go in and out of being, somehow; appeared MIA in the crevices and shadowy places of his face and form.

Bullshit. There was enough spookiness in this world without planting some where there wasn't fresh manure.

"Ain't no train passing through here, my friend." Garrett came up close, so his body'd cast a shadow over the seated one, grant him some shade. "No train passing anywhere, come to mention it."

The other rose then, like a heap of sticks conspiring themselves upright. Garrett was surprised to see that the old dude was taller than himself.

"Don't I know it," the old man sighed, again in that voice like a night wind passing.

"Where you goin'?" Garrett asked.

The old man looked out uncertainly beyond Garrett, at the orphaned land, and the flat horizon, and whatever mysteries lay beyond. For the first time, Garrett got a good look at the man's eyes, saw they were pale white, too.

*Sweet Lord of Contagions, he's flat-ass blind.*

"You got any people?" Garrett ventured, with growing concern.

"A boy . . ." the other answered vaguely, the sound all dust.

"He know where you are?"

"No. . . . But I know where he is."

"Well, lemme just help you there," Garrett said, stifling a fruity belch. *Damn* that fourth brew, and the damnation heat, and the friggin' gnats that accompanied you everywhere, swarming like your own personal wedding veil. He extended a hand. "I'm Garrett Lambert."

"Call me Marcus . . ." said the other, and though he was blind his hand reached out and clasped Garrett's firmly.

It was all cobwebs, and dust and ashes, with not a living thing in it.

And as his life flowed out into this blind, ravenous seeker after one certain, most *special* boy, Garrett Lambert had time for just one final, piquant reflection. . . .

Man, he'd thought that concert in '68 with the Lizard King was pure stone weirdness.

But it wasn't a patch on *this.*

In the time of early morning, Enid Blindman emerged out onto the porch of the house May Catches the Enemy had secured them outside Pine Ridge—part of the housing tract, she'd explained, that had been built after the twister had come through and cleared out the trailer park that had been on this land, just after the turn of the new century and before the Change. Since then, most of the people had cleared out, too, so there were plenty of places on which you could hang a VACANCY sign.

Enid found Papa Sky sitting patiently there, shaving a reed for his Selmer. He marveled as the old man's fingers moved deftly from long practice, not needing the distraction of sight.

Enid settled next to him, began tuning his guitar.

"Pretty brisk for you to be out here," he said.

"Hadda say me some goodbyes," Papa Sky replied. "Ely went winging off back East."

"I'da figgered you'da gone with him, the two of you being so long on the road and all."

Papa Sky was quiet a bit, mulling the days of their time together. "Nah. . . . He needed some alone time to think on things, get comfortable with who he is 'stead of who he's been."

Enid gazed off past the low buildings to the gentle rise of the valley and the snow-dusted plain beyond. "Way I hear Cal tell it," he said, "Stern was one mean *hombre* once upon a time. Took some major *cojones*, you takin' on reforming him."

"Well . . ." Papa Sky shook his head dismissively, then raised the Selmer to his lips and started in, mournful and lovely, on "Someone to Watch Over Me."

Enid joined in, fingering the maple jumbo with complexity and grace, and Papa would've sworn it was Django if he didn't know better, only even finer, truer still.

Finally, they came to a stopping place and let the last of the sweet sound drift off into the dawning air. A meadowlark trilled far off, answering their song with his own.

*You gonna come clean, Old Man?* Papa Sky asked himself. *Or you just gonna let your axe do all your talkin'?*

He felt his heart pounding like a kettledrum fit to burst. But he knew it wouldn't, knew he had a good many years yet left in him, even if he could remember back to when the only sound movies had in them was what music you could make with your own two hands.

"Don't you go thinkin' I was no saint or nothin', son," Papa Sky said with a fierce rumble more intense than he intended. "I took on Ely Stern 'cause maybe I figgered, after all the wrong he done, all the folks he hurt, if he could earn a second chance . . . well, maybe I could, too."

Then Papa Sky told Enid Blindman just who he was, and who Enid was, too.

# SIXTY

## The Sound of Rain

Dawn came with tumbled clouds and spitting rain.

Melissa Wade awoke from a troubling dream in which she was changed into a thing of wisps and luminance.

Then, looking at her hands gleaming in the darkness of the room, she knew it was true.

She began to weep softly, and rocked herself as she floated in the air above tumbled covers.

She looked about her and did not recognize where she was. The bedroom was mostly bookcases crammed with paperbacks, a few pieces of IKEA furniture, a computer. The room was dim, the blinds closed against the dawn, but she could see clearly enough in the light that sheened off her own body. Atop the desk beside the computer, she discerned a framed photograph of herself; of the way she had been.

The door opened and Melissa turned away, wiped her eyes quickly.

"I heard you moving around," Theo said behind her, and his voice had an odd roughness.

"Where am I?" Melissa asked vaguely, still coming out of sleep.

"My place," Theo said apologetically. "I hope you don't mind."

She turned to him then, and was surprised to see how dazed he looked. Not to mention scratched, cut, beaten, disheveled and shell-shocked.

And that didn't even take into account that he was no longer human.

She saw that he had moved to block her from seeing the photo by the computer; embarrassed, he turned it facedown behind him. Melissa smiled to herself, feeling warmed for the first time. It was still Theo, after all.

"Do you remember what happened?" he asked tentatively.

She searched her memory, found painful shards there.

"Jeff . . . ?" she asked.

He nodded, neither of them wanting to say the word. Tears welled in his luminous big eyes. "I'm sorry, Melissa. I'm so sorry."

"What about the others?" she said when she could, and her voice was high and thin as birdsong.

"Made it back," Theo said. His mouth twisted into a melancholy smile. "Guess the good guys won. . . ."

*The good guys.* Melissa didn't even know who the good guys were anymore.

But no, she realized, thinking back on the evening before, that wasn't true.

Theo was a good guy.

Theo, who had followed her and found her, who had held tight to her against the worst ravages of the Storm . . .

Who had killed Jeff to save her.

Theo loved her, had always loved her.

Had Jeff loved her?

She thought he had when he'd sewn that dead stone into her flesh, when he'd delayed her becoming what she truly was.

But was that to save her . . . or merely to save what he needed her to do?

She knew the answer. And what she had held within to warm herself for so very long turned dead as that stone.

Theo spoke then of incidental things, of the town's power being down, the gems lifeless and possessed of no miracles now. Their cozy enclosed universe of electric lights and gasoline engines had collapsed like a spent balloon.

Eventually, he said, they might be able to turn it around. But only time would tell.

She was studying him closely now in the glow of her own being; his sensitive features despite the change, his delicacy.

"Do you know what you'll be doing next?" she asked him.

He shook his head. "Maybe an extended sabbatical. Head out in some direction, see where I fit in."

Melissa nodded at that, and felt something born in her different from what she had felt for Jeff, for every man of a certain kind since her father.

It was a change beyond what had turned her into a flare, far deeper, and it opened up something new in her, a world of possibility.

That might in turn grow into . . . what?

Only time would tell.

Rain beat against the room's single window. She found her way to a chair beside him and settled into it, although it took her more effort than to hover above it.

"I'd like it if you could stay awhile," she said.

Theo said nothing, but his eyes were all the answer she needed.

"The rain's coming down harder," Melissa observed after a moment. The window rattled as she spoke.

"I always did like that sound," Theo said, and the two of them sat quietly and listened to it for a time.

# SIXTY-ONE

## Magic Time

*Life is loss,* Cal Griffin had once told himself, amid the drifting flakes of ash coming off Magritte's funeral pyre, by the waters of Lake Michigan. But he might as well have said, *Love is loss,* for the many lessons his life had given him.

Looking about him now, though, around the big table in the flickering candlelight redolent of vanilla, as they all shared a final dinner together—his sister, and Inigo, May Catches the Enemy, Larry Shango and Mama Diamond, Colleen and Doc, and Enid Blindman and Papa Sky—he felt confident he could add, *And sometimes, it's not.*

They had weathered the Storm together, beaten it back and emerged with the only treasure that really counted, the human one.

Over in Iowa, Atherton was sweeping up after the whirlwind, and here outside Pine Ridge, Walter Eagle Elk and the other survivors were emerging out of the Stronghold into the good, fresh air, secure that nothing lurked any longer within the Six Grandfathers to steal away their lives and souls.

"Hey, quit hoggin' the oregano," Howard Russo demanded of Colleen, reaching across the table with his spidery grunter arm.

"Tell me," she said, slapping his hand away, then sliding him the jar, "are you this rude because you're an agent or a grunter, or both?"

"Lay off the grunters," May Catches the Enemy shot back, laughing and warmly eyeing her son. "Can't we all just get along?"

Inigo had chosen the place for their last meal and, being a kid, it stood as no surprise that he'd selected the Pine Ridge Pizza Hut. It had been shuttered since the Change, but Morris Cuts to Pieces had opened the place up for just this occasion, had fired up the woodstove and managed to cobble together a pretty decent pizza, all things considered, although chunks of buffalo steak were still a pretty sad substitute for pepperoni.

Odds were damn good he'd be seeing his fair share of business from now on, Cal reflected, considering that Rafe Dahlquist and Theo Siegel and Melissa Wade and the rest of the physics team from Atherton were now ensconced within the mountain (thanks to a portal opened up courtesy of Herman Goldman, bachelor-at-large), working alongside the rehumanized scientists of the former Source Project.

Ironic that, considering Theo and Melissa were now a grunter and flare respectively; two of the posthuman species, working alongside untransformed men and women to unlock the secrets of this fierce new universe.

Only dragons were unrepresented. But then, none of this would have come to pass if not for Ely Stern's intervention.

Would they ultimately manage to tame the Source Energy, perhaps seal it away again?

Who could say?

But, whatever the outcome, it would no longer be magic; it would instead be what it had always been, truthfully—merely a further realm of science.

"You look thoughtful," Colleen said to Cal. "Quit it."

Cal grinned, and took another slice of pizza.

Later outside, Cal found Christina peering up at the night sky. Now that the moon was on the wane, Venus and Mars shone out clear and bright, in this sky that was as black as Lady Blade's gleaming hair.

It was a mild night, and Cal realized that whether the winter was gentle or fierce, spring would soon enough be here. He wondered if the seasons would return to some semblance of normalcy, or if they would remain as unpredictable as they had been of late.

"The future's just a ghost, you know," Christina said, aware of Cal without turning back to look at him. "What you think you're gonna have, how you think it's gonna be . . . Just some mirage that waves at you in the heat, but you can't ever touch it."

Cal nodded, and thought of the life he once thought he'd have back in Manhattan, working for Ely Stern, watching Tina rise through the ranks of the American Ballet Theatre or some other pre-eminent company.

A phantom, nothing more, that had haunted and eluded them, like the future Jeff Arcott had envisioned of the Spirit Radio bringing a new birth of freedom to the land, with himself as its guiding spirit and patron saint. Arcott had pursued that illusion until it had destroyed him, rendered him a ghost, if he remained anything at all.

And all of them one way or another had been driven, shadowed and bedeviled by the memories of ones they'd lost, or never had at all.

Past and future, phantoms all . . .

*Time to let go of all the ghosts,* Cal thought, *and at last come out of the Ghostlands.*

*Which was the whole world, until we let go . . .*

"I can still be a dancer," Christina said, to the night, to the stars. She turned to Cal, her feet never touching the ground, smooth as liquid. "Just a different kind, a new kind."

"How'd you get so smart?" he asked her, drawing near.

She wafted to him, the only ghost her smile. "I was raised by smart people."

His boots crunching on the parking lot gravel and the call of larks filling the daybreak air, Larry Shango found Mama Diamond on a bench outside the SuAnne Big Crow Boys and Girls Club. Now that folks were reclaiming the land, Chick Big Crow had been able to open the center again; this facility that federal money had built and that she'd dedicated to the memory of her daughter, a high school basketball star who'd spoken out against drugs and alcohol, who'd inspired hope in her people; the daughter lost to a traffic fatality before everyone in the world had shared in one great disaster.

"Guess not everything funded by the government was all bad," Larry Shango said as he approached Mama Diamond. She was bundled up sitting in the brisk sun, watching Indian kids surge onto the playground; kids exuberant with the joy of being in the open again, of being alive.

"How old are you, Mr. Shango?" Mama Diamond asked as he settled beside her.

"Let's just say thirties and leave it at that."

"I'm old enough to be your mother . . . or grandmother, if I'd gotten an early enough jump on things."

Shango smiled. "You applying for the job?"

"We've been looking after each other for some time now. No need to start sticking labels on everything."

They were still for a time, with the stillness each had cultivated over the years to shield themselves from people, to keep invisible and apart, but which now had evolved into easy companionability.

Finally, Mama Diamond said, "I've been ruminating a tad . . . thinking over what we're living for."

"That's a big subject for so early in the day."

Mama Diamond looked off to the mountains in the distance, the eroded cliffs that ringed the Badlands. All those fossil bones in the rocks, all those creatures that were born and raised their young and died . . .

In times past, Mama Diamond had scraped those bones out of their resting places, had wrenched her shining gems from the living earth, and thought them her fortune.

Her cache of gems was slag now, turned to slurry when Atherton went into meltdown. But she didn't mind. Looking back, she realized that what she'd considered her living for so many years had hardly been living at all.

The mountains talked to you, if you were quiet enough to listen; she'd known that even back in Manzanar. But there was a new thing they were telling her now, a deeper truth.

All those generations down the ages, young and old, looking out for each other, surviving and making a life . . .

She mulled it over, watching tawny boys and girls clamber over slides and jungle gyms, arc high on swings. "May Catches the Enemy found her boy Inigo. . . . Papa Sky's hooked up with Enid now. . . . That young Cal Griffin's got his sister Christina back, who I guess was pretty much a daughter to him all along. . . ."

As autumn waned and winter arrived, their whole wayward adventure through Wyoming and Iowa and South Dakota had revolved around reunion between parent and child, whether actual or surrogate, old or new. In this transcendent, shifting world, the only choice for them all was to be caretakers of one sort or another, good mothers and fathers, good stewards; to love each other and not falter, to be uplifted by their mutual need and regard, to be *better* than any of them had ever seen reason or need before to be.

Larry Shango raised an eyebrow. "You're saying we better get busy raising a family?" he asked Mama Diamond.

Mama Diamond turned her dragon-young eyes to him, and the wetness in them caught the morning sun. "I'm saying we found one, Mr. Shango."

In the late morning, they all gathered once more, outside what had been the Visitor Center, to compare notes and make their plans.

"I've heard some mighty fine things about that Preserve Mary McCrae's got running," Papa Sky told Cal. "Figgered I'd mosey on down, have me a look-see. 'Sides, me and Enid can give 'em a concert they'll *never* forget."

Enid nodded, saying nothing, affectionately eyeing the old blind man—who, Cal could see now that he knew the score, bore Enid more than a passing resemblance, once you got past the affectations of clothes and hair.

"Yeah, me too," rasped Howard Russo, who now sported Hugo Boss sunglasses between a porkpie hat and a striped suit that would give a drunk-tank lush the white shivers.

Larry Shango opined that it was getting on time for him to pay a call back home, to see how the President's son was getting on, in the care of Shango's first and second and third cousins—not to mention the great-aunts and other assorted relations, who he felt sure remained every bit as rooted to the sultry bayou swamplands as their fathers and their fathers' fathers had been.

As for Mama Diamond, Burnt Stick held no further allure. If anyone chose to lay claim to her store and the dead bones sleeping within, more power to them. Her attention now lay on returning to reclaim Marsh and Cope from where they were stabled, then continuing on with Larry Shango to meet his clan, who—if Shango's twenty-year avoidance of them were any indication—would be noisy and contentious, boisterous and cantankerous . . . and joyously *alive*.

"I hear the ground's so wet there, you can't bury a soul," Mama Diamond observed.

Shango nodded. "Even in the tombs, you put someone in, they rot away to nothing. Then you just jam more folks in."

Mama Diamond smiled inwardly. A land that dissolved its dead like an Alka-Seltzer in water, that took them into the bosom of the earth and left nothing behind, not a scrap to pry out and shine and hoard.

That suited her just fine.

"If it's just the same to you, Calvin," Doc Lysenko chimed in, "Colleen and I have gotten rather used to your company. We thought perhaps we might continue sharing your road, for a time."

"Assuming," Colleen added, "you ever get around to telling us what that road happens to be."

Cal shot his sister a glance. "Well, seeing as we've come this far from New York . . ."

He let Christina finish it. "It seems kind of a waste not to keep right on going."

"Don't tell me," Goldie piped up. "You're goin' to Disneyland!"

"Been there, done that." Cal said, deadpan. "But the Pacific has its appeal . . . depending on what we find."

"Hmm . . ." Herman Goldman considered, glowering. "In the words of Yogi Berra—or was it Samuel Goldwyn?—I could say, 'Include me out.'" He grinned, extending Cal a hand. "But what would I do for laughs?"

*True enough*, Cal reflected. Since their time inside the mountain, Goldie had been laughing a good deal, as though a weight had been lifted, as though he'd come back to himself . . . or more than himself.

"I could open up a portal à la Goldman," Goldie offered. "We could be there in a jiff."

"That'd kinda take the fun out of it," Cal responded. "I mean, it's like flying instead of taking the train."

"Neither of which is an available option at this particular moment," Goldie observed. "Although, given the progress of the assorted boffins from Atherton, I'd say both will almost certainly make a comeback in the very near future."

No rush, Cal thought, at least as far as he was concerned. Time to go slow awhile, to have a little respite from the cell phones and boomboxes, the voicemail and internal combustion. Bring back health care, sure, running water and all the blessings of the modern age, but let's take a holiday.

A holiday . . . what a concept.

It had been a never-ending battle across the U.S., from the five boroughs to the Windy City to the Great Plains and this sun-beaten land. Cal felt like a heavyweight near the end of his days, still battling but having lost all his agility and spring, with nothing left but scar tissue and a growing inability to talk.

Could he really let all that go?

Marcus Sanrio might not be dead, after all, might still be roaming the back roads somewhere, weakened and lieutenant-less but at large. And either way, there might be other Bad Things out there, almost certainly *would* be.

In time, they might have to again put on their armor, buckle on their blades.

But Cal also knew it was high time to get a life.

He caught himself looking at May Catches the Enemy, who stood nearby in the shadows with her son. She brought her emerald eyes to meet his, and held his gaze there.

At last, Cal managed to say, "I suppose you'll be staying."

She looked questioningly to her son. Like Howard Russo, he wore shades and layers of protective clothing, but with considerably more restraint and style. He rubbed his chin contemplatively.

"I've never seen the ocean, Mom," he said finally, sneaking glances Christina's way. "I'd sure like to."

May Catches the Enemy, who was also Lady Blade and the Widow Devine, smiled knowingly.

On the ancient plains, under the sky that went on forever, Christina danced, and Enid Blindman and Papa Sky and Goldie played. Not to ward off anything or to forget anything, just for the sheer damn joy of it.

High above within the clouds, cruising in thermoclines exhaled by the sun-heated earth, the dragon peered down with raptor-keen eyes that could readily observe without any of them having the least knowledge of his gaze.

He felt a warmth that came, not from the fiery furnace kindled within him, but from another source entirely.

"Love" was not a word that Ely Stern ever used, and he did not use it here.

But even so, looking down on them, on the ones he had brought to this unforgiving land, the ones he had safeguarded and endangered, confounded and inspired . . . he smiled.

Then he banked in a great wide arc until he caught the wind and was uplifted by it.

Soon, he was far away, heading east.

10/14/00
DEMCO